CHA

OF THE

SOUL

CHARIOT
OF THE
SOUL

LINDA PROUD

GODSTOW

·PRESS·

First published 2018 by
Godstow Press
60 Godstow Road, Oxford OX2 8NY
www.godstowpress.co.uk

978-1-907651-13-7

Set in Kuenstler 480 and typeset by Jean Maughan
Cover design by Geoffrey Parkes and Linda Proud

Printed and bound in Great Britain by
Hobbs the Printers, Totton, Hants

The paper used in this publication is procured from
forests independently certified to the level of
Forest Stewardship Council (FSC)
principles and criteria.

Dedicated to the trees and truth-tellers of Britain

'There is another world but it is in this one.'

W. B. Yeats

CONTENTS

GLOSSARY

GAUL
Massalia Marseilles
Durocorteron Reims
Lugdunum Lyons
Avennione Avignon
Valencia Valence
Augustodunum Autun
Augustobona Troyes
Gesoriacum Boulogne

BRITAIN
White Way, Albios Way Fosse Way (started at Ilchester and ran to Lincoln. Vespasian extended it south to Exeter).

WEST SUSSEX
Noviomagos Chichester

HAMPSHIRE
Ford of the Alders (Venta Belgarum) Winchester
Isle of Vectis Isle of Wight

BERKSHIRE
Calleva Silchester

OXFORDSHIRE
Ford at Two Rivers Oxford
Sanctuary of the Wheel – henge under Keble College, Oxford
Sino Dun, Old Mother's Buttocks Wittenham Clumps
Cuma's Hill Cumnor, Oxford
Hill of the Albios Horse Uffington (Oxon previously Berks)

WILTSHIRE
Kennet Avebury stone circle, Swallowhead Spring, Silbury Hill, Kennet longbarrow

SOMERSET (THE SUMMERLANDS)
Hot Springs of Sulis Bath
Peddre Dun Ham Hill
Mendip mines, Vebriacum Charterhouse
Creech, Ile – places near Yeovil
Gifl Yeovil
Lindinis Ilchester

GLOUCESTERSHIRE
Kyronion Cirencester (Bagendon)
Elm Grove Ditches, near Bagendon
Clevo Gloucester
Rim of the Cauldron Cotswolds escarpment around Birdlip
Hills of Cuda Cotswolds
Seven Springs Seven Springs, south of Cheltenham

LEICESTERSHIRE
Venonis High Cross
Crow People's land Charnwood Forest, Outwoods
Lands of Llyr Soar valley

NOTTINGHAMSHIRE
Vernemeton Willoughby-on-the-Wolds

WARWICKSHIRE
Three Bridges Tripontium (site near Rugby)

DORSET
Mai Dun Maiden Castle
Bol harbour Poole harbour
Isle of Vectis Isle of Wight

DEVON
Isca Exeter

ESSEX
Camulodunon Colchester

PLACES MENTIONED, NOT VISITED
Lugh's Dun London
Isca Exeter
Verlamio St Albans
Lindum Lincoln
Siluria southern Wales
Brigantia Yorkshire, Lancashire, Northumberland, Durham
Ewyas Shropshire
Ordovicia and Decanglia northern Wales
Caledonian and Pict lands Scotland

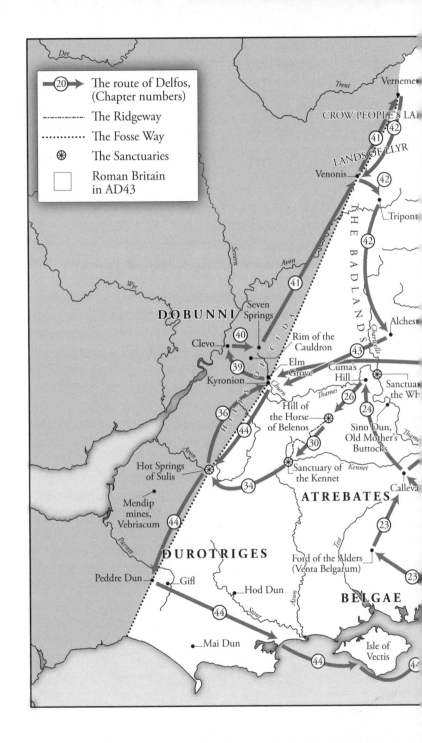

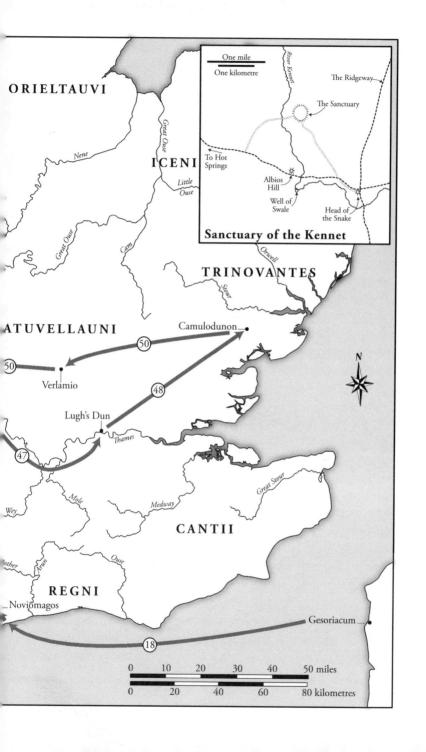

ORIELTAUVI

ICENI

One mile
One kilometre

River Kennet

The Ridgeway

The Sanctuary

To Hot
Springs

Albios
Hill

Well of
Swale

Head of
the Snake

Sanctuary of the Kennet

Nene

Great Ouse

Little
Ouse

Cam

Great Ouse

Orwell

TRINOVANTES

Stour

ATUVELLAUNI

Camulodunon

50

50

48

Verlamio

Lugh's Dun

47

Thames

Wey

Mole

Medway

Great Stour

CANTII

other

Arun

Ouse

REGNI

Noviomagos

Gesoriacum

18

N

0   10   20   30   40   50 miles

0   20   40   60   80 kilometres

FOREWORD

I have long admired Linda Proud's superb novels about Renaissance Italy, which have allowed me to enter the life of Florence under the Medici, with the excitement of the rebirth of Platonism and the flourishing of an artistic culture unique in human history. Of course there is copious documentation for the Quattrocento and Cinquecento, and the four great novels, a trilogy and its prequel, combine imagination with solid history to a quite remarkable degree.

Chariot of the Soul has set her an even greater challenge, for what we have of the history of early Roman Britain amounts to a few pages by writers who had never been to the island, and whose comments are, in the case of Tacitus especially, certainly mired in prejudice. Archaeology and epigraphy (inscriptions) can add a bit, and the excavations at Bath and especially Fishbourne as well as recently at Alchester, Oxfordshire, have been a revelation. We can at least begin to bring into the light a ruler who is briefly mentioned by Tacitus for his loyalty to Rome and, on an inscription recording the building of a Temple to Neptune and Minerva at Chichester, West Sussex, a mile or so from Fishbourne palace, is described as 'Great King in Britain'. Tiberius Claudius Togidubnus may have been as important in the history of civilisation and polite culture in Britain as was Lorenzo de Medici in Florence, and it is the great achievement of Linda Proud to rescue him as an individual we can come to know. He deserves no less.

In the past pre-Roman and Roman Britain has been presented far too much in simplistic terms, in which the inevitable battles, baths, amphitheatres and samian pottery take centre stage, but for those who lived in the first century of our era there was much more to lives that were at least as rich and varied as our own. These people lived in a vibrant religious and artistic society, open to new philosophical ideas from as far as Greece, and at last we have an author who does them justice. This book does for early Roman Britain what John Cowper Powys did for the end of Roman Britain in *Porius* and, like that great novel, it is a masterpiece.

Revd Professor Martin Henig FSA

1

KNOW THYSELF

1

BEHIND CLOSED DOORS

It was the last stream in Gaul, the kind of stream you would offer things to, clear and fast-flowing with waving reeds and water fowl. After resting here, we would pass through the gates of Massalia and go to the port for a boat to Ostia. Lying on my stomach on the bank amongst the horses sipping water, I, too, drank then dipped my head below the surface, lowering and raising it three times in honour of the god of the place. On the third time, I felt a gentle tug and the bronze horse I always wore on a leather thong slipped from my neck. I saw it go to the bottom, trailed by the wavy line of the leather thong, to disappear amongst dense reeds. I reached in, desperately feeling around, but the mere effort of looking made it impossible to see in the eddying silt and my bronze horse was lost. I knew, with the instinctive knowledge of a ten-year-old, that I was to leave my past, my Britishness, behind me, and go forward into the Roman life.

'Oi! Young-un!' called one of the soldiers. 'Togi-whatever-your-name-is, stop playing about. We're leaving!'

On the long journey down through Gaul I had picked up the rudiments of Roman. I knew well enough what he was saying and was alive to the lack of respect being shown to the son of a king. Quickly and formally offering up what had been taken, I gave my beloved bronze horse to the spirit of the stream and rose to rejoin the party. The amulet had had the curving lines of the white chalk horse on Albios Hill. Flat, as if cut out of metal by shears, it had been made for me by an old bronze-

3

worker in Calleva who wanted to show me the magic of casting, how lumps of copper and tin are melted in the unbelievable heat of the crucible and poured into the mould like liquid fire, to cool into a horse. My horse. Now all I had left was a bag of clothes which, once I reached Rome, would never be worn again: the tunics and breeches of a barbarian.

Almost four weeks on the road, part of a large train of merchants under military escort, I had kept company with an old Gaul who dealt in woollen plaids which, made by British weavers, sold for high price in Roman markets. He was growing rich on Rome, his life immeasurably improved by trade. He loved the concepts of city and civilization, and impressed upon me my good fortune at leaving Britain to live in the very heart of the greatest empire the world had ever known.

I had been there when it happened, when my father said to the delegation, 'Tell Emperor Tiberius he has my full loyalty.'

'And as collateral...?'

'The word of a British king is enough!'

'Not to an emperor. You need to demonstrate your loyalty.'

I looked up at my father, proud of him in that moment for standing up for himself. We were used to merchants using our harbours, and paying our tolls, always accompanied by a unit of soldiers, but these official representatives had come specifically to visit the king of the Atrebates, king of the south coast.

'Well then,' said Verica, 'I offer you my son as hostage. Should I ever prove untrue to my word, do as you like with him.'

My body betrayed all the feelings I strove to keep hidden. Fear and a catastrophic sense of betrayal flushed on my skin and made my limbs shake.

'But you will look after him,' Verica continued, 'put him to a good home, give him a good education?'

'The finest. Hostage he might be, but he will come out of it a Roman citizen if he – and you – behave.'

Now other colours played on my skin. A Roman citizen...!

The boat from Massalia landed at Ostia and from there it was half a day's ride following the Tiber to the bridge that crossed to the main gate of the imperial city. The river was filthy, muddy brown in colour with debris caught in the banks or floating towards the sea. As I looked into its murkiness, I saw a dead dog floating downstream. That is no way to treat a holy river! The stench of the Tiber had me retching, but for the merchants and soldiers I had travelled with it was the smell of home.

In my boyish stupidity, I had imagined Rome as a cluster of round houses ten times the size of our own: everything the same as at home only much, much bigger. Rather than a gigantic oppidum of thatched huts, however, there were marble temples and basilicas seemingly piled one on another. Not that all the buildings were of marble, many were made of brick. But for someone who had never seen anything higher than one storey, to whom ceilings and floors were foreign, even brick tenements were a wonder. Escorted by two legionaries, I walked up the Palatine Hill to where the house of Antonia sat on its terrace looking out towards the river and beyond.

Antonia, niece of Augustus, considered it her civic duty to play host to foreign dignitaries. The guest previous to me had been Herod Agrippa of Judea. She was beautiful but humourless, a woman of tight mouth and firm morals (never trust appearances was a lesson I learned early) and had me carefully instructed in how I was to behave: rise at dawn; do as you are told; study every morning and exercise every afternoon; and never, ever say anything about anybody. If I was ever caught telling tales about any member of her family or her household, my corpse would be thrown out on to the streets to feed the rats. She pinched my ear, hard, as she delivered this imperative for discretion. At first I thought it was something expected of all young boys, and that lady Antonia, niece of Augustus, was terrifying, but soon I discovered that the rule of silence applied to everyone, and that it was not Antonia who was the source of terror. Every member of the household went softly about their duties, and if anyone needed a conversation, it was held behind closed doors with no slave present.

Behind closed doors... There was a cubicle towards the back of the house where the door was never opened. I was lodged in a small closet nearby and I think it was on my first night there that, already made sleepless by my distress, I heard scrabbling. I thought it must be the rats come to eat me and, when I did finally sleep, it was to awaken in a shamefully wet bed, for which I received a beating from the lady herself. The following night I heard it again, scratching and, I thought in my fevered anxiety, sighing. Soon I was alert to the sound even during the day, of someone shuffling, or was it crawling? Someone too weak to stand or cry... No one ever went in that room and the only thing that came out of it was an increasingly putrid smell. It became the location of my frequent nightmares (it still is, sometimes). Antonia became so incensed at my nocturnal leaking that she had my mattress removed and made me sleep on the floor.

Not long after I arrived, she reinstated her son in the house. A mature man, Claudius had been living in the house of his grandmother for some years, a kindly woman who was not offended by his bodily infirmities. I think this was my first clue about the moral rectitude of Antonia, for what kind of mother is socially embarrassed by her child? Antonia had no love for Claudius. If she hoped age might have made him more tolerable, it hadn't. Although past forty he still dragged his right foot and had all those tics and twitches she found so hard to look at. He was a jerking wretch and as far from his father's image as it was possible to be — which led of course to rumours of his being from the seed of a demon.

I needed tuition and that was the one thing poor Claudius was good at: teaching. So Antonia put us together to get me educated and to keep him from the dicing tables. What she didn't expect is that, man and boy, we'd get on so well. The day I arrived, fresh from the land of hovels and pig sties, I had been so overawed by the House of Antonia that I had mistaken a wall painting for a doorway into a garden and banged into it. Antonia grieved. She had gained another idiot. And that was what drew Claudius and me together, that sense of not fitting in. He treated me, at first, as his adopted son but, later, it was more like exotic slave.

He was tall with a pleasant face, and when sitting down you wouldn't know there was much wrong with him other than a tremor in his head and a runny nose. The first time he came to collect me for a morning of study, I was already coming out of my room to meet him and noticed that he kept his distance from the locked door, making an arc in his approach as if round an obstacle. His twitches became exaggerated and he kept his head averted but his eyes swivelled towards the door. Because of the rule of the house, I never dared ask what – or who – was in there but, ten years old and impressionable, I came close to developing a few twitches myself.

When I was taken to the park for exercise, or to a temple, or down to the Forum, I kept quiet as instructed but picked up what I could and learned that the Emperor Tiberius had been living for years on the island of Capri while the city was run by the Praetorian guard under the command of Sejanus. Now Sejanus was dead, and Tiberius was back. No one said that name with any joy. Somehow, more instinctively than anything, I knew that here was the source of the terror.

Claudius and I both found comfort in study, locking ourselves away with codices and scrolls that he either owned or borrowed. I was not only illiterate, I had never so much as imagined a book before I arrived in Rome. I had a lot of catching up to do but soon proved myself to be an able and willing pupil, and Claudius patiently taught me how to read and write using the works of Livy, Sallust, Cicero and Caesar. Whether we were reading history or geography, it all related to Rome, for Rome was — is — the centre of the world. I learned about its foundation almost eight hundred years previously and its growth into a city ruled by kings; I learned about the Republic when, having abolished monarchies, Rome was ruled by the Senate. Following the dictatorship of Julius Caesar, Rome was governed by the people led by the princeps, the First Citizen. It had been under Augustus, uncle of Antonia, that Rome had become an empire, and anyone related to Augustus was, in all but name, royalty.

'Kings, then!' I said to Claudius, pleased with my ability to see cycles in history.

'Nonsense!' he replied, but never gave a satisfactory explanation as to the difference. It seemed to me that both kings and emperors are succeeded by sons or by usurpers and are often killed in the process. Tiberius himself had only recently survived a plot to assassinate him on Capri, a plot hatched by Sejanus and his betrothed, Livilla. I can't remember how or when I found out that Livilla was the daughter of Antonia and sister of Claudius. It had only been a few weeks before my arrival that the plot had been exposed by none other than Antonia herself. Sejanus was summarily executed and thrown down the Gemonian stairs. I'd seen what was left of his body myself by the Temple of Concord. The man who had ruled the Empire in the absence of the emperor had been reduced by the mob to lumps of meat being fought over by dogs.

I wanted to throw my arms open to the Forum and shout, 'And you call this civilization?' Instead, I threw up.

My arrival in Rome coincided with the start of what turned out to be six years of reprisals as Tiberius dealt with anyone associated with Sejanus, and who hadn't been? Antonia, by exposing the plot, had demonstrated her innocence but to prove it she had dealt with her daughter Livilla herself.

The sounds from the locked room, which must have begun with screams to be let out, grew weaker and weaker until, one day, they stopped. The day after that, the door was open, as were the windows, and every piece of furniture or fabric removed to be burnt. It was over. 'Vale, Livilla,' said Claudius standing at the door and looking in, his face a mask.

Antonia protected her family throughout the reign of the man who had everybody spying and informing on each other. Claudius and I spent those six horrible years living in the past with our study door closed to the present. In my studies, I learned how the Empire was spreading out across the world in every direction. Claudius referred to anyone beyond the Empire as a 'barbarian' although, as I learned Greek, I discovered this simply meant bearded or hairy. Nevertheless, being tall, fair-skinned and tattooed, I equated myself with this despised race. Happily I grew out of the bed-wetting but only to take to scratching at my tattoos, first with a fingernail, later with a knife, in some insane effort to be rid of them. It did not do to be singled out in the Rome of Tiberius. Antonia made me stop, having a slave bind my hands both day and night until I solemnly promised to leave myself alone.

I enjoyed studying history. Unlike the stories of the hearth I had heard at home, these ones found in books seemed to have authenticity. They were true, unembellished accounts. The stories of Caesar, in particular, which related to his conquest of the Gauls, fascinated me. But, as Claudius warned, just because it is written doesn't mean it is true. 'The veracity of history depends on who wrote it and why.'

We studied Greek together through the works of Plato and Aristotle. Perhaps not so appealing to a youth as the stories of Romans versus barbarians, yet the wisdom percolated through me like a hidden spring and, though I had to drag myself to study on the Greek days, I also had to drag myself away at the end. There were Platonists in the city – there was everything in the city, every foreign cult had its altar on the Aventine – but the philosophy of the day was Stoicism, made popular by Caesar's contemporary, Cicero. 'Virtue is the only good,' he had said. 'The sage alone is free.' 'Only the wise man is rich.'

'Discuss,' said Claudius.

On the death of Tiberius, Rome came out from under the water like a half-drowned man, rejoicing in having a new emperor, Gaius. Gaius, but known to everyone as Caligula who, as we were to discover within the year, was an even greater source of terror than Tiberius. Antonia, at first lauded as a saviour by the new princeps, was soon side-lined, her tight-lipped, disapproving virtue too much for an emperor who wanted a life constrained by no one. Unable to bear the truth, that the descendants of the Divine Augustus were all proving to be mad tyrants, she took her own life.

To escape ghosts, Claudius sold the house and bought something smaller on the Esquiline Hill. The sale gave him the funds to make him eligible as a senator. Kept out of public eye all his life, he dreamed of office, whereas I, increasingly convinced that the only escape from the madness of civilization was neither advancement nor suicide but Stoicism, persuaded him to let me attend the classes of Lucius Seneca.

2

THE NEW SUN

On the day the Sun came amongst us I got caught in seething crowds and arrived late to class. Weighed down by heavy scrolls, it was hard to get through to Seneca's room under the colonnade. The lesson was half-way through when I pushed the door open with my hip and clattered in to the serene classroom overlooked by a bust of Socrates. The theme was indifference and my fellow students were sitting with eyes lowered, listening to Seneca claim that there is nothing in this world worthy of our attention. 'There is no need to get agitated by anything,' he said, 'not by a student arriving late, nor even being that student arriving late.' I lowered the scrolls to the ground as gently as I could but one slipped my grasp and fell with a smack of bronze casing on stone floor. I glanced up and found Seneca smiling.

'Loss of possessions, for example,' he continued, 'injury, sickness, bereavement. Let nothing disturb your equanimity.' He looked up again at the sound of distant, ecstatic cheering from the Circus Maximus where Helios the God was riding the circuit in his golden chariot. Adulation swept across the city like a wave of heat. I was only eighteen years old. The idea of being absent from a sublime event, the desire to race out and participate, buzzed like a mosquito but I took a deep breath and ignored it.

'All evils are obvious agitations,' said Seneca. 'But what of the subtler distractions? Desire, for instance. Guilt... What is it that, right now, is hooking your mind like a barb? Interest?

Curiosity? Morbid fascination? Do you not long to know what Helios the God looks like?'

We kept our eyes lowered and concentrated on the practice of indifference.

'After all, it's not every day a god comes amongst us, but right now, as we sit here contemplating eternal verities, he's out there, in our own city, bestowing sweets upon his devotees.'

Some of us grinned.

'Look within,' he continued sternly. 'As Socrates said, the unexamined life is not worth living. What claws at you inwardly, so subtly that you have got used to it? Suppose, for instance, you are deformed in some way. What is there you can do about it, other than learn to be indifferent?' He glanced round the room but saw no deformity. Except mine.

'Suppose you have tattoos, indelible tattoos that make you look odd.'

I withdrew my arm inside my tunic, not only to hide the design of an eight-spoked wheel but also the scars that distorted it.

'Perhaps,' he continued, 'you would seek to cover them with your clothing; or even to scrape them off with a knife. The only escape, however, is through control of your own mind.'

I let my arm re-emerge and I stared at it as if it were some-one else's. A blare of trumpets from the rostra, however, began our unravelling. Against the music of trumpets, horns and pipes, and the rumble of the crowd, our teacher raised his voice. 'The only thing of any value is virtue, the only thing worth being interested in is virtue, the only thing one should have in mind at any time: virtue.' A good-looking young man, son of a senator, suddenly jumped to his feet and, declaring we were being disrespectful to the Princeps, strode to the door. As he opened it, the heat and noise blasted in. I caught a flash of gold, the clinking tramp of a unit of Praetorians passing... And yes, of course I was interested. It was hard not to tap your feet to the incessant rhythms of the procession. As I redoubled my efforts, another two students left, yelping like hounds off the leash as they burst out into the Forum.

To shut out the world I went deep down. It was a trick my druid mother, Innogen, had taught me to help me withstand, say, the pain of having a tattoo drawn, or the fear when you are up-ended in a cauldron of boar's blood. 'Go under water,' she had said. 'See the reeds, the murk, the webbed feet of a swan passing overhead. Sink down, sink lower, go to the bottom of the lake...' It was as if she were speaking to me now. I slowed my breathing, sitting root still while one by one my fellows failed Seneca's test. Every little while there would be agitated shuffling, a sudden expletive and another student of Stoicism running out of the door. By now I was sitting on the bottom of the lake, unmoved and unmoveable. The solar music attending the god pulsed in my ears. The roar of the crowd, the applause, the cries of delight. *Virtue is the only good, the only good,* I repeated to myself, as if each phrase were a weight to keep me down. Then an image arose of the true god of light, Belenos himself, rising out of the waters... Image or reality? And that was the name that came to me, Belenos, not Apollo as the Greeks and Romans would have him. Image or reality? Perhaps both...

As a boy I had often seen things invisible to others. My father said I'd been dropped on my head as a baby; my foster brother told me I was a changeling child of the Shee, you had only to look at my pointed chin and high cheek bones. But while I lived in Britain, I was not abnormal: there were many others to whom the Otherworld was open. Here in Rome they said I had second sight, like Scipio Africanus, who had been able to see the future in dreams, but I had learnt to make no mention of my visions. I watched Belenos-Apollo fill the universe with golden light and tried to persuade myself that even the supernatural is an indifferent... My last remaining companion whined piteously, scrambled to his feet and ran out.

The piercing calls and whistles of the crowd brought me back up to the surface. If they were suddenly louder, it was because

Seneca had left his seat and was standing at the open door to watch the spectacle. I joined him there and listened to his lame pretences that he was observing tyranny in action. Then his kind face crumpled in a smile. 'You win, my young Briton, as always.' That was good to hear although it was not true, I did not always win. As a boy I had lost almost every race to my foster brother. 'Where do you go when you disappear like that?' Seneca asked.

'To a place my people call the Otherworld. I suppose you think that's superstition?'

'No. Just another thing to be indifferent to. Interesting one, though. I would have you show me the trick of it sometime. Oh Jupiter, here he comes, the god himself.'

Wearing a golden mask, a cuirass of gold and a golden crown radiating sunbeams, Caligula was standing in his chariot with his arms raised to the exultant crowd. It was a day in early spring but the sun in the sky had heat in it and obligingly glanced off the god in a dazzle. 'Here I am!' the god cried. 'Helios, the New Sun! Fall down and worship me, your living god!' I'm not sure which was more alarming, this ridiculous apparition or the moaning people reaching out their trembling arms towards him. You'd think, wouldn't you, that Rome was a reasonable place? Full of intelligent men capable of making an empire of the whole world? You'd think so, on your way here at the age of ten. Then you'd arrive and find nothing was as expected. The magnificent republic was well and truly gone and we were in an age of madness. It had been only after his death that Augustus was called a god; he never proclaimed himself divine; nor did his successor Tiberius. What pit of lunacy had we sunk to?

'When a man is so vain as to consider himself divine,' said Seneca, 'he risks the wrath of the true gods.' He turned back inside. 'Well, I'm not surprised you won. The rest of them — merely the sons of senators more in control of their slaves than they are of themselves. I don't expect any of them will still be with me in a year's time. The next fashion in philosophy will have caught them and they will be wearing hair shirts or be on diets of seafood, but only for the short time before the next fashion sets in. Hypocrites. Like Claudius.'

'Claudius? My Claudius?'

'I hear he was at the baths last night, forcing himself on a woman but too drunk to do the deed. That is disgusting. Sometimes I look upon citizens of Rome and wish I were a barbarian.'

I raised an eyebrow at that.

'Barbarians are properly raised to the virtuous life,' Seneca said, 'and are taught to be brave beyond what any other man can endure. I'm sorry I drew attention to your arm.'

'It was a useful lesson. Standing out from others, looking "odd" as you call it — it's something I find very difficult to be indifferent to.'

He took hold of my arm and studied the scarring. 'Looks like you tried to flay yourself.'

I took my arm back. 'It was many years ago.' I stooped to retrieve the heavy scrolls I'd collected from the imperial library for my mentor, Caligula's uncle Claudius. 'What have you got?' Seneca asked, reading the labels at the ends.

'Polybius.'

'Happy reading for me, then, while you are gone.'

'Gone where?'

'To buy yourself a slave at the flea market,' he said, taking his purse from his girdle and counting out its contents. 'It's not fitting that you, the son of a king, should fetch and carry. Two hundred and sixty-four denarii. Won't buy you a knackered donkey. Still, do what you can.' He put the money back in the purse and handed it to me. 'Perhaps the gods will be with you.'

They would have to be. It was about a tenth of the going rate for a good slave.

'The flea market,' he repeated, 'down by the river. That's the place for bargains.'

I looked out across the Forum. 'Have you seen what's between me and the river?'

'Excellent practice for the aspiring Stoic. Learn to move through the crowd as if you were invisible.'

With that, he shut the door on me and the world.

I chose each step carefully, looking for gaps between men like oil finding its fluid path. I tried not to notice the deranged faces pressing in on me, of artisans and courtesans, of mothers wrapped in mantels or priests of Bacchus wearing rouge and kohl. It was hard, but even harder to be indifferent to the sense of smell, that universal stink of stale body oil mixed with sweat. I squeezed my invisible way around the Forum and passed close to the Temple of Castor and Pollux where Helios the God was descending from his golden chariot attended by close companions, one of whom I recognized.

Adminios, son of Cymbelinus, surely. It must have been a decade since I had last seen him, standing aloof at some festival where I was wrestling his youngest brother, Caratacos. Remote and aloof. A 'Romey'. One who had adopted Roman fashion and culture. One who had friendly relations with the Empire. A Romey, like his father; like my father, also, Verica of the Atrebates. Any king or chieftain of Britain interested in trade and prosperity was a client of Rome. Adminios, yes, king of the Cantii people: no one else was quite as bandy as him. And there I was, he who had been indifferent to the epiphany of a god, now caught like a fly by curiosity. Wondering what Adminios was doing in Rome, dreaming myself back in the past, back in Britain, hating all the sons of Cymbelinus but Adminios most because he was ten years older than me and aloof. When someone in the crowd inadvertently stomped on my toes in his hobnailed sandals, I railed at him. So, here I was, not half an hour from my lesson and back in the world of pain and anger. A failed Stoic, I limped off down an alley leading to the river.

Loneliness. That was something else I was finding it difficult to be indifferent to. Sometimes I would wake in the night and find myself teetering on an abyss of nothingness. The loneliness of exile, of not being able to speak your own language. I needed someone not only to carry scrolls but also to be a companion. British slaves, I am proud to say, are few — or they were then — and I had scant hope of finding one in the flea market but there, behind a pile of old furniture and a stall of broken horse trappings, was a puny individual with long black hair looking like a cornered weasel. I went close to read the placard hanging round the captive's neck.

CALLS HIMSELF MANDRED

YEW RIVER TRIBE, SEA PEOPLE, SOUTHERN BRITAIN

GOOD AT WAY-FINDING AND CHARIOT DRIVING

OBEDIENT BUT LACKING IN ALL RESPECT FOR HIS BETTERS

DEFORMED IN THE LEGS

'Not much call for way-finding and chariot driving in the city,' said the dealer, 'so he's going cheap. I'm not going to lie to you, he's a handful.' He poked at the Briton with an iron prod. The wretched captive did not respond to the provocation but just stared at the ground. I've seen caged animals like that, who have given up the fight.

'Any other negative qualities you may have forgotten to mention?' I asked.

'Only that he's like one of them Stoics and they don't make good slaves. Look.' He prodded the short man again, harder this time. 'How can you control someone who has no fear?'

'So how cheap is he?'

'I'll let you have him for five hundred denarii. To be honest I ought to pay you to take him off me, but I've got to make a living.'

'Five hundred denarii?' I examined the slave as you would a horse, running my hands over his limbs to check that they were sound. As I did, I noticed red, raw chaffing on his neck from the iron collar. 'I'll give you two hundred. You say he is lame after all.' I could see nothing wrong in his thin legs. 'In what way is he lame?'

'He came all the way from Britain shackled in irons. Arrived ruined. But it was the only way they could stop him diving into the sea. Wild thing.'

'Two hundred.'

'No.'

'I'll give you two hundred and fifty.'

'Get off with you. You're robbing me.'

I walked away and had got further than I'd expected before he called me back and, holding out his grubby paw for two hundred and fifty denarii, handed Mandred over like a dog on a chain. As the slave stepped down off the low platform he'd been standing on, he lurched forward. At first I thought he was going to fall, but that was the way he walked, stumbling forwards into each new step.

The dealer, who kept a twig of rosemary in the corner of his mouth, smiled with his teeth clenched, a smile which said he'd got a very good deal, but he'd warned me, hadn't he? A smile which said that all men except himself were fools.

'Sea people — Durotriges?' I addressed my new slave in what I could remember of the Durotrigan dialect but, getting no response, tried several other dialects. I'd forgotten more than I'd realised. For eight years I'd spoken Roman, read Latin and studied Greek. And now, in my own Gaulish tongue, I spoke gibberish. In silence, Mandred followed a foot behind, stumbling along head down in his strange gait. The oddest and most pitiful thing about him was that he kept his hands clasped in front as if they were bound. Far from being surly, wild, independent or free, he followed me like a dog that had gone stupid with gratitude. I took a risk and gave him the chain attached to his iron collar. 'Here, carry it yourself.' As I hoped, he did not run but then, how could he?

'Thank you,' Mandred said, in Gaulish. 'Master...?'

18

'My paternal name is Togidubnos,' I said, inviting him to walk by my side.

'Striking Deep?'

'That is its meaning. A warrior name bestowed by my father but here I go by the name of Delfos, my cradle name given by my mother. The Romans find it easier.'

If he was lame it was from walking on his toes. The slave shuffle.

'Togidubnos... Your father... would that be Verica?' he asked, frowning.

'Indeed, yes, Verica, King of the Atrebates.'

'As was,' he said.

I stopped and turned. 'What do you mean? Has he died?'

'No, he lives, but in exile. Have you heard about the battle for Calleva? No?'

'Such things are not considered news in this city. Has it been lost?'

'Aye. The Atrebates were driven out of their oppidum and their lands.'

I blanched.

'Verica retreated to Noviomagos and, once he'd recovered from his wounds, crossed to Gaul. He ran from Britain like a cat.' Mandred pulled a wry face, reminding me that, though we were both Britons, we were not of the same tribe. He, Durotrigan, could not help but make clear his feelings about Verica's cowardly flight.

'Who was it? The Catuvellauni?'

Mandred nodded.

'Cymbelinus?'

'No, he had just died. Adminios was his rightful heir but the rest of his sons went on the rampage, threw off all the trappings of the Roman life, turned on Adminios and chased him into exile.' Again that twisted look of disapproval, as if the Durotriges were the model of the virtuous society, which assuredly they were not.

19

'He's here. I saw Adminios this very morning, with the Princeps.'

It made sense now: the main benefit of being a client of Rome was the promise of military aid when required. Adminios must have come seeking help to regain his territory. That was the Roman deal. Give us your tributes and your royal sons as hostage, and we'll help you in times of trouble. Unfortunately, Adminios was seeking help from a man not renowned for keeping his side of any bargain. Gods don't do deals. Adminios would have to resort to oblations and sacrifices.

'Do the Catuvellauni possess all our territory now?'

'Not all. The Belgae still have Ford of the Alders and are keeping and protecting Noviomagos.'

'But our capital at Calleva is gone?'

Mandred nodded.

'Our horse herds?'

'Gone.'

Calleva, the oppidum in the woods. Suddenly I was assaulted by memories of people, family, home, of favourite trees, pet dogs, my secret den, my father's treasured stallion. If the king had fled, then my tribe was no more, and no one had thought to tell me. The only clue had been the sudden cessation of my allowance a year before, and I suppose I should have worked it out for myself, or at least made enquiries. By the time we reached the Forum, the crowds had dispersed, intent on supper after the excitement of the day. Now the place was just its usual bustling self, people picking up bread, cheese and fruit from small shops on their way home.

'Where are you going?' asked a familiar voice from behind me, 'and what is this mutt carrying his own lead?' I turned to face Claudius, standing in conversation with a group of senators.

'My slave. I've just bought him to help me carry your books.'

Claudius's face was always mobile with involuntary tics, yet I recognized a sudden squint of anger, and that he was keeping it within bounds. 'Well you won't need him where you're going.'

'What do you mean?'

'Did you not hear the words of the god from the rostra? Helios intends to shine on Britain.'

My stomach lurched as if the ground had fallen away beneath me.

'Oh?' I said, struggling to feign indifference. It was one of Claudius's pastimes, to knock Stoics off their stride. He was like a boy with a catapult among a flock of birds. He practised the stoical disciplines himself, but he could not bear hypocrites. He brought his face close to mine, to watch for those blinks and twitches that betray true feeling. His breath smelt of sardines and coriander. 'He says it's time we conquered the barbarians and brought civilization to the wild north.'

Since I agreed with him — after eight years in Rome I had come to see my people through Roman eyes, as naked savages of the bogs — I simply nodded and said, 'True.'

'Naturally, he shall want Britons to advise him.'

'Alas, I remember too little of my homeland to be of any help.'

'But you speak the language and are the son of a king.'

'A king in exile.'

'In exile? Verica? Is that why you've been living this past year solely on my generosity?'

'According to my slave.'

'Nevertheless, I shall have no hesitation in recommending you to my nephew.'

Was he wanting to be rid of me? For buying a slave?

'Come to me the moment you are back at the house.'

I found Seneca where I'd left him, staring into space as they say Socrates was wont to do. He roused when I touched his arm and blinked in surprise at my purchase. Without saying anything, he picked up a scroll and laid it across Mandred's arms; one by one he piled them up, waiting for the one that would prove the slave's undoing and make him drop the rest. Mandred did not flinch. He took all the scrolls then said to me, 'Is that it? Lead on, then.'

I laughed and took a few back from him. 'I bought a man,' I said, 'not a pack horse.' Besides, I did not wish to risk things of such value on a man who lurched in his gait. We shared the burden.

'Is all well with you, Delfos?' Seneca asked. He too watched my face as I answered but his gaze was more that of a doctor than a torturer.

'I've heard Caligula intends to mount a conquest of Britain.'

Seneca laughed. 'And you think he will succeed?'

'Of course not. Which is even more reason not to be part of his entourage.'

Seneca's fluid face passed from humour to concern. 'Whatever you do, avoid that. The world is mad enough without keeping the company of maniacs.'

On the way back to the house of Claudius, I stopped at a blacksmith's forge and had the iron collar cut off Mandred. He was already in pain from the chaffing. Now he had to sit still while a file went back and forth very close to his neck. He bore it all with impressive equanimity.

3

IN BED WITH MESSALINA

When I arrived back at the house, I met Claudius's young wife in the atrium. With one appreciative glance I noted that her figure had not suffered from the recent birth of her first child. She took a step towards me but said nothing, only rolled her eyes and pulled a face to indicate I should avoid her husband, but how could I? I was under orders. Since Messalina stood in my path, I had to brush past her to take the scrolls to Claudius in his study. Her scent wafted like that of meadow flowers crushed underfoot. I cleared my throat, told myself to be brave and, entering Claudius's study, walked into a very caldarium of anger where his fury was making the walls sweat.

'Who said you could buy yourself a slave?' he demanded. 'Did you not think to ask me first? Where's he going to sleep? Am I supposed to feed him?' He gave me no chance to make any reply; I stood with my head bowed, waiting for him to subside. This was the first time I had been on the receiving end of his famous temper and I knew that it was not really about Mandred. Eventually the flames died down to a smouldering, muttering discontent as he rearranged his desk. As gently as I could I explained that Mandred had been a gift from Seneca.

'You should have sought my permission first!' he squalled, firing up again. 'What's wrong with a porter if you need help carrying?' Once more he subsided. His mood was like a hypocaust furnace being stoked by an incompetent child, all flarings and smoke. 'What did you bring from the library, anyway?'

Mandred stepped forward and carefully placed the scrolls of Polybius in front of the Dominus whose head shook as if he were negating everything he said. His freedman and secretary, Narcissus, made a neat pile of them on the desk. 'What's the matter with his legs?' Claudius demanded, nodding at Mandred.

'He spent too long in shackles.'

Claudius himself walked with a limp. A genuine limp, so far as he was concerned, and not some left-over stiffness from a long sea voyage. He studied the labels on the ends of the scrolls and drew one out. Narcissus helped him open it.

'Are you a Gaul?' Claudius asked Mandred in Gaulish.

'Briton.'

'Same thing. I'm a Gaul.'

'Claudius was born in Gaul of noble Roman parents,' I said to Mandred. 'Likes to think he's a barbarian. He also claims to be one of the last of the line of Augustus. Can't have it both ways, can we, Dominus?'

Claudius smiled crookedly as he began to read. Believing the squall was over, and that I was going to live another day, I took one of the scrolls to my desk. My own desk. I don't think I was fonder of any other aspect of Roman life than having a desk and being able to read and write.

I read out a passage to Claudius about Dis Pater, for this was a god who fascinated us both. According to Julius Caesar in his book on the Gallic wars, the Britons claimed descent from him, but Dis is a Roman god of the underworld and I had not been happy with my native home being associated with hell, not least because we had no such concept of a place of the dead. For us, souls pass into new bodies and don't hang about in ghostly stagnation. Our Otherworld is, well, other... I had a theory that Dis Pater was a corruption of the Greek *Zeus-Pater* — Father God — and Polybius was confirming this.

'It's Jupiter!' said Claudius. 'Same etymology, surely. *Dyaus ... dyu-pita* or something like it.'

And this was Claudius, that man of many facets, at his best. Alone at our studies, alone surely in our interests, we snuffled like happy pigs amongst the leaves and mast of knowledge.

'According to this,' he said, pointing to the text he was reading, 'Britons fight naked with their hair spiked with lime. Is that true?'

'Yes, and we decapitate our enemies and use their skulls as cups,' I said, teasing him.

'By Apollo!'

'No, it's not true,' I laughed. 'At least, I don't remember seeing such things myself.' I brushed my face to clear the vision of tattered old heads hanging on ropes at my father's doorway.

'But it is true,' said Mandred, who was not given to behaving like a slave, 'and we use their brains for slingshot.'

Claudius snapped upright. 'A slave who dares to speak?'

'And in Roman,' I said, looking appreciatively at Mandred.

'Brains for slingshot?' Claudius was intrigued.

'Brain balls,' said Mandred. 'The brains of enemies pounded up in a mortar, bound and hardened with a mixture of lime and rolled between the palms of children.'

Claudius's eyes widened at this strange, crippled fellow's boldness and brilliance.

'It seems I bought something of a bargain at the market,' I said with a laugh to break the tension.

'Polybius speaks truly,' Mandred declaimed, speaking now in oratorical Latin. 'Even gods think twice about taking on Britons.'

'You're not a druid, are you?'

Mandred assured him he was not.

'He may stay,' Claudius mumbled, his head shaking as if he meant the opposite, 'for as long as you're both staying, which won't be long. My nephew will be wanting your services in his expedition.' He suddenly gazed into space as if at ghosts. 'And mine, no doubt. He'll want to summon me to pick my brains.' Now his head began to wobble violently on his neck. Since the accession of his nephew, Caligula, he had lost much weight and all his tremors had become exaggerated. He glanced up at me with pleading in his eyes. 'I'll have to suffer one of his dinner parties. He'll make me stand up and give the history of Britannia while he and his guests pelt me with fruit stones like last time.' Now he blinked rapidly and had to hold his hands steady on the desk. 'Will you come with me?'

I could think of a thousand reasons why I shouldn't.

'Please, Delfos. You can distract them. A tall barbarian, a practising Stoic proud and aloof at the orgy. You can tell them yourself everything they want to know about Britain.'

'Why should I betray my people?'

'Because you're one of us. Aren't you? I expect he'll want you with him on his expedition, to show him how the land lies, that sort of thing.'

'Dominus, you know that I crave a quiet life. Can you please make sure I am not included in any expedition?'

'I thought you wanted to go home.'

Before I discovered Stoicism, I had had a tendency to home-sickness. It had long since passed. 'Not in these circumstances,' I said. He smiled. Now, in retrospect, I wonder about that smile. It was always closed-mouth and slanted with Claudius; I don't think I ever saw him throw back his head and reveal his teeth in laughter; nor did his eyes ever crease up. When he smiled, he remained watchful. I felt the chill of fear I'd felt meeting him in the Forum. Did he know? And if he did know, when was he going to act?

When I left his study, I saw the door to Messalina's chamber standing open but, feeling that I'd tempted Providence quite enough, I slept on my own that night and when the light tap came on my door, had my new slave send her away.

From the time of her marriage to Claudius the previous year, Messalina governed her husband more thoroughly than ever he'd been governed before, his desire making him slave to her caprices. I remember my first sight of her. The shape of her, the scent of her, the sound of her... I was only seventeen at the time and, though I appreciated my newly-adopted Stoicism as a theory, in practice, well... I told myself this was what Seneca meant when he spoke of 'preferable indifferents' but of course it wasn't. I was a hypocrite from the moment I met her and uncaring of what crimes I must now commit against the man who was giving me his hospitality and a fine education. Three nights out of seven, she had come to my small room at the back of the new house against the hill to experience the embrace of a barbarian three years her junior and twice her height. I overcame any guilt I might feel by convincing myself that I was doing Claudius a great service by making her life tolerable. After all, being in bed with a man thirty years older than you is bad enough but with Claudius, it must have been like sleeping with a frog, all spasm and drool, kicking legs and fishy breath.

Do not harbour any idea that I deflowered a virgin or corrupted a young mind. She made the first advance, and she let it be known she had other lovers, the prime one being the Princeps, Caligula himself, who found it amusing to bed an aunt who was several years his junior. Only once a month did Messalina go to the bed of her husband and that solely for the purpose of procreation, which soon worked. At first I had worried that the child would prove to be mine but she reassured me that she knew precisely who the father was, and that it was who it should be. By what arts she knew these things, or controlled nature, I never found out. Once the pregnancy had begun to show, I stopped our liaison. Now, after a short period of confinement, she was making it plain that she wanted it to resume. My fear of her husband and resolve to avoid her lasted only one night. On the next, I had Mandred let her in.

'Oh,' she said, 'we have an audience?'

'We can trust him.'

She slipped into my bed, dousing my passion with the news that the Princeps was making enquiries about me. 'He wants native Britons to help him with his plans for his expedition.'

I felt my skin creep. 'What did you tell him?'

'Oh...' she nuzzled me with her nose. 'How clever you are, how Roman you are, despite your tattoos, that kind of thing. Of course I told him you have a brilliant mind and are bilingual in Gaulish and Roman and know a good many dialects.'

'Well, thank you!' I said, sitting up. 'Anyone would think you want me to go with him, to certain death!'

'Caligula is clever. If I'd down-played your virtues, he would have guessed why and it would have been bad for both of us. Don't worry. This is only the first part of my plan.'

'It's not true, about the languages. I've forgotten Gaulish. I am bilingual only in Roman and Greek. And I'm a philosopher, not a soldier!'

She smiled, as if to say, 'You're not even a philosopher.'

I was too tense now to sleep.

'I thought philosophers advocate courage,' she said, propping herself on an elbow.

'They do,' I moaned, 'I am not as good a Stoic as I would like to be.'

'At least you're honest,' she said, kissing my patterned shoulder and drawing me down again. I buried my head in her hair, loose on the pillow. I kissed her now here, now there, pausing from kissing her navel to tell her what an omphalos is.

'It means a central place, but only in the symbolic sense. In reality it can be anywhere. On the human body, for instance, it is quite far south.' As in Britain. The omphalos, the place where this world joins the other one, where forms gain spirits and spirits gain form.

'I tend to find men who think too much incredibly dull,' she said. I took her mind off that thought by kissing her again on that warm, soft navel that trembled under my breath. After that, things were far from dull.

28

It was spring. Warm air flowed in through the open window carrying the scents of jasmine and nut blossom. We had not met for several months while Messalina recovered from the birth of her first child, a daughter who, I had been relieved to learn, looked just like Claudius.

'I think he knows,' I said, falling back on my pillow.

'Caligula?'

'Claudius. He wants me to go on this expedition. Wants me out of the way. Wants me to go with Caligula to fight my own people.' My breathing was fast and ragged. 'I have to avoid it somehow.'

'There is a mission going to Greece to put up statues in the temples. With your qualifications, you are even more fitted for that than the British expedition. That is step two of my plan, to convince Caligula of it.'

'Greece?' I sighed. That out of all these ills could come a good...

'It won't be a culture tour,' she said. 'The statues you'll be putting up will be of the Divine Gaius, Caligula's own image. The Greeks will be outraged.'

'Nevertheless...' Since I had begun my studies in philosophy, Greece had become a mythical land of truth and goodness in my soul. It had given birth to so much wisdom...

Messalina said she would arrange it. Twenty years old and mistress of the affairs of men. Relieved, I snuggled down with her.

Mandred shook me awake at dawn. A secretary from the imperial palace with two of the Praetorian guard were at the gate to the house. Of course they had come for Claudius, to bring him an invitation to dinner, but my guilt had me springing from my bed, scrambling into my clothes and escaping through a small door in the enclosing wall that led out on to the hillside. Mandred stumbled after me, saying things about cowardice.

After a day spent hiding amongst tombs, I went to Seneca's house. He studied Mandred's neck and an infected abrasion with concern and called for his wife to bring a salve.

'The blacksmith was careful,' I said, 'but it was close work.'

'Indeed,' he said, dabbing on the ointment. 'Did you flinch, perhaps?' he asked Mandred. I told him that my slave did not know the meaning of the word.

'Is there such a thing as a natural-born Stoic?' I asked.

'Only amongst barbarians.' Seneca stood back and returned the salve to his wife. 'Well done, Delfos. You spent my money well and have found a man wiser than yourself. What are you doing here? Servants of Claudius came earlier, looking for you. Apparently you're springing about like a nervous goat.'

'It's Caligula. He makes a coward of me.'

'I would say that you are wise to avoid him.'

'The Praetorians came to the house at dawn. I was in Messalina's bed. What would you do?'

'Me?' he chuckled. 'I wouldn't put myself in that position in the first place.'

'Now I realise it wasn't me they'd come for. Claudius is so reluctant to attend Caligula's banquets that invitations are delivered by armed guard. But after a night troubled by dreams, I believed they had come for me to lead the expedition to Britain.'

Seneca laughed heartily. Throughout that fine spring day as we sat in the shelter of his topiary, he probed me with questions to find out if there was anything underlying my aversion to going home. I folded over, trying to discover the source of my unease, and all I could think of were the rows my mother used to have with my father, the shouting, the inflamed curses, and Verica thundering back like Zeus himself. I remembered also the cold dampness of the place, the blandness of the food — every day brown stuff ladled out of the cauldron — and the constant state of alertness, always on guard against the next raid on your livestock, the sudden rush into the stead by mead-fuelled warriors looking for booty, looking for women...

'I don't want to go home,' I moaned.

'Why? You've always extolled your native land, compared to which Rome is, to use your words, a cesspit of decadence. So why now the reluctance to go home?' The questions kept coming as he sought to prise open my soul like a clam until I revealed the truth.

'Life in Britannia...' I said, 'is barbaric...'

'And so it is,' Seneca agreed, 'a seething cauldron of men lost to their passions: bandits, rustlers, rapists, warriors who have muscle where their brains should be.' His words stabbed at me and I writhed.

'Answer my question,' he said, 'are you Roman or British?'

'British,' I said through clenched teeth.

'Up until now, I think we both thought of you as Roman.'

From being a barbarian child, resentful at living in the capital of the oppressive Empire, I was soon wearing the clothes and speaking the language, as convinced as anyone of civilization's superiority; a city boy. But Seneca's insults against my people poked a stick into where my barbarian self lay curled up and dormant. My soul stirred.

'So, now, we can properly begin our examination of your problem. Caligula may call for your help on his expedition. That makes you feel wretched, as if you were betraying your people.'

'Yes.'

'But what if your people were to benefit from a Roman presence? There has long been trade between southern Britain and Rome — your tribe in particular — but our merchants have to have strong escorts from the military. Peace would be to everyone's benefit.'

'It would. But if there were a battle, which side should I be on?'

31

'It is the duty of a man to defend his family, his home, his tribe.'

'Is it? Then you are saying that I must go home with the imperial army and, once there, turn round and defend my people against them?'

Seneca nodded thoughtfully. 'It is a problem, isn't it? Let me reflect on it awhile.'

I didn't return to the house of Claudius until after dark and found him in his study dabbing at his nose and reading about the druids. He had dined at the imperial palace. 'I'd asked you to come with me, had I not? But could I find you? Not at all. Absent all day at places unknown. And that's how you repay my kindness to you.'

I apologised and told him the truth, that I had no wish to bring myself to his nephew's attention, not while he was recruiting. The sniffling Claudius glanced up and I saw again that other Claudius within, the one with intelligent eyes. The one who wanted me gone.

'How was it?' I asked.

'Inquisitorial, to put it mildly. I told my nephew what I know, mostly from what I've been reading in Polybius about the Britons. I also told him I have two druids in my house. He was very interested to hear that.'

I felt the sweat break out. 'Neither I nor Mandred are druid.'

'You need to look more closely at that shifty slave of yours. And you are half druid, are you not? Tell me what you know about them. I read that they have the power of judgement,' Claudius said, 'they are the lawgivers and law keepers.'

I nodded in agreement.

'They have the power of religion. They are the priests and take charge of sacrifices. They have the power of healing. And they have other, stranger powers, too. Divination. Magic. Some report shape-shifting, turning one natural object into another. And communication. It's said they can communicate with each other quicker than the fastest messenger on the speediest horse. They are masters of singing and can send messages via mountain tops. Is any of this true?'

I remembered those strange calls, louder than a wolf, more expressive than an owl, running across the land from dun to dun, penetrating a forest like a frost. And the long-distance whistles, ascending for announcements of birth, descending for death. I had blocked such memories to avoid pain and home-sickness but now, after Seneca's prising into my soul, I was open and vulnerable. I began to tremble but Claudius did not notice.

'Why is Caligula so interested in the druids?' I asked. 'You'd think he'd want to know about the warriors and how they fight.'

'No doubt they fight the same as any other barbarian: stupidly. When it comes to battle, the Romans will win. It's resistance that concerns Caligula, and the druids are the very seat of resistance. Get the druids and you get Britain, I told him.' Claudius was one of those curious men who wish to destroy the very thing they find most fascinating. Or, to put it another way, find fascinating that which they wish to destroy.

While other men had riotous supper parties getting drunk on couches (I always assumed they dined lying down to save themselves a fall), Seneca and I preferred to dine alone, sitting cross-legged British-style and feeding ourselves on figs, cheese and moral problems.

I asked him, 'When is it right to resist?'

'When your state is threatened by an enemy.'

'What if the enemy is stronger?'

'Then it would be advisable not to resist. Men beat their chests, bulge their eyes and storm in the name of freedom when all they are is angry. Look into history, lad, and you will find that many national heroes were but self-seeking warlords.'

I knew this indeed to be the case, with only one or two exceptions.

'But if the people are oppressed by the enemy, should they not rise up?'

'You cannot be prescriptive about it. It depends on the time, the place, the people. You will only know in the moment, whether honour or freedom are worth the sacrifice.'

'Surely they are always worth it.'

'Thus speaks a barbarian. You have the benefit, of course, of an afterlife worth having. That helps. The only time a Roman will choose death is when life becomes intolerable.'

'As with lady Antonia?'

'Indeed. But as to your question, if it relates to resistance to Roman incursion then think twice. Don't forget I'm Iberian by birth and ancestry and I thank the gods for my Roman citizenship. If you are worried about your homeland, and want a model for how its people should behave under occupation, read Strabo on the history of Hispania. It's a story of peaceful merging of two cultures. And if you want a hero to worship, look to Viriatus of Lusitania.' He helped himself to a handful of almonds. 'You have a miserable choice,' he said. 'Either to go with the Princeps and oppress your own people or become their champion, a very short-lived one, in all probability, but with a mighty reputation assured. What's it going to be?'

I buried my face in my hands and spoke the truth in an incoherent mumble.

'What was that?'

'I said I'd rather walk away into the forest. I don't want to make such a choice!'

He gazed at me with sympathy. 'There is, perhaps, a solution to your problem. There is a mission leaving shortly for Greece to put up statues of our Divine Princeps in the temples.'

'I know,' I said, looking up. I've asked Messalina to get me on it.'

'Well, I had a word with Caligula's secretary and told him that you would be of enormous value to the mission, for you have the language and are familiar with the wisdom of the Greek philosophers. It will be a difficult mission, although not as difficult as it is proving to be in Judea, where the Jews are flatly refusing to put statues of emperors in their temples. But the Greeks…'

'They are more malleable?'

Seneca humphed. 'They are wiser. They will let us set up our sacrilegious abominations then remove them once we've gone. Rome will know, but Rome will do nothing. The Greeks, you see, are our superiors. We won the war, but they won our minds. How did Horace put it? Captive Greece captured her wild conqueror. No, they won't resist, but they'll be hostile. I told the secretary that the mission would benefit greatly from the inclusion in its number of a young noble who can speak their language, especially if he is not Roman himself.'

Only Seneca ever referred to me as 'noble'. To everyone else I was exotic at best, uncouth at worst. 'Who's in charge?' I asked.

'Praetor Vespasian. A man of integrity whom Caligula wants out of the city. You will like him.'

Seneca spoke again to the secretary and convinced him that putting up statues of the Divine Princeps in Greek temples was a far better use of me than my acting as a translator in Britain. 'I reminded him of the reception we receive when we try to put up statues in Judea,' he told me later. 'He paled and agreed. You can expect a formal invitation.'

Thus, as Caligula set off north at the head of his legions to conquer Britain, I was on my way east, to be conquered by Greece.

4

ATHENA

If the philosophical schools are next to the gymnasia, it is to remind us that, body and soul, we are in need of exercise. I enjoyed wrestling and running but when it came to military training I had pleaded to be in the cavalry. My desire was granted and I'd spent much of my happy youth in the stables and practice paddocks. I had had to learn to use a saddle, to resist plaiting manes or decorating animals with dangling amulets but instead to take my pleasure in grooming those dark brown hides to a gleam, something impossible on any British horse. Sometimes in my fantasies I was at home, riding the hills on a Roman horse, commanding all before me, especially that ear-grating braggart, Caratacos of the Catuvellauni. I only had to mount a Roman horse to feel myself superior, no matter what my background. Thus, on the mission to Greece, I rode with the Noble Youths in attendance on Praetor Vespasian and, in doing so, felt myself superior even to Greeks.

We rode up from the port to the city of Athens. Despite having lived nine years in Rome, I was unprepared for my first view of the Parthenon, the great temple high on the rocky Acropolis. The size of it, the soaring size of it half way between earth and heaven: it was easy to believe that Athena herself dwelt there. Led by priests and neophytes clashing cymbals and blowing on pipes, our formal procession began at the Temple of Mysteries, which marks the beginning of the Sacred Way from the Acropolis to Eleusis a few miles to the north.

Eleusis… almost every great philosopher I had ever studied had been an initiate of the Mysteries, Plato, Socrates, all of them, but our mission did not have Eleusis on its itinerary. 'How far to Eleusis?' I asked our interpreter.

'Not far. To the coast and around the gulf, not far.'

Vespasian turned in his saddle and gazed at me through narrowed eyes. 'Delphidius! Keep your mind on the business,' he said. For him, 'Delfos' was too informal, 'Togidubnus' unpronounceable. I pulled my thoughts from Eleusis and concentrated on our immediate task, which was to install a statue of Caligula in the Temple of Athena. A small detachment of Legio IV Macedonica tramped in two files, one either side of a wagon bearing a statue of the emperor as we went up, past so many gorgeous temples and treasuries to the summit where the soaring columns of the Parthenon reached up to the sea-blue sky.

The gateway, itself as big as a temple, opened on to the fore-courts and pavements of Athena. Rome had made a sceptic of me but, as we came to the steps up to the temple, suddenly I rediscovered my awe of the divine. There was no building in my homeland where you had to crick your neck to look up at it. I felt overwhelmed by scale, like a farm animal that has strayed into the open forest. I gazed up at the figures of men and horses and gods crammed into the triangle of the colourful pediment, taking in what I could in a moment for there was no opportunity to stop and stare. I wanted to fall to my knees and weep at the achievements of the Greeks, to throw myself prostrate before them crying, 'You are the masters! Let me be your slave!' Instead with impassive face I followed the Praetor.

The clashing of cymbals and gongs accelerated as the doors to the temple, four times the height of a man, were drawn open. They opened so smoothly, so in time with each other, you would think winged spirits were the door-keepers. And there she was, Athena, standing in the centre of the temple under a deeply coffered ceiling, dwarfing us all, including our statue. The priest standing on her plinth was the height of her golden knee. Gold and ivory, that was the first impression, a mountain of precious stuffs, although I later learned that the real gold had been stripped by Romans on a previous visit and had been eplaced by gilded bronze. Her blue eyes in her lofty, helmeted head, stared out over all Athens, the city she had won in a contest with Poseidon. On her breast plate, a pendant image of Medusa to turn to stone any man who gazed there. Her peplos of golden folds was cinched at the waist by a belt of two entwined serpents, with another serpent, coiled and erect, beside her shield. On her outstretched right hand stood a figure of Nike, the goddess of Victory, looking like a doll although she was the same size as us. To gaze up at Athena, the work of the divine Phidias, was to feel small and inconsequential against the gods. Our party stood in awed silence staring up at the goddess, apart from Mandred who just stared at the floor, his hands clasped in front of him.

The high priest called us forward and began to intone prayers to Athena. We made our gifts of wine, flowers, the blood of a sheep slaughtered at her altar, the scent of burnt flesh. Praetor Vespasian begged her forgiveness for the trespasses of our predecessors, saying they were barbarians, promising future harmony between Rome and Greece and formally asking her permission to put a statue of the emperor in her temple as a mark of this accord. The gifts made, the haruspex examined the liver of the sheep in a silver dish and announced that Athena looked kindly upon the new god. I could not help but wonder what the outcome would have been had she not.

The bronze statue of Caligula was ceremoniously brought in and mounted on the plinth that had been prepared; it stood there, one arm outstretched, a midget in the shadow of Athena. Vespasian would write to the Princeps, telling him how the divine emperor and the goddess gazed at each other eye-to-eye in love. When at last all the interminable rites had been performed, Vespasian and his officers turned to leave. We needed to be in the mountains before the summer heat began to rage and could not linger even one more day in Athens. He marched out of the temple, looking like a god himself in a bronze cuirass moulded to the shape of a hero's chest. The Greeks bowed as he passed.

I was acutely disappointed. I wanted to see everything on the Acropolis, the temples, the sanctuaries, the great theatre of Dionysus; and beyond, the Tower of the Winds which, they claimed, marked time in hours. I wanted to see the agora below, where Socrates, Plato and Aristotle had taught. What was the point of coming all this way and not seeing anything? Not pausing for a moment to look? Clearly Vespasian had no sense of wonder. The sun was hot on the back of my head but a breeze playing round the Acropolis cooled me. From the forecourt, as I looked out to olive trees and cypresses dark against the parched and shimmering land, something moved inside me, as wind in the barley. I dismissed it as mere emotion. I was, I thought, close to being exhausted by the heat. Practising stoical resignation and the surrender of desire, I remounted and followed obediently in the wake of the Praetor, descending the sacred hill with my fellow Noble Youths.

Returning to the Temple of the Mysteries, we set off on the Sacred Way which led us towards the sea. Swaying gently in t he saddle, I entered the trance of the march as we followed the coast on the Corinth road. And there in the distance, a temple high on its rocky prominence. Eleusis! I felt like a man drowning in a river, being pulled down by weed into a new reality. Vespasian's only interest in the place, however, was that it marked the fork in the road that would lead us to Delphi. The unit marched past the temple mount without stopping. I glanced back over my shoulder to look at the temple now behind us and receding. Close-to it had been impossible to see because of its high surrounding wall; it was only now that I could fully appreciate its immensity.

I could not continue riding looking backwards, especially feeling so stricken with disappointment. I took a deep breath, let Eleusis go and faced the future, a future Vespasian was approaching with the steady determination of a plough. He was not the kind of man the future would surprise; he was the kind of man who would surprise the future. He beckoned to me to join him and I rode up.

'There's no need to look so hard-done-by,' he said. 'I've saved you from humiliation. If we'd gone into the temple, you would have found yourself excluded. Barbarians are not allowed.'

'Why?'

He shrugged. 'Something to do with Greece being invaded by Gauls.'

'That was three hundred years ago.'

'Long memories, the Greeks, and a great respect for history.'

In the days it took to reach Mount Parnassus, the summer rose in waves of desiccating heat. At the foothills we left half the unit with the wagons carrying numerous statues of Caligula to make camp and await us, the other half loading just one marble statue on to a small wagon pulled by a pair of white oxen that could negotiate the vertiginous path up the mountain to Delphi. The sun above was relentless – even the animals were sweating – and as it bounced off the barren, limestone rocks, the half-blinded and wincing Roman escort struggled to keep the wagon on a path best suited to donkeys. It lumbered with effort, its heavy wheels grinding on the stones, but the higher we went, the fresher the air became and the heat began to diminish.

For some reason the Praetor had singled me out as a companion. Vespasian was ten years my senior, advancing nicely on the *cursus honorum*, the sequence of office, and you'd have thought we had little in common. Perhaps his low birth and high office, and my high birth and no office, equalised us.

No, it wasn't that. It was this, although I risk vanity to mention it: Vespasian and I share a love of integrity. While others advance themselves by currying favour, by bribes and intimidation, Vespasian always chooses hard work and right action, and he recognized the same love of virtue in me. He is gruff, blunt and has no time for philosophers, and yet he is one – one of the best.

'Delphi is one of the most sacred spots in the world,' he said.

'Used to be. They say the Oracle is silent now and has been for a hundred years. Delphi lives on its past.'

'Are you saying gods die?'

'I have read somewhere that Pan died during the reign of Caesar —'

A shower of loose stones clattered down the mountainside. My horse reared and I tightened the rein to prevent it bolting. Vespasian's horse was as solid and dependable as its rider, 'unspoilt by good breeding' he said. He was of the opinion that you need a broad stock for sound offspring, that mongrels are always to be preferred and I understood that he was speaking about the imperial family. The Praetor sat on his steady horse and watched the stones bounce on the path, over the precipice and into the abyss.

On the wagon our marble statue of Caligula, yellow-haired, pink-faced and blue-eyed, laid with its raised arm pointing at the sky. The wagon groaned; the hooves of the oxen slipped, unable to get a hold on the loose stones; the expressionless statue rocked in its strappings. Vespasian halted the wagon, made the men tighten the ropes while a couple of legionaries brushed the path clear. 'Don't want to lose our divine emperor,' he said, 'or, more importantly, any of you lot. Be careful, stay safe.'

We continued up the path that, as it began to level off, broadened into a paved way. There was a cloud of distant dust on the road behind us and Vespasian halted the column to allow a messenger to catch up. He had news from Rome. The expedition to Britain had failed. My heart fluttered like a dead bird showing life.

Vespasian listened to the news with his face grave and straight and increasingly mask-like. We were told that Caligula's legions had mutinied and refused to cross Oceanus to the land of beasts and monsters, that Caligula had mustered them on the beaches of Gaul and made them collect seashells for war trophies. 'You'd expect more from a god,' Vespasian said to me quietly as we rode on. 'How can we raise his image now without the Greeks laughing at us openly?'

Mandred was lurching along on foot beside my horse and, leaving the Praetor to ride on alone with his glum misgivings I dismounted to walk beside my slave. It seemed to me the proper way to approach Delphi, on foot. I had always longed to see this place, given that I seemed to share its name. The Greeks considered it to be the great omphalos, the navel where earth and heaven meet, where Man is close to the gods; sanctuary of sanctuaries, shrine of shrines. Every nation has its omphalos, determined by its haruspices, but the one here at Delphi claimed to be the centre of the world.

As we neared the sacred sanctuary, we passed more and more temples lining the path, a path now transforming into a well-laid processional way. The Roman legionaries had become ragged and Vespasian paused for everyone to catch up and fall into step again.

'I heard,' said Mandred, 'that before he was appointed to lead this embassy, Vespasian was the magistrate in charge of street cleaning.'

'Well, he served as quaestor in Crete for a year but before that, it's true, he was in charge of street cleaning. No one else would take that job. He's that rare thing, an honest man who does his duty, remaining loyal to Rome even when Rome is humiliating him.'

'Is it true the Princeps stuffed dung down his toga and laughed in his face?'

'No. Caligula was enraged when he saw an alley full of muck and ordered it to be thrown at the magistrate in charge. He didn't do it himself.'

I gazed reflectively on the statue being carried into Delphi. We were going to present it to the Temple of Apollo, along with a matrix for as many bronze heads of the Princeps as the Greeks would care to make. 'Advise them to make many,' Claudius had said. 'For the Princeps is the new god and they must worship him above every deity of Mount Olympus, even above Apollo himself, even above Zeus, if they wish to retain what freedom they have. Consult the Oracle while you are there in Delphi. I have a question for it.'

'But you told me the Oracle is silent these days,' I'd said to him.

'Yes, that is true, but you may still consult even if you don't get an answer.' He had laughed and sprayed me with spittle. Claudius had a mouth like the atrium of a bath house, full of puddles.

A bath house... could I hope for one of those at the end of this journey? Since leaving Athens I had 'bathed' in way stations – just a quick oil and scrape – and felt thick with dirt. A hot bath was what I longed for, even though it was so hot here it would have been more comfortable to bathe in ice. No, a bath must always begin with hot water. Each time I stepped into a bath house, I relived the wonder of my first visit when I had arrived at Rome, the steam which cleanses and relaxes, the informality of the fellow bathers – all status left in the atrium along with our clothes – the oiling of the skin by some dark and silent slave, the scraping of the strigil to remove all the accretions of dirt. And then the cold plunge. I had screamed the first time, the shock, the shrinking of my member to near nothing: I was only ten and had precious little to shrink. But what began as a shock soon became the ultimate delight. These days I limited myself to one bath a week: a love of sensual pleasure is not the way of the philosopher. According to Seneca, even once a week was sheer decadence: he never went to the baths at all. 'To boil down the body and sweat it thin is pointless and effeminate,' he said. But he also said, 'Abstain if you can, but if you can't, be moderate.'

At the final bend in the road before the sacred sanctuary was the gymnasium. Here, surely, was a bath house? But formality obliged us to ride on, following the Sacred Way to the Temple of Apollo and the welcoming ceremony that awaited Praetor Vespasian.

5

KNOW THYSELF

In its glory days, there had been three Oracles at Delphi to deal with the crowds, and men at the back of the queue rarely got to put their questions of great matter. It is much diminished now, although you would not think so from the wealth displayed there. The marble of the sacred precinct had been scrubbed to a white glare. Treasure houses and temples painted red and blue were dominated by the Temple of Apollo soaring above them and above that, behind the sanctuary and like a great fan on the hillside, the theatre. Over the gate that opened on to the forecourt to the Temple was a legend engraved in fine Greek letters: GNOTHI SEAUTON. I stood gazing up at the famous injunction, feeling almost faint to be here, under a legend that had been contemplated by Pythagoras, Socrates, Plato, so many kings, even Alexander the Great. The formal visit of the Roman delegation to the temple would be on the morrow, but I was finding it hard to restrain an impulse for a preview.

Mandred, as usual, was staring at the ground.

'Look at that,' I said. 'Look up, Mandred.'

He raised his eyes but not his head. 'What does it say?'

'Know Thyself.'

He flinched then and made a quick brushing movement as if to be rid of a fly.

'What does it mean to you?' I asked.

'That I'm a slave and should remember it.'

'I've always understood it as "know your place, mortal", or, "be prepared to discover the uncomfortable truth".'

Mandred turned his head sideways like a bird and gazed up at me. 'You're knotting your mind with too much thinking, Master. Know Thyself. It's easy. You're a good man. That's what it means. So, enter freely.'

His face was flushed as if with fever.

'Have you been bitten?'

'Perhaps. I'll wait here for you.'

'I'm not going in, not until tomorrow,' I said and steered him away. As we walked through the streets of Delphi, looking at the buildings sacred and profane, the flush on his face subsided.

Somehow, when you are leader of a Roman unit, the legend over the gateway does not have the same powers of attraction and repulsion. GNOTHI SEAUTON.

'What does that mean?' Vespasian asked me.

When I told him, he smiled and rode through the gate. I have never known a man to sit so easily in his saddle. His equanimity was almost immediately disturbed, however, by the blatant robbery being practised in the courtyard where tethered beasts lowed, bleated or clucked. Rather than be presented with our sacrificial animals we were told we must buy them.

'Greeks!' muttered Vespasian, instructing his optio to buy a goose. The optio persuaded him to do as expected of a great commander and buy a fine, black bull. Vespasian, feeling the pinch of the expense, grunted in agreement and turned to me. 'Do you have a question for the Oracle, Delphidius?'

'Claudius gave me one.'

'But not the money I suppose.' Vespasian nodded grimly to his optio, who selected a small ewe as befitting a barbarian prince. Accompanied by our sacrificial animals, we entered the temple.

The statue of Apollo is not towering like that of Athena in Athens but man-sized, if like me that man is Keltoi (as the Greeks like to call us). It is tall, but not gigantic. Its power rests in its beauty, which takes the breath away. Marble carved into flesh, with the structure of bone, muscle and sinew visible. Naked but for a silken mantle thrown back over his shoulders and draped over his outstretched arm, Apollo has just let an arrow fly from his bow: he is in the act, we are told, of slaying Python.

Our statue of Caligula was much the same height and size. Although the drapes of his white and purple toga were a masterful piece of stone carving, they looked crude next to the naked stone flesh of Apollo. The two statues were mirror images of each other and clearly ours was influenced by theirs; each figure rested with his weight on one leg, only the opposite leg, Apollo on his left, Caligula on his right, each with an outstretched arm, the opposite arm. They would look good side by side, Apollo facing the rising sun, Caligula the setting sun. Had all this symmetry of stone and symbol been deliberate?

The machinery to erect Caligula was already in place. The statue was lifted on to one of two platforms on something resembling a balance. Sandbags were added to the other platform to raise him gently. It was all done slowly by one muscular, oiled and glistening man, an act of theatre in the lamp-lit temple. Once the foot of our statue had reached the height of the waiting plinth, he swung the apparatus gently, moving it into place. Did I see something then, or is hindsight playing tricks? At the time I registered movement, a shadow flitting past in the gloom. The strongman lowered the statue into place; for a single moment, it rested there, then it slithered forwards. My heart stops now, just thinking of it. As when you fall and cannot save yourself, so we could not save Caligula from crashing to the floor. The outstretched arm smashed to dust, the body cracked in two places, the head rolled away. There was shouting and violent oaths from the Romans. I rushed to the plinth to see what had happened and found several small balls of marble like slingshot, some on the plinth, most on the floor and still rolling.

'Sabotage,' I said to Vespasian as he joined me. I expected him to explode and order a massacre of priests. I did not know him well enough. He looked around, found a ladder, took it and placed it against the statue of Apollo. Drawing his sword, he went up the ladder and with one stab beheaded the beautiful, curly-headed god, which is to say, he levered the head off its pin. More theatre – the heads of statues are often made separately from the torsos and he had merely found the join just beneath the swathe of mantle. Still, it had the desired effect and the Greeks were now crying out as the Romans had done moments before. The strongman went up the ladder and removed the head of Apollo, I have to say, reverentially. Once it was down on the ground, he carried the head of Caligula up the ladder to put it on the pin protruding from the neck of the god of Delphi. It was a good fit but it was a travesty. The smooth, tanned features of short-haired Caligula facing the wrong way on that beautiful nude. There was something obscene about it.

'There, all is mended,' said Vespasian, wiping the dust off his hands. 'Get a stonemason to glue and mortar the join.'

The priests stood in a huddle of outrage around the head of Apollo. I crossed to them and said in a low voice, 'Put it in the treasury. We'll be gone soon enough.' The high priest recovered himself quickly, made apologies to the Romans for the wicked act that had been done and thanked Vespasian for the wisdom of his solution. The ceremony picked up where it had left off.

We were shown the omphalos in the tiny, dark adyton of the temple. The omphalos is a stone half my height which, they told us, fell from heaven in ancient times to show men where the centre of the Earth is. It has been over-decorated, of course, chiselled with patterns and festooned by centuries of devotion, yet I was moved by it, this centre or navel of the world. The middle of maps. Approaching the inner sanctum, we were presented with our sacrificial animals, now garlanded with ribbons and chains of flowers. Behind a shimmering curtain, rites of purification were being performed and the air was heavy with the fumes of laurel leaves, myrrh and barley meal that burned on the altar of Apollo. At last the curtain was drawn and Pythia revealed, a gaunt woman who, though obscured by veils, was obviously older than I'd expected. She was led to the crevice in the rock over which the temple had been built and helped to seat herself on a tripod. There were no queues at all, apart from our short Roman one where Vespasian took the lead. A gong was struck and its reverberations allowed to linger in the air, followed by another of a different note, then another in Pythagorean harmony. Incense arose from the crevice where once a natural steam had come. The room was dark except for a few lamps whose light gleamed in the oiled hair and the gilded laurel leaves that the five attendant priests wore as crowns.

Another priest came forward and took Vespasian's young bull to the altar where, after prayers were intoned, it was dispatched with one swift cut across its throat. The priest collected the blood in a large bowl.

'Your question?' Pythia asked the Praetor.

'When can I go home?' he asked.

The priests around the Oracle quivered at his disrespect.

Pythia gazed at him balefully. 'Not before you rule the world,' she said.

Vespasian stiffened, as if he had just had his dreams revealed. He brushed aside the priest who offered to interpret the Oracle. 'I paid enough for that bull,' he said, striding away. 'You're not milking any more out of me for any "interpretation".'

I was fourth in the line. When I got to the Oracle, I kept hold of my ewe on her leash and refused to relinquish her to the priest who had stepped forward bearing the bowl and knife. I waved him away. The sound of the gongs stopped and I could see Pythia's eyes staring through the gauze veils. 'You must make sacrifice,' the priest hissed.

'I intend to. I am going to take this beast and set her free on the mountain. If divine Apollo wishes to speak to me, let him speak.'

Wild glances were exchanged and frantic whispers, then the gongs began again. I presumed they had weighed up my impiety against my being part of a delegation from Rome and decided, as fortune would have it, to humour me.

Pythia, her head down and eyes closed again, invited my question.

I asked the question of Claudius, a question which had made me wonder what his intentions might be. Still, it was a good question: 'Should good men act to rid the world of evil?'

Her eyes flashed open. 'Ask a question on your own behalf, not another's,' she said. I was impressed. I was also thrown and, although I brimmed with questions as pertinent as that of Claudius, I waffled about the troubles in my land and whether I should go home. A vague question deserves a vague answer. Pythia raised her head, squinted at me then began to inhale the incense deeply. She seemed to fall asleep, her head sinking on to her chest, but then a low moan came from her, followed by a voice. 'I, Apollo,' she began, and then burst forth into prophetic utterance, her body apparently taken by a seizure which grew wilder by the moment until she flung herself from the tripod, dangerously close to the deep fissure in the rock, and was only saved by the dexterity of the five holy ones attending her. Everyone seemed taken aback by the strength of her frenzy as she spoke with the voice of the god in wild, incoherent cries that were taken down by a scribe.

'This will need interpretation,' said the priest, leading me aside. Pythia's eyes were fastened on me; I held her gaze, but the priest came between us. I was taken to a small recess where I explained I had no money, but the interpreter was offended and said he worked in service of the god, not profit. He translated the words of Pythia into hexameter verses telling of great troubles ahead which were written down by a scribe. As I say, vague questions deserve vague answers but the wooliness of this one seemed to contradict the drama of Pythia's oracular utterance.

'Theatre,' muttered Vespasian as I pushed past clutching a small roll of papyrus and desperate for fresh air. I left the temple shaken to stand in the shade of an olive tree and open the roll. Troubles for whom? When? Where? I was not impressed by the verses and thought that, for a god of poetry, Apollo could have done better; what had shaken me was something about Pythia, some earthy rootedness that distinguished her from the chorus of priests with their rites designed to create fear. I found I believed in her where I did not believe in the temple. I found it hard to forget her gaze: who was it truly who had been staring at me through those fine nets?

After an afternoon rest at our lodgings, I went down the mountain to the wrestling school at the gymnasium, eager to keep up my practices, but could find no one prepared to sully his hands grappling with a barbarian, so I passed on through the wrestling school and went to the so-called bath which was more like an outdoor plunge pool. It was deep, circular and had no roof, no caldarium, no tepidarium – just the frigidarium with water as blue as the sky and glancing with sunlight. I jumped in making a big splash, followed by Mandred who made a bigger one. We rolled and tumbled and I marvelled at my slave's freedom of movement in water. We were watched with seething disapproval by some Greek patricians standing at the side. I could not tell whether their objection was to my playing at being dolphins with a slave, or because, as was obvious by my tattoos on shoulder and arm, I was a barbarian, someone excluded from a mystery cult that accepted even women. I only saw the fizz of their annoyance hanging like a cloud of steam over the bath. Ignoring them, Mandred was floating on his back and staring at his own feet with an expression of disgust.

'What is it?' I asked, but he rolled over, dived under the water and grabbed my knees. When we came up spluttering and gulping for air, the men were appealing to a woman to help clear the place of these 'pollutions'. She was as dark and knotty as a yew, her hair still black despite her age – she must have been fifty or more – her eyes shiny as olives. She was dressed in a simple chiton; her arms, with their gold armbands above the elbow, were scrawny but powerful, all sinew and hard muscle. She had suffered: it was etched into her face, her suffering, but not the usual kind of love and loss; it was the suffering of self-sacrifice.

She stared at me like Nemesis, reflections dancing up her body in scallops of light and dark. And I knew the power of that gaze, had experienced it only the day before. She did not beckon to me, she just turned and walked away, leaving me compelled to follow. Having passed through the changing room, where Mandred helped me dress hurriedly in a clean tunic, I found her waiting in the forecourt of the wrestling school, ignoring the philosophers who taught there as if they were just herb-sellers in the market of wisdom. She led me out of the gymnasium to cross the Sacred Way, taking a path that led to the rocky face of the mountain. Coming to a dark crevice where water was trickling out over a streak of green slime, she turned to confront me. I could see that the spring seeping out of the rock became a stream that ran down through a culvert under the Sacred Way; I realised with horror that it formed the pool where I had just been bathing.

'The water you disported in was sacred,' she said as if to confirm the thought. I blanched. 'Respect our land, our gods, our traditions, Roman.'

'I am not Roman, I am– '

'You are Togidubnus of Britain. Barbarian but Greek-speaking. The god bade me bring you here.'

Had I known the source of water in the pool I had been playing in with Mandred... Sacrilege! No wonder those old patricians had been full of muttering complaint. The bath at the gymnasium had only one purpose and that was purification.

I went to my knees before her, head bowed. 'I am guilty of desecration,' I said, 'and make no excuse. Please, I beg you, give me some rite of purification that I may honour the god and avoid his wrath.'

'Rise up, Togidubnus. The god would have you swear henceforth to honour water in all its forms. Whether Ocean or River, Spring or Well, you will honour water. Make the promise and drink from this sacred, ancient spring of Kastalia.'

Solemnly swearing to serve and protect water, in the person of the spirits and nymphs of each locality I found myself in, I cupped my hands and drank. I think now, looking back over the past few years, I have done my best in this but, like Apollo and his poetry, could have done better. The water had the smell of violets, so sweet that I wanted more, but knew I must resist.

'What you heard and saw yesterday in the temple is mere theatre,' she said. 'For many years now the Oracle has been silent.' She took some laurel leaves from a pouch. 'People still come to Delphi expecting advice and so we give it. Our treasuries are no longer as full as they once were, but they are still rich; we live on the gifts of kings and, like anyone else, we wish to survive.' She held out a large, shiny leaf to me. I shook my head.

'Eat!' she commanded.

I took the laurel and began to chew.

'Once the god spoke through the crevice over which the temple was built,' she said. 'He spoke through the Oracle. But then his voice grew faint and, in time, stopped altogether. All the Oracle could hear were the sighs of the earth and silence. But at this spring, we can still hear. We tell no one. We want no temple built here at the spring; no body of priests leeching the seekers; no cryptic riddles and false hopes. We intend to keep this Oracle pure.'

'We?'

'My grandmother, my mother, my aunts, my sisters, my daughters, all the generations of Pythia.'

'Why are you confiding this to me, a man, a stranger from Rome?'

'But not from Rome. You come from that place which stands between this world and the next. What do Romans know? They believe that men can be gods and that the dead become ghosts. But you, Briton, you know and have visited the Otherworld. And you know that the portal is water.'

As she spoke these words, I did know it; or remembered it, remembered having heard it from mother, aunt, grandmother.

'Drink,' said Pythia.

I drank of that lovely water again and could feel it running down inside my throat and into my inner parts: from the deeps of the earth to the deeps of myself the water ran.

'Again,' she said. 'This time inhale more deeply.'

I lifted more water, breathed in, felt my head swim in the perfume of violets, and drank.

'Again,' she said, 'but this time only inhale the scent, then give the water back.'

One moment I am listening to the incantations, half Greek, half nonsense, of this wizened woman, the next I am falling down, down to the bottom of the lake, into the Otherworld where I open my eyes in the middle of battle, my shield arm exhausted from the onslaught of Roman spears and swords, my sword arm even more tired from slashing right and left, dismembering, butchering, taking life. I feel neither exultation nor revulsion, only a determination to live. Those squat soldiers coming before me, with their breastplates and shield walls, are like turtles. They look invincible until my sword finds the neck. Sweat runs into my eyes; by the time it reaches my lips, it tastes of blood. Yet I will live, will live. And then comes the dark. I swim in it as if in a thick and stinking bog, a sucking quagmire of shame pulling me down. I want to drown in it, to blot myself out forever, I who have lived up to no one's idea of a hero. I turn over, go face down into the black water and drown myself. And then it is deeply calm, an underwater kind of calm, a floating in the sea kind of calm; the kind of calm where you realise that there is nothing in the world that can harm you.

A voice. 'Commius!' I try to ignore it.

Again, 'Commius!' Is that my name? I thought it was other. A third time: 'Commius!'

'Yes?' I answer.

'Make it right!'

My eyes sprang open. 'Who speaks?' I asked.

'Apollo,' said the priestess. 'It is Apollo who speaks to you, who calls you, who offers to answer the question you have yet to ask, the question of your heart. Go home, he says. Go home, O homeless one, O orphan, go home to your mother and marry her to your father.'

'They are already married,' I protested. 'You said there would be no riddles.'

'Let its meaning unfold, what has been said to me by the god. It will reveal itself when you go home. It will reveal itself in reflections.'

6

THERE CAME A MAN FROM ELEUSIS

I left Pythia at the spring, where in a cloud of dancing midges she was chanting words of devotion to its nymph, Kastalia, and joined Mandred where he had been waiting for me. I said nothing about the prophecy I'd received although he was clearly longing to hear about it. It was growing dark quickly and to distract him and myself both, I pointed to the sky as we walked up the Sacred Way under a firmament of silvery stars, tracing out the figure of the Scorpion which dipped its tail in that stream the Romans call *via lactea*. It was painful for Mandred to stretch his neck so we lay down on some turf and stared at the heavens. It is a thing of wonder, but I felt it necessary to catch it in some net of understanding. 'According to the Greeks, it is the milk of Hera as she feeds Herakles.'

Mandred said nothing.

'According to my studies,' I told him, 'the *via lactea* is one of eleven circles that encompass us, the zodiac, the meridian, the horizon, the equator...'

'Oh,' Mandred grunted. 'You study too much. Is it not enough to see this and feel your heart bursting with the mystery of it? Why do you have to know everything? It seems to me that nothing can be truly known until it is dead, until you can poke about in its entrails with tweezers. And by that time, knowledge itself is dead.'

'Are you sure you are not druid?' I asked.

'If I were druid, I'd be naming every bright dot in the sky, not just the Scorpion.'

We rose to continue up to Delphi, omphalos, the centre of the world, under the light of stars. Entering through the gates, we came back into the world of noise; Romans and Greeks mingled in the streets lit by winking lamps enjoying the cool of the evening and the local taverns. I walked through the throng. We live under fixed stars and wandering planets and have the arrogance to believe we amount to something, but we are all just gnats over the pool. Even the stars will die in time, even the gods. Everything is transient. Where then the eternal? Deep in my soul the answer throbbed and could not express itself in words.

At one tavern near the great temple I saw Vespasian eating with his officers. He called me over to join them. It was a habit of his, never to dine apart from his men, and they loved him for it. I thought I might tell him about the true Pythia and the prophecy, but he was in an ill mood. 'Where have you been?' he demanded.

'At the baths.'

'You were aptly named by your mother, lad. She knew a wet fish when she saw one.' He rose to stride up and down to ease an attack of indigestion. 'This greasy food! When can I go home?' he thundered.

His aide, who knew better than to say anything glib about ruling the world, told him he had seven days of formalities and some mock games to endure before we moved on to the sanctuary of Zeus at Dodona, from whence we would return south, cross over to the Peloponnese and thence to Olympia with the last statue to be installed in Greece, after which we would overwinter in Corinth before returning to Rome.

'The answer to your question,' the optio said, portentously, as if he were an oracle given to revealing straightforward facts, 'is early next year.'

I never understood Vespasian's desire to be home until another evening in another tavern when his optio, in drunken indiscretion, told me about his mistress, the very beautiful Caenis, a slave woman who I knew for she had been secretary to Claudius's mother, Antonia. 'Love of his life,' the optio said, propping himself up at the tavern bench.

'I'm not surprised,' I said. Caenis had been the goddess of my pubescent dreams. 'But didn't he marry a few months before we left?'

'Yes, Domitilla, a year ago. But it's Caenis he dreams of. He hates delay. He knows he can't go home, not before winter, but he'd much rather be on the move than stuck anywhere, like here in Delphi, being honoured by hours of tedious wrestling matches and chariot races.'

When we moved on, a week later, Vespasian's mood mellowed. Stuck in one place, he was like an unmilked cow; on the move, he became his affable self, cracking jokes and winning respect not only by his actions but by his dogged adherence to his rustic accent. Vespasian was not a man to pretend to be other than he was, the son of a family of debt collectors and money lenders. Furrow-browed, bull-necked, thin-lipped, he was a soldier of the old school, a man who shared the values of the Republic but who lived under emperors. Whenever we set up camp for the night, or took lodgings, he created a room of immaculate neatness with no personal possessions on show except one thing: a handsome silver cup.

It was while we were visiting the major temples of Sparta during the autumn that I discovered what the cup was, when he took it down from its place one evening to perform a rite in honour of the dead. Every particular of the rite, including the oblation of wine from the treasured cup, he performed with love, a remarkable sight in this gruff, no-nonsense soldier: love and tenderness.

'It's his grandmother's birthday,' his optio explained to me. 'It was her cup.'

When we finally arrived at Corinth, the wind from the sea was making piles of fallen leaves. The city, with its forum and basilicas, its amphitheatre and fountains, felt like home to Vespasian. With his cohort he settled into barracks for the winter and it was my turn to be restless and impatient. Corinth is no place to be when you have no money of your own. With the officers' quarters a place for the worship of Bacchus and whoever the god of gambling is, I retreated into study of Plato, where I read about initiation into the Mysteries, not that he said much. It was all veiled in secrecy. After the autumn equinox, we'd met many on the road who were Mystai, returning changed from their experiences at the Temple of Demeter in Eleusis. Men, women, children of all classes, making the return, the pilgrimage to home, wearing crowns of woven barley corn. Riding with a unit of the Roman army, I was accustomed to seeing other travellers looking shifty. They kept their heads down, unless they were trying to sell you something, cowed by the very thought of the lash. But not these. The Mystai feared nothing. Souls forged in the fires of initiation. I longed to know more but the initiates were sworn to secrecy and Plato, like all other authors, offered only gleanings.

To cure me of boredom, Vespasian insisted I join the military drills and weapons training. I was fit enough, given my practices in wrestling, but the boredom was exacerbated by all that marching, turning and marching back again, and the stabbing of lynched pigs. So Vespasian set me to help with the annual tax gathering, sitting at the tables in the Temple of Hermes to take and count coin. Corinth is responsible for upper Attica and I took the coin of men from far-flung places who had made a difficult journey to pay their dues to Caesar; much of the coin had travelled even further and I was dealing not only with local drachmas and staters but discs of silver from the furthest reaches of the Empire and beyond, some so small I could only pick them up by licking my forefinger and pressing on them.

I came across one of my father's own from Britain stamped VER REX. A vine leaf with the triple-tailed horse on the back. I lingered over this one until a Thracian complained about waiting in the queue. Some men I had to send to a money-changer, to translate their currency into something the Romans would accept. Farmers wanted to pay in kind, but thankfully not at my table. The flutterings and bleatings and air-choking chaff of agricultural tax were confined to the local temple of Demeter.

If any were resentful of the tax, it was difficult to tell given that the expression of glowering annoyance is as fixed on the Greek face as the quiet smile on their statues. As the days passed, however, I began to feel a creeping awe for Roman administration and the order it brings to lives. These men paying their dues were paying for new roads and the mainte-nance of old ones, roads made safe by frequent patrols; for the rebuilding of temples and even cities, such as this one of Corinth; for the great increase in trade and prosperity that the Romans had brought to them. Greek history was one of war, state against state, but now they were living as one nation under Rome. Names were recorded in the census, births, marriages and deaths, and each man had an official identity: he was known beyond his tribe.

On those days and weeks of money-counting, I saw not only the brisk efficiency of the Romans gathering their taxes, but also the merciless acquisition of wealth from a subject nation, and some of the things I saw, the beatings and mutilations of those who could not pay, sickened me. Yet... yet... every now and again I glimpsed the beauty of order and discipline, the beauty of law. It seems to me a 'preferable indifferent' to live in a well-ordered nation rather than a disordered one. The question is, how much is man expected to pay for it? And what happens when, through no fault of his own, he can pay nothing? The face of justice is beautiful, that of injustice hideous, and at the tax tables I saw both.

At the end of each day, I presented the master of the table with piles of coin that I had sorted according to type and value with military precision and received a small remuneration from the great Empire in return. Not enough to pay for the cheapest hetaera, but enough to be able to eat with friends in a taverna occasionally, to return Vespasian what I owed him and to pay for doctors to examine what was now a lump on Mandred's neck, grown from the chafing of the iron collar. It did not pain him but it had become livid and bled easily if knocked. He kept it covered with a soldier's red scarf I'd obtained from the unit's supplies.

One day in the early spring there came a man from Eleusis to pay the taxes imposed upon the great temple. As I reached out for the bags of money he put on the table, his eye fixed on the scarred wheel on my left forearm. Presuming he'd recognized me as one of the barbarians forever banned from the Mysteries, I spoke to him in fluent Greek to put him at ease. When I left the tables at the end of my shift, he was waiting for me.

'A tax collector with wisdom on his arm?' he said.

'This? It was made at the behest of my mother,' I said. 'It's a chariot wheel, the wheel of Taranis, our sky god, the wheel of the sun.' I gazed at it, annoyed by it, annoyed by the scarring, annoyed by a blob of soot that formed an ingrained black spot at the end of one of the spokes, a fault in the execution by my mother.

'It is an eight-petalled flower, a double poppy, familiar to any initiate of Eleusis.'

'A status from which I am banned.'

'That rule was made generations ago, when your people were rampaging through Greece sacking our temples.'

I flushed, embarrassed by this history. How I had squirmed in my lessons with Claudius, although he was always careful to say that the armies of Brennus had been 'a faction' of the Gauls. Nonetheless, it was the reason why Caesar's wars in Gaul had been so savage.

'The last battle, at Delphi, left the place in such ruin it was all but abandoned until the Romans built it up again,' said the man from Eleusis. 'It is good to be reminded of such things when it comes to paying our taxes.'

I hung my head in shame but he lifted my chin. 'Make it right,' he said.

'The faults of my ancestors?' I asked, stunned.

He smiled – there was a happy look to this man, as if the drama of life was just part of a play that was essentially comic. 'Your blasphemy. You are defiling our temples with images of a mortal man, and a mad mortal at that. You need to make it right with the gods. Seek absolution.'

I traced the wheel on my arm, comparing it with the eight-petalled flower in bronze that he wore as an amulet. 'I have already made a vow to Apollo.'

'What is your name?'

'Delphidius.'

'Your true name.'

'Togidubnos, son of Verica of the Atrebates,' I said, feeling my spine stiffen.

'Pythia sent us a message. Though you are a barbarian, though it is closer to the time of the Lesser Mysteries than the Greater ones, you are to be initiated. Apollo wills it. Your destiny is entwined with that of your people. *To misterion*, which is to say, keep silence. Do not speak of these matters to anyone, not until you are spoken to. Can you leave your tax collecting for four days?'

I sought Vespasian's permission, expecting him to deny my request with a snort of mockery but when I asked him a light shone out of his eyes, some part of his soul usually kept so well-hidden. It seemed that, were he not in charge of this Roman unit, he would drop everything to ride with me himself to Eleusis. But he just nodded and said, 'Four days. No more.'

The Greater Mysteries, which last for nine days in the autumn, involve long and ecstatic processions from Eleusis to

Athens and back again, a road of some twenty miles, the Sacred Way which I had first encountered on the approach to the Acropolis. No dancing or shouting for us, however, as we went on horseback on the road from Corinth, no drunken calling to the God of Wine. When the multitude of initiates from all over Greece and beyond arrive in the great hall of the temple of Eleusis, they participate in sacred dramas and undergo ordeals of death and rebirth. For me alone there was to be a much-reduced initiation. 'You will become a seed,' said my guide. 'You will be buried, you will sprout.'

It rose up before us in the distance, that high wall of the fortified temple. As we rode, he recounted the story of Demeter and her daughter. 'After Persephone was snatched by Hades as she picked spring flowers, her mother stormed amongst men and gods, demanding her daughter's return, but the gods refused until she began to burn up the land and threatened to kill all humanity. Without men, the gods would be starved of praise. As the wheat and barley withered in the fields from the heat of her despair, Zeus capitulated and persuaded his brother, Hades, to return the young woman who was now his wife. Hades tricked Persephone into eating a pomegranate seed and, by that means, bound her to return to him for three months of each year.'

I was puzzled. From all my reading of the ancient poets, I thought Persephone was with Hades for six months each year, corresponding to autumn and winter. Now I was being told it was three months, corresponding to high summer. 'She is the goddess of seed,' he told me. 'And when do we sow? In the autumn. She protects the seeds, looks after their germination, stays long enough to see the shoots appearing and then, at the time of flowers, returns to her husband. You will be a spring sowing, but there is nothing lost in that.'

As we entered the temple precincts, I was told that I must remain silent about everything heard within those walls, so I shall say no more. Only that, following the trials of darkness in the Plutoneion, the terrors of the night vigils, the trance induced by drinking kykeon, the burial, the watering with sacrificial blood, and ultimately the Vision, I emerged as new life. Look at a seed as it bursts asunder and the new shoot emerges from the cleavage, white, tender, but with the power to penetrate anything lying between it and the light. It is an image of my soul on that, perhaps the most significant day and ritual of my life. A yellow thread was tied round right wrist and left ankle to remind me of the Two Goddesses, the Light and the Dark, the Above and the Below. It was unusual to be initiated alone but apparently not without precedent. All it took was for a god to will it.

As I left the temple, feeling that nothing would ever trouble me again, I found Mandred hopping with agitation. He gave me the news kept from me while I'd been enduring my ordeals: Caligula had been assassinated. Vespasian was on his way back to Rome.

My calm heart lurched into my throat. 'When did he leave?'

'Embarkation takes days. We may catch him yet at the port.'

And so I, this fearless initiate of the Eleusinian Mysteries, raced back to Corinth like an abandoned dog in chase of its master.

7

RETURN TO ROME

Vespasian was at the port, waiting until all his troops had filed on to galleys before boarding his own. Though his face was stern, he seemed relieved to see me. I was certainly relieved to see him. He told me, 'The new god is dead, assassinated like Julius Caesar, stabbed by many at once.' The latest news, a fortnight old by the time it had reached Greece, was that the situation in Rome was unstable. Who could say what the situation was now? In early February, it was not the sailing season, but the weather was fair and the wind easterly and Vespasian was in no doubt we had to return to Italy.

'I sent a messenger to Eleusis but he was told you were in Hades and not to be disturbed.' A light danced in his eyes; stern of mouth, merry of eye: the death of the Princeps had put him in a good humour. The last thing he did on Greek soil was to arrange for a messenger to go to Delphi and tell them to restore the head of Apollo.

'I presume,' he said to the messenger, 'they did not destroy it as I instructed. As for Caligula's head, tell them to kick it off the mountain.'

There is no point being impatient while at sea. Yes, you can whip the oarsmen to row harder but, once the sails are up, you are at the mercy of the wind's caprices. On many tedious days it was strong enough to move us but not at any speed. Vespasian paced the upper deck of the bireme, rehearsing his actions in the future, what he would do if he found Rome under the rule of a usurper, or returned to a republic. The men laid bets as to who the new princeps would be: each one of them destined to lose his money. Vespasian paced, muttering to himself, now dreaming he was in command of the Praetorian guard, now in flight from it. The uncertainty of the future — even of the present — the uncertainty of not knowing caused him agony. For the entire journey he slept only in quick snatches.

Sometimes we would see ships on the horizon, going from Italy to Greece, and he shouted as if he could possibly be heard, but they passed by, too far away to hear us, carrying news that would reach Corinth sooner than it would reach the man trying to race home. As at last we approached the toe of Italy, the captain told Vespasian that the winter seas were too rough, the tides too strong in the Straits of Messina. We would have to go around Sicily to reach Ostia. The captain was lucky to survive Vespasian's wrath, but once his rage was spent, Vespasian could see the sense of it. Better to arrive late and alive than sooner and dead.

'Did you ever meet him?' he asked me one day as we stood together at the prow, staring at the ruined temples standing out on hills along the coastline of Sicily.

'Caligula? I made it my business to avoid him. I've always lived with Claudius who, with his mother Antonia, preferred a private life away from the imperial palace.'

'Yes,' he said quietly, 'I knew the lady and her house.'

And her secretary... I thought. After the optio had told me the story, I had thought back to my days in the House of Antonia, remembered the lovely secretary, Caenis, and thought I could even remember the young magistrate who would find any pretext to visit the house. I remembered Antonia complaining that whenever he came, he seemed to require her to write a letter.

'If only half of those stories about Caligula were true...,' I said. 'Antonia killed herself because of the shame her grandson was bringing upon the family. Yes, I avoided meeting him face-to-face, but only just. It was because he was seeking me out to join his expedition to Britain that I joined your mission.'

'Some would call that expediency,' he said.

'Seneca called it wisdom.'

Bull-necked and thin-lipped, Vespasian stared out at the passing temples of a lost empire. 'Who's your money on?' he asked.

'I don't gamble,' I said. 'But the favourite amongst the men is Caligula's nephew, the son of Agrippina.'

'He's only three! How did it come about that princeps is an hereditary office? The men of the Old Republic will be moaning in their tombs.'

'If men could only govern themselves, it would matter less who is the leader,' I said.

'More Seneca?' he asked wryly. 'I don't gamble, either, but I'm telling you with the conviction of an Oracle that we're r eturning to chaos. A city needs a leader; even a bad leader is better than none. And what is true for a city is ten times truer for an empire. Ever seen a spinning top wobble?' He squinted at the fallen columns of temples that had been built when the Greeks ruled here. 'How fortunes change, flipping and flopping like fish out of water,' he said. '*Heus!*' he shouted suddenly to a passing fishing boat. '*Quid novi?*'

'Caligula is dead!'

'And?'

The fisherman shrugged. What did it matter to him who came next? Where the sardines were, that's what mattered. It was not until we were sailing into the port of Ostia that we heard. '*Heus!*' Vespasian shouted to the captain of a passing merchant ship going from port to port down the coast. '*Quid novi?*'

'He's still alive, just.'

'Who is? Caligula?'

'Who? Where have you sailed from? Beyond Ocean?'

'Corinth!'

'Woah! How was that crossing?'

'*Who?*' thundered Vespasian. His officers joined him, eager to know the result of their bets.

'Tiberius Claudius Caesar Augustus Germanicus,' the captain called as his ship passed ours. 'Claudius! You'll be busy in the city. It's a never-ending riot.'

8

SENECA AT HOME

'Should good men act to rid the world of evil?' I often wondered about that question Claudius had me put to the Oracle and the vague answer it had elicited about 'great troubles ahead'. Had he been part of the conspiracy to bring down Caligula? Was he, in fact, as surprised as he claimed to become princeps? The man now wearing the oak-leaf garland and glorified with the name of 'Caesar' was the choice of a military wishing to avoid being ruled by a three-year-old but he was far from being a popular choice. With the city still in ferment even a month later, we feared he would soon meet the same end as Caligula and the soldiers of Vespasian's unit were employed in support of the Praetorian Guard who were keeping a strong presence in and around the imperial palace.

I did not consider it wise to bother him at such a time with a trivial question as to where I should live now, nor did I want to have to tell him what the Oracle had said. But the real reason for my reluctance was learning that Messalina was about to give birth again. Our last night together had been nine months before.

I went to the house of Lucius Seneca on the Esquiline hill in a sweat of fear, convinced that, on the birth of the baby, I would have to flee the city. I expected to find Seneca relieved by the death of Caligula, who after all had once commanded the troublesome senator to commit suicide. If Seneca had survived that, it was because he had convinced Caligula he was about to die anyway so they should let Nature do the job. Seneca always seemed to be on the brink of death. He was one of those people who surprise you each time they survive winter for he was sickly and prone to attacks where he had to fight for his breath. He was struggling to breathe when I arrived at his house and was far from dancing at our release from mad tyranny.

'Freedom,' he wheezed when he had recovered a little, 'is not the death of your enemy, or the rise of your friend to power. Freedom is in being unmoved by changes in fortune and circumstance.'

I nodded, agreeing with him as I always do, theoretically. 'The city is boiling with stories about what happened,' I said. 'There are as many versions as there are people with opinions. What do you know to be true?'

'Caligula is dead.'

'Seriously, Lucius. Who did it?'

'I am being serious. Don't meddle with these things; don't turn them over in an idle mind. Concentrate on what's important.'

'What is important?'

'The state of your own soul. That's where you have some power to influence outcomes. That's the only place you have power.'

'And how do I achieve a calm soul in this storm?'

'For a start, be very careful what company you keep. You are right, there are many versions about what has happened, and not a few of them feature your lady love. Even more, your mentor.' He held my eye to ensure I listened to what he had to say. I could hear the breath rasping in his throat. 'Keep away from the house of Claudius; keep away from Messalina.'

'I have no intention of bothering either of them. I'll be beneath the notice of Claudius now, and Messalina too, given the rise in her fortunes. I don't suppose she'll retain any interest in me. Unless...'

'Unless?'

'The child is born with blue eyes. Then she might wish to see its father.'

'Is it *you?*'

'I don't know. Could be.'

'Pray to the gods that it is small and dark! Did anyone see you come here?' he asked, suddenly cautious.

'I made sure no one did. Only your slaves.'

'We can trust them, as presumably we may trust your man, for you know how to treat a slave well. I want you to stay here and not go out until we know.'

Of all Romans, Seneca was the most virtuous. 'A man must practise what he avows or be a hypocrite,' he said after a light supper. He and his family lived simply, ate in moderation, never drank to excess, never did anything to excess, yet his house was not a bare-walled cell of abstemiousness. It was the pleasant house of a pleasant man who loved his garden and the finer things money can buy. The walls were decorated with scenes of animals and birds in nature, the floors with geometric patterns, and the colours of green and blue tinted the very air. The tinkling water of a small fountain in the atrium greeted visitors and put them at their ease. He'd 'fallen into riches' he said, 'as other men fall into poverty.' His father, a wealthy orator, had bought him the house and he himself made a moderately good living through the offices he held. He did not waste his wealth on banquets and briberies. His wife, Cornelia, heavily pregnant and due to give birth any day, kept the house ordered and tranquil. Perhaps because of his neediness, Seneca had a way with women: his mother, his aunt, his wife — all showed him extraordinary devotion. Or there again, perhaps it was simply because he was kind to them and solicitous of their own welfare. He fussed about Cornelia, plumping cushions for her and making her sit on a couch with her feet up.

We passed a week or more in domestic solitude in this house on the hill, looking down on the turmoil in the streets while the city went through the continuing aftershocks of the change of princeps. Seneca gave mornings over to the financial business of government. It seemed to me odd that he taught philosophy in the Forum and did his official work at home. I could understand how a little pool of peace would do the Forum much good, but I couldn't see how a triclinium full of politicians would do the house any good at all, but Seneca said it kept the household awake. 'Peace,' he said, 'is another name for torpor if you're not careful.' That he was in the Senate at all was a wonder, given that his family were merely of the *equites* class, but he had his aunt to thank for that. She had used her influence to set him on the first rung of the *cursus honorum* with an appointment as quaestor attached to the state treasury. That was another of the contradictions of Lucius Seneca: the man who advocated poverty was very good with money.

Living with him, I had the rare opportunity for conversations in philosophy in beautiful surroundings. Sometimes others — what he called his 'more serious students' — joined us. One of them, a half-starved young woman called Julia, he met alone, claiming that he was above feminine distraction while the rest of us were not. It seemed odd to me that a woman should be interested in philosophy at all, until I learned that she was a sister of Caligula who, implicated in a plot to kill her brother, had been banished to a rocky island and had nearly died. Her Uncle Claudius had called her home just in time and her wretchedness had driven her to the house of a man who would not only teach her how to rise above fear but be kind to her while he was about it. Seneca fussed about Julia as much as he fussed about Cornelia.

He and I were sitting alone one afternoon on an upper terrace of his garden in the shade of oleanders when he asked me to tell him about my travels in Greece. I dwelt on the difficulties of travel, the undefeated pride of the Greeks, the lack of good baths. I told him about Vespasian, the praetor on the rise. 'A good man despite his humble origins,' I said, not thinking.

'As am I,' said Seneca. 'Or at least, try to be. Of what use have all my lessons been if you still presume that goodness depends on breeding?'

Eager to change the subject and avoid further embarrassment, I asked him what *Know Thyself* means, and then he had me as a hawk a mouse. 'You went to Delphi?' He spoke the name with the same awe he betrayed when saying 'Socrates' or 'Pythagoras'. 'Don't spare my feelings. I can only make this journey through you: tell me everything you saw and heard. Forget about the stony roads and arduous voyages. Tell me about Delphi. And Athens.'

I began with Athens and told him of the agora where Socrates had taught, where Plato's Academy — although much debased — still is, the Parthenon, its sculptures and the statue of Athena, so golden, so gigantic. 'She holds in her outstretched palm a figure of Nike who is the height of a man,' I told him, and his eyes widened like a child's. When I finally reached Delphi in my account, his breath was shortening and I feared a renewed attack of his malady but it was only his excitement at hearing about the Temple of Apollo, the Oracle and the omphalos. 'You enter the temple forecourt through a stone gateway with *gnothi seauton* engraved deeply in the lintel,' I said. 'What does it mean, *Know Thyself?*'

'Logos, the spirit within all things, that is the self to be known. The divine breath of the world. It is the only thing to be known. It is who we truly are. Of what use is worldly knowledge when we don't know who we truly are?'

It was as I told him about Pythia at the spring that he began retching for breath. It wasn't only his malady: it was envy he was struggling to overcome. I realised suddenly that, *to mysterion*, I must remain silent about Eleusis, although I suspected he knew the significance of the barley-coloured threads I wore.

This time he did not recover but began turning blue. I shouted for help and Cornelia hurried into the garden. When Seneca had come close to death in his twenties, his aunt, whose husband was the Prefect of Egypt, had taken him to live in Alexandria for ten years. Ancient Egyptian methods of healing had provided many therapies for his condition. Cornelia had him brought indoors to a room where they placed a censer filled with smouldering herbs that gave off a warm, spicy fragrance. Cornelia sat with him, encouraging him to breathe slowly and as deeply as he could.

'Too damp here in the winter,' Seneca told me between inhalations. 'Too close to that foetid river. I should go back to the hot, dry air of Alexandria.'

When finally the attack was over, Cornelia had the kitchen make him some hot chicken soup, another therapy discovered in Alexandria, but this one Jewish. When it arrived, she commanded her husband to eat it all up, and to use a spoon like a civilized man. 'Yes, dear,' he said, and slyly watched her to make sure she left the room, at which point he relaxed.

He never laid on a couch but, like me, sat cross-legged on the floor to eat. He dipped his spoon into the hot broth and watched the liquid pour off the sides. 'Please,' he said, 'continue with your account.' He sucked on the spoon and immediately got soup on his tunic. 'Oh, now she'll be at me,' he said, brushing at the stain. A slave went off to fetch a napkin.

'Perhaps we should leave it for the present?'

'Tell me now,' he said. 'There may not be another day.'

'You are a good Stoic,' I said. 'A practical man dedicated to living well. Why do you get over-excited when I mention gods or oracles?'

'Stoicism is the best way of finding happiness, but happiness is not everything. When I was your age, I savoured many systems of philosophy and counted that of Socrates the best of all. He's rational, yes, and exercises the mind the way a gymnast exercises the body, but he was initiated into the Mysteries. Did you go to Eleusis?' he asked in an almost reluctant whisper.

'I was initiated alone in a special ceremony,' I said, and he exhaled like a puffball that has been kicked. 'I'm sorry,' I said.

'Yes? For what? My failure in dispassion?'

'I'm sorry I've received things that Fate should have reserved for you.'

He stretched his neck while the slave tucked the napkin into his tunic. 'Thank you for reminding me that this is the work of Fate,' he said. 'Yes. She has other things reserved for me. I dread to think what they are...'

I smiled.

'Of course,' he said, 'you can't tell me anything about it.'

'Nothing.'

'Not even in private.'

'Nothing.'

'To your beloved tutor who has given you so much...'

'Stop wheedling.'

'Oh yes,' he continued, waving his spoon like a baton as he returned to the original track of our conversation, 'Logos, the spirit within. The one god of all. Socrates did not worship the gods the way the superstitious rabble do, but he could see and hear what was invisible to the rest. In the philosophy of the soul, he was of course influenced by Pythagoras. I would have been a Pythagorean myself, you know,' he said, 'except my father forbade it. I made the mistake of telling him that I no longer ate meat because it encourages the habit of cruelty. That touched a nerve! He took it as a personal affront, said the practices of the Pythagoreans were too extreme, the meatless diet "too Jewish".' Seneca laughed. 'Idiot! If only he knew what faith Jews put in chicken soup!' He dipped in the spoon and made a horrible slurping noise. 'But I was obedient — first law of a good philosopher: obey your father.' Giving up on the spoon he raised the bowl to his lips and drank.

'In all circumstances?' I asked. 'Even when he is wrong?'

'Even then. Except of course in this instance he wasn't wrong. I didn't understand until later that, at that time, there was danger of exile or even execution for the practice of foreign rites. No wonder he didn't want a vegetarian in the house!

Now, tell me at least about Pythia. Hold nothing back. I promise I will keep breathing.'

And so I told him all about my meeting with her at the Kastalian spring, about the fragrance and the trance and, perhaps because he was prepared, he did keep breathing. He nodded silently, reflectively, as if wishing he lived in another time and place, say Greece four hundred years ago. Just talking about it was putting me back into trance. The day was warm and the first scents of spring were in the air, that smell of earth as it is warmed by the sun and the chill of winter withdraws. Song birds were trilling...

There was a rising clamour outside in the street, and shouts of 'It's a boy!'

Seneca snapped upright, momentarily thinking that Cornelia had given birth, but then he realised. 'Messalina...' he said, going back to the spoon to get the meaty bits at the bottom.

Now it was my turn to find it difficult to breathe. I sent Mandred to enquire on the baby's health. And, discreetly, its appearance. The time that passed before his return seemed long. At last he arrived, panting.

Small. Dark. Beautiful brown eyes. Like his mother.

Seneca smiled at me. 'The gods are with you. You are free to leave.'

'But if I preferred to stay?'

'You are free to do that, too, and would be most welcome.' He touched the thread at my wrist. 'Lucky boy. You lucky, lucky boy.' He gave a long, theatrical sigh.

'Surely a good Stoic knows no envy.'

He tapped me hard on the brow. 'Do you not understand yet? A good Stoic is one who, experiencing envy, knows how to deal with it. Anyone who does not feel the passions, well, he is a dead thing.'

He went to the Senate the following day, to offer congratulations to the Princeps and his wife on the birth of their son. He detested the Senate, considering it nothing more than a club for social climbers. 'If I'd only had myself to consider, I would have had nothing to do with it, for a wise man abjures all office,' he told me as he was being dressed in his toga. 'However, like a republican of old, I believe a man has a duty to his city, and that he is responsible to others, not just his immediate family but the family that has been and the family yet to come. We were of humble origins. Did I not owe it to everyone to change their fortunes?'

'And no regrets since?'

'Riding two horses is possible only when they are both going in the same direction. Am I a hypocrite? I often fear it. But it seems to me that we have two choices. One is to stick to our principles and take the consequences, probably living a short life but a famous one; the other is to play our part in society and do everything we can to influence those in power to the good. While I admire so much the heroes of philosophy, I have chosen the second path. Does that make me a hypocrite? Was it the choice of a coward? On all such matters I consult my own soul. I rush into nothing. I reflect; I ponder; I weigh everything up and make my decision. And as a consequence of that, here I am, a philosopher in high office, a good house and enough wealth never to know want!'

'If you were a stronger man,' I said, 'I am certain you would have chosen the hero's path and now be living in a cave. As it is, you've chosen to prolong your life as much as you can. And I'm glad of it. You have to live as long as possible, for the sake of the rest of us. We need your wisdom.'

'My dear young friend…' he said, patting me on the shoulder. 'You're a tonic. You are chicken soup for the soul.'

9

THE ARREST OF SENECA

I had not forgotten Pythia's injunction to return to Britain;
indeed, like flags in a wind, all signs and omens pointed north,
but I had no desire to go home. With the failure of Caligula's
expedition, Britain remained a barbarian backwater. My father
was in exile. Who knew if I even had a home to go to? But,
truth be told, I had no wish to exchange wine for ale, sunshine
for blanket cloud, books for fireside stories, it was as simple
as that. Rome settled with Claudius for its princeps and life in
the house of Seneca was happy. We spent our days ambling
in the countryside, dining together, visiting his friends, going
to the theatre when there was a literary drama in performance.
He particularly enjoyed the Greek tragedians and would put
aside everything to see Medea or Oedipus Rex. During the
hours he spent in the Senate, or on senatorial business, I
studied privately, either reading Plato in Greek or the history
of my peoples in the works of Caesar and Strabo.

Caesar had written of proud barbarian kings paying homage
to Rome, and it was still going on. A delegation from the
Brigantes tribe arrived to pay honour to Claudius and reassert
an alliance that had been made in the time of the great Caesar.
The new king of the Brigantes, however, was a woman,
Cartimandua. I still had not presented myself at the palace and
thus was frustrated when she arrived, for I longed to see her up
close. As it was, I went down to the Forum to watch her from
afar, standing in the streets with the crowd enjoying the shock
of this exotic vision, this Cleopatra of the north. I had Mandred

mingle with her entourage to see what news he could get of the Atrebates but he came back with nothing, not even reports of their extinction. It was as if they had just disappeared. A heaviness came down upon me and I returned to Seneca's house working hard to free myself of it. He once said that the only time we have the right to fear is when a lion is snarling in our face. Ideas and speculations are just that, and Stoics must guard against them.

Noticing at once that there was a cloud upon my soul, Seneca took out the surgical instruments of Reason and probed me with questions. 'What is it about this queen that has brought you so low?'

'Nothing. I am indifferent to her.'

'So, then?'

To cut the inquisition short, I told him that I couldn't find any information from her entourage about my family and my tribe. It was the not-knowing, I confessed. 'I think I would almost prefer to hear that they're all dead. Then I could grieve. And live here forever.'

Seneca frowned, wondering at which point virtuous dispassion becomes vile apathy.

'I'm not uncaring,' I said. 'I am just trying not to cry.'

'Cry over what? Lack of news? I think it's about time you thought about obeying the Oracle. It is time for you to go home and find out for yourself how things lie,' Seneca suggested. 'It's rather a cosy life, this, isn't it? Easy to practise stoicism in such conditions. If you really want to practise your chosen path in philosophy, you should stop hiding. Always better, I say, to go and meet Fate rather than wait until she comes to you. Always better. You find her in a much softer mood.'

Once a week we undertook 'a day of poverty' to prepare ourselves for a change in fortune, because that is what fortune does: change. On those days Seneca gave the servants a holiday and enjoined his family — including me — to serve each other. We fasted during the day and at night slept on the hard floor.

Mandred relished these nights because they were the only nights he got the chance to sleep in a bed (mine). I told him that he should be joining us on the floor. He said if I wanted to practice stoicism I should offer myself up as a slave. 'We practice it all the time.' And so, as I lay down on the hard stone floor, trying not to remember my first year in Antonia's house, he rolled around on my mattress and plumped the bolster, groaning with pleasure.

Despite the ache it put in my bones on such nights, Stoicism appealed to me. I liked the practicality of it, a philosophy for body and mind together, founded on precepts of right action and justice, a system which uses reason to restrain the appetite. A man living such a life should be above criticism, yet running about the city were rumours of Seneca's hypocrisy.

With the return of Julia and her sister Agrippina from banishment, one of the first acts of benevolence of Claudius, old factions began to stir and new ones to form. It was put about that Julia was having an affair with Seneca, a rumour that surely started life as a joke. Let me be witness: there was no affair. Julia came to his house for private instruction in philosophy. If you've had an insane tyrant for a brother, who ravished you and murdered one of your sisters, and had now been murdered himself; and if your arch rival, Messalina, had just come to power, you seek escape. Not physical escape. Escape of the soul. Julia sought detachment from this world of terror. Seneca gave her private tuition and that was the mistake, that it was private. Seneca said not to worry about rumours; we could trust our new princeps. His other mistake was listening to Julia's accusations that Messalina was committing adultery.

'Messalina? Is it true?' he asked me.

I swallowed so hard it was surely audible. 'She may have been free with her affections once,' I said, 'but she seems to have changed her ways since the birth of her children.'

'Not according to Julia.'

I turned away to obscure my face while I dealt with successive eruptions of envy and anger. Realising I had fallen into the trap of listening to gossip, I calmed down and turned back to find that Seneca was at his desk, writing to Messalina about the dangers of adultery, couching it all in very general terms, just in case she was ever tempted, et cetera... For one who would be wise he could often do unwise things and, despite my begging him not to, he sent the letter. He would be the first to say never let passion govern your actions, but he had taken sides in the war of women and it was to cost him his freedom.

It was high summer in that first year of Divine Claudius when they came for Seneca at his country house, to put him on trial on a charge of adultery with Julia. He was in the country, keeping out of the public gaze, while he fought with his own passions. His infant son, born just a few months earlier, had died from a fever. Cornelia looked as if she would never recover. He had to be strong for her if nothing else. He spent hours reading and sometimes would jump up to walk out alone in the countryside. I had no doubt he wept as he did so, but whenever he returned he had sloughed off the misery as a snake its skin.

One day he returned to find a tribune with a unit of the Praetorian Guard waiting for him. His face rippled momentarily with emotion and then was placid again. 'Look after Cornelia,' he told me as they took him off in a carriage.

After a short trial he was found guilty and sentenced to death. The State took his pleasant properties but magnanimously allowed him time to put his affairs in order and arrange for his family to go to his brother's house. As he left, unshackled and apparently willingly, Seneca gave money and objects of value to his slaves and servants. To me he gave another bag of coin.

'Should be enough to pay for lodging for one year in the city,' he said, 'but if you would be wise then obey the Oracle and go home. It's not as cosy here as we had hoped. Stop fighting Fate.'

He wagged his finger. 'She doesn't like it, you know, when she has to come and get you herself. Always go to Fate, always. As I am doing.' He stepped back discomfited when I suddenly fell to my knees and clutched the folds of his toga, sobbing like a child.

'Don't concern yourself about me. This could be a quick death and better by far than choking on phlegm in a public place.' That was the death he feared most: fighting for breath in the Senate with everyone laughing at him as he died.

It was time that I stopped discussing Stoicism and began to practise it. Stepping over my fears, I sought audience with the Princeps. There he sat, on the curule chair upon a dais, looking dignified, as he always did when seated. The wreath of oak leaves was slightly askew since his was a head not made for crowns, the brow too wide, the ears too protruding, the hair too sparse.

'Ah, Delfos,' he said brightly. 'Why have you been avoiding me?'

'Not avoiding, Caesar. I just presumed you would be too busy.'

'Never too busy to spend an evening with you, my young friend.' His jerks and twitches seemed much diminished. Some have said he had put them on to make himself appear harmless to Caligula, but I don't think that is the case. The role gave him confidence in himself; the first half of his life he had been bent and cramped by the charge of 'idiot' that his own mother had put on him; now he was straightening up and revealing himself to be a capable ruler. 'We never finished our study of Polybius. And now that we've seized Seneca's goods, we have dozens more volumes to read. It's as if we'd discovered the contents of the Library of Alexandria. I've had to make another room in the palace available just for his books. We never know what's coming do we?' he asked. It was just the kind of trap

82

Caligula used to lay: seducing an old comrade with apparent friendship and then snapping his neck when he was stupid enough to speak as a familiar.

'Caesar,' I said, retaining formality, 'I've come to appeal to you on Seneca's behalf.'

'Well, don't.'

'He's a good man, you know he's a good man. How many suppers have you shared with him? And you need good men about you now.'

'Do not presume...'

'This trumped-up charge. Why?'

'It pleases my wife. She hates philosophers. I don't know why. Do you know why, Delfos?' With his eyes upturned, he seemed to be asking the question of the ceiling.

'She's irrational,' I said quickly, glad to be avoiding his gaze, for surely guilt was glowing on my hot face. 'You know he's innocent, Claudius,' I said, momentarily forgetting my place, but the Princeps looked down at the sound of his name, and it seemed his eyes were pleading with me. The man who had once been almost friendless was now surrounded by friends he could not trust. When he looked at me, he looked beyond all that had happened, to the time when I was all he had.

'I will consider your petition as favourably as I can,' he promised.

According to the gossip of servants Messalina had no argument with Seneca: his was merely the most preposterous name she could think of when accusing Julia of adultery. And Julia's crime? She'd been rude about Messalina's new hairstyle of tight rolls that took three hours a day to achieve with curling irons and gold pins. Apparently Julia had said it made Messalina look like a dead sponge.

Perhaps my intervention had some effect, however, for Claudius suddenly commuted the death penalty to relegation to the isle of Corsica. Julia was exiled to an island more deserted than Corsica, and even more barren than the one she had nearly starved on. This time she was dead within the year for want of food.

I went to see Seneca in prison before he was taken to the port, to tell him about the cheap, clean lodgings I'd found. He was sitting on the floor looking serene. 'Relegation!' I cried, determined to stir up some passion in him. 'To Corsica!'

'It's not Rome,' he agreed, with a gentle smile, 'but a mountain in the sea, rough and coarse. No one for company but a few shepherds and their goats. No pleasant walks, just steep and stoney climbs. A hut for a home. But I shall have the night sky for a blanket. Delfos,' he said, taking my hand, and drawing me down to his foul straw. 'I am delighted. I am galloping into poverty. What more could I want? All those days of practice will now bear fruit. I shall be able to fast and sleep on hard floors without trouble.'

'And Cornelia?' I asked to upset his equilibrium, which was cruel of me. His eyes lost focus momentarily.

'So you've changed your opinion?' I asked. 'You no longer think the better way is to participate in affairs and influence them for the good?'

'Well, had I the choice... But I've given up on Claudius,' he said. 'He's proving not much better than Caligula.'

'Not that bad, surely?'

Seneca's hand tightened on mine. 'Believe me, he is.' He fingered the yellow thread thoughtfully then let me go. 'I had hoped to become tutor to his son in due course, but the gods have decided otherwise. Now I shall have the sky and rocks to study and my collected tenets of wisdom to practise. I am content, Delfos. Of course I shall miss Cornelia, but my brother will look after her.'

'You'll be screaming for urbane company within the week.'

'Let us see if that is true. Quintus Sextius wrote that he sometimes wanted to throw himself out of the window, so frustratingly difficult is the philosophical way of life. Well, let us see. It's being made easy for me. I'll not be surrounded by any temptations, except perhaps sloth. But I'll have my writing to keep me busy, and no distractions. No distractions! I am, I do believe, looking forward to this.'

He who could hold the Senate spellbound by his words was so convincing that I found myself asking if I, too, could accompany him to Corsica. He laughed. 'You, my boy, are to go home. Pythia said so.' And then an attack began.

'Guard!' I called at the iron gate to his rock-cut cell. 'Guard!' When the man came, I told him that Senator Lucius was dying for lack of air and that we had to get him outside. Seneca was clawing his tunic from his chest, his fingers and lips turning blue as he retched for breath. 'He's not going to try and escape,' I said. 'Look at him!'

The guard, a beaten-up lump of brawn who was probably an ex-gladiator, picked Seneca up like a child, carried him into the open courtyard and stayed with us until the attack subsided.

'You never know where you're going to find a good heart,' my teacher gasped as he recovered, nodding gratefully at the guard. 'Goodness is natural, Delfos. Remember that. The soul of man is naturally good. I thank you both.'

He was dispatched to Corsica the following day. I prayed the sea breezes and mountain air would suit him well.

10

VERICA

I received a message from Claudius saying I was to move into the palace. For, as he said, 'it is not fitting that the son of a king lives in a mean tenement.' Not as enamoured of the simple life as Seneca, I moved from my lodgings into a small but luxurious apartment without protest. Yes, yes, yes, I intended to return to Britain, but every day I found another good reason to put it off, the main one now being the onset of winter. Meanwhile Claudius needed my company. Any reluctance I might feel in living in the household of the one who had banished my beloved teacher was overcome by that teacher himself, speaking in my mind. 'Do not avoid evil: influence it to the good.'

I met Claudius alone in his chamber about once a month to discuss our studies, what he called 'my Etruscans and your druids', but I also often joined him for supper on those nights when there were guests. Other than that, I led a lonely life in marble halls, dreading a summons from Messalina and then getting annoyed when it never came. I was yesterday's flavour, yesterday's fashion. She no longer had a taste for tattooed barbarians. And I no longer found her desirable.

There is much that has been said about Messalina, about her appetite for men so voracious that it made prostitutes look like virgins, about her vanity, her superiority, her complete power over her weakling husband. Like all good rumours, they had the seed of truth but that was all. Whatever I may have felt about her, the woman who had caused Seneca to go into exile, the Messalina I saw in the palace during the months I was there was a mother of two small infants, a girl and a boy, whom she fed herself, a woman more devoted to her duty than to her pleasure. Yes, she had a contrived and ridiculous hairstyle that was being adopted by every matron of Rome — many of them having to resort to wigs to achieve it — but the wife of the princeps is in a strange position; she is neither queen nor empress, just a consort. Messalina was twenty-one-years old and crowned herself with curls.

One benefit of living in the imperial palace was access to the imperial bath house, the main pool being in a sumptuous hall of porphyry and onyx with gilded pillars, where the water was frequently changed. Most bathed in the afternoon; in the evenings I had the place more or less to myself. It was almost a year and a half since Claudius had come to power, the beginning of that month the Romans have named after Juno, when I was there one evening, dabbling in the fragrant water. Only slaves were present. While Mandred snoozed on a marble bench, cleaners and attendants were getting the place ready for the following day. I paddled about under the vaulted ceiling of stucco where shadows trembled over paintings of gods. As night came on, sconces and lamps were lit and the polished stone walls took on the patterns of light. I was reluctant to leave the water. On land I was an awkward thing, just like the dolphin I had been named after, but in the water I was safe and happy and unaware of passing time. My trance was broken by a sudden entry into the hall and a commotion at the end of the pool. Palace guards were dragging in a naked barbarian. Mandred stirred and exchanged a puzzled glance with me.

Whether the humiliated wretch was a Gaul or a Briton, I could not tell, but presumed him to be some petty king who, until his arrival in Rome, had believed his title meant something. He struggled in their grasp, apparently frightened of water. 'Come on, you hairy ape!' one thundered, his words echoing off the walls. The violent squall of curses and invective that came in response were in my own dialect.

He was an old man, late sixties, spare in form and sinewy, no loose skin. In this city of paunch and bulging flesh, it was good to see someone so lean. As they tried to take the golden torc from around his neck he fought like a captured ferret, twisting, turning, snarling and biting.

'Do you want to drown?' demanded one of the guard. 'Take it off, you idiot! You don't want your head pulled under the water, do you?' Bitterly, the king removed the torc, placed it with care on a marble seat and gave himself back to the guards. Taking an arm and a leg each they swung him out over the water, back and forth a couple of times to gain momentum and then threw him in. I think he was in mid air when I recognized him. Why at that point? I don't know. Perhaps it was the way his face was contorted in such fury. I ducked beneath the water and swam to the shadows at the far end where Mandred helped me out.

'Who is it?' he whispered.

'Hush!' We slipped out to the next room which was the cold bath, but I skipped that and made for the changing room.

'It's my father.' I took the towel Mandred held out for me.

'Verica? Here?'

'He must have come to see the Princeps but needed purifying before coming into the Presence. No doubt his beard stank of animal grease and old ale, his body of, well, whatever the unwashed smell of.'

'You have no fond memories of your father,' Mandred observed as he dried my back and helped me dress.

'I'm not saying Verica never bathes, but his idea of keeping clean is a daily splash in a stream and, once a moon, full immersion in a lake or, in winter, a good sweat-out in a steam hut. A pool, a man-made pool: he must have thought he was being sacrificed to the gods of the Otherworld.' Verica had spluttered and splashed like a cat being drowned.

'Why didn't you make yourself known?'

'He had lost enough dignity without knowing I'd been witness to it.'

'Purification' to the Princeps did not mean only physical cleanliness: the soul must be clean too, of any idea that kingship counts for anything in Rome. Verica was in the process of finding out how insignificant a client king really is. Only when humiliated would he be fit for his meeting with Tiberius Claudius Caesar.

I was summoned to the audience chamber the following morning, for a formal reunion with King Verica of the Atrebates. I noticed that his skin looked scrubbed and his long grey hair was strangely fluffy but I remained solemn and grave as we were reintroduced to each other.

'Well, quite the Roman!' he said, looking me up and down warily. 'Are you a citizen?'

'Partial. I have Latin rights but can't join the army or wear a toga.'

'Can't join the army? What do you do all day?'

I told him, with some pride, that I studied, mostly history and philosophy.

His lip curled with disdain.

'And I wrestle,' I said. 'And am training as an equites.'

'What's an equites?' he asked but, before I could reply, our awkward exchange was broken by the entry of Claudius. The Princeps limped across the floor in a hurry to reach the curule chair where, once seated, nothing appeared to be wrong with him. A magical chair, he told me once, that made emperors out of fools. He sat there gazing now at my father now at me.

'Clearly you take after your mother, Delfos,' he said, treading on the bunion that was my relationship with my father. Verica did not bristle as I expected, however; he just stood there with a stupid look of gratitude on his face. I felt ashamed on his behalf that he had been smartened up for this interview. Better if he were standing there in his plaids, his hair hanging in felted clumps. The bath had robbed him of his dignity.

'I think,' said Claudius to me, 'you need to interpret for your father?'

'You speak no Roman?' I asked Verica in Gaulish. He turned and his silly smile became a frown.

'So, King Verica,' said Claudius blithely, 'I was saying how Delfos obviously takes after his mother.'

'He says I clearly take after you,' I said to Verica, then remembered, when Claudius chuckled, that the Princeps spoke Gaulish perfectly well. Claudius was enjoying himself at our expense.

'I thought sending him here would make a man of him,' my father grumbled. 'Instead he's studying to be a philosopher. Whatever that is.'

'It's a wise man,' said Claudius in Gaulish. 'Delfos is far from that, but a good student, yes, the best.'

'Togidubnos,' Verica corrected him.

'Togidubnus, indeed. Mouthful, eh? Striking Deep. What does that mean? With the sword or with the stylus?' Claudius dabbed at his mouth. 'Sit, my friend, take refreshment and tell me the cause of this visit.'

Verica sat as bidden and told the Princeps all that had happened to his people since the time of the Great Caesar, how his father Commius — known by us as 'Kommios' — had been given lands from the south coast up to Thames river and built his capital at Calleva; how he had had an alliance with Cymbelinus, king of the Catuvellauni north of the river, who had his capital at Verlamio; how both of them had stayed true to their friendship with Rome. 'We knew we were both there because of the Great Caesar, who had transplanted our tribes from Gaul to new lands, that we were if not vassal kings then representatives of Rome. We liked to think we lived the Roman way and were civilized, at least compared to the wilder tribes of Britain. We were always a bridge, a trading gateway.'

Claudius nodded. 'So I understand.'

'Cymbelinus had four sons. Only one of them, Adminios, was willing to continue in the way of his father. The other three... When Cymbelinus died two years ago, they declared themselves hostile to Rome.'

'For what reason?' Claudius was genuinely intrigued. 'Why should anyone be hostile to Rome?

'The taxes and tributes,' Verica said simply. 'It is my belief that they are fair, given what we receive in return by way of trade. And protection. That was the arrangement made with the Great Caesar: if ever we were in trouble...'

'Yes, yes. Tell me about these three sons.'

Verica described them in order of age, Togodumnus, a man in his mid-thirties who held Verlamio. Arvirargus, a few years younger and holder of the capital of Camulodunon. And the youngest, mid-twenties, Caratacos, 'Who, needing a capital for himself, took mine.'

Claudius winced. 'These names. They are sharp in the mouth, like splinters of bone. Caractacus,' he repeated, getting it wrong.

'In most litters the youngest is a runt; this one was a leader. From his childhood...' Verica glanced at me. I kept my head down and nodded, remembering that overbearingly loud and vain boy who had dominated every game or race at the festivals. 'Always in charge,' my father continued. 'From the moment of his birth, he tyrannised his own family. He's the one who caused the change of allegiance. Adminios was old enough to withstand him but Caratacos, not given to being challenged, responded by driving his eldest brother out of his own terri-tories and taking them for himself. He'd already taken mine... Calleva. There was a battle for it just after the death of Cymbelinus and I lost.'

So it was true. My native place of birth was now the capital of Caratacos of the Loud Mouth.

'After that I retreated to Noviomagos on the south coast,'

Verica continued, 'where I survived about a year before the Catuvellauni pushed me into the sea. I crossed to Gaul, intending to come to Rome, except Adminios was ahead of me. I thought I'd leave the work of supplication to him and stayed with kinsmen in northern Gaul. With my own eyes I saw those proud legions of your predecessor on their way to liberate our lands from our enemies. But then, a week or so later, I saw them on their way back again, cowed by failure. They didn't even set sail! Not knowing what else to do, I settled and made a new home in my ancient homeland. I would be there still except that Fate has brought you to the throne of the great Empire. A man of justice at the pinnacle! Thus I have come to you to beg your help in restoring to me what is lost, and restoring to Britain the peace of Rome. Restoring, yes, for while we traded freely with you, and our kings and queens swore allegiance to you, we prospered. Caratacos in his pride has destroyed the peace.'

'Is everything lost?' Claudius asked.

'No, we have retained the port town of Noviomagus, thanks to my foster son, Katuaros, and the units of your infantry who are there defending the port for the merchants.'

Claudius, who had become hunched in the chair, straightened up. 'I have heard your petition, Verica son of Commius. I feel inclined to help you but need to take the decision to the Senate. You will hear from me.' He dismissed us with a limp shake of his wrist, a gesture that had several times brought an end to the life of a gladiator or cantankerous senator. For us it just meant, 'leave me.'

I had a private supper with my father that night. For once and perversely I abjured sitting cross-legged to lie on the supper couch, propping myself up on an elbow and extolling the virtues of eating lying down.

'Pah!' said Verica, sitting on the floor. He was too old to sit cross-legged now and sat with his legs splayed out before him. He told me of the battle of Calleva and, the way he told it, it seemed odd that we had lost. It was betrayal and trickery that had got the better of the Atrebates, not strength of numbers. I felt grief, though, and images came readily to mind of a happy boyhood spent in the 'oppidum in the woods'. As for seeing Caligula's army pass by on its way to Britain...

'I decided to stay where I was, let the Romans sort it out and then go home once the Catuvellauni had been destroyed. That's all I needed, their destruction. I could do the work of rehabilitation myself. So I waited, but not for very long, because they all mutinied, didn't they? This killing machine that is the Roman army, all too scared of ghosts and monsters to go across Ocean. So then I really did not know what to do, until Fate took a hand and rid us all of that lunatic princeps.'

'It wasn't Fate,' I said. 'It was several assassins.'

Verica shrugged and held up the rubbery leg of a small octopus to gaze at it with disgust. He put it on the side of his dish until he could bear it no more then pushed it off. A waiting slave hurried forwards to clear up after the barbarian.

'This is a foul and reeking city,' Verica said after his fourth goblet of wine. 'Have you tried those latrines?'

'Of course.'

'What a stench. So unhealthy.'

'Much better to crap on the forest floor,' I said, smiling.

'So much better. You get to feed the plants and the worms and can clean yourself with lovely soft moss. Not sponges. Sponges on sticks! Shared by all!'

Now I had to laugh, because I'd had as much wine as he had.

'They are so proud of their sewers but when I was shown the Tiber this morning, I could see all the mucky water flowing into it. That's where the sewers go. And people throwing their rubbish in it, into their holy river! That's like throwing rubbish into the Otherworld! How do they get away with it?' He poked around his dish of seafood and ate what he recognized, but not without a grimace. 'And last night, they made me take a bath.'

'Really?'

'They said I stank, and I probably did, because it's a long time since I'd had a sweat-out, but to make me immerse myself in stagnant water! Water, no doubt, as full of piss as a tanner's sink. Don't tell me those Romans don't piss in the bath. Course they do! Rome is a foul and reeking place, like all cities, and as it's the greatest of them, it stinks the worst. Ugh!' He pushed a transparent and whiskery prawn off his dish. One of the more quick-witted slaves had brought a dog into the chamber to clean up after the king.

As we parted, Verica noticed Mandred for the first time. 'Durotriges...' he observed. 'Another dog in the room.'

Mandred kept his head down and bore it well. Since acquiring him, I had taught myself to overcome the prejudice I bore against his peoples. I'd never told him that children of the Atrebates were coaxed into obedience by the threat of the Durotriges coming in the night to chop off their limbs and eat them. That people of the south coast were of a different order to the Catuvellauni. The Catuvellauni were a noble tribe gone bad; the Durotriges were never noble. They were so belligerent that they could form no nation under one king, only a noisy and argumentative federation of tribes that squabbled like starlings. They were born of the hard rock of the southern coast, our neighbours to the west against whom we were always fortified. I presumed that the Catuvellauni would be leaving them well alone. I often itched to ask Mandred about his upbringing amongst the savages but he always made it clear by subtle shifts in his being that he had no wish to discuss the past.

11
ACROSS OCEAN TO DIS

11

THE NEW LEGATE

'After deep consideration,' said Claudius to Verica, 'it is the opinion of the Senate that it is not in the interests of Rome that your lands be harried by warlords and inimical tribes. We have enjoyed trading with you since the time of the Divine Julius but now it is becoming too dangerous and too expensive. Therefore we have decided to come to your aid. But I want you to understand this, we are not about to move eighty thousand men across the Empire to sort out a petty squabble between British kings. If we help you, in return for our aid, Britain will become a province of the Empire.' Verica turned puce under his beard but he remained silent and listened to the plan Claudius outlined. 'We shall not seek to annexe all the British Isles, just the southern part. We'll leave the hostile primitives to their mountain ranges and set up a line of forts to create a new frontier.'

I was impressed. Claudius was clear and authoritative: such a contrast to the woolly idealism of Caligula, indeed, such a contrast to his own previous self. Claudius was turning out to be a leader even his mother would have admired.

'Shall we get Calleva back?' I asked.

'It is my intention that it returns to the Atrebates.'

'On behalf of my people,' said Verica hoarsely, 'I accept.'

'What do you mean by your people?' Claudius asked. 'The Atrebates or the Britons?'

'The Atrebates, of course. And related tribes such as the Morini, the Ambiani, all those who go under the name Belgae.

But I cannot speak for the Cantii, the Durotriges, the Dobunni and the rest of those in the south.'

'I need you to be able to speak for them. I want you to go home in advance of the army and negotiate peace. Your son will help you. I deem it your sacred task, Delfos, to save your people, and by your people I mean all Britons, from a bloodbath.'

Claudius put me to work studying the records of the two previous expeditions, the limited one of Julius Caesar and the aborted one of Caligula, to find out why they failed. It was not long before I had identified lack of planning and the use of inappropriate legions. They had been drawn from the deserts when what was needed was men used to marsh. Claudius nodded when I reported back to him, took note of what I said and passed it on to the generals he had commissioned.

The plans for the expedition were to be half a year in the making, and the legions chosen were familiar with large rivers and their crossings. Germany, which had been finally subdued by Claudius's brother, was able to give up three legions from the Rhine: the Twentieth Valeria, the Fourteenth Gemina and the Second Augusta, the latter renowned for brutal subjugation of rebellious Gauls. The Ninth Hispana was relocated from the fens of the Danube. Likewise with the auxiliaries, Claudius was careful to choose those with useful skills such as the Batavians who can swim in full armour. Orders went out for these four legions to leave their forts and muster on the coast of northern Gaul.

Every day Verica was called in to answer questions. Although he could understand a little of the Roman tongue, he could not speak it. At first I acted as interpreter in these meetings but having me speak his words put him in a foul temper, so foul it was tactfully suggested by Claudius's secretary, Narcissus, that I step away and leave it to a professional interpreter. The mood between my father and me was no better in leisure times; when I suggested I give him a tour of Rome to show him its architectural wonders I was sourly rebuffed. By the end of the first month he had moved out of the palace grumbling about soft mattresses and bad backs. Claudius had a friend who was a Gaul by birth who had recently bought the famous gardens of Lucullus on the Pincian hill. The vast estate had run down badly over the last generation and, with its broken statues, dry fountains and topiary gone wild, was an image of the futility of wealth. Death comes to all, even fabulous gardens. But it provided an agreeably shabby retreat for Verica which, apart from the odd grotto or marble seat, could pass for a forest. He had his round tent put up in the shade of some overgrown oleanders where he could relax with a view that was green in every direction. But when the mounting heat and mosquitoes of summer drove the imperial family and household out to a villa in the Bay of Naples, Verica, his tent and his son went with them.

The tireless planning for the 'expedition' continued wherever we were. After much deliberation Claudius had elected Aulus Plautius to command the army while putting Didius Gallus in charge of the cavalry. Three legionary legates had been appointed — Sabinus, Geta and Frugi — all of them, like Plautius himself, sound men of some integrity. Although the legate of the Second had yet to be appointed, as the personnel became settled we began to concentrate on strategy. Sometimes Claudius conducted the meeting but the man in overall charge was his secretary, Narcissus, an ex-slave but now a freedman and Roman citizen who had a mind like a well-honed blade. While Claudius had a tendency to forget names, Narcissus did not. He remembered everyone in full praenomen, nomen and cognomen as well as any relevant detail, anything he could enquire about. How was the ailing mother, the pregnant wife, the daughter about to be betrothed? How was the brother the senator, the son the student, the esteemed father? Narcissus was accompanied everywhere by a small white dog; in any other man, that would be cause for ridicule. Narcissus's dog, however, had senators and legates bending down to scratch him between the ears, feed him treats and praise his goodness. *'If you want to advance quickly on the cursus honorum,'* one wit said, *'pet the dog.'*

It was in August and in an airy room of the villa, given to the business of Britain, that Narcissus announced the arrival of |the newly appointed legate of Second Augusta and I looked up to see the thin-lipped, compassionate face of my friend Vespasian. In his formal introduction, Narcissus introduced us as, 'Verica son of Commius, King of the Atrebates, and his son, Togidubnus.'

Vespasian, knowing me better by my cradle name, looked me up and down as if seeing me anew. 'Grandson of Commius?' he muttered. 'I hadn't realised.'

It was a claim to fame I never made, not wishing to be associated with my notorious grandfather.

The placid brow of Aulus Plautius furrowed as if a plough had passed across it. 'Commius...' he repeated. 'Commius the Gaul, whom the Divine Julius planted in Britain?'

King Verica was nodding. 'A great friend of Rome, my father,' he said through his interpreter.

'But...,' Aulus Plautius fingered his throat, feeling for bristles, 'that was nearly a hundred years ago. Commius was your grandfather, surely?'

'My father sired me on a twenty-year-old when he was seventy-nine,' said Verica. 'Long-lived, the Atrebates, and fertile to the end.'

'This is the Commius who agreed to anything the Romans wanted of him, so long as he never had to meet a Roman?'

Verica nodded proudly. 'Hence being planted in Britain, but of course, there were Romans there whom Caesar had left behind to look after things. My father bumped into them at every turn.'

'Long time ago,' said Narcissus, smoothly, 'all a long time ago.' Addressing those gathered, he explained that the purpose of this meeting was to study the geography of Britain in advance of the army.

Claudius spoke. 'We have the guidance of history. Our Delfos, here, is well read and knows by heart the accounts written by the Divine Julius. And King Verica has the knowledge of experience.'

'Britain is a hilly land, a rocky land and, in the north and west, a mountainous land,' said Narcissus, 'and between all these rises are the dips, so many rivers, marshes, estuaries, streams and lakes that, in some places, the houses are built on stilts.'

I avoided catching the eye of my father in case we laughed. There are houses on stilts, for sure, but what Narcissus was giving was a patchwork picture made out of the stories of historians, factual reports, hearsay and rumour. As he spoke, we got the picture of a wild, windy, rain-swept land infested with naked barbarians tattooed from head to foot and you could see the eyes of legates rolling as they wondered how best to defeat such an enemy with their well-ordered legions wading across difficult terrain. 'It is worse than Germania,' Narcissus said. 'All we had to do there was burn the forests. It is worse than Gaul. It is the last refuge of rebels and druids who, escaping the Empire, decamped to Britain. They are bitter, querulous and would rather die than submit to reason. That is our enemy, is it not, King Verica?'

'The druids? For certain. I banished them from my territories. Always conspiring behind my back, thinking they knew better. You can never trust a druid.'

Claudius was listening to Verica and not to the interpreter; the interpreter merely confirmed what Claudius had already understood: druids were not to be trusted.

'We have been civilized in the south since the time of Caesar,' my father continued. 'The south, at least in the central part, is hilly and fertile and the people are, on the whole, as gentle as the land. Our enemy, the Catuvellauni, are not wild barbarians on the rampage so much as good men turned bad. Under the leadership of the sons of Cymbelinus, they have become rapacious, greedy horse thieves...'

Claudius nodded. 'It is true. Southern Britain is allied to Rome for the purposes of trade and most of their kings and chiefs are loyal to us. It is beyond the mountains west and north that the barbarians of our nightmares lie.' Narcissus whispered to him and Claudius corrected himself. 'I was forgetting the Brigantes of the Pennines and their beautiful queen who last year came all the way to Rome to pay me honour. But beyond them, yes, the hairy savages of Caledonia, and in the west, the squat and vicious Silures and Ordovices. What we have enjoyed since the time of Caesar,' Claudius concluded, 'is the territory of southern and central Britain acting as a buffer between barbarism and civilization. It is that part of Britain that we look to annexe to the Empire for its protection and for the continuance of trade. Verica has assented to that and has undertaken to go in advance to win the support of his fellow kings and chieftains. What we need to do is to ensure a quick, clean intervention with as little blood spilled as possible. Thus I have commissioned all of you, O best of commanders, to effect this conquest.'

Maps were unrolled and heads bent to study the topography of a land that had only ever been crudely drawn. Verica told them about the hills, hills everywhere, and most of them fortified. 'We call them duns. Not all of them remain fortified. Many have been abandoned since the time of the Great Caesar, especially in my territories.'

'How come?'

'That civilization the Princeps mentioned,' said Verica wryly. 'Once we got a taste for trade, we gave up the livestock raiding. At least most of us did. And then came that thieving throw-back, Caratacos.'

He explained the location of the various nations, peoples and tribes that make up Britain. The Catuvellauni here, the Trinovantes there, the Iceni up here. It was talk I'd hoped never to hear again, for it so occupies the mind at home, knowing where everyone is within our constantly shifting boundaries, that there is barely room for any other topic of discussion. Growing bored I studied a large circular map painted on the wall that had Rome at its centre and the Empire spreading out in all directions. On this map, the foot of Britain hung in the north in an area labelled BEYOND OCEAN. The main part of my country was off the map, beyond the beyond: the land known as Dis. I wondered at my own boredom. Here I was, part of a small and very select group determining the fate of a country, my country, and all I wanted to do was yawn. I needed air.

Out in the garden, I met Messalina walking with a slave who was guiding little Claudia Octavia in her first steps; Messalina herself was carrying her infant son. I stopped to exchange greetings, which were stiff and cool, for I was not yet stoical enough to forgive her for the false accusation of Seneca and avoided her gaze by making much of the little girl. Messalina, who I had once desired so ardently, had become an indifferent. She looked the same, she smelt the same, but I knew now the blot on her soul. She took on the baffled look of a lap dog that has been shut out but I remained curt, frosty. 'He reminds me so much of you,' she whispered as I bade her farewell and walked off. I turned and walked back to study the baby.

'Why have you sent no message?' I asked, coming close to lift the cowl of the swaddling to see something resembling a pickled walnut.

'Claudius knows,' she whispered. 'Unable or unwilling to find an excuse to kill you, he's sending you to Britain. Don't expect to come back.'

'He looks like his father,' I said.

'Of course he does.'

'I mean Claudius.'

'Yes, so do I.' Her eyes were feasting on me. 'Delfos...'

'I am happy to go home,' I said. 'We may be painted barbarians but we don't have innocent men sent into exile on charges trumped up by women.'

With that I went back to the meeting where I found Plautius wanting to know what loyalty we might expect from these southern tribes and Verica telling him that, while all were loyal to Rome, many were scared of Caratacos. 'Some have signed treaties where he has promised to leave them alone in return for an annual tribute. They will feel honour-bound to supply fighting men to support the Catuvellauni.'

'So will anyone fight on the side of Rome?' Plautius asked.

'Presume not. But you can also presume they will be happy to lose.'

'What does that mean?'

'It means they will abide by past agreements and relish new ones, made with Rome.'

Plautius scoffed. 'You think we will make allies of men who have fought against us? We shall make them slaves. It is your work,' and here he stabbed at Verica with a forefinger, 'to convince them of that before any battle. Anyone who changes sides before battle will win our respect and protection. Anyone who changes sides after battle, after losing a battle, can expect a quick death or slavery. That's the choice. Make sure they understand it.'

Plautius, the senator who had been appointed to command the army, was of all the men in the room the only one born for the office he held. The rest, upstarts, ex-slaves, new men. Plautius was old Rome and seemed to have been carved in marble. It was hard not to look for imperfections as attentively as his slave must search for them each morning, hoping for a spot, a curly whisker in an eyebrow, nose hair, anything to spoil the pale beauty of his face. It seemed impossible that hair could be trimmed so immaculately: the line across the back of his neck must have been drawn with a bricklayer's level. The nearest a beard came to his jaw was a certain blueness in the evening. His slave told mine that if it got too blue, Plautius would have another barbering before dinner. As for the baths, well … the things slaves discuss.

Plautius made my father, standing next to him, seem even hairier than he was. Verica's once thick locks were now thin and matted, but you could still see the vestige of the old colour and knew that once he'd had a great mane. He was like faded cloth, still strong in the thread but drained of its dyes. His eyebrows had whiskers springing like briars, his ears seemed full of thistle seed. There was no trim at all to his beard and bristles grew where they would on his cheeks, even one at the end of his nose. The difference between the two men was that of a Roman topiary garden and a British weed patch.

'And these fortified hills,' Plautius asked. 'How are they defended?'

'The summits are encircled with very deep ditches,' Verica replied, 'one, two or many, a high bank with ramparts, palisades. All the defences are concentrated on the weakest point, which are the gates.'

'Do people live in these enclosures?'

'In some places but not in others. They were built long before the time of Caesar and are intended to mark territory and protect against raiders. Used mostly in the summer months, they are often little more than livestock pens, but sometimes, if water is available, settlements have grown up. But all of them provide refuge in times of danger, and everyone will resort to them when you arrive.'

'What weapons do they have? How do they fight off an attack?'

'As I say, it all happens at the gates. The rest of the ramparts are easily defended since few can get up and over those steep ditches and embankments. At the gates, however…' Verica described how attackers were funnelled by the clever ditch-work to expose themselves to the bone-breaking assaults from slingers; how those who got to the ramparts were met with a rain of javelins, and how those who got over were met by swords. 'But if you can get the gates, you have the dun. A dun is only as strong as its gates.'

Plautius looked at Vespasian with a smile seeping into his face. 'How long would it take us to subdue a dun?' he asked the legate.

'Do we have use of ballistas and scorpions?'

'Catapults, crossbows, every machine of war we require.'

'About half a day.'

Verica coughed to hide a choking sound. Plautius smiled at him. 'Your Britons can fling what they like at us. We don't have to come within reach of your stones to bring down those gates.'

I could almost read my father's mind; his face remained impassive but I sensed his dawning realisation that he was unleashing on his people an enemy who fought without honour.

'Bloodless,' said Plautius. 'A bloodless victory if, as you say, we only have to take the gates.'

12

PLANNING

The strategies that emerged from a succession of such meetings were complex and subtle. Verica and I were to go ahead of the army to persuade the southern Britons to surrender. The four legions, matched in number by auxiliaries, would follow about a month later. There was much discussion about landing places but it was finally decided not to follow Caesar's route to the east coast, where he had lost forty ships. Caesar had had poor reconnaissance; Claudius had Verica, who persuaded him that a southern landing in his own harbours would be safer and worth the extra days at sea. And, of course, it would enable a quick march to Calleva, which surely was the Roman's objective?

Plautius reading itineraries... '*From Noviomagus to Calleva, go north-north-west to Venta Belgarum, following the coastal plain, keeping the sea to your left, crossing two rivers at fording points.*' It sounded so straightforward, apart from 'Venta Belgarum' which I had to explain to Verica was the name the Romans had given Ford of the Alders. He let it pass, being more concerned to make Plautius realise how tricky those river crossings were, but Plautius put more faith in the written word than the spoken one. '*From Venta, go north-north-east, two days march over rolling hills and gentle valleys, all cleared for farming, towards the river flowing east.* Is that the Thames?'

'No, the Kennet. The Thames is half a day further but also flows east. That is the great river, which effectively is my northern border, dividing southern Britain from the rest...'

'No doubt there is a bridge.'

Verica laughed.

'Well,' said Plautius, irritated, 'if there isn't now, there soon will be.'

Verica was in too fine a mood to be troubled by immaculate senators. Enquiries had confirmed that Noviomagos was still secure under the command of Katuaros. 'Now he's a real warrior,' Verica said in my hearing. 'The tallest tree in the grove. A very beech of a man.' He had always favoured Katuaros but I did not mind as much as he presumed I did. I had been as relieved as he was to hear that my foster brother was safe. After the death of his father, Biccos, at the battle for Calleva, Katuaros had become Verica's second-in-command.

On my own I studied those itineraries, mostly Caesar's, and tried to absorb their meaning, for it seemed to me that a list of settlements and features in the landscape is just a string of beads, telling you nothing of what lies in between. As a child of Britain I had been hefted to the land, a shepherd's word for how a ewe trains her lambs where and where not to wander. My brothers taught me how many strides it is from the river to the heath, from the Calleva gates to the slab bridge over Stony Bottom Brook, where the king of the slow worms lives, or up to the standing stones in Broom Woods which, they said, move about on nights of full moon. The aunts taught me the names and locations of plants, what to eat and what not to eat. The uncles taught me how to stalk prey in the woods or on the rough heath. My mother introduced me to all the shrines and sacred places within a day's walk and told me the names of the local gods. My father took me up Beech Hill to show me the view, such as it was, and have me believe that everything in sight was his. Between them, they walked me in all directions until I knew the land well enough that I could walk alone.

And so I got to know the hills and valleys and long stretches of marsh, the forests, woods and groves, sacred wells and shrines. And the boundaries. Hefting is real. Although a boundary is often invisible you step over it at your peril. I never felt imprisoned by it; secured is the better word. Within your boundaries, provided no one was bursting through to you, you were safe. As soon as I was old enough, even a little before, I walked on my own but it was only when my foster brother joined us that I dared to attempt the three-day walk to our southern limit that was the sea. That was the extent of the Atrebatic lands, between the Thames and the sea. And such was the fine cobweb of interconnections within the Atrebatic tribes that, if I wandered too far and got caught by the night, someone would take me in and send word to my father in the morning.

The boundaries east and west were less fixed. Neighbouring tribes jostled for possession and the boundaries moved as if the territory breathed in and out. Even rivers did not provide barriers but had to be protected from nearby hills. That was where our warriors got their practice. The aim of a warrior? Sometimes it was defence but other times it was to burst through the boundary of another tribe's territory and take the livestock.

The hefting is real. The Atrebates had only been in Britain three generations, but I was so hefted to the land that when the Romans came to take me away, I felt as if I were being ripped from it like a sapling pulled up by the roots.

'When we have Calleva,' Plautius was saying, 'the main body of the army will go east to wipe out the Catuvellauni but one legion will go west to deal with anyone who has not sworn allegiance to us. We can rely on Cartimandua to hold the north.'

Claudius followed this plan as it was drawn on a sand bed — Caesar himself had noted that southern Britain is a triangle, with the south coast as the base and Venonis as the apex — and there it was in sand: the next addition to the Empire, with the sacred track we call the Albios Way, the way of heaven, designated as the new frontier. I remembered it well, the sacred path busy with pilgrim processions, the liminal boundary between this world and the Otherworld. To be designated from now on as the boundary between barbarism and the civilized world…

'And which legion subdues the west?' he was asking.

'Second Augusta, under Vespasian.'

Vespasian remained expressionless whereas Sabinus, his elder brother who commanded one of the other three legions, looked stormy, knowing that all the glory would be in the west. Vespasian had been singled out as the man most likely to establish the new frontier of the Empire.

Still staring at the map and the line that was the Albios way, Verica said, 'It's not a boundary at the moment.' He explained that it ran across the territory of the Dobunni governed by King Esius.

'Is he friendly to Rome?' Vespasian asked.

'Would be if he could be,' said Verica, 'but he's in thrall to Caratacos and has to pay him tribute to be left alone.'

'That, then,' said Plautius, 'will be your first goal, to get the support of Esius.'

The general who would be in charge of the cavalry, Didius Gallus, was a priest of the Temple of Jupiter. During the festival of lamps in the month of Augustus, he invited Verica and me to his house to discuss the gods. 'Let us be straight with each other,' he said. 'As a priest of Jupiter I have concerns over and above military matters. When Rome takes a territory, we endeavour to respect the local gods. For that reason, I need to know about yours. While every people, every locality, every feature in the land has its own genius, there is a pantheon of gods that the Greeks call "Olympian" but who are universal. They will be present in Britain, whatever they are called there. When Rome conquered Greece we understood that we shared their deities. Their Pallas Athene is our Minerva, their Poseidon, our Neptune, their Hermes, our Mercury and so on. Some grammarians say that, with the oldest gods, the names appear to come from the same source. So, for instance, Jupiter and Zeus are one and the same. What is the British counterpart of the Father God?'

There was a lot of pausing in this conversation as I interpreted for both of them. Verica's attention had been taken by a bowl of figs, so on his behalf I said it was Dis Pater. 'Claudius says it's a corruption of Zeus-Pater, the Father God, who for us is Jupiter.'

Didius Gallus raised his eyebrows. 'Fascinating... Do you know any more equations?'

I shrugged. 'Apollo-Belenos is the only one I can think of. The greater gods have dedicated temples, but it is the lesser gods the people worship. The gods of field and marsh, spring and lake, tree and animal.'

'We need to go about this carefully and intelligently, so that your people do not feel their gods are being supplanted by ours.'

'Or built over,' I said, remembering the plans for military roads and camps.

'What are you saying?' Verica asked through a mouthful of fig. Where a Roman would have used a plate and a small fruit knife, he had sunk his teeth directly into the soft skin and now had fig flesh in his beard. This he wiped off with his hand, and his hand he cleaned by sucking on it. I sensed horror in Didius, but he concealed it well.

'We're talking about the gods, father,' I said.

Verica preferred to see off the figs and asked for no further interpretation.

'The whole matter is delicate,' said Didius. 'Mistakes can be made. I shall be there, to make sure the Romans do not tread on British — or divine — toes, but I need your help. I need you to tell me about your gods, give me their names, describe their attributes.' This was the kind of conversation I relished, and

111

we spent the rest of the afternoon comparing British deities with Roman ones, making pairs of Apollo and Belenos, Nodens and Mars. 'Although personally I think Nodens is more Mercury than Mars,' I said. Verica fell asleep, his head back, mouth open and snoring; until, waking with a sudden cry of pain, he ran for the latrine.

'Please excuse my father,' I said, beyond embarrassment. Didius leant forwards.

'Don't ever let him know you are ashamed of him. I speak as a father.'

I noticed, as I was meant to, the eight-petalled amulet of Eleusis hanging on a chain usually concealed beneath his toga.

'Do you have the cult of Demeter in Rome?' I asked.

'We have the cult of Ceres, with a temple on the Aventine hill, but it's a plebeian affair. Anyone in Rome who wants to be initiated must travel to Athens and Eleusis at the appropriate time. There are not many of us. I hear you were initiated in a solitary ritual at the wrong end of the year.'

'Apollo willed it.'

'So I hear. I believe it is part of his will that you do this work for us in Britain, of bringing the gods into harmony. It is a great and subtle work. I think your father is not capable of it, but you...' He fell quiet when Verica returned looking abashed and saying that Roman food upset him.

When our interview ended, Didius asked why my slave was wearing the red scarf. I showed him the lump on Mandred's neck hoping that, as a priest, he could help. Didius pushed at it, noted that it caused no pain and said it was nothing serious. 'Just a cyst. Have it dealt with back in Britain. Your druids have better physicians than anything we can offer. Our quacks would just cut it out and cauterise it.' Mandred stared at him with haunted eyes.

To take Mandred's mind off his problems, I took him to the races at the Circus Maximus. He watched the mighty chariots, said they were lumbering beasts compared to our light and nimble vehicles, and claimed that as a boy he had been champion of the local races. 'I used to run the pole,' he said. You have to be more than nimble to run the shaft that joins the cart to the yoke. You have to be braver than brave. We went home, he stumbling as usual, falling forwards into each step, his dreams as crippled as his body.

When Julius Caesar made his first attempt to invade Britain, he had sent the Gallic chief Kommios in advance to persuade the British chiefs to surrender. Now we, son and grandson of Kommios, were to attempt the same. Only when the time for departure approached did I begin to question how easy it would be. Verica seemed to think the chiefs would all drop like ripe pears at our feet, but I was having qualms of entering enemy territory with a small escort and nothing more. 'Oh, stop worrying, pup. I know them all. As soon as they hear the Romans are coming, they'll rise up in a body against Caratacos. There isn't a single tribe that hasn't suffered from him and his rapacity.'

Claudius was not quite so confident. 'There will be resistance,' he said. 'Caractacus will be calling on them as men, calling out the warrior, calling out the proud Briton. How did Horace put it? *Dulce et decorum est pro patria mori.* Sweet it is to die for your country. That's what he'll tell them, and they'll be too much in a blood-rage to question it. So you need to speak to the kings and get them to see reason.'

'Reason?' I asked.

Claudius stared at me long and hard, except that there was a violent tic in one eyelid. 'This is a mission of peace, yes, an expedition, a liberation, a mild intervention to re-establish trade. You can tell them that, but better if you tell them that to resist Rome would not only be certain death, but an unpleasant one. If the Britons resist us, if they put up a fight, they will be slaughtered, man, woman and child. There will be no mercy.'

I quailed at the ferocity in him. Was this my scholarly and inquisitive mentor speaking? Or is it true that a role rules the man?

'There will be rivers of blood: all your holy springs and wells will turn red and be polluted. Your houses will be razed, your soil poisoned, your women raped, your babies roasted on spits, your horses blinded, your dogs crucified. We will show no mercy and nothing will be left.'

There was a silence in the room that crackled. Claudius's thunderous expression softened, like the sun coming out from behind storm clouds. 'But if they do not resist us, Britain will thrive, will grow rich on trade. All that natural mineral wealth that you fashion into objects and put into streams for the gods! Let it be sold. Let your people be rich. There will be villas and bath houses and fertile, lush farms. All will be well if you will be governed peacefully by Rome. Tell them, Delfos, persuade them of this truth: to resist would be futile. It would mean annihilation. Of course,' Claudius added, 'if you are Catuvellauni, all those things are going to happen to you anyway, so you may as well resist. We don't want to go all that way without a fight!'

I was so shaken that I cannot recall what followed. I found myself staring at the floor and wondering at its manufacture. Was it a mosaic? I was not sure, for the fragments of stone were not tesserae but had been carved into shape and pieced together into a geometric pattern. The joins: a masterpiece of stone carving. An optical illusion where squares looked like squares until they suddenly looked like circles. I squinted at it. Intarsia, yes, that was what it was called...

Vespasian drew me away, leaving King Verica with the other legates.

'It was rhetoric, Delfos,' he said as we passed through the vestibule. 'I've been in the army all my adult life and I've only ever seen barbarians do those things, not Romans.'

'I saw dogs being crucified here just a few weeks ago.'

'Ah, well, that was a religious rite. We fight honest battles and win by our superior strength and strategies. It was rhetoric.' He laughed. 'Don't let Seneca see you — all pale and trembling, like a girl who's just lost her virginity.'

'Seneca's in Corsica,' I muttered, nodding to the guard at the gate as we left the palace.

'Ah yes, so he is. You see? Barbarians would have buried him alive in a desert for such flagrant adultery, but we just send him to an island famous for its grapes.'

I smiled at this. It was true that Seneca had exaggerated the picture of Corsica as a wild and almost uninhabited rock, but he was a writer first and foremost, and writers live by words and use them to create dramatic effect. It was something Claudius had just taught me, and something I clearly needed to learn. There was no point in my going home and telling the Britons not to resist what was only a liberation. What would that achieve? No, there must be threats, and any threat worth its salt must include impaled babies and crucified dogs. Vespasian could see me coming up from the deeps and was waiting for me at the surface, his rubbery face creased with laughter.

'Me? Crucify dogs? Come on!' He turned to speak to Mandred who was limping along behind us. 'You told me once, when we were in Greece, that you were of the Durotriges.'

'I am,' said Mandred without looking up. 'That I am.'

Wanting information from Mandred, Vespasian took us back to his own house for dinner — a small place in a seedy part of the city — and once again we were poring over a sand-bed, but in much better detail. Mandred showed Vespasian where the territory of the Durotriges lay, on the south coast, to the west of the Belgae, drew in the rivers and the strings of mighty hill forts. When he told him that the Durotriges held the Isle of Vectis, which shelters our harbours from the sea, Vespasian considered that to be of vital importance.

'Sounds like a task for the Second Legion, to clear that island.' Vespasian's plans to take back the Isle of Vectis from our ancestral enemy was, for me, the defining gesture of the Roman expedition and one of the main reasons why I was in favour of it.

'This evening,' I said to Mandred on the way back to my chamber, 'you've listened to Vespasian's plan to subjugate the Durotriges without expression. How is that?'

He shrugged.

'Have you no feelings of loyalty towards your people?'

'As much as they have for me,' he said. 'Who do you think sold me into slavery?'

'What happened?' I asked.

'My family were poor and needed the money.'

Did I believe him? I think not, but I was sensitive to his reluctance to say any more and let it drop.

By the time the imperial family moved back to Rome in the autumn, and Verica was back in the gardens of Lucullus, legions were being moved, merchant ships requisitioned, siege engines constructed, armour forged, swords made, instruments of survey gathered and gargantuan supplies of dried biscuit and bacon stockpiled. Then, at Saturnalia at the end of December, Verica and I were suddenly told to prepare to depart for Gaul. In the *winter*? It was necessary, we were told, to have as much time as possible for our negotiations with the British chiefs before the Romans landed.

Our boat for Massalia was waiting at Ostia when, in a small, private ceremony at the palace, I was given two gifts. One was Roman citizenship. 'You are of age, now,' Claudius said, 'and it is time you took the name your father gave you.' He held out a signet ring to me as a sign of his imperial favour and pronounced me 'Tiberius Claudius Togidubnus.'

In my mind's eye I could see my mother wincing.

'And with this honour,' he said, 'I grant you the power to sign treaties on behalf of Rome. Take our peace to your people, Togidubnus.'

Verica, who had not shared in this honour, gazed at me with ice-cold eyes. He was even more annoyed when, clopping over marble floors, came my other gift, a horse from the Maremma. He used to have a horse like this, called Tiberius, but had come south on a small British horse called Amabel. I wondered what had happened to his stallion.

'This is the father of your new herd,' said Claudius, running his hand over the horse's sleek flanks. 'What will you call him?'

I was too taken aback to think, but the name that came to mind was 'Scipio.'

'Good name,' said Claudius. 'Elder or Younger?'

Scipio Africanus the Younger, the one who in a dream saw the insignificance of Rome in the context of the stars. 'The Elder,' I said.

Claudius, still stroking the horse, made sure that I understood that 'Africanus' was an epithet given as a reward for the conquest of Carthage. 'He didn't have African blood, whereas this fine, fine young stallion does, hence his height.' And so we fell into one of our easy discourses ranging over time and place, causing Verica to leave, complaining of a back ache and saying he needed to lie down, not stand about listening to history lessons.

While we were in Ostia a boat arrived from Corsica carrying a letter for me. Seneca gave a detailed account of the habits of sea birds nesting on lime-streaked cliffs, of fragrant drifts of juniper, myrtle and wild herbs, of plants he had never seen before, shy nodding things that somehow survive high up in rocky scree, of the songs of shepherds and the simple pleasures of a diet of goat's cheese, seafood and olives. Apparently Corsican wine agreed with him very well. He described the vivid sunsets over the sea and sunrises over Italy. Half way up a mountain you can see Rome on a clear day, he said, but he was happy not to bother to make the climb. His most lyrical passages, however, were reserved for the night time. Seneca was spending his exile studying astronomy. Each clear night he sat outside under the stars, learning their courses around the pole star, identifying planets and constellations. The sky at night was, he said, 'Nature's masterwork'. As for his breathing, he had had no attacks since that near fatal one in prison. He didn't have to tell me he was happy: it was in the seed of every word.

13

THE LONG MARCH

The road north across Gaul from the port of Massalia, tamped
down by marching soldiery over the years, is a clean, hard
surface that follows the course of the Rhône. Way stations are
each a day apart, the distance between them being determined
by the terrain. Sometimes we covered eighteen miles in a
day, sometimes only seven, but we always reached the fort. We
were escorted by a cohort of the Second Augusta, the scales of
their armour clanking in rhythm as they marched, but we, the
king and his companions, were allowed to ride. Verica was
on his elderly and faithful Amabel, a blond-maned roan with a
russet coat so dusted with white hairs that in some lights she
looked blue, in others purple. I rode Scipio. The Horse of
Heaven couldn't have had a better pace and each day I thanked
Corotiacos, god of horses, for this gift from Claudius.

The main body of the legion was coming from the border
with Germany and we aimed to meet them in a month at
Durocorteron, capital of the Remi territory, and proceed with
them to the mustering at the port of Gesoriacum.

'When do we eat?' Verica asked, not long after starting off.

'Tonight,' I said.

'Tonight?'

'It's eighteen miles to the fort. I believe there is no intention
to stop along the way and cook up a stew for five hundred.'
I smiled at the thought. 'No hot mead to go with it, or nap to
sleep it all off afterwards, just walking.'

'Walking?'

'Well, riding for you and me.'

'So when do we crap?' my kingly father asked.

'If you need to, we can stop, and you can go and feed the plants and worms.'

I was teasing him, of course, and we stopped for regular short breaks, with a rest at midday to eat our rations. Still, my father was not used to having his day arranged for him by someone else.

'Togidubnos!' he snapped. 'I need to eat! Now!'

Mandred, astride our baggage mule, opened up our rations and handed him some bacon. Largennius the centurion passed by and prodded Mandred so hard he fell from the mule. 'No riding pack animals!' he barked.

'He can't walk any distance,' I protested, leaping down to help Mandred to his feet.

'I can't think why you bought a cripple for a slave. Was he going cheap?'

'At least he's only crippled in the legs,' I thought, 'not in the soul.'

'Send him to the back of the line,' said the centurion, 'to the baggage carts.'

I stood aside with Scipio and Mandred while the cohort marched on. At the rear, I took the Roman saddle off my horse, stored it on a trundling cart, and introduced Scipio to the British way of riding: bareback. The horse was uneasy, especially with two of us, as we caught up with Verica towards the front, but then settled into the pace. Even horses enter trances on a march.

The soldiers marched and even the clanking of the kit they carried came into rhythm. No one spoke but sometimes there was the sound of a hawk and spit, sometimes a fart and a protest from the man behind, but mostly it was just walking, walking, walking. They were somehow able to suspend normal life and go into this locomotive state. When it rained, everyone cloaked-up and the percussive tramping was augmented by under-the-breath muttering and cursing and squeaking boots. A winter march was a rare thing, but this cohort, from a legion that had served in Germania, marched on through rain and, some days, snow, and I swear missed not a single beat in their pace. This discipline was both impressive and frightening. The men seemed to have only one purpose, which was to fulfil the will of Rome. I'll say one thing about these fighters, however, and that is, if they survived battle, they were long-lived. We had no concept of veterans in Britain, but then we had no concept of a marching army, either.

Although we had been together half a year, Verica and I had yet to have a conversation in private. I'd hoped and expected that this journey would allow me to get to know him better, and for him to come to know me. I had imagined us riding slowly along, side by side, gently disarming our hearts as we grew to trust each other; I had imagined a time when, in complete ease, I could ask after my mother.

Verica, however, swathed in sheepskin, preferred to converse with weather gods, Taranis in particular, offering them extravagant sacrifices if only they would let him alone. He left a votive image at every shrine we passed but it did no good; by the time we got to Avennione, the mistral was blowing, a north-westerly wind roaring down the Rhône valley to bite our ears and noses. Every step of the way was good practice in Stoicism. I refused to complain, even inwardly, but simply noted that I was cold, that I was wet, that I was tired, and left it at that. At each fort where we made an overnight stop, while the soldiers queued for baths, latrines and their meals, Verica had his cart unloaded: two oaken chests, his round tent, some hides and the weapons. That's the way of the barbarian, to be mobile, all treasures portable. As one of the Noble Youths, I could use the officer's bath house, and did so, the steam and the scraping making me whole again after each arduous day, but they were rudimentary, these baths, and the water was over-used. On that stay in Avennione, when I went to bid

Verica goodnight I found him sitting sodden in his tent, hunched in blankets after a wash in a stream, saying rain water never did anyone any harm and that I, Togidubnos of the Atrebates, had grown up a woman, which made his warrior companions laugh.

'How can you sleep under ceilings?' he continued. 'I would lie awake all night if I were you, just to be on my guard. What men put up tends to fall down. Trees. You can trust trees to stand, not much else. Never trust a man. Never trust a ceiling…' He buried down under his hides, his spear and shield hanging from a post, clutching the end of the chain that bound his treasure chest. I left him in his tent while I, with more than a hint of superiority, went for a bed in the officer's quarters. The ceiling there was brick vaulting, apparently held up by magic. Blaming the waxing moon for my sleeplessness, I spent the night staring at the bricks looming over me.

'It's not natural, is it?' Mandred asked, equally — or perhaps loyally — sleepless and reading my thoughts. 'How do those bricks stay up?' I tried to explain how vaults and tunnels are made but Mandred suddenly clambered to his feet and stumbled outside to sleep under the stars.

'They can fall, you know,' I said to his retreating back. 'Stars can fall.'

He came back within minutes because of the cold.

And if it wasn't baths and ceilings, it was staircases that turned Britons into mules. I suppose I once felt that way myself, but I said nothing of this when I scorned Verica's fear of ordinary flights of stone steps. I stopped short of calling him an ignorant barbarian but it was implicit in everything I said, so it was no wonder that he wasn't very talkative and seemed to close down each time I tried to tell him things about my life, of Claudius and Seneca, of the philosophy of Socrates. The question about my mother that nagged in my heart remained unasked. Half way along that endless valley, its broad river busy with Roman cargo barges, I was leading up to telling him that

I was an initiate of the Eleusinian mysteries when suddenly he rounded on me, saying the reason he slept on the hard ground in a tent each night was only partly because it was good for his back: in truth he wanted respite from me. 'When I sent you to Rome,' he snarled, 'I expected you to come back educated. What I wanted in my youngest son was a wise law-giver and a friend of Rome; what I've been given is a bigot. Who was it who taught you to despise your own father?'

The weather began to improve and by the time we reached Valencia on the eleventh day, spirits were rising. Gaul had been Roman since the time of Caesar, that is, nearly one hundred years. You'd think, to judge by the basilicas and forums of the southern towns, that it had never been anything else. The marble temples seemed as rooted as oaks and the amphitheatres a natural part of the countryside. All along the river there were shrines, mostly dedicated to Bacchus. Verica wasn't interested in Roman gods or their places of worship and did not respond when I pointed out the beauties of a Corinthian column or a pediment in the Greek style. 'Gods don't live in palaces,' he said, as we left one town for open countryside, 'they live in the woods. But where are the woods here? All cut down.'

I doubted whether there had ever been woods in this particular steep-sided valley of the Rhône. Perhaps the hillsides once had trees, but the Romans had cleared everything away for the planting of vineyards. In rows as straight as an army on the mustering ground, the vines in their winter twigginess covered the slopes, rows straight up and down and straight along: grids of grapes. Seneca would have loved to have seen this, keen as he was on viticulture. He would have considered this valley perfect and gone on at length about the need for the presence of mountains and water and the flow of cool air to make the best wine. I thought of him getting as far uphill as his lungs would allow on Corsica to investigate the local vineyards. I missed him acutely.

Verica's head was hunkered down between his shoulders. I began to ride apart. After sharing my horse with Mandred for several days, I'd secured him a place in the baggage train, riding in Verica's own cart, which left me free to ride where I liked in the column. The centurion, Largennius, seemed willing to pass the time in conversation, and I indulged my Roman while I still could, telling him about Seneca. He himself was a devotee of Serapis but he was interested in Stoicism, though he considered it godless. 'These people,' he said, flinging his arm out to indicate the fields that, at the end of January, were empty except for crows, 'what religion do they have?'

'The ancient one, presumably,' I said.

'We took over their gods, gave them ours, but they show scant regard, oily little barbarians.'

'I, too, am a barbarian,' I reminded him.

'Yes, but a Briton, not a Gaul. Hairy, not oily.' He smiled jovially, as if he'd paid me a compliment. I passed a good amount of time telling him the history of the Gauls in Britain, of which he was obviously ignorant. 'Some tribes migrated to escape the genocide but my tribe, the Atrebates, moved later, transplanted by Caesar.'

'How come? Why were your lot favoured by Caesar?'

'My ancestor, Commius, was loyal to Rome.'

'If he was your ancestor...'

'My grandfather.'

Largennius grunted at the improbability of it. 'If that's true, then it's even more necessary to keep quiet about it, at least while you're in Gaul.' Largennius thought Britain must surely surrender of her own accord to the expanding Empire. 'I would, if I saw what was coming, and surely they can see it? Besides, who would want to live in pig sties when you can have proper houses? I can't understand what precious thing it is they're protecting. My family is Spanish and we've done nothing but thrive since Rome conquered us. If we'd won, I'd be ploughing fields or milking cows. Look at me now, commanding this great body of men.'

Dropping back down the line, I fell in with British company. Verica's bard, Fergos, was travelling in the rear, having his eye on one of the women in the baggage train. He crooned to her in Gaulish but she was batting him off like a fly, so he brought his horse into step with mine.

'Have you not a wife at home?' I asked him.

'Aye, and precious little chance of seeing her again. Or so I thought. Now here we are, going home with an army!'

'Well, just a cohort.'

'But we're picking up the rest of the legion, aren't we, at Durocorteron? And the army at Gesoriacum? Like a snowball gathering snow. Who'd have thought it? When we left, all was lost.'

'What was it like? What really happened? Why did Verica flee to Gaul?'

'After Calleva fell, we retreated to Noviomagos and lived there for about a year. Verica put all resources into digging dykes and ditches around the settlement, but then it was not raiders we had to worry about but the poor harvest. We were seriously weakened by it. Caratacos cut us off from Ford of the Alders, raided our grain stores and took the horse herd. We had to parlay — no choice. If you can call it parlaying. Caratacos rode in, dismounted, dragged Verica from his house by the hair, down to the harbour, and put him on a boat going to Gaul. Anyone prepared to go with him had no time to think about it. The companions he has with him now, them and me — we all jumped on board without a second thought. The rest stayed to face slavery or death. The ordinary people, the land-tillers, they stayed of course, tied as ever to the soil. It was just the warriors who had to choose, and most of them jumped on board. The only things we had were our horses and our weapons. Verica had a couple of treasure chests full of coin he always kept ready for flight. Canny of him... Otherwise, we left everything behind, farms, cattle, wives and children, everything. One son, two daughters, me.' He started to hum a melancholic air.

'What about Katuaros?'

'He was at Ford of the Alders, having become chief of his tribe on the death of his father. Verica sent a message asking him to protect Noviomagos if he could. And he could, so we've heard.' The raid by Caratacos had not been backed up by forces of any great number. It had been just a raid. It was food they wanted, not land. 'He strengthened the defences of Ford of the Alders then went south to look after Noviomagos.'

'And he's withstood Caratacos ever since?'

'Seems so.'

'Verica thinks he should be king.'

'There's only one king-in-waiting, and that is you.'

Following the early death of my half-brothers, it was true, I was the only male left in the bloodline of Kommios, but in Britain it was rare for kingship to pass gently from father to son. Usually it passed via murder, battle or, in better times, through election by the druids. Some quiet deathbed ritual involving the passing over of a torc — well, I'd never heard of such a thing.

Fergos continued his tale, telling how Verica had gone from tribe to tribe across northern Gaul, renewing old kinships and looking for new lands for the Atrebates to settle. 'It seemed the only way, to migrate back to Gaul. Verica thought the Princeps would not help us, that our cause was too petty, but then we heard that Caligula was helping Adminios. Not that it came to anything.' Fergos had a way of laughing that made his nostrils flare with disdain. 'I'll make a song about that sometime, how the Roman army was defeated by fear of sea-monsters and the ghosts of Dis.'

'And my mother,' I asked him. 'Is she at Noviomagos?'

'Not anymore.' Fergos got down from his horse to walk. 'Feet or bum, bum or feet — what a choice. Will this march never end? Gods give me a chariot. We could have been home by yesterday on chariots.'

'Where then?'

'Gone home,' he said and, whistling to the woman of his fancy, gave her a long, slow wink. 'Want a song, my lovely?' She kept her head down and trudged on.

14

BARDS AT NIGHT

It was Parentalia when we arrived at Lugdunum, at least officially. For the Gauls, however, it was the eve of Imbolc, the first day of spring, the festival of returning light. As we entered through the great marble gateway of the city built by Romans, lamps were being lit; lamps on windowsills, in niches, on altars, in shrines, hanging in the windows of every house and tavern in that great city which, founded as a colony for veteran soldiers, had grown into the administrative centre for all Gaul. We were escorted to a palace that was being made ready for the arrival of Claudius when he rode north to Britain later in the year, but a suite of rooms had been made available for this British king. This British king who then offended hospitality by having his tent raised beside the fountain in the formal garden.

The imperial legate, governor of all Gaul, had a small, private bath house but I was told that the public baths were better. Verica threw me an angry glance as I went off with a slave, saying that he preferred to bathe in living, breathing, sacred water. Water you can drink. The large and sumptuous bath house was busy and queues formed for each of the three halls. Voices, both Gaulish and Roman, echoed off the vaulting, some banter, some jokes, some grievances.

The war for Gaul had been a vicious affair; in battle after battle the Gauls had been defeated until one man put up a mighty resistance by uniting the tribes. Now here they were, progeny of those Gauls, naked in steamy water and discussing building projects and investments. Presumably they were the grandsons of those who had collaborated with the Romans, for those who had resisted would have been slaughtered or led off in chains. The lesson seemed clear to me: do not resist. If a mighty river surges towards you, go with the flood or else be smashed.

As I laid on a bench for the oiling, I looked at the scarred tattoo on my forearm. I had made myself bleed trying to scratch it off but nothing would remove from my skin those indigo stains of the eight-spoked wheel I'd received on the eve of my departure for Rome. Innogen had drawn the design herself with the juice of oak gall for the priest to make indelible with his pin pricks. *Let this be your guide. You will understand one day.* In Rome it just seemed barbaric magic and whenever I could I kept it covered. But at Eleusis it had meant something. I dozed under the massage; on the point of falling asleep, it seemed I knew the answers to the most profound questions but when I snapped awake, this vaporous truth was lost to me.

The imperial legate being away, seeing to troubles in Gallia Aquitania (pockets of resistance remained, even a hundred years after the war), we were looked after by the quaestor. A native Gaul, he wanted to discuss with anyone who would listen the desire for Gauls to govern themselves. He quizzed me on the sympathies of Claudius. 'He was, after all, born in this city.'

'Yes, but to Romans of the house of Augustus.'

'Even so...'

The quaestor's Roman name was Junius Maximus and he made much of Verica as the son of Kommios, the willing associate of Caesar, the Gaulish collaborator. But Verica changed the subject, complimenting Maximus on the beauty of his wife and children.

'And your wife?' the quaestor asked Verica. 'Did she remain behind in Britain?'

'She died about three years ago.'

A good Stoic never betrays his feelings and while the men fell to talking about the wisdom of remarriage, how a man needs the kind of company in his old age that a concubine cannot give, I struggled to keep my food down. What had happened to her? Why had I not been told? I half choked on the desire to jump up and batter out the brains of my father but good Stoics do not do that kind of thing. I chewed, I swallowed, I took another mouthful, but I never looked up. I knew he was watching me.

And she seemed to be watching me, too, with her eyes the colour of bluebells, her wheaten hair done into plaits and coiled round her strong, broad head. 'Why didn't you tell me?' I asked her inwardly. 'Surely you knew,' she replied. 'That time when I began to appear in your visions. You cannot see the faces of the living in the sacred pools.'

'Yes, it's never too late to marry again,' Verica was saying. 'My father took a girl of twenty when he was seventy-nine. I was their child.'

The quaestor, who was by now in his cups, leant forwards and tapped the back of Verica's hand. 'Ah, yes, Kommios,' he said. 'Turn and turn again Kommios. Janus of the northern Gauls.'

Verica side-stepped this remark like a donkey who'd seen a snake. Claiming weariness, he rose and went early to his tent.

'I hope I haven't offended him,' said Maximus. 'He doesn't seem to want to talk about Kommios. But that's not so surprising, is it? Who could have an ancestor like that and hold his head up?'

'What do you mean?' I asked, genuinely baffled.

'Kommios switched sides, did he not?'

That was such common knowledge that it seemed to go without saying. Bidding the quaestor a good night, I followed Verica out. My mind on Innogen, not Kommios, I went walking in the dark, so hard and fast that Mandred panted with the effort to keep up. As the night drew on the barbarian soul of this Roman city was revealed in a million tiny lights, guttering in the draughts, making the shadows lurch drunkenly. At midnight we went to the bridge that crossed the Rhône and Saône at their confluence.

The people came down in snaking processions from all quarters each bearing an earthen lamp with a flame dancing on its snout, fed by a wick floating in oil. Children at jetties and landing places along the banks gave out small dishes decorated with evergreens and early blossom woven into wreaths into which the people could place their lamps as offerings to the goddess of each river and then, leaning out over the dark water, send the lights floating on the current until both rivers were flickering gold.

Gathered round a fire on the bank, local bards sang songs in Roman about Vercingetorix and the siege of Alesia, how the rebel leader of the Gauls had been defeated by the great Julius Caesar. These bards, fully Romanized, sang of the battle from the point of view of the victor, songs in strict metre, lacking passion. When they came to the part where Vercingetorix was defeated and dragged off to Rome a slave, the bards could have been singing about the procession of the months or a recipe for honey cakes. Fergos sat in a dark scowl holding his harp as a warrior holds his shield, ready for action.

One by one the governor's staff and any Roman officers present rose to leave until, close to dawn, only the Gauls remained. It was cold but they wrapped themselves in their mantles and kept close to the fire where the flames illuminated their solemn faces. Then the real songs began, songs of resistance, authentic songs of Vercingetorix. Blood-stirring tales sung to plucked lyres with refrains shouted by all present, raucous and proud. The sound of resistance is half a heartbeat faster than normal and makes you breathless. Of course I responded to its wild rhythms, my body quickening to the excitement of rebellion; I imagined myself standing up against the oppressor and risking my life for freedom.

I hoped no one in the vicinity knew me as the grandson of Kommios. But as the story of the siege unfolded with the night I heard what I'd never been told as a child. Kommios had turned. And turned again.

'I confess, Fergos,' I said, 'brought up in the women's house, I did not hear our Song of Origins often enough.'

'Or listen with due attention,' my father's bard said pointedly.

'Admitted.' It had been a rare thing for me to share the fire in my father's house with him and my half-brothers. My mother had lived apart in a house of her own. While the men were drinking malted ale or mead, telling tales of heroes and boasting of their own exploits, Innogen and her women were about other business, chanting softly some ancient spell or rite, mixing brews in the cauldron that could heal wounds, singing together some hymn invoking spirits. I grew up in a whispering world scented with herbs and rustling with presences, more or less oblivious to the tales of our ancestors, at least on my father's side.

'But this version of the story is not in our Song of Origins,' Fergos said. 'Verica won't have it. Says it brings disgrace on the family.'

So it was from these Gaulish bards that first heard the story of Vercingetorix calling for help, and Kommios coming to his aid.

'But how did Vercingetorix do that?' I whispered to Fergos. 'Call for help? He was besieged in Alesia.'

Our bard looked surprised at my ignorance. 'He just called. From the walls. *Help!*'

And the call went out across the land, passing from hill top to hill top, across all Gaul to jump Ocean to Britain. *Help!* When all the Gauls rose up as if one body and moved towards Alesia, they were led by a British chief. Called Kommios.

'But he was a friend of Caesar!' I said low. 'Caesar had given him those lands in Britain!'

Fergos raised his eyebrows but said nothing. It was coming to his turn to sing, and what I heard as the sky began to lighten was a song that had never been sung in the land of the Atrebates. With a strike across the strings of his harp and his head back as if he would sing to the moon in its last quarter, he began his tale of Kommios who, after he had helped Caesar, was accused of conspiring with the Gauls. Kommios was lured by the Romans into a sham meeting with the intent to dispatch him but he escaped and vowed never to associate with Romans again.

'*Never with Romans again,*' crooned Fergos and the gathered bards echoed the refrain, stomping on the ground. The following verses told of Kommios responding to Vercingetorix's call for help and leading the assault on the Romans besieging Alesia. He did not win, of course, but escaped again, this time into Germania where he led the revolt of the Bellovaci. Eventually he met the Romans in open battle and was wounded in the thigh but escaped yet again. Perhaps he was beginning to tire, for he sued for peace and promised Mark Antony that he would go where he was told to go, so long as he never had to meet a Roman again.

'*Never meet a Roman again,*' sang Fergos, and the gathered bards slapped their knees. '*Never again!*'

'What happened to Kommios?' I asked when Fergos had finished.

'He moved permanently to Britain, established his capital at Calleva and had three sons, destined ever to be at war with each other.'

'Can history repeat itself?' I asked. 'Kommios was sent to Britain by Caesar to persuade the tribes not to resist. Exactly the same mission as I've been given.'

Fergos smiled. 'There is little similarity between you and your grandfather. You are not king, nor are you a warrior. How, then, can history be repeating itself?'

'Why does Verica not allow these songs? You'd think he'd be proud of his father.'

Fergos shrugged. 'He prefers the version of the man who was constantly loyal to Rome.'

And I? For that night at the confluence of two rivers, I was increasingly proud of my rebel grandfather.

After Lugdunum, the road goes north-west, following the valley of the Saône. For days Verica and I barely spoke, he sinking ever deeper into his own world. The going was easier now, the only difficulties being small rivers we had to ford, many of which were in flood. The further north we went, the more temples of gods gave way to shrines where local deities such as Grannos are worshipped. *Granno my friend; Granno my father; Granno my mother.* A hundred years after being annexed by Rome, the Gaulish soul lives on.

As we neared Augustodunum, a lonely rider, long-haired, dour, came out of one hinterland to cross the road of civilization and enter another, trotting across in front of the marching column. There were several blackened heads dangling from the neck of his long-tailed and rangy horse, jiggling and clicking together as he rode.

'Do we still do that?' I asked Verica.

'Do what?'

'Take the heads of enemies?'

Verica humphed and shifted on his horse. I was beginning to worry about Amabel. Her wide-set eyes were losing their light and her ears, usually erect and alert, had become limp. At the end of that month of long marches, Verica began to complain of backache, forever shifting on the saddle, straightening and slumping. He wanted to get off and walk, but he had become so slow now that he would have gone at the pace of the baggage train, which was inappropriate for a king; Largennius the centurion offered him a seat in a four-wheeled coach carrying women at the rear, which set Verica off like a bear trap. He immediately remounted, but I told Verica that, for Amabel's sake, he should take the *raeda*. He dismounted once more and began to walk, leading his mare by the rein, shaking off all offers of help, growling that what he needed was a chariot. No one was going to carry him along in a box with curtains, not if he could help it. 'I haven't exactly lost the use of my legs.'

After parting from the river, the road made its inexorable way through forest and hills, a land of gentle streams and waterfalls where there were shrines at every few paces, whether to the god of a river or to the niskas, the spirits of well, spring and cataract. Verica stopped at each one to leave an offering in the water. Now suffering from blisters, he got back on Amabel, but she had not rested enough. A physician at a small fort gave him a tincture of willow bark that seemed to help him sleep overnight but, as soon as the journey resumed, the jolting increased the suffering of the king while his horse limped along with her head low.

By the time we reached Augustobona both rider and horse were done. I caught Verica at one point remonstrating with the man in charge of the baggage train, who was refusing to put the little horse on a cart, and it was clear then, as the quartermaster bore down on the king, where authority truly lies in this Roman world. There was a grove not far outside the city. In the evening Verica went there with Amabel, two broken creatures going to meet the goddess Epona. When the king returned, he was alone. Fergos told me later that Verica had had his men dig a grave and that Amabel, after her sacrifice, was buried with full rites.

The road went on across hills until we looked down on Durocoteron, the round fortress that was once the omphalos of the Remi people. All around it like a skirt were the camps of the Second Augusta, waiting for us. For nearly a week I had been lulled back into barbarian dreams. The green of the hills and the trees had called the boy out of me. But there it was waiting, the Second Legion in all its bright splendour. Rome.

Legate Vespasian stood none of Verica's nonsense and for the rest of the journey to Gesoriacum my father had no choice but to travel in the *raeda*. As he could have it to himself my father agreed. Drawing the silken curtains closed he was borne along the Via Agrippa, making his presence known by frequent grunts and strange hiccupping noises. I looked in and found him kneeling on the floor, his face buried in a cushion on the seat and weeping. He claimed it was the pain. I suspected it was the horse.

15

VERICA'S TREASURE

The road to Gesoriacum skirted the territory of the Atrebates, our ancestral home. As we sat together one evening in his pungent tent, Verica put the small oaken chest between us. 'It's time you knew what I keep in here,' he said. 'The land of our fathers is just a few miles south, at a place called Arras.' He undid the chain and lifted the lid. Inside were his silver armbands, a ceremonial torc with ball finials made of heavy gold, a much-depleted store of votive images to leave at shrines and a collection of chariot fittings, terrets and bridle rings. These he looked at morosely as all that was left of his life as a king. Opening a small leather pouch, he emptied it into my hands.

'Here you are. You've wanted them long enough. You can have them now.' Twelve tiny silver coins: his collection of first strikes. To strike a coin in Britain means you are a king with Rome on your side. In this collection there were coins of Kommios and his three sons: a stater of Tincomaros, one of Eppillos stamped 'Rex', and several that were Verica's own. There were images of a vine leaf and the horse god Corotiacos, and one which had a torc on one side and the image of the Emperor Tiberius on the other. I had loved these coins when I was a child and felt the same passion now as I handled them, not for the kings or torcs but that leaping horse that is the emblem of our peoples.

As a child I used to go at coins like a jackdaw, the common coins used for trade, picking them up when father was out and flying off with them to my own little nest, a den of fern and twigs I'd made in the woods. Whenever it was noticed that there was a deficiency in the treasury, I was made to reveal my horde and take a beating like a man. Now, having become that man, I picked up one of his silver coins and examined its design like a tax collector. On one side a portrait of the god Belenos-Apollo apparently made out of balls of mud and, on the other, the triple-tailed horse. It was the horses I'd collected, not the metal.

'Beautiful,' I said, handing them back to him. 'But just money.'

'Money? These are not money! The traders, yes, they use coin for money on the basis of credit and debit.'

I had heard much about credit and debit but had never understood it; all I knew was that it is best to avoid money-lenders or coin-changers: you always come out worse for the deal and my time at the collecting tables in Corinth had proved it. Verica chose a coin and held it out to me. I looked at him questioningly.

'Take it. Take it!'

I took it.

'Ha!' he said. 'Now you owe me.'

'What do I owe you? This stater? Here, have it back.'

'No! You owe me two staters!' he said. 'The one I have given you, and the cost of the loan.' He sat back, satisfied that, to judge by my expression — a mixture of bewilderment and sudden understanding — that he had taught me a valuable lesson.

'According to Seneca,' I said, 'money should be nothing more than a symbol of trust.'

'How so?'

'I am a farmer who wants wine but you, the wine seller, doesn't want my cow, so I sell it to someone for ten staters which I then give to you for an amphora of your best. That value does not exist in the metal: it represents the value of cow and wine. Trade. The coins act as a symbol of trust. I give you these for your wine; you use them to get whatever it is you need and want. Money is trust between men.'

Verica hawked and spat. 'That's the Roman way. It's different amongst our peoples. Now this has value,' he said. Reaching into his wooden chest he brought out the ceremonial torc of twisted gold wire, which I presumed was what he was referring to.

'Melted down, it could buy a lot,' I agreed.

My father stared at me dumbfounded. 'Melted down? This was your grandfather's! It is the sign of a king and beyond value!' He put it to one side and brought out the heavy iron bar he'd been looking for and let it fall on to the rushes. It sent up a cloud of grass dust that danced in the firelight. 'Now iron has value, and can be melted down.'

I could see what he meant. Iron is the product of mining and smelting. It is hard work. It can be turned into swords and tools. Yes, iron has true value.

'The gold is beyond value, these little silver coins have pretend value. The only metal worth hoarding is iron.'

'So why did you beat me when I stole the coins?'

'Because they were mine! Coins are for giving away. I give them to fellow kings; I give them to my warriors who do not want to be encumbered by booty or a herd of cattle. What these are is what they represent. Only a king may strike coins and to have a mint means you have territory. These coins say that I, Verica, am king of the Atrebates.' He grew reflective. 'Worthless now, apart from their silver content, my mint no doubt in the possession of Caratacos who is busy stamping his own image on metal.'

'He'd have to be king to do that.'

'True.' He put them back in their leather pouch and drew the string tight. 'We do not need coin. It is mere show. Our economy is based on generosity, not debt. When I travelled south to Rome, I stayed freely in the houses of chiefs and kings, was fed and clothed by them, as I have always fed and clothed any guest of mine.'

Wrapping up the iron and stowing it away, he carefully lifted out from the bottom of the chest two objects of similar size and shape, swaddled in fine linens. These he unwrapped with reverence, but I knew at once what they were. Two heads. One had been embalmed, its eyelids and lips stitched up. It was old and leathery but you still got an image of the man it had been, brave and firm of purpose. Swan feathers had been woven through his still-black hair. The other had not been embalmed, just left, and all there was of it now was a grey skull; even though bone, you could see the man had died in distress. The lower jaw was missing; skin still adhering to the face hung in shreds of bristly leather and somehow, just looking at the skull, you could see the mortal face creased up in its agony. It bore no decoration other than a label of engraved lead that said it was a gift from Emperor Tiberius to Verica, King of the Atrebates, loyal friend to Rome, 'the head of the rebel Vercingetorix'.

I trembled when I realised who it was I was staring at. It didn't take any effort to guess the identity of the other. 'Kommios?'

Verica nodded. 'The head of your grandfather, passed to me by my eldest brother, and in time I shall pass it to you for veneration in the family house.'

It was then I realised that my separation from my family, which had been intended to be temporary, had become absolute. I could not envision a time when I would decorate my house with the heads of my ancestors, or the skulls of my enemies, ropes of them pinned upon my door as trophies of battle. In my ten years away, I had become a Roman, and it was as indelible on my soul as my tattoos were on my body.

Something was glinting within the box, half-buried by the votive images. I reached in and, taking hold of its long handle, removed a bronze mirror the size of my face. I was about to

look in it when Verica snatched it away, saying, 'Don't!'
I glanced at him askance. 'You'll see her,' he said, his eyes
averted.

'I want to see her.'

My father groaned and his head moved from side to side.
'What do you know?' he asked, looking up briefly, and his eyes
were distant, those of a stranger.

'About what?'

'What did she tell you? About our marriage? Come on! What
did she tell you? Because I am certain she made no pretence of
it being a love match or even something politically expedient.
What did she tell you?'

'Nothing!'

'Liar! She would have wasted no opportunity to turn you
against me.'

I could remember nothing, except that I grew up in a house
where my father was not welcome, the house, the inviolate
house of my mother, where no man was welcome apart from
her son (which is not to imply that she did not welcome other
men, but it was always out in the open, in the grove or under
the night sky). 'She told me nothing, but I heard the story from
others, how you snatched her during a raid on her people.'

'Lies, lies, lies.'

'So, tell me the truth!' I demanded.

Verica said he had gone to the Ford of Two Rivers and the
marshy pastureland between the Thames and the Charwelle,
known to the ancients as the Sanctuary of the Wheel. 'A very
sacred place, but I was just after horses. Do you remember
Tiberius?'

'Of course.'

The thought of his horse plunged Verica into painful
reminiscence. 'That was the year I met her, the same year that
I received the gifts from a grateful emperor, the gifts of a horse
and the head of my father.'

'Why was the Emperor Tiberius grateful?'

'For my loyalty of course,' said Verica quickly. 'It was the finest gift, that tall horse so dark he was nearly black, that tall, mighty horse who I named Tiberius...' He looked stricken. 'I only had to sit on him to command all men. I must have looked like a god. But he was not meant for riding. He had more important business. He was going to be the bloodline of a new herd, a herd the like of which had never been seen in Britain. Tiberius was going to be my fortune. As he was, when you think about it.' Verica started to put the coins back in the purse. 'At the Sanctuary of the Wheel, our native horses run wild. They are fine beasts, sturdy, reliable, but small. Perfect for pulling chariots. If I could get some brood mares, put them into a paddock for Tiberius to pleasure, it could be that I'd get the best of both in the offspring, something sturdy, reliable and tall. And it worked. The firstborn was Amabel. Came out odd colours and still short but the right shape. Like you, a cross-breed born odd.'

'How am I a cross-breed?' I asked, astonished.

'Half Atrebates, half Dobunni,' he said without blinking, but that is not what he meant. He meant half-Romey, half-druid.

'Do you remember my herd, boy? It was not the largest herd, but it was the finest, thanks to Tiberius.' He stared into space as if he could see it again. I remembered it, too, the Callevan horse fields.

'What happened to Tiberius?'

'Caratacos took him. It's why he came to Calleva, to get my stallion.'

Stoicism frees you from your emotions, keeps the soul free of their taint. Now, suddenly, in the back of my throat I could taste anger, resentment, pure hatred for Caratacos, all burning like bile.

'And do you know the worst thing?' Verica said, poking me in the arm. 'He killed him. He didn't want the Roman line. He said he was liberating British mares from Roman stallions.

That witch sister of his, Theana, she sacrificed Tiberius. A horse sacrifice lasting three weeks.'

Now I was finding it hard to breathe because Tiberius, who, like Scipio, was a dark chestnut from the Maremma with big, broad feet, was the most beautiful horse I had ever seen. I had grown up with him. He'd arrived the year before I was born and my father was right, the king did look like a god when he sat on the Roman stallion. As I had grown up with the horse, so I had grown up with the idea that Rome was a centre of beneficence, from whence came great gifts.

I became restless, wanting to go to the stables and check on the welfare of Scipio. I sent Mandred, telling him to give my stallion some hay.

'The Sanctuary of the Wheel,' Verica said, going back to his story. 'It was our favourite place to get brood mares; it was our favourite sport to lasso a young horse, mount it and ride it. That was for the young ones, remember, boy? Young and light. It was there, and on that day, that I caught Amabel's mother. My purple and silver darling.' He was falling into melancholia. 'That's who Amabel was, fruit of the union between Tiberius and a mare I called Eponina.'

'I noticed in our planning sessions that you took care to convince Claudius and the generals that there is nothing of interest in that area.'

'It's a no man's land, sacred territory where three tribes meet. It's the least I can do to atone for the crimes I committed there. I was breaking a sacred law in capturing horses but everyone did it! If we didn't do it, the place would have been overrun with horses. Horses and druids. There was a college of healing there, beside the great Wheel, and in pursuit of horses we got too close to it. And then I saw her, this tall woman striding out from the temple, raising her arms and shouting curses at me, terrible curses, trying to drive me and my men away. All on her own. My men were laughing, goading me, telling me to show her who was king, and so I rode at her, expecting her to run, but she stood her ground. Ah! Such beauty! It was like your first deer. Just as you raise your spear, you see the beauty in its eye, the sleekness in its coat, the glowing life of it. So it was with Innogen. Even as I rode at her, intending to knock her off her feet, throw her in the dirt and remind her who was king, I saw her beauty as something divine. I pulled the rein, diverted course and glanced past her. Then I turned and went back. I said, will you come with me, woman? I see you keep cowards for company — look at them skulking in your deep-thatches. But you, you have spirit. Come with me and be my queen. In reply, she spat at me, straight, not into her hands, straight at me. I beckoned to my horse-catchers and they came, threw a halter round her neck and bound her hands even as she struggled like a wildcat. I tried to lead her away but she would not walk. My men called on me to drag her until she surrendered her pride.' He fell into a brooding quiet.

'Did you do it?'

'She was never going to surrender, so I got down, threw her to ground and possessed her, there and then, in the Sanctuary of the Wheel. I shoved her against one of the stones in the shadow of the Pole of the Nation, the great pole that links Earth and Sky, and took her from behind like a stallion a mare.'

I almost choked at his sacrilege.

'I can see what you're thinking, that my misfortunes began in that moment, and you are right, they did. I brought her home with the rest of the brood mares but by the time I got to Calleva, I was full of fear and regret. I tried to make amends. I wanted to marry her properly but she had to be forced into it as into everything else, shouting that she was an old Briton, truly royal, and me just an upstart, land-grabbing Gaul. I dragged her to the grove but the priest refused to do the ceremony, saying I had desecrated the Wheel and a daughter of Dobunni kings.'

'I heard you killed the priest.'

144

'So what if I did? A king cannot brook disobedience. You have to keep order. We were married by my own authority. I brought her mother to live with us, that is, to live with her, because from the beginning she insisted on living apart in her own house, the women's house, which she filled with Dobunni witches. Sometimes I woke in the morning and found I could not move, or that there was no milk because the cows had run dry and no eggs because the geese were not laying. All the work of her women. I should have burnt the lot of them.'

I was puzzled for none of this matched my memories. I saw my grandmother hogging the fire to soothe her aching bones, sitting on a log stool, her legs wide apart, skirts drawn up, inner thighs enflamed, as she told me stories of dragons and magic cauldrons. I saw my mother standing before the loom, sending the shuttle through the opened warp threads as she sang a weaving song, each song having within it a mnemonic for the pattern, the heddle rods clicking as she lifted them up or down, changing the warp threads each time. She said if you ever stopped to think about what you were doing, you'd lose the pattern and the threads would tangle. You sing, she said, to the Shee, and they do the weaving for you. My favourite pattern of a band and three lines was the song of the Mother and Three Daughters. It was a house of magic, for sure, but happy magic, not the malefic practices Verica was describing.

'How did she die?' I asked.

'A scratch on the elbow. Hard to believe, eh? Just a little scratch she didn't notice until wound fever set in and the poison was too advanced for her medicine magic to work. She could not heal herself. She was back in Kyronion by then. After you went to Rome, she returned to her own people. King Esius sent me word to say that she had died of a fever and that I would not be welcome at the funeral rite. And that was that.' He shifted on his seat and straightened his back. 'Two mares I captured. I loved them both. And their foals.' He glanced up at me and had that look of a wand stripped of its bark,

145

naked, vulnerable and oddly pale. 'I suppose I never made that plain.'

'No,' I said, 'no, you did not.'

'You must realise that every time I looked on you I was reminded of the worst of myself.' Verica picked up the heads to put them away. 'Nobody loves you,' he said to Kommios and the swan feathers trembled in his breath. 'Nobody understands.'

'Understands what?' I asked.

Verica held the heads aloft, one in each hand, both facing me. He raised up that of rotted, disintegrating Vercingetorix. 'Here, the hero.' Then that of Kommios. 'Here, the collaborator. Yes, yes, that's what they say of him, that he turned, changed sides. But he never did, not my father. Look into his honoured face. This is the face of loyalty. Remember it, my son, remember it.'

16

MUTINY AT GESORIACUM

The last march was over twenty miles and it was night before we reached Gesoriacum. The next morning I went up to the windswept hill above the harbour to look out on the short stretch of water which, before Caesar, was known as Ocean at the Edge of the World and which, in the minds of most Romans, still was. Below was the naval base and shipyard on the estuary of the Liane and, behind, the immense camp of a gathering army. Although the commander-in-chief and three legions had yet to arrive, the Fourteenth Gemina was busy extending the perimeter to include a barracks for eighty thousand, working in long lines to dig ditches and build more walls. From this standpoint I had a vision of all that planning we had done in Rome coming to fruition and thought it beautiful, but it was a vision that was to evaporate more quickly than morning mist.

Back down in the harbour, I stopped at a shrine to Neptune on the waterfront to make a libation, pouring a cup of wine into the pool of the God of the Waters. The winter was proving unusually long here in the north and they said it was worse in Britain, that grain pits and hay barns were empty. This was good news for merchants, who calculated a rise in prices for the grain they carried. The rich would not go hungry.

I walked along the straight lines of tents, past a parade ground where soldiers of Gemina were practising formations, past horse lines where cavalrymen were feeding and grooming their animals. Smoke rose from various fires into still air, one of those quiet sun-on-frost days making brilliant all the colours of armour, leather and cloth. In the taverns and over gaming boards, hardened veterans told young recruits about vicious sea monsters, the bad omens in the skies and the wild men waiting for them on the cliffs of Britain.

'They are painted blue and their hair stands up on end.'

'Their screaming curdles your blood.'

Other rumours suddenly began to circulate, no one knowing their source, but soon the soldiers were telling each other, 'The curses of the druids can travel for miles and kill a man in his tracks.' 'There are witches among them, wild women, who could turn us into frogs.' 'They pick you off, the way the lions pick off deer, taking the weakest. The last in line of any column will die without making a sound.'

The rumours spread through the ranks like poison and you could see their progress by the droop in confidence. Once when we were boys of about seven, my foster brother and I had been wriggling over the downs on our stomachs to spy on a party of Dobunni hunting boar in the valley with a pack of excited dogs. Katuaros claimed to have the power of enchantment over dogs. I didn't believe him but when one of the hounds scented us and we were in immediate danger of being discovered, Katuaros somehow drew the dog to him. It came sniffing through the long grass, tail beating the air, and did not bark when it found us but regarded Katuaros with large, inquisitive eyes. Tapping it three times on the snout, Katuaros removed its sense of smell. 'It's not cruel,' he said. 'It only lasts three days.' One by one the dogs came to us through the dry grass; each one was tapped by Katuaros and he knew which ones he'd done because their tails went down. Soon the hunters were whistling in vain for their hounds, with increasing urgency. We could hear their consternation. 'In three days the pack will find its masters again,' said Katuaros, 'but they will have spent three days happy and free.' He began wriggling back the way we came and I followed, full of wonder. I was never sure whether he really did have power or if it was just the paralysing effect of his self-confidence.

As I walked the camps, I could see where the rumours had been, could see soldiers whose martial tails had stopped wagging, who had lost the scent of glory. Verica said it was the work of druids. 'The Romans say the druids have been exterminated in Gaul,' I said. Verica snorted. 'So they like to think. Anyway, who is to say this is brewing mutiny is not the work of druids from Britain? No one ever explained why Caligula's expedition had failed, but I'll wager the same thing happened to them. Poisoned whispers. Druid work.'

When the Twentieth Valeria arrived from Germania, their legate almost immediately lost control, his troops infected by fear. Aulus Plautius arrived just as the army was collapsing into anarchy. Lines became mobs. Ordinary soldiers were shouting at their centurions, the centurions at the tribunes. Aulus Plautius exhorted the troops, bellowing from the rostrum on the parade ground, only to be drowned out by jeering. The more he struggled, the worse it got for him. Shields became drums, short swords, hammers, and the clamour was thunderous.

Vespasian was frustrated. He knew how to get men to obey and was not shy of using the scourge if necessary, but he was too new to the role to better the commander and merely did what he could to keep his own legion in order. Vespasian did, however, prevail on Plautius to send to Rome for help.

'That will delay us a month at least!' Plautius protested.

'This is too serious to let pride get in the way,' Vespasian risked saying. Plautius took it well and agreed.

Vespasian had a word with us in private, strongly advising us to sail. 'This is becoming so inflamed, your life could be in danger.' But sailing before the equinox was precarious and we had to wait for a favourable wind. It was beginning to look like a choice between death on land or death at sea. While we waited for a captain ready to take the risk in sailing, we stood on the headland below the lighthouse to watch the newly-built fleet arrive, the biremes with their long-beaked prows rowing towards us over the cold seas, sails reefed, like leggy insects with folded wings walking on the water. In rhythmic harmony of rowing, they nosed their way into the estuary of the Liane to disembark at the harbour — there to find themselves in the middle of a mutiny that had gone quiet, that was in the seething stage after the initial clamour, when secret meetings were being held beyond the camp, when the mutineers, like the generals, were just waiting. The marines joined the soldiers at the gaming boards. And listened to what they had to say.

Plautius called us to him. 'Tell me,' he said, 'have you identified any druids among the Gauls here in camp, spreading stories about sea monsters? The power of story! Our men are drilled for years into deadly fighting machines but still gibber at tales told at the hearth.' Verica said it was true, there were indeed druids in the camp, sowing the seeds of mutiny. I looked askance at him, for there was no proof of this, but my father was convinced and did not have to see something to know it was there.

'Vespasian thinks you are in danger here,' Plautius continued, 'and I am inclined to agree with him. You will sail on the next tide, favourable or not.'

If Plautius selected German auxiliaries to accompany us, it was because he thought they would be less alarming to the natives than short, dark, obviously Roman legionaries. He gave us cohors II Germanorum, killers in animal pelts who would, he said, blend in with the background so much better. A cohort of five centuries? I was surprised at the number for a mere escort. News from the harbour was that an easterly wind was expected. We would embark with the soldiers the following night and expect to put into harbour three or four days later.

I went to Vespasian's tent alone. 'Plautius has arranged for us to sail tomorrow.'

'Yes, good.'

'What if,' I said, 'while we are at sea, the army goes home? What if this expedition is no more successful than Caligula's?'

'We do not allow such ideas,' Vespasian said.

'What if,' I persisted, 'I find myself in Britain without you behind me?'

'In that case, make your peace with the gods and hope for a better life hereafter.' He smiled his thin-lipped, bright-eyed smile. 'Do not worry, Delphidius,' he said. 'I will not let you down.'

'But will you at least look after my horse? Can I leave Scipio with you?'

He rose from his seat and came round his desk to take me by the shoulders. 'No,' he said, eye to eye. 'I understand your fears. Scipio is head and shoulders above the rest and will be the desire of every passing horse thief. He will also mark you out. But what would Seneca say?'

'That I should never have accepted him in the first place.'

'Can you deny the gift of emperors? I think not. Besides, you wanted him. So now you have to take the consequences of your desire.'

'That is precisely what Seneca would say. What if I gave him to you as a gift?'

'Tempting, and laudable. But no.'

Verica was growing increasingly morose and blamed the cold for it. 'Ice moon,' he muttered bitterly. We had left Rome in the month of Janus. It was now the month of Mars. As we had progressed north, I had begun to hear the old familiar names for the months, for Gauls name the months not after gods but after the weather and life on the land. We had left Rome in the month of Anagantios (Stay-at-home moon) and were now in Ogronios (Ice moon). In the camp I heard both calendars in use. Beyond the Ocean, there would only be the one.

Verica now had pains running down his legs into his shins. His back had been broken, he said, by the journey. He could not sit, stand nor lie; his only relief was in constant movement and he shambled about groaning until he was so tired he collapsed into sleep. To distract him and keep him moving, we spent the night wandering through the swelling camps of the auxiliaries listening to foreign tongues: Pannonian, Dalmatian, Syrian, Thracian, Anatolian, Cretan, Numidian — men of the desert, men of the mountains, men of the forest. Each unit of the auxiliaries had its own preferred weapons, tribal emblems and costume. While the legionaries were armed with a short sword and shield, and each wore his plated armour and iron helmet, among the auxiliaries were lancers wielding javelins, horse archers with quivers on their backs, slingers from the Balearic Islands who, with their round pebbles, could kill without drawing blood; there were those who could swim in full armour; those who could do the Parthian shot, apparently retreating only to twist in their saddles and let fly lethal arrows at their pursuers. To wander through their barracks and listen to the babble of auxiliaries was to know the Roman Empire for what it is: disparate and often exotic peoples bound under a common law. But though the languages differed, the underlying sound was the same: disaffection, growling rebellion.

The following day was one of bright sunshine with pennants along the harbour fluttering in a good easterly. We met our cohort in the late afternoon, preparing to board a small fleet of corbitas making ready for a night sailing. We shared our ship with a unit of them. Their grim and unshaven faces were thrown into deep shadow by their helmets. These were prime fighting men, used in advance of the army to frighten the enemy, especially led by standard bearers wearing bear skins, the head of the beast covering their helmet, its bared teeth on their brow. The Germans settled where they could to spend the long voyage gambling with dice.

'Up anchor!' called the ship's master and our corbita caught the ebb tide in the estuary and floated out to open sea. Old, steady on the water, square-rigged with a swan-shaped stern, it was just large enough to take us and half our escort on the top deck. The sea was choppy and waves slapped the ship. At once all the stories I'd ever heard of violent Neptune, sea-monsters, sirens and whirlpools rose up; I even began to believe that wild natives would be waiting for us on the headlands and beaches of Britain. I wondered if I should go and try to calm the men but decided it would be better to try to calm the god and gave myself to prayers and invocations. When men are sick, they lean over the edge. When horses are sick, they vomit on the deck. Scipio was not sick. As if aware of his role as the horse of a Stoic, he endured the journey without murmur even when, half way across the strait, we were pitching violently through a storm of spray. Holding on to Scipio's bridle with one hand, and with the other anything fixed that would stop us sliding across the flooded deck, I was struck again by that alarming *what if?* that could puncture any man's courage. What if the Roman army went home? We would be alone and cut off in Britain. The brutal Germans, throwing up as violently as anyone else, were our only protection. I spoke to a centurion, asking him what their orders were should the mutiny prove successful.

'We are to return to Gesoriacum at once,' he said.

It was only once the storm had abated that I fell asleep, and that only for a short while, asleep on my feet, standing with my face buried in Scipio's wet mane, to dream of hairy Hyperboreans with blue faces waiting for us on the white headland.

17

ACROSS OCEAN TO DIS

My father and I stood looking down into the water while I poured an oblation of wine into Ocean. Verica approved of my devotion with a nod. 'Always honour water,' he said. He was weak now and vulnerable, no longer the tyrant father. He spoke as if to free his soul of burdens.

'I expelled the druids from our territories,' he said, returning to the subject like a dog to a flea bite.

'Why did you do that?'

'I told you, they're not to be trusted.'

I stared at him until he weakened, for a Briton is obliged to value the truth and, therefore, to speak it. We have trees dedicated to truth-speaking, altars, stone seats, rites and ceremonies. A truthful man, we say, is a healthy one. Verica grunted with annoyance. 'Very well. I threw them out because they excommunicated me when I snatched Innogen.'

'From a druid college.'

Verica shrugged as if he could not help that. 'I couldn't undo what I'd done. How could I? I suppose I should have accepted the judgement of the druids and made the reparations they demanded, which were harsh but not unjust. But your father is a proud man, Togidubnos, and kings must be above the laws of priests. So I banished them from my territories.' A sudden spasm in his thigh had him bending double and he rubbed hard at his leg until he could straighten up again. 'I sent them across the borders to other groves, but a druid curse knows no borders and it was then that our territories began to shrink. I expelled the druids and as a consequence I have been expelled by the gods, unworthy of kingship. Yes, that sounds just. The gods call on me for reparation, and I will make it soon enough.' He glanced at me. 'You were conceived in violence. You are the spawn of rape and I am sorry for it. But think of this before you condemn me, had I not raped your mother, you would not have been born.'

The truth of this winded me.

'I hated you for it,' he continued, 'blamed you in some way, although how could it be your fault? But there you were, a constant reminder, until we sent you away.' He looked out across the sea. 'For your own good,' he added.

'My own good?'

'Your brothers, your half-brothers, Marcomaros and Reginu, would have killed you before you came of age. I barely stopped them killing each other. But that is the way of kings in Britain: it's the survivor who wins. As you know, I killed Eppillos.'

'Your own brother? I thought you drove him off!'

'Ha! That's Fergos's version. I killed him in hand-to-hand combat. Him or me. It's the way of kings. I had no thought about it until your mother came into my life. Suddenly, at Calleva, there was a house of women, with a child who leapt with joy like a dolphin, so Innogen said of you when you were in her womb. As a boy you ran free on the downs and in the forest, a precious thing of beauty. You reminded me of my evil; you also reminded me of my good. I loved you, Togidubnos, never doubt it. I still do.' His head hung low on his chest and his voice became muffled, but I heard him say, 'I understand why you hate me.' He raised up again. 'I don't know how much longer I have, but do your work in Britain and then leave. Do not walk the way of kings.'

The strengthening wind buffeted the sails, snapped at the rigging and nipped our noses; even though we were packed amongst the troops on the upper deck, it found every way through our wrappings to chill our bones. I could hear splashing and went to the edge of the ship to see a pod of dolphins swimming with us, leaping out of the water on shallow arcs, leading us on a path across the waves to avoid monsters. Verica joined me and poured some wine into the sea for the god of dolphins. 'He at least hears my pain and forgives me.' He glanced at me to see if I did, too.

'What if,' I said, thinking of something else entirely, 'what if the mutiny triumphs and the legions disperse?'

Verica humphed, expecting little more from Fortune.

Suddenly a white line, which at first I took for mist, appeared on the horizon and my stomach lurched with excitement. It was what I had seen when I had looked back when sailing away from Britain: that great chalk headland rising out of the water. The wind bore us towards it quickly and it grew until it was dwarfing us. Now my heart felt sick, too, and I could not understand it. Was this the joy of homecoming? Is this how Odysseus felt after ten years lost at sea? But the home I knew no longer existed. Because of all I had heard and read, I expected the skyline to be bristling with the spears of warriors but the only thing on the top of the cliffs was grass. There was no one on the headland; on the shore, a few women and children picked up crabs.

The corbitas tacked along the southern coast. It would be another two or three days before we found harbour. Verica was trying to dull the pain with wine and the more he drank, the more garrulous he became. 'I lost the battle of Calleva, yes I did, lost it. I ran away. They swarmed across Thames river, the Catuvellauni, and overwhelmed our defences, the carnyxes howling, the chariots racing round our walls, the warriors hollering. All the rocks we could sling at them missed, so fast did they ride. Their flaring torches lit our thatches and smoked our people out, women carrying infants stumbling through the smoke. Bloodied and defeated, I ran. I had to run. There has to be a king.'

Although I wanted to question this, I nodded.

'Marcomaros fell with a Catuvellauni spear between his shoulder blades and Caratacos took his head. Reginu was captured and sold into slavery. He killed himself within the day, I heard. There was only one hero and that was Katuaros. He, too, fled, but not before he'd taken ten heads. I am old and what days of glory I had are long gone. Now I have only humiliation for company.' Verica fell quiet for a moment, his bandy legs flexed to ride the pitching of the ship.

'Marcomaros was going to be my successor and, after him, Reginu. But my two sons are gone. Who now shall be king after me?'

I sighed. 'Well, you have warned me against it. Besides, I do not have the will. You must consult the druids. They will tell you who should be king.'

'I told you, I drove the druids off. What do they know anyhow?'

'They know that true kingship does not lie in crowns or golden palaces, that a wise king is free from fear, an evil heart, and ambition.'

'You and your philosophising, always quoting someone, never speaking for yourself. I don't like it when you trip along beside me, full of your own virtue, a conscience so polished that I can see my own miserable reflection in it. To be happy all I need is a few good jokes, a jug of mead, a good roast, and maybe a compliant woman. Who cares what Seneca said? And yet you look me up and down in silent judgement and find me wanting. You despise me, think I'm a failure. You'd rather spend an evening with that crippled dog you bought in a plebeian market than with me.'

I rode the hurt. It was the wine talking. The wine and the pain. The sore back and the broken spirit.

'I am Verica. It was foretold that my blood would found a new nation but I cannot bring to fruition the seeds I have sown. I do what I think is right. I want my people to be free. The Atrebates, feared by their enemies, loved by their friends, keepers of borders, respecters of shrines and sacred temples, law-givers.' Stretching to ease his back, he belched. We could hear below the grunting of the oarsmen and the occasional whip lash. 'Who needs druids? They just complicate things, giving people another choice when their only recourse should be the king. The Atrebates need no druids. I allow in their priests for great festival days and that's it. I don't need them round me, pricking me like horseflies, finding my faults. It's not for priests to keep kings in check!'

'That's a tyrant speaking. A wise king listens to the priests.'

'So you say, you runt of mine, half king, half witch. How can you reconcile yourself into one man?' He groaned with pain both inner and outer. 'The Sanctuary of the Wheel. The hidden omphalos.'

'What of it?'

'The centre of our nation, which no one is supposed to know about. Everyone thinks it's at Venonis, the place of the great assembly, but the druids know the true centre is at the Sanctuary of the Wheel at the Ford of Two Rivers. The place of round tombs and stone circles and the Pole of the Nation.'

I queried this. Did he not mean 'nations' in the plural? No, he said, it's singular, the pole of one nation, the druid nation. 'The trunk of an ancient oak, planed into a pole and carved with dragons. The navel of Britain, and the pole that joins Earth to Sky. The druid college there – School of Night, they called it. That's what I'd heard.' He paused for awhile, then continued. 'I wanted to marry her, to make it right. The more enraptured I became by her, the more guilty; the more guilty, the more enraptured. I had to have all of her, soul as well as body. After a few months I went back to the Sanctuary to make things right, somehow. I was received with hostility and told I was banished from the grove, excommunicated, unwelcome at any druid rite. And so I banished them. The Sanctuary of the Wheel in the vale of the willows and the alders — a no man's land where three tribes meet, the true omphalos of

Britain – but I cleansed it of druids. I was strong then. No one argued with me. Now the horses have the place to themselves.'

'The druids may have returned in your absence.'

'Perhaps…' He took a great lungful of air and expelled it in a sigh. 'What can I do to make things right?'

And now something happened that was disconcerting. My father began to cry. Tears leaked from his watery eyes and his voice caught. 'My life is a failure. My wives did not love me; the druids hate me; my people despair at my weakness. This is your father, boy, a defeated king, a weak man, a failure. I have my fianna still, Katuaros, and my hangers-on. I am still king, after all, and there are plenty to fawn on me, those fame-lickers who must keep company with kings, but I can see through them all. I look upon an eternity of loneliness.'

I could think of nothing to say. My collected gems of wisdom failed me and I was forced into an awkward silence.

Verica took me by the arm. 'When I die,' he began.

'No one dies of back ache,' I said irritably.

'When I die, take my ashes to the Sanctuary of the Wheel and give me there to Thames river. That was me. I was Thames. Your mother Charwelle. We met at the Sanctuary. Give me back to Tamessa. Let it be my atonement.'

I thought too much powdered willow-bark was affecting his mind.

The sinking sun bled into the sea ahead of us. I turned to look backwards. The chalk cliffs, now distant, had taken on a rosy glow and the combes and estuaries were already in the shadow of night. Small boats bobbed in the harbours of fishing villages and gulls shrieked over the remains of the catches. The captain dropped anchor in a large bay for the night since it was too dangerous to sail that close to land in the dark. The moon rose full and made a silver lake of the sea.

When finally my father fell asleep, I joined Mandred on the floor of the deck.

'What ails you?' he asked.

'Nothing. I am well enough.'

'You are pale and trembling, distracted like a man in love.'

And he was right, that was what was wrong with me. Seeing Britain was like catching a glimpse of your beloved in the distance and anticipating the meeting. My knees were knocking. I sat with him for the rest of the night, listening to the creak of the boards and the agitated slaps of the sail, longing for the morning. All around me men snored. I thought I would never sleep.

III

THE TEMPLE OF SOUND

18

NOVIOMAGOS

Verica toed me a little before dawn. 'Awake, awake,' he said as if I'd been lying in. I rose up glad to be free of the dream I'd been having in which my father had been hanged by his people from a willow tree, drowned in a water meadow and set on fire, the triple death of kings. 'Can you believe it?' he said. 'By all the gods, I am coming home.'

Screaming gulls followed in our wake as we crept along the southern coast towards the next headland, a burial ground for many a boat which we negotiated with the help of local pilots. Hearing them shout in my own dialect… They were Regni, a southern tribe of the Atrebates nation. As we rounded the last headland before port, my heart was pounding but then the tide turned and we had to wait half a day before we could slide past the Sacred Isle into the creeks of Noviomagos. Half a day within view of the Isle of Vectis and the hostile Durotriges; half a day with Mandred keeping his head down and his gaze on his feet. It was clear by now that he was not so much uncaring of his own people as frightened of them. Then, with the turning of the tide, a sea fret rose up. We have mist and fog in Rome, of course, forming in the valleys and making islands of the hills, but nothing like this felted cloud emanating from the sea to suffocate the land.

The captain arranged for local boats to take us ashore and as each man left the corbita he was swallowed by the fog. The German soldiers went one-by-one down rope ladders and were rowed away into oblivion. Out of the mist came a sound as of seals singing. I asked my father, 'What is that sound of seals singing?' and he said, 'It will be seals, singing.' But if it was, how come he could not hear them himself?

We disembarked at last, following after the surveyors and engineers, the king and his son climbing down the ladders to reach a flat-bottomed boat that we couldn't see until we were in it. The oarsmen pushed away from the corbita and headed up the main creek, the pilot calling repeatedly to the landing jetty and steering us according to the replies. The splash of our oars brought us closer and closer to land while the pilot kept calling. It was eerie, these disembodied voices in the fog. Suddenly the land voice was very close indeed and at once our boat was bumping against the jetty. At the quay we could just about make out wharfies in their leather bonnets unloading cargo of wine and oil from another flatboat.

Verica's first step on to the land was hesitant and faltering and I moved forwards to help him. He didn't shrug me off as usual but leant on me, staring helplessly into the fog. When my father had arrived in Rome, he was an elderly man. By the time he disembarked on home soil he had become an aged man. It seemed to have happened overnight, as when a flower loses its sap. It's still recognisably a flower but its head is bowed, its leaves limp, all vitality gone. Verica the king, the sinewy, scarred warrior who once had a voice that could tan hides, had become an old man. There was a tremor in his step. He was stooped. When I put out my hand to steady him, he didn't brush it away. There were voices: captains of the unit building grain stores for the army to come, talking with the senior centurion of our German cohort, discussing whether to wait for the fog to lift or to go on into Noviomagos. They decided we should go on, that as long as we could see the track, we wouldn't get lost.

Even as we set out the fog began to thin as if it couldn't follow us ashore but must retreat now like a stray dog who had joined us only for a while. A small flock of songbirds skimmed from bush to hurdle in advance of us, leading the way along the track as we tramped towards the oppidum. Thus we walked into Noviomagos, my attention divided between the needs of my father and my cold, wet feet. British mud — I had quite forgotten about it. It was oozing through the gaps in my Roman sandals.

For the people of the settlement, we appeared out of the mist like their worst fears materialising. They fled within the palisades, screaming and shouting, 'Invasion! Invasion!' The heavy wooden gates of Noviomagos were closed in our faces.

The centurion shouted up at the guard in the gate tower, 'Your king has returned!'

'Our king is within!' the guard shouted back.

'This is Verica!'

'Verica?' There was a pause and a babble of conversation. Then, 'How many are you?'

'Just the king, his son and an escort.'

'Show yourselves!'

Verica and I stepped forward. Another babble and voices of assent. Then,

'Who are the soldiers we see with you?'

'Cohors II Germanorum. An advance unit of the Roman army that remains in Gaul, awaiting a fair wind.'

Someone was sent for. Eventually the tall gates creaked open and there he stood, the warrior king of Noviomagos, in full armour, sword drawn and ready to meet the enemy in single combat.

'My son!' said Verica, shambling forwards, his arms reaching towards him.

'My king!' replied Katuaros, falling on one knee to receive Verica's hands on his head. His eyes widened when he noticed me. 'Delfos? *Delfos!*' He leapt up and I was reunited with my foster brother in a near-fatal bear hug.

The oppidum returned to noisy life as people went back to their work in forge and weaving house. As we passed they stopped to stare but displayed more curiosity than joy at the sight of their returning king. At first I thought it was something in my eye, some streak of dirt, but then I saw a woman's face, my mother's, surely, on a figure who, weaving around huts and pens, tried to keep out of sight while following our course. My eyes must have widened.

'What is it?' Katuaros asked.

'Ghosts,' I muttered.

'*Ghosts?*'

I was about to say something about speaking metaphorically but remembered the measure of my brother. 'Nothing. I was mistaken. A glimpse of a woman I mistook for Innogen.'

'I was crestfallen when I heard about her death,' he said, then held out his arm against mine, white against pale brown, and wondered if there was anything more sallow than an Italian in winter. 'You're the colour of olive paste.'

'Better that than chalk,' I retorted, banging against him, shoulder to shoulder. I had feared this reunion but the only thing between us was the affection we'd had as boys. Katuaros had a tattoo of a ram-headed serpent coiling down his sword arm from shoulder to wrist: it had been interrupted by a white slash of knitted skin.

'That's a brutal scar,' I said.

'A gift from Caratacos. At Calleva.'

In Rome men establish their status with badges of office; here it's with scars, and if you can put a name to one, and a fearful name at that, so much the better.

'Nearly took my arm off,' he said, and I wondered at the envy surging up in me.

Katuaros was taller than me, and I am not short. He was broader on the shoulder than me, and I am not puny. He was bolder than me, and I am no coward. His hair was long in the British style but his face clean-shaven in the Roman one, a feature shared by his fianna, the war band that accompanied him at all times: in a fusion of British and Roman styles, all had long hair and none of them wore moustaches.

The last time I had seen Noviomagos it had been a simple port market with a few traders leading their flea-bitten mules along muddy tracks in what appeared to be one large, disordered camp. If we call our settlements 'camps' it is because, up until the time of the great Caesar, we had been an unsettled people. We might stay in camp a hundred years or more, but always with the knowledge that one day we must move on. It is for that reason, and not primitiveness, that we build in wood rather than stone. So when I say 'camp' I mean a large cluster of round houses occupied mostly by farmers. 'Oppidum' is the name the Romans give to our larger settlements, usually the hill camps (which we call 'duns') but now also, since Caesar's time, to the new settlements that have been built on the plain. Oppida all have the same function: they are places of trade, administration, law. So my story is the tale of travel between oppida such as Noviomagos, Calleva, Kyronion et cetera. But understand that, between the oppida there are many smaller settlements, usually of one extended family, which we call steads; on every hill and in every valley, smouldering houses thickly thatched and embraced by nothing stronger than woven fencing. In times of trouble the farmers sought refuge in the oppida but otherwise Britain, with her rolling hills and water-logged vales, is a place of fields, paddocks and steads of those round hovels we call deep-thatches. We do not have the same attachment to a locality as the Italian or even the Gaul. Our attachment is to life, whether in this world or the other, and so we make sacred the groves, the streams, the lakes, the trees and find that, wherever we are, there is a holy place.

The oppidum of Noviomagos was encircled by palisades and divided into four quarters by two streets crossing in the middle, bringing some semblance of a plan. The huts, however, were still those made of a chalky drum wall of wattle and daub and roofed by a great, thick sweep of thatched reeds. Everything was round: huts, stores, beehives, bread ovens, pens and paddocks. Progress is difficult when grandmothers complain bitterly of having corners in their homes, 'where evil spirits may gather'. When Verica had built a very long timber hall in the Roman style at Calleva, his mother had refused to move in but had camped in the open air until they had built her a nice, round deep-thatch within its own compound. 'What's the point of all this expense?' she had shouted, jabbing her finger at the terracotta roof tiles being shipped in from Italy. 'We make our own walls with laths, spit and dung, our own roofs with reeds from the river. Our floors are the milky skin of Ana the Mother. Do you think you're going to have me tread on images of gods made of little bits of broken stone? Well, I will not do it! Sacrilege!' And if mothers and grandmothers resist, progress can be held back for generations.

With the rootling of pigs, and boundary disputes between neighbours, the plan of circle and cross had become obscured during Verica's absence and we squelched through mud on a sinuous route to the king's house in the north-east quadrant. As round itself in plan as the sun and the moon, and with its old, grey roof reaching down almost to the ground, it looked like a big sleeping hog in a family of smaller sleeping hogs. The porch was made of carved tree trunks joined by beams and topped by a massive pair of bull's horns. Verica regarded his house with what seemed to be awe, for he had never expected to see it again. No matter that it was just a rude hut, it was his rude hut, restored many times and somewhat neglected in his absence, and decorated with the heads of his enemies. For good luck as he passed through the porch he rattled a rope of scalps that hung by their dead hair. 'I'm home, you bastards,' he said to the spirits of his Catuvellauni enemies. 'Didn't expect that, did you?' Verica the King puffed up his sunken chest like a mating bird, threw his blue mantle over one shoulder, adjusted his sword and, holding up the ceremonial torc of Kommios, marched into his house bearing it aloft.

I took off my ruined sandals and left them outside under the thatched eave.

'Indifferent?' Mandred asked, noting my look of disgust at the condition of my feet. This was one of his less endearing qualities, noticing my failures.

Indifferent? Far from it. I walked into the dark house with its pounded and uneven floor, its glowing hearth and dog irons. For sure it was sumptuously furnished with couches covered with elaborate plaids, shelves piled with dishes and goblets imported from Greece and elsewhere, rich hangings keeping out draughts and many lamps making the very air glitter gold and bright bronze, but even exotic spices burning in censers could not mask the smell, the stench of smoke, tanned hide and urine. I was home and my plummeting spirit was pulled down to the ground like a weighted warp thread on a loom.

19

HOMECOMING

A stranger would have been repulsed, but I was not a stranger. The smell of blackthorn burning. The smell of leather and hides — the same the world over, you would think, but these were the skins of the deer, sheep and cattle of Britain and just a whiff of them reminded me of the rainy summers of boyhood spent too long indoors. As for the mead, hissing as a slave warmed it with hot stones, the scent of its spices stung me with longing. Home. This acute pain: this is how it feels to belong somewhere. The kinsmen stood in silence, heads bowed, while Verica walked through on a path as straight as a pin across a brooch, holding aloft the golden torc. He took his seat, a bronze bell was struck and the torc of Kommios was fitted by a servant round Verica's neck.

Greet your king! The bard called.

Hail the king!

Hail the king!

All hail the king!

Katuaros took from Verica the head of Kommios, placed it in its niche and joined the circle of 'uncles', as we called all elders. Without expression they watched me slowly pour a libation into the hearth fire and ask to re-join the tribe.

'The Atrebates welcome back their son, Togidubnos,' Verica said, and the stiff faces of those around me broke into smiles. I sat on my haunches among weathered old men I recognized, who reached out and patted me as if I had somehow been naughty but was now repentant; as if being sent to Rome had been a punishment. 'Welcome home, boy,' said one. 'No doubt,' said another, 'you have learnt a lot, but now you can forget it all again.'

Slaves came in carrying between them a heavy, steaming cauldron and hung it over the hearth to heat up a stew that had been cooked in it. I did not recognize any of the slave women. My mother had taken hers with her when she returned to her people. A heavy-hipped woman poured Italian wine into my silver goblet, presumably both she and the wine the spoils of a successful raid on the Durotriges and their harbour warehouses.

While we were eating, sitting cross-legged on couches, the uncles spooning stew through their beards, an aunt stormed into the house, snatched up a ladle from the cauldron and set about Fergos, beating him over the head, screaming at him for abandoning her. He cowered under the hot spray from the ladle and begged forgiveness: he hadn't known he was suddenly to leave, hadn't known that he was to return. 'I am a faithful servant of the King!' he protested. Her anger subsiding, she flung her arms around him and sobbed.

I remembered many of Katuaros's fianna from when we were boys together, although now they had names drawn from the cauldron of names and bestowed with admiration upon each other: Cow-crippler, Gelder, Wolfbane, Ten Horns and Mouse-ears, who did indeed have very small and furry ears. It was one thing to accept the mission given me by the Divine Claudius, quite another to persuade this bunch of cattle raiders of the value of Roman rule but, if I could, it would start my mission well. As they quaffed unwatered wine like ale, I stood to speak. I did not intend to adopt the stance of a senator before a bunch of ignorant barbarians, but I fear that is how I appeared to them, each Gallic word I so carefully sought sounding stilted and unctuous, punctuated by the long, long pauses of a man who would consider every phrase, checking it for truth and accuracy, before enunciating it. I was lucky they didn't pelt me with dog turds.

'For almost a hundred years,' I began, 'we have had a special relationship with Rome. Since the friendship between Caesar and Kommios, our house has enjoyed great benefits. We have prospered from trade with the Empire and have largely adopted Roman ways.' Although you wouldn't notice it to look at us, I thought, glancing at the warriors on their couches. 'Now everything is out of balance and we have lost that prosperity to the thieving Catuvellauni. It is part of the agreement we made with Caesar that Rome will lend her support should we be threatened. Now that we are threatened, Rome intends to hold good to her word.'

There was much snorting at this. 'Why would they come all this way just to fight our battle?' asked Wild Pig.

'You are right, it is not generosity on their part. They want to restore balance to keep the trade going.'

'They want our *pottery*!' His sarcasm was justified, for the Atrebates had little by way of mineral or metallic wealth. Even our pottery wasn't anything special.

'What we have,' I reminded him, 'is our harbours, our coast-line, our boats to carry away what they have gathered from other territories: iron, lead, silver, salt and grain. The wealth lies in the lands of the Corieltauvi, the Dobunni, the Brigantes, but only we have the means to transport it to Rome. We, and the Durotriges, have the sea. That is our wealth. That is why it is in the interest of Rome that Verica be reinstated as king here, king of the harbours and king of the waters, our very own Neptune.'

'The princeps,' said Ten Horns, 'what's he called?'

'Claudius.'

'Kerlordios.'

'Claudius.'

'Is he king, this Klordios? King of Rome?'

'No. Princeps means first citizen. First amongst equals.'

'Huh!' said Verica, remembering the size of the imperial palace. 'They despise kings,' he said. 'Treat us with no respect. But their princeps is more king than I am. King of kings.'

Mouse-ears asked, 'How do they decide who is the princeps?'

Why, I thought, the Praetorian Guard drag out the first man related to Augustus they can find, even a snivelling wretch hiding behind a curtain. 'It used to be by election, as here, but these days succession tends to be hereditary.'

'So if they take us over? We'll be ruled by the princeps?'

'That is not the intention. They want to restore things to how they were and rid us of anti-Roman factions. It will be a liberation, not a conquest.'

'But if they do take over,' persisted Mouse-ears, who was not half as gullible as I'd hoped, 'what will become of us? If there are no kings, there will be no fiannas?'

'No kings?' piped Verica. Clearly the idea had never occurred to him before.

'Whatever happens,' I conceded, 'there will be kings. And kings' fiannas. It could be that, for awhile, we are governed by a proconsul, until everything is settled.'

'The worst, the very worst, that could happen to us under the Romans,' said Katuaros, 'is that we become employed in administration.'

This made them all laugh.

'Administrators!' roared Ten Horns.

'You'll have to learn to write,' said Katuaros.

'So will you!'

'No more cattle raiding?' Wild Pig's plaintive question brought silence to the hearth. I realised then the enormity of what I was asking of them: to give up a way of life as old as the stars, a way of life that had created them.

'There will always be kings, and kings always need guarding. Your positions are secure, and your income will be in coin, not booty.'

'Do we get to keep our swords?'

I said that that was beyond doubt.

Over the afternoon Verica reported to the uncles the planning sessions we had been party to.

'How many are coming?' they asked him.

'Forty thousand, with as many auxiliaries.'

'Sounds like an invasion.'

'The Princeps was adamant: it is an expeditionary force with the task of restoring peace to Britain. The Catuvellauni will be driven back to their original territory. That is all. As Togidubnos said, it is our harbours the Romans want, our access to trade.'

Katuaros now spoke, directing himself to me. 'If I understand you correctly, you want to negotiate peace. That is, you want us to talk our way out of trouble. What did they do to you in Rome? Geld you? When we were boys, I had only one serious contender in the wrestling ring: you. Only one boy could knock the sword from my hand: you. The only thing I could do was outride you in races. They sent you to Rome for your education, and now you come back drained of your warrior blood recommending we talk to everybody. *Talk?* Are you mad? Where is your pride, man? Have you no sense of shame?' He spat on the ground. 'Delfos! What did they do to you? They've sent home a gelding to live among stallions.'

The fianna, who had spent the afternoon trying to imagine themselves living the Roman way of life, now started hollering and jeering. I leapt to my feet.

'And you, Katuaros,' I shouted. 'Why are you here with the uncles? Keeping safe and warm in Noviomagos? Why aren't you riding to join Caratacos in the defence of our land?'

'*What?* You think I should join Caratacos?' He grew twice his size and turned the colour of ox blood. He held up his scarred arm. 'This is why! This and the death of my father!'

'Listen,' I said. 'What is your choice? For all your warrior spirit, you lost at Calleva. Yes!' I shouted over his squall of protest. 'You lost! Calleva was lost! You escaped the enemy, you escaped death or enslavement. What now is your choice?

You think fighting is the only way; what I learnt in Rome is that it is not. Talking. It takes longer but leads to lasting peace and settlement. Surely,' I said, addressing everyone now, 'that is what we truly want? The Romans are on their way. It is not their intention to massacre us and possess the land. They just want, they *need*, the trade. Are we going to be wise and start negotiating, or are we, like that hot-head Caratacos, going to rush into certain death brandishing our magical swords? That's the choice.'

Some of the older men looked up at me, their leathery faces creased in smiles. Wisdom comes with age, they say, and they wondered to see it in a young man. It was the warriors who took persuading, but gradually, gradually I won them over. Just as I got their agreement to the plans, there was the sudden sound of a snap like a log in the fire. I looked up in alarm, but Verica smiled. 'It's just the old house. Has trouble in the joints, like me. But it bends with the seasons, breathes in and out, not like your marble halls. There's probably a goat on the thatch.' The house was made of good daub on a frame of hazel and ash with rafters and purlins of sturdy oak. Of oak, too, the supporting circle of pillars carved with writhing serpents. But it was made long ago, long before Verica took possession and, since his exile, it had been badly neglected. Thatch must be renewed at least every nine years.

The night drew on. Men went out to stretch their legs, to exercise or go riding as the sun went down. I sat warming myself at the fire, looking around, stirred by the images, serpentine lines, great curves, overlapping moons and suns etched, hatched or painted. It was there in the jewellery, there in the woven fabrics, on the carved pillars, caught in layers in the long, steel swords. I understood the geometry now, where I hadn't as a boy. Then it was just the patterning of my world; now, compared to Rome, it was the patterning of the Otherworld, of Annwn, of water. Euclidean geometry is solar; ours is lunar. You have to learn to read it as men read the heavens.

175

On a wooden dresser was a triple-legged bucket that had fascinated me as a child. It was made of yew staves all but covered by three bronze bands, on the top one of which was a frieze of figures. The iron handle was fixed to the bucket by two heads, one male, wearing a vertical disc ending in two great lobes, a mistletoe crown, the other, female, wearing a wreath of oak leaves.

The patterns on the bronze band seemed random — a wheel caught in a lozenge, a knot of berries, a pair of horses up on their hind legs, which were jointed wrongly, or so a Roman sculptor might think, and dismiss this as a crude barbarity, not knowing it was an image of horse dancers celebrating a wedding. Medicine man and medicine woman, stallion and mare, demonstrating to the shy bride or ignorant groom what was expected of them. It was the high point of most weddings and, done by those who had a good understanding of farce, made everyone scream with laughter; done by those with a higher understanding, it induced the silence of awe...

The waning moon was high in a sky flecked with rags of cloud by the time the men returned to a house transformed for feasting. Slaves carved meat from a boar roasting on a spit in the compound and carried the meat in on large trenchers that they laid before the king and his companions. There came a long groan in the roof, but Verica and his warriors ignored it. 'The house has a voice,' said Katuaros.

'It's a little husky,' I said, tapping the pillar I leant against to check for beetle.

'Who isn't? It's been a long, hard winter, with precious little sign yet of spring.'

I chewed on boar and venison spit-roasted and pork from the cauldron. How brown my native food is: I missed the astonishing colours of a Roman dish, but the tastes took me back to those days of eating outdoors, of my first hunt at the age of nine and drinking the hot blood to show that I had reached the first degree of warrior. These memories were setting up a vibration in my gut like a high-tuned string on the harp. I knew if I were not careful, I could be in tears in what Seneca would have called 'a mess of nostalgia and sentimentality' and that would never do in the house of King Verica. Men who have drunk the blood of a boar do not weep.

The mead was stronger now and we all competed to be the last man awake. There were a couple of bouts of single combat to settle old quarrels, but the swords were blunt and the fighting so lacking in drama that some men slept through it, chin on chest, their snores rippling their lips. The younger ones kept awake — as did the king, although in his case it was because of pain.

After the Tale of the Cauldron from Fergos, sung to the ringing accompaniment of the harpist upon a lyre strung with wires of silver and gold, one by one the younger warriors arose to entertain the company with tales of gods, of springs flowing where the Albios Horse struck the ground with a hoof, of the day the sun chariot did not ride the sky, old stories but no less entertaining for all that if told by a gifted teller, a warrior raised by a grandmother who knew the tales and a grandfather who knew the rhythms and forms of telling. And so the companions of Verica stood one by one to tell their tales of shape-shifters or decapitated giants who carried their talking heads. When it came to my turn, I gave them the tale of the Cyclops from Homer's Odyssey. At first they listened with some hostility, for they clearly expected me to have come back from Rome with nothing but disdain for my own folk, but gradually I won them over with my telling and when it came to Odysseus blinding the Cyclops with a stick sharpened in the fire, they roared in approval.

As the company began to sink with the fire, and those still awake grew reflective, Katuaros came and sat down beside me.

'Brave words I've heard from you today. But what I hear from the sea is of mutiny. Are the Romans coming?'

'There is mutiny, stirred up by druids, they say, but the commanders are men of strength and resolve. They will come.'

'And if they don't?' Katuaros leant forwards questioningly.

'If they don't…?' I muttered. I could not imagine my native peoples suffering me to live. 'They will come,' I said, as much to convince myself as him.

20

KATUAROS

The rain came in the night, a background roar like a cataract, but inside the house I felt as cocooned and safe as I had as a child. There was an upper gallery just below the smoke line and there we bedded down, three to a stall, our feet pointing in to the centre like the spokes of a wheel. The wind howled around the compound; men went out to check on the bleating animals, shouting to each other in the rising gale, but despite its creaks and groans the house seemed solid enough: I had tapped most of the pillars and found no beetle. I slept through the noise of the weather and woke in the morning to the stench. The reek of smoke — although the king had the best of woods for his fire yet still I woke up with eyes red and sore. The close sweat of men sleeping under the airless cover of furs. The stale fat from last night's roast. The pungent stink of urine. Rome is no perfume shop but I'd forgotten the olfactory assault of life in Britain. With a thumping head I crawled to the ladder and went down to get air outside.

A great puddle had formed at the threshold and I lifted the hides on a grey dawn teeming with water. The rain came off the roof in sheets and under the porch it was like standing behind a waterfall. Inside the house men were beginning to stir, to stagger upright and relieve themselves in the floor gutter but I preferred to go outside, using the overhang of thatch as a shelter. Katuaros was already there, his breeches down round his ankles while, hands on hips, he pissed into the rain. 'So,' he said, 'what's it like being home?'

I couldn't tell him about the oppression of spirit brought about by mud and gloom: he would have taken it as an insult. Instead I told him that I was uneasy because I didn't know who to trust. 'You, for instance. For over two years you've been chief here, not knowing if Verica would return, yet you give up the king's chair without a struggle. What's it like for you, Verica coming home?'

'Galling,' he said, drawing up his breeches. 'But I'm not going to kill your father, or you come to that. Believe it or not, I'm too fond of you, even if you don't trust me.' He pulled his sword out from where he had wedged it into the thatch above his head, turned it edge-on and stared at me across it with mean eyes, then broke out laughing. 'If I am the sheen in the metal: you are the sword. Your father does not look well. It will not be long before you are our king. You, my brother,' he said.

I felt ashamed to have distrusted one so loyal. 'I have no wish to be king,' I said as he pushed Firebreath back into the thatch. 'One sees things differently in Rome.' From his expression, I imagined him thinking, Oh yes, here it begins, Rome, Rome, Rome. 'Presumably you would rather beat out your own brains than hear anything about my travels?' I asked.

'We hear of nothing but Rome here,' he said. 'Merchants arrive in the harbour every day and treat us like idiots, offering us their wine for our precious metal, but we love their wine so we deal with them, dine with them, listen to their tales of the wonders of Rome. I think you'll find we know it all.'

When he had first arrived at Calleva at the age of five, sent by his father Biccos, chief of the tribe at the Ford of the Alders, I had treated him with caution, expecting a bully as cruel as my brothers, but he had won me over in a matter of days. Bold, brave and invariably good-humoured, this was the brother I had always longed for; we became inseparable, until Verica cleaved us apart by sending me to Rome alone.

We sat down on a log under the eaves and stared out at the rain. Men in seal skin capes hurried to cow byres to do the milking. 'What happened at Calleva?' I asked as Katuaros drew out his knife to idly carve sinuous patterns in the log.

'Not hard to tell,' he said, the customary opening to a romping tale of amazing feats in battle. 'The Catuvellauni charged in like a pack of starving wolves, led by those hag-born sons of Cymbelinus...' I listened to how Katuaros had fought off Caratacos, man to man in single combat, the strikes he'd used, the strikes he'd parried. Perhaps I was looking incredulous for his boasting stopped suddenly, like the rain. 'My father was visiting Verica at the time,' he said, more in the tone of a truth-telling. 'A visitor. A guest of honour. Togodumnos speared him like a pig.' He inhaled loudly. 'You remember Calleva... We thought the woods and the steep drop to the valley in the east were enough to protect us. A few dykes, some ramparts... The Catuvellauni were through the gates before we knew what was happening.' He told of the run to arms, of his hands sweating in his haste to buckle on his sword and pick up his shield, of the screams that had begun to sound in the oppidum before he could scrabble out of the hall to meet the foe. It had been his first battle. Hand-to-hand he had fought Caratacos, the steel of their sharp swords ringing. He pulled back the sleeve of his tunic to show me the whole of that white scar made by a blow that could have taken off his arm, the scar that had disfigured the magnificent ram-headed serpent I remembered him receiving without a whimper in our coming-of-age rites. 'I kept my shield but I dropped Firebreath,' he said. 'Caratacos would have killed me then without a thought had it not been for Biccos. As I fell my father jumped in and took him on. He'd have won, too, but for the spear in the back from Togodumnos. No sense of honour, that one.' Katuaros spat into his hands and rubbed them together hard. 'May his seed go sour, make his bitch barren and poison him from within. But I was up again and had Firebreath. Verica called us off, shouted for us to run. To run!' Now Katuaros spat on to the ground. 'I'll never forgive him for that. We should have fought until we died for what was ours. Yours. Not leave it all behind. That would have been an honourable death.' His carving forgotten, he sat with his head hung low. 'We lost everything, the herds, the grain, the women...' He suddenly stabbed the log with his knife. 'I'll never forgive Caratacos for killing the stallion. I wouldn't forgive him for any of his crimes, but for killing Tiberius I curse him.' He looked across to where our horses shared a manger of hay. His, a son of Tiberius, was shorter than mine and dappled. 'It'll take generations to build the herd, but we can start again with your Scipio.'

'We are hardly in a position to breed horses! We need to be settled first. A good reason not to resist the Romans.'

'Perhaps the best.'

'Do you think ill of Verica, calling on the Romans for help?'

'He should not have run from Calleva, but at Noviomagos he had no choice. Caratacos dragged him to the harbour and kicked him off to Gaul. Do I think ill of Verica for calling on the Romans for help? I do not. Whatever it takes to squash Caratacos like a midge,' he stood up, keeping his head bent to avoid brushing his hair against the overhanging thatch. 'The Romans owed us anyway.'

'Owed us for what?'

'Driving out the druids.'

'Verica said he did that because they excommunicated him.'

'Partly. But mostly because it was the wish of Rome.'

'I presume Caratacos wanted Calleva because he needed a capital of his own?'

'When Cymbelinus died, he left Verlamio and Camulodunon to his eldest sons. Caratacos was without land so he took Calleva. Wonderfully strategic, our oppidum in the woods. It was his first step in his push towards Kyronion and the west.'

'He wants Kyronion? I hadn't realised he's after such a great swathe of southern Britain.'

'A great swathe?' said Katuaros. 'He wants all of it. All of Britain. He forced your father out, he's got the Dobunni in a head-lock. He wants to be King of Everywhere. All that stands between him and total possession is the Durotriges to the south-west and the Brigantes to the north. Everyone else, including the Trinovantes in the east, are more or less vassals of the Catuvellauni now. We didn't realise his ambitions until it was too late.'

Having with some effort got his knife out of the log and back in its sheath, he drew Firebreath out from the thatch again. By some trick of a master sword-smith, the steel blade was run through with serpentine lines of pale grey. 'Are the Romans really just coming to do us a favour? Or are they coming to stay? Who's to say which evil is the better one?' Straightening his clothes, he rearranged his plaid, woven in the Belgic stripe at Ford of the Alders, and kissed the blade. 'You say there will be no more kings. What about us, the warriors? Must I break her up, my lovely, and give her to the gods, without any Roman blood on her?' He put Firebreath in her scabbard.

'That would be most advisable,' I said, following him inside to a breakfast of black pudding being cooked up on the fire. The rain had begun again so after the meal we retreated to our sleeping stall in the gallery and sprawled on the hides. I tried to tell him about the philosophers I'd studied with but he just lay there, propped up on an elbow looking at me, his eyes smiling as if he were being amused by a child showing off. I remembered then why I'd been happy to leave ten years ago, since I could find none apart from my mother who had shared my curiosity in the world.

'Books...' he said. 'Wisdom is in the rocks, the streams, the light. Why would you need to read about it? What is there to know that you can't find sitting in front of you?'

I wanted to talk about knowledge, having an idea to teach him how to read. He spoke Roman passably well but he had never learnt his letters when we had studied together under my father's slave, Turnus, saying he had no use for them.

According to the druids, reading destroys memory, and Katuraros had used that as an excuse for being idle.

I suggested I might at least teach him the alphabet in a first step towards literacy but he shrugged it off. He thought that it was me who was deficient in education, that the best system of teaching and learning is through stories, and that the most useful occupation on this rainy day was for him to tell me about the near-fatal cattle raid he'd led on the Isle of Vectis, a mad adventure involving boats and panicking bovines which ended up making Katuaros richer by ten bullocks. 'Your father was good to me, let me keep almost everything I won,' he said. Dependent on the spoils of war and the gifts of Verica, he showed me his treasure chest which was rich in coin, broken torcs, some fine silver brooches and bronze knives. He told me about his stash of captured weapons, his horses, cattle and skulls, but said he would give it all up quite happily in exchange for a parcel of land.

'Do you want to be a farmer?'

'Well, when I say parcel...'

'You mean a large parcel.'

'Quite large.'

'The size of a kingdom?'

'Yes, that sort of parcel.'

'As large as ours once was, stretching from here to the Thames and west as far as the old Stone Temple?'

'Yes, that's what I mean by "parcel".'

'You want to be a king.'

'Born to it.' He grunted as he realised what he'd said. 'King of the Belgae, that is, not the Atrebates.'

'Verica wants you to inherit here.'

'I know. I love that old dog. But it's yours, rightfully yours.'

'Yet I do not want it. If Britain becomes part of the Empire, perhaps I'll find myself a role in its government.'

Katuaros pulled a face of supreme distaste. 'What have they done to you?'

'Imagine. Imagine waking up each day not worrying about how that day will end, to be able to plan with some confidence of outcome, to farm in the anticipation of harvest. Imagine that.'

'It is to imagine myself roaming the world looking for a fight. Of what use to me is a settled life?'

'Do you have no secret hankerings for your own farm, a good wife, sons?'

He laughed. 'I would die of boredom. I want a parcel of land large enough that it would take an entire year to travel round it, staying now here, now there, settling nowhere. But tell me, if you do not intend to become king, why have you come home?'

'To warn everyone not to resist. Anyone who stands in the way of Rome will be destroyed. They are invincible.'

'The man who seeks to lengthen his life by all means is a coward and will go to the Beyond without honour. How do you intend to go about this savage land persuading others to betray their own souls?'

'It will not be difficult, I think.'

Katuaros laughed. 'I'll remind you of that when I pull your head off a Durotrigan spike. How would you like it embalmed? Cedar oil from the orient would be my choice.'

He was right of course, and I was being stupidly optimistic. 'My first target is going to be Esius of the Dobunni.'

Katuaros agreed. 'Good. You'll need him.'

'He's a kinsman of my mother, so I am hoping he will listen to me.'

'He'll listen, but he may not hear. Caratacos beheaded his wife before his very eyes and said he would do the same to him if he were ever to betray him. So Esius has to pay an enormous annual tribute. He may listen, but will he change sides? I doubt it.'

'Does he have sons?'

'He has no children except a daughter, and she's in hiding somewhere.'

'Rome intends to stay and will make the Albios Way the new frontier.'

'Then you need Esius. When does the army plan to arrive?' he asked.

'Any time after the equinox. It depends on the winds and the tides, but the aim is to subdue Britain by Lughnasa at the latest. My task is to negotiate peace in advance, starting with Esius and then going on to Venonis, negotiating with any chieftain I meet on the way, but meeting all tribes together at the Great Assembly.'

'And what if you get that far and the Romans have still to arrive?'

Sweat broke out on my brow. My nights were becoming sleepless wondering what I would do if the Romans failed to arrive — stay or flee? Would I have the choice?

'They'll come,' I said.

Katuaros leaned forward, deeply serious. 'You will need the gods with you, and good fortune. It is the dark half of the month and no time to be setting out on such a venture.'

'Since it is equally possible that the Romans could arrive in two weeks, Verica and I need to set out straight away.'

'Take the divine road, Delfos. Go with the gods, not against them. Do not leave during the dark half.'

'When is new moon?'

'In ten days.' He sat back. 'Then, I hope, we shall see some sign of spring. There was snow here right up until last week and many lambs were lost, frozen to death at a day old. There is famine across the land and famine brings out bandits — you will need me and my fianna.'

'I have a whole cohort of Germans auxiliaries.'

'Do you? I thought their purpose was to protect Noviomagos, not you. As soon as he learns that the Romans intend to land here, Caratacos will make a desperate push to secure this harbour.'

'What if the Romans land in the east?'

'You said they were coming here.'

'But what if Caratacos thinks it's the east? We need to spread some rumours, get his war bands going in the wrong direction.'

Katuaros looked sideways at me, as if he did not approve of deviousness as a weapon of war, but, mindful of what druids were doing at Gesoriacum in spreading fear, I considered my plan like for like.

'So,' he said, 'ten days to wait.'

It seemed to me impossible. I was ready to go and wanted to go now, but he was right. One must trust the gods. I thought I might spend the time making sacrifice and reading omens but Katuaros had a different idea, at least for the first day. He moved towards the ladder to descend. 'It's not enough time to train you up again in arms, but we can get you properly dressed.'

'I don't need training in arms,' I protested, following him down. As we went to the weaving house, I described the drills Vespasian had put us through in Greece and he snorted, saying that learning how to walk in file was hardly the way to become a warrior. It was as if the intervening years had not been: we walked side by side, deliberately banging into each other, our touching shoulders a sign of our affection. Mandred, as faithful as a hound, hobbled along behind, but he looked sullen and abandoned, and his limp had clearly worsened. His hands also were clasped in front of him again, as if shackled.

'I like the idea of a Durotrigan slave,' Katuaros had said to me on our reunion. 'The only thing that lot are good for, slavery.'

I turned to say something encouraging to my slave but as I did so, I caught sight of that figure again, blackened and bowed like a dying plant, hurrying through the stead as if on the same course as us.

'What is it?' Mandred asked.

'Who is that woman? If it is a woman.'

'How should I know?'

187

'You'd know a druid if you saw one.'

'Would I? Perhaps. If I saw anyone at all. I think you have something in your eye.'

I grunted. It could be true. There were enough smuts in the air.

In the weaving house, I asked Mandred's opinion when I tried to choose between various lengths of plaid, all of the Atrebatic stripe. The women left their looms to fuss about me, holding different samples in drapes across my chest, snatching handfuls of fabric and making me feel its quality. They had me feeling wool until my hands were as greasy as theirs. Is there any warrior in the world as conscious of his appearance as a Briton? Katuaros was trying the plaids himself, just for fun, enjoying having the women touching him and telling him how handsome he was. I could have chosen something plain, as Mandred wanted me to, but Katuaros was adamant that I must wear the tribe's colours, so I chose a blue one of fine wool with the thin crossed lines of red which is our pattern. 'Expensive, I know, but as befits you,' he said. 'It will do for summer. We'll get you something even more expensive in the autumn.' I also ordered some breeches in their softest cloth that he'd recommended, the kind that end at the knee, and a tight-fitting hip-length coat of wool. When we left, it was to go to the leatherworker for a pair of British boots and a good belt, and to the bronze smith for a large buckle. Katuaros studied and compared some elaborate ones and was showing a preference for images of Cernunnos, the antlered god who holds a ram-headed serpent. 'Does it have to be decorated?' Mandred asked. 'Plain would do the job just as well at half the cost.'

Between Katuaros and Mandred, I was being pulled apart by the horses of ostentation and abstinence. In the end I bought a plain buckle and smiled at my offended foster brother. 'I must tell you about the Stoics some time,' I said. As we left the market, we came upon the practice grounds where the warriors were tumbling about in what passes here for exercise.

'Come on,' said Katuaros. 'We need to get you fit, scholar.'

We stripped down and, arms out and legs splayed, began to move around each other, he snarling, me impassive. I had not spent my days practising with sword and sling, had not broken in ponies or driven chariots over the downs, had not hunted for meat nor built walls or dug ditches. I had the soft skin of a library man, but I knew how to floor a broad, tall Briton. 'Where did you learn that?' Katuaros gasped, flat on his back and winded.

'Wrestling school, where the philosophers teach.'

Each morning I took Scipio on a training ride not to the harbour but to the shore with its expansive view to the horizon, as if just being there I would see before anyone else the Roman fleet on its way. The training was as much for me as the horse; together we cantered the strand, picked our way over mudflats and negotiated fords, training for our journey and our role.

On the beach small children collected mussels. They got used to me, this stranger on the Roman horse, and began to watch for the ships with me, but all we saw was grey sea and foaming waves breaking on the beach. It was still days to the equinox and thus improbable that we should see the fleet, but I was coming to believe I never would, no matter how hard or long I stared. The smallest of the children, perhaps five years old, skipped about wearing a slimy wreath of seaweed and, picking up a whelk shell, would ask me, 'Is this one? Is this a mussel?' I worried for him. Worried for us all, in the dim light of an uncertain future. The sea whispered its amorous secrets to the shore and cared not.

21

BLACK RAVEN

We spent the dark half of the month, the unlucky days, feasting, drinking, bragging, boasting, as if this remnant of the Atrebates had every expectation of overcoming Togodumnos and Caratacos at the next challenge without any help from any Romans. I could pass such long hours easily enough in Rome, provided there was someone to converse with on the nature of the stars, the secret of a happy life or the meaning of Plato's *Timaeus*. Here, now, I was remembering how it felt to be a bored child.

When the weather allowed, I was out and engaged in restoring an old chariot of the King's that I'd found in a barn. I had the wheels re-tyred with new iron, replaced the hide thonging of its floor and put the treasured fittings back on, happy to have something to do. When I practised harnessing the horses and driving the chariot, I found that the memory of how to do it was still with me. I only had to stand with the reins in my hand for it all to come back. Verica's herd had reduced to a small paddock of throwbacks. I took the best, a pair of sturdy cobs with long manes and beautiful eyes, to pull the chariot. When I took it out for a practice run, Mandred always rode with me as shield-bearer; when my memory faltered, or even when it didn't, he gave a constant stream of advice. He was, in his opinion, something of a champion. 'I used to run the pole,' he said, as if suggesting I might like to try the manoeuvre that was beyond all but the bravest. 'Did you,' I replied, ignoring the unspoken challenge.

When the weather got too bad, we stayed indoors with all the good grace of bears with toothache. One afternoon when I was trying to teach Katuaros to read simple words such as 'canis' and 'ursus', we were called to the King.

'Come here, you son of a witch,' said Verica at the gaming board that was set up for Black Raven with pieces of gold and silver exquisitely wrought. 'Still remember how to play?'

He had taught me when I was a child but could never resist winning, even against an ignorant seven-year-old, and was forever capturing my king and crowing in triumph at his victory. But about two years previously Claudius, hearing about Black Raven, had asked me to teach him. I had thought this would be my opportunity to take advantage and win, but not at all; within days, Claudius was at my gaming pieces like a thrush at snails. But he did what my father had never done and showed me how to win. 'You need to understand,' he had said, 'that pieces change in nature and function. Take Messalina for instance. She is my wife, she goes to the baby and is her mother — same woman, different relationship. With her own mother, she is daughter, with her slaves, mistress.'

'Goes to another man and she is lover,' I thought, at the risk of betraying myself with a blush.

'And so it is with this game,' said Claudius. 'Take this little fellow. You think he's a warrior. Well, he is a warrior, to begin with, and you've been planning to use him in an ambush — yes, you have! — but stuck here, he's a defender of the king. Now, go for that ambush you planned. There! You see? Forgetting that he's now defending the king, you've moved him and, well, you've put yourself in a very sticky position.' Having done what Claudius suggested I do, I had opened myself to attack. 'Wheeee!' he said, kicking my warrior off the board. But it had been a valuable lesson and I was on my guard now for the devious ambushes of my merciless father.

On the black and white board, seven squares by seven squares, battle commenced. 'You're Caratacos,' he said, making it morally difficult for me to win. I moved in on his defences slowly. Slowly the golds and the silvers moved forward a square and then back a square, as we sought each other's weak spots. With the game threatening to last all day, we broke off to eat and returned to it after the meal. Verica was tiring and forever shifting about to ease the pressure on his spine, but also I think he was over-confident. I saw that he'd forgotten that one of his pieces was playing three roles. I set up an ambush four moves ahead. Four moves later, I snatched his king. Verica roared. I grinned, presuming it was a roar of delight that his son had become a worthy opponent, but no, it was the caterwauling of sheer petulance. He blamed it on the mead, for I'd been drinking watered wine and was still sober whilst his eyelids were drooping. 'So,' he said, recovering his temper and remembering the laws of gaming, 'you are entitled to a boon. Is there anything you wish to ask of me?'

'Tell me about my mother.'

'I already have. What more do you want?'

'Anything. My memory is hazy. I remember a strong-boned and beautiful woman who knew everything there is to know about herbs. But tell me more about her.'

Verica watched me carefully, eye to unblinking eye. 'I haven't told you the truth,' he said. 'She didn't die of a scratch. I killed her.'

I have drunk the blood of a boar I thought as I said, calmly, 'Why?'

'She betrayed me. She slept with another.'

'It's the queen's privilege.'

'Not Caratacos.'

I felt winded.

'Hurts, doesn't it?' said Verica. 'The one who steals our horses, our women, our land, stole our queen. I raised a band, went to Verlamio, pulled her from his bed and slit her throat.'

He was still staring at me, so intently that I did not see the question shouting to be asked, *Why didn't you kill Caratacos?*

192

Marry my mother to my father! Did the Oracle at Delphi have any true meaning? Had I been deceived by Pythia? Then a goddess arose in my soul, one I had become acquainted with through Greek plays: Nemesis. Her drawn and savage face appeared before my mind's eye, calling for vengeance. An act was being called from me by gods beyond bargaining and propitiation; the ancient ones, the most ancient of ancient ones.

'You can kill me if you like,' said Verica, seeing what was behind my eyes. 'I'm dying anyway. But I wouldn't make it easy for you.'

'You sired me in rape; you have orphaned me in murder. Why shouldn't I kill you?'

'Because you're a coward. Look at you, as soft as a eunuch, jumping like a cat every time the hall beams creak. I raised you as a warrior and you've spent ten years wondering about the meaning of life. You couldn't even lift my sword, couldn't draw it from the scabbard.'

I leapt up and drew his sword in one flowing movement and pointed it at the old man's breast. Verica's eyes widened with approval. 'Go on then, use it.'

'Not yet,' I said, raising it. The light of the fire gleamed in its chased bronze hilt, in the dull polish of its steel blade.

'If you want this kingdom, you're going to have to kill me,' he said.

'I keep telling you, I have no interest in being king.' I handed him back his sword.

'You are unnatural! If you do not kill me, I shall kill myself, then will destruction be unleashed upon this house and the Fates will drag you down.' Slowly his chin dipped until he was staring at me from under his brow: the panther was about to spring. I stood back a stride and drew my own sword, a short Roman blade and no match against that long sword of iron alloyed with charcoal, born in fire and hardened with hammers. 'Come on, then, old man.'

The Roman sword was only good for stabbing people so I used my agility to draw Verica to the side of the circle where, with a quick movement, I helped myself to the long sword of a man asleep and clearly dreaming of his lover. As the blades met in long, downward slashes, the company of sleeping warriors awoke with a start to see the kingdom being fought over once again. Verica was failing, staggering backwards under the force of my strikes. One more slash and I struck the sword from his weak and trembling grasp but then stood back in the stance of mercy.

'She died begging to live,' the old king snarled, calling me on.

I was about to swipe off his head without further hesitation when suddenly Mandred got in the way. As if numbing prey, he struck my hand. All power fled from me. The sword dropped to the ground.

'You are in the grip of ancestors,' he whispered fiercely. 'Be free. Be yourself. Show your father the mercy he never showed others.'

I nodded in agreement and kicked the sword back towards its owner.

'Mercy?' Verica snarled. 'It's an act of weakness! May weasels eat your eyes, you runt of the litter. Milk sop! Son of a witch!'

I tried to remember every piece of good advice I'd ever had from Seneca about quelling the passions.

'Runt! Last-born! Do you know why I sent you away to Rome? Because I couldn't stand the embarrassment of having you here. While good men were dying for their land, you were talking, talking, always talking, trying to find out the secrets of the universe. You are lamentable! I call upon Cernunnos to pull out your innards, roast them on the spit and eat them before your pasty eyes, you god-forsaken last of the brood!'

'Do not be provoked,' Mandred whispered. 'Keep your head down. Do not meet his eye. Let his curses curl over you like water.'

194

'DRUIDS!' the King screamed. 'Both of you! DRUIDS! Didn't I cast them all out of this kingdom years ago? Those creepy man-trees who think they have authority above kings, those leaf-haired, branch-armed, twig-fingered wizards! You are their whelp!' he shouted at me. 'You are not a warrior, no, never were and never will be! What will happen when I die? Who will inherit here? For it will not be you, you beardless piglet! You should have killed me, should have killed me, then one day you might have been king.'

'I do not wish to be— '

'But no, you drop your sword like a coward. Like a priest. LIKE A DRUID!'

He rose, relieved himself in the house gutter and, shrugging off the attentions of servants, lurched up the ladder to his stall. 'I can do it, I can do it,' he insisted, weak in the left leg and limping. When he stubbed his toe against a rung of the ladder, he blamed the ladder, shouting at it as if it were a slave in his way. I went up to my own stall to lie there sleepless, murdering my father in a dozen different ways.

When at last I slept, it was to dream of drowning in blood.

We were nine and ready for that rite that turns boys into men. Starting with invocations to Cernunnos, god of the hunt, and Moccus, god of the boar, we set off with the warriors into the woods that surrounded Calleva, crashing through the undergrowth, our hounds wild in pursuit of a scent. Katuaros made the first kill, a mature male, small-eyed and snarling. He hurled his spear and took the life. Spurred on, I followed my own hound on a new trail and came at last to a sow backed into the undergrowth. Flooding with compassion, I called my dog off, leashed it and tied it to a tree. I was on my own. I could easily have let the animal go, but I did not. I had to become a man. So… I slid off my horse and walked towards the trembling, spitting creature, knife drawn. I would not use the dog —throwing himself against his tethered collar, howling with frustration — and I would use no spear. I went forwards. She lowered her head. With no tusks, she was not a killer, but a charge could knock me dead nonetheless. I held her with my eye, softly, softly speaking to her, telling her not to be afraid, and at the moment of hesitation, if not trust, I slipped my arm round her neck and drew the knife across that tough, bristly hide. I watched her death throes. I caught her life blood in my drinking horn. I became a man.

Later, back in the camp, all the blood from the hunt was collected in a cauldron. One by one we boys were picked up by the heels and lowered head first into it, where we swallowed a mouthful before being pulled out. One boy struggled wildly in the grip of the priests and screamed for his mother. He was exiled from the rank of warrior; so, too, another boy who, although submitting without noise, when he was pulled out and put back on his feet, wet himself. So head first into the blood I went, and it ran into my nose and throat so that I was drowning in blood but I was not to fear and not to struggle. I closed my mind down to the beat of my heart and, just as fear began to rise up like a thunderhead on the horizon, I was drawn out. I opened my clogged and sticky eyes to see Katuaros sitting on the ground, stretching out his tongue to lick his own face, looking as satiated as a dog after the kill. After the rite of immersion, we burned the creatures in our sacrifice to the gods. We had come of age.

I awoke when the creaking began in the middle of the night, a creaking that was not going to stop, a creaking that became a terrible groaning and then a sudden crack. Roof beams moved, purlins snapped and the sleeping platforms tore apart and tipped towards the ground. The house was twisting, like a warrior brought down by a spear. It was falling to its knees. My first thought was, *Earthquake!* My second, *Catuvellauni!* I fell with my bed, crashing down on those sleeping below. After me came the thatch. There was a dull crumpling of bronze and iron as cauldrons, pots and hangings, firedogs, shields, spears and war trumpets buckled under the tremendous weight coming down. Sometimes you hear of a sow who rolls over in her sleep and squashes her litter. Thus it was in the house of Verica.

Mandred pulled me out from under the choking thatch and shoved me towards the doorway — so many trying for that narrow door at once — but we got through just as the old house gave a final groan, sighed like a dying, headless giant and collapsed.

Outside there was uproar. It was dark, the wind was buffeting, the rain stinging. Women screaming. Men crying out. Warriors without a battle, except with decay. Katuaros appeared, cloaked in thatch and coughing. 'Sire?' he shouted into the dark. Then everyone stopped, became quiet, for we could see nothing. 'Sire? Sire?'

There was no sound, no muffled calls for help, no cries or groan, just a sodden silence. Wretched and helpless, everyone took shelter where they could until dawn which, when it came, came reluctantly. The rain ceased but the sun stayed abed with no thought of getting up. There was nothing to shine on here, just a silent pile of wet, black thatch. We pulled on the reed bundles, clearing everything away, and after a morning's work had found nine bodies and one man still alive but so badly crushed that someone cut his throat. Amongst the corpses, Verica, King of the Atrebates. With a rope around his neck. And I knew and understood what he had done as surely as if I had done it myself. Against the sacred laws, the King had killed himself and in so doing had brought down his house. Only in its physical form, perhaps, but I understood it deeply: the line of Kommios would find its end in me. Whether I had sons or not was immaterial: the royal house of the Atrebates was finished. And there she was, suddenly, that wraith, that Nemesis, whose face I still could not clearly see even though she stood beside me.

'Whither now, Togidubnos? Whither now?'

22

THE LAST RITES OF THE KING

In that year, the spring equinox occurred a week before the new moon. At dawn everyone gathered in their houses with the doors open to perform the rites to the rising sun and welcome light back into their homes. After the prayers and oblations, we gathered to carry Verica on his ceremonial shield, not to the sky platforms but to a giant pyre we had built of the remains of his house. We carried with him the body of his faithful bard, Fergos. The funeral place should have been high on a hill on the chalk ridge, in some lofty dun or even at Calleva, not here on the coast, but there was no choice. We built the pyre just outside the ramparts. I lit the kindling and watched the flame crackle through the poles, boards, broken wattle and lathes, running in sparkles up thatching reeds, a sluggish start with the dampness of the material, but men on bellows got it going until suddenly it was a roaring conflagration that was burning our faces with its heat. We chanted our offerings to Fire and thus he went into the next life, my unlovable father, his bronze and leather shield over his face. There was no pity nor regret in me until Katuaros took me aside.

'What he told you about Innogen, it wasn't true. He didn't kill her. She left him when he banished the druids and went home to her own people. I heard she died sometime later of an infection.'

'So why did he tell me he'd murdered her?'

'He wanted to die at your hand. Clearly he wanted you to be king. According to our most ancient traditions, he believed his death would restore the land. You refused to do the deed of sacrifice, so he did it himself.'

I remembered something Seneca had told me once, that no matter how oppressed we are, we all have one sure route to freedom: we all have a vein we can open. But what was acceptable to Romans was unacceptable to Britons. To take your own life was to usurp the work and will of the gods: there would be retribution. 'He could not tolerate the pain. I don't think he'd slept properly for weeks,' I said.

Gathering Verica's ashes, we put them in the small bucket of yew and bronze. To keep the people settled, we sacrificed to the tribal gods and built a new house for the new king. 'Who that king shall be,' I told the uncles and the tribe, 'is not yet known. I wish for us to return to the tradition of electing our kings. Katuaros and I are leaving for Venonis and the mid-summer gathering.'

'We shall follow later,' said the eldest of the elders.

'No, not this year. It is not safe to travel so far. We shall represent the tribe and consult the chief druids, asking them to elect a successor to Verica. For this much I can assure you, while I am in command here, the druids are welcome to return.'

I didn't know why I said this. It came to me in the moment, as the surest way to calm the frightened population of Noviomagos, and that is what it did: a murmur went round them like a breeze on a summer's day. All that they had suffered in the loss of Calleva had come upon them because of Verica's sin. Now I, his only surviving son, was putting things right. Making good.

'What shall we do when the Romans come?' an uncle asked me.

'Rejoice,' I said. 'We are leaving Cohors II Germanorum here for your protection against hostile Britons. You don't need any against the Romans. They are our friends, our liberators. Lay rushes on the roads to welcome them.'

The centurion in charge of the cohort took me aside later and demanded to know by what right I was inviting the druids to return. Did I have permission to offer such a thing? I puffed up before him, just the way Verica used to do, and said that, until the Romans occupied this land, I was in charge here. I. My father's son.

'Kings!' muttered the centurion, walking away.

Katuaros glanced at me appreciatively.

Men of the tribe gathered intending to beat the drums to tell the land that the old king was dead. Drums through the valleys, beacons on the hills, everyone in the Isles would know by the following day that Verica was dead. Katuaros stopped them. He asked that no beacons be lit, no riders sent out, no news of the death of Verica given until the birth of the new moon. 'The old king dies with the old moon. It would be wise to be quiet during the remaining dark days.'

He took up the bronze bucket, now sealed with a lid. 'He wished his body to be given back to water?' he asked me.

'Yes. He told me once in Gaul that, when he died, he wished to be given to Thames river at the confluence with Charwelle.'

'That's at the Sanctuary of the Wheel. We can go now; dark days or not, it would be propitious. From there we can pick up a road to Kyronion.'

Before we left, we performed a rite to Nodens, god of travellers, to protect us as we journeyed during the unlucky days, and another rite to the gods of the house to keep the place of the king. Under the direction of Katuaros, the people had built the new house, twice the size of the previous one, in just a few days. The women were still thatching the roof when we hung up Verica's ceremonial sword, shield and helmet with the rest of his regalia. Although they were bent and damaged, we decided to display them as they were and not have them mended. The oaken chest had been rescued and was given to me. I took all the coin to take with me; as to the rest... With due ceremony we took out the skull of Kommios and placed it on a shelf where it would be attended by an eternal lamp. A new chair was being carved. Katuaros said I should leave my boots and, when the house was complete, they would be left on the king's chair to act as a promise to the people that I would return.

I duly left my Roman boots in the new house. As for the skull of Vercingetorix, there was much debate. A few wanted it to share the shelf with Kommios but some were concerned how the Romans might interpret that and recommended we bury it. In the end, we hung it up outside the house with the trophies. It could hide there among the enemies until we had settled under our new overlords.

Among Verica's effects, rescued from his house, was a small marble bust, the head of a young boy that would not have looked out of place in any fine villa in Rome, but here looked incongruous. 'Who made this?' I asked.

'Verica commissioned it at Calleva, where there was a sculptor trained in Rome.'

'Who does it portray? Anyone?' I thought it could be a generic head, perhaps of Ganymede or some young boy-god.

'It's you, Delfos. Meant to be you. Your father loved you more than you know.'

I gave a bitter laugh and left the head behind in the new house.

Verica had possessed about twenty slaves, mostly Durotriges he had taken in various battles for the Isle of Vectis. I offered them their freedom, which some took and left at once for home. Others stayed, much as animals remain in cages when the door is left open. The exotic slaves who could speak neither Roman nor Gaulish, whom Verica had bought from traders, were more difficult to deal with. If you release some animals into the wild, you send them to certain death. In the end I decided to retain them, offered them a wage and the chance to marry and settle in Noviomagos.

One of the freedmen I kept was a harpist from Germania called Draumur, a man of some forty years with long, lank hair braided with thongs and beads. He appeared to be unable to speak Gaulish or Roman, but there again, he didn't respond to any German dialect that I knew, either. He was neither deaf nor dumb, just taciturn; not so much unable as unwilling to speak.

'Do we know anything about him?' I asked Katuaros.

'I've always assumed he's an escaped auxiliary. Probably some cowherd or shepherd who got recruited by the Romans but couldn't bear it.'

'Which tribe?'

'Chatti, I think.'

The name rang a distant bell.

'He's strong and can defend himself well enough, but his real strength is the harp.'

Draumur wore strings of beads round his neck and both wrists (a convenient and comfortable way to carry spare harp strings). His language was gesture and facial expression, sometimes emphasised by an agitated clicking of beads as he tossed his hair back. What I noticed most about him, however, was his affinity with animals and children, as if he could love anything that was not an adult human. He made a quiet fuss of horses and they repaid him with trust and affection.

Before we left, I had a private discussion with the centurion. The latest word from Gaul was that the mutiny was now in full flood.

'Has any help arrived from Rome?'

'Not yet.'

'Do you think it will come?'

'I do. The mutiny will fail.'

'And if it doesn't? What will you do?' I asked and was shocked to hear that plans for withdrawal were already in place, not only for the German cohort but also for any soldier who had been sent in advance to secure Noviomagos, dig dykes or build granaries. If the army turned for home, these men would sail to Gaul on the fleet of corbitas that remained at anchor in the sound.

'And I?'

The centurion said my name had not been mentioned in any plans for retreat. My stomach lurched, as when you step forward to find that the ground isn't where you expect it to be. I recovered my equilibrium and held council with the uncles. 'If the cohort retreats, we could be left very vulnerable,' I told them. 'We may not survive. What then?'

'The gods will be our protection,' they said, putting much faith in the return of the druids.

I went down to the shore with pots of grain as gifts for the mussel children and told them I was about to depart and go north.

'Your ships are not coming?' they asked.

'Oh, yes, they are definitely coming but I don't know when. Will you be my lookouts? As soon as you see them, send word to Noviomagos, yes? And then, little ones, hide a while until the soldiers have passed through.'

Katuaros and his band of warriors were waiting for me at the western gate, singing a travelling song and drinking ale to strengthen their spirits for the journey. When everyone had mounted, Katuaros led the way out of Noviomagos, riding bareback on his dappled crossbreed. Draumur rode on Scipio, the only person I would trust my horse with, and Mandred and I followed in the chariot.

Thus I left behind the Roman cohort to travel alone with three companions — Katuaros my foster brother, Mandred my slave and Draumur my freedman — and the half-dozen warriors who made up Katuaros's fianna. It seemed to me best to make ripples, not waves, as I moved through Britain. But as we set off, I felt deep fear, not so much of what we were to face, but of what might be happening, or not happening, behind us. If the Romans did not come, I was riding into a hostile land, and there would be no way back.

23

TO CALLEVA

We went first over the hills to the Ford of the Alders, the native home of Katuaros. Once three fortified duns close together, now it was a settlement in a river valley between three hills. It had been my grandfather Kommios who had overcome the local rivalries to create a unified oppidum that traded with foreign merchants. It flourished and would have continued to do so but for the return to the old ways after the death of Cymbelinus. On the instruction of Katuaros, the defences on the hills were being restored. Thus far the Alders tribe had fought off several Catuvellauni raiding parties but were not confident they could withstand a concerted attack, should Caratacos decide to make one. With all the efforts being directed towards defence, the arable fields had been neglected and we had brought two wagon-loads of grain for the starving people. The elders gave Katuaros a hard time, saying his duty was to be with them, not with his foster father's people. He looked wretched under their onslaught of criticism.

'You know how I have ridden back and forth this past year. With Verica in exile, the Atrebates were in even more peril than you. If they fell, your destruction was certain.'

'But Verica is back now,' they said.

Katuaros glanced at me and I assented with a nod.

'Verica is dead,' he said. There was a rustle of shock. 'We did not call it. This is his son, Togidubnos, and together we are taking Verica's remains to Thames river.'

'After that, you will come home,' they told him.

'After that, I will accompany Togidubnos on his journey to Venonis. With the Romans on their way, you will have nothing to fear from the Catuvellauni; even now they will be thoroughly distracted and not wondering how many foals or calves you have.'

The elders agreed grudgingly. They told us that, even during the dark half of the moon, the tracks had been busy. Warriors, they said, were running about like disturbed ants. 'First we hear that the Romans are coming to the south; then that they have mutinied; then that they have not; then that they are going back to Rome. The fighting men are going hither and thither but mostly they are going home, tired of chasing about when there is so much to do on the land.'

We asked them where Caratacos was but they did not know. Perhaps Calleva. Perhaps not. 'With his brother, Togodumnos, at Verlamio,' was the general belief.

To sweeten the atmosphere, I had Draumur play his harp at the fire and his audience was quickly mellowed. He was as good as a bard, they said afterwards but I told them that, so far as I knew, he was self-taught.

We continued our journey after new moon, travelling more easily now that we knew that the lines of warriors we saw on ridges were heading for home, not looking for us. The track to Calleva went across open country in this green land of ample bosom, past fields being belatedly ploughed for a spring sowing, paddocks where pregnant mares cropped hay from mangers, pens where lambs gambolled, steads where geese raised fluffy goslings under the low eaves of deep-thatches. Returning fighters were shape-shifting into farmers again, farmers who did not care if we were Atrebates but raised their hands in the brief greeting that is the hospitality of the road. We were few; we posed no threat; they called upon the local gods to bless us and we passed safely on.

After one day travelling through dense forest, we came out on shaggy pasture where we camped for the night in a small beech wood. We decided not to use a fire even though the air was chill and Katuaros threw me an old mantle to wrap myself in. The feel of the wool, its smell of sheep grease and herbs worked their magic and I slept as soundly as I had when a child in my mother's arms. It was nine days after equinox and we'd had no word at all from or about the Romans. It was tempting to forget about them, and about the Catuvellauni, and live like a child under the wing of the Mother. After a breakfast of cheese and a salad of dandelion, sorrel and wild mustard, I walked into the woods, following the sound of water: a babbling, gurgling brook somewhere close by. Finding it at last in a ditch beyond an earthen bank, I knelt and dipped my head to drink. Mandred found me there later, 'just staring into the water as if you had been turned to stone.' I was running my hand through the lush weeds of the brook with their lucent greens, saying, 'It's so alive.'

'Are you in the Otherworld?' he asked gently.

'Where does one stop and the other begin?'

'Some places are thin.'

'I'm beginning to think all Britain is "thin" as you call it.'

'There are gates everywhere. This may be one of them, although no image of a god has been placed here to make this a formal shrine.' He took from the pouch he carried on my behalf one of the votive images I'd inherited from Verica, a small silver torc the size of a thumb ring.

'Offer it to the water,' he said. As I did so, Mandred made a brief invocation of gratitude to what my father would have called 'living water', this elemental being who jumped and splashed over its bed of stones. It seemed Mandred was a master of spontaneous prayer.

'There is about you, my friend,' I said, 'something which is becoming increasingly pronounced and noticeable now that we are home.'

'Britishness,' he replied, creating clouds of garlicky, lemony scents as he limped away over the sward. 'It seems strange to you, that's all. You'd forgotten.'

Not wholly forgotten. We continued on our way, crossing this lush land of a thousand hues all called 'green', where the shadows of clouds run over the flanks of the hills like dark spirit horses.

As we crossed the downs, I looked to the horizon and began to recognize certain bumps and notches, some natural, some put there deliberately for the sake of way-finding, all familiar and part of my hefting. Memories of my birthplace rose up like will o' the wisp: the cry of a friend imitating an owl, my first dog, Bello, my mother sighing with frustration when she had to unpick a few rows on the loom. The shape and smell of the autumn leaves my grandmother laid out for me to name. The easy ones: oak, holly, ash; the more difficult ones: beech, birch, hornbeam, alder and elder. Windows in my memory were being flung open by random sounds and smells. The sun was mounting the sky when the oppidum of Calleva came into view in the distance, a low hill to the east just visible above the trees where the smoke of innumerable huts coiled languidly in the still air. Calleva, my home, my world. Calleva, now the capital of Caratacos. There was no sign of any Catuvellauni warriors, not even look-outs. Was that complacency on their part, or absence?

We skirted the woods, keeping the trees between us and the oppidum. My woods, called Willow Woods to distinguish them from Broom Woods and Ash Grove. There was the heath, my heath, and East End Brook. Names so prosaic, so poetic. High field, Low field, Aunty's stile; names to make boys snigger: Windy Bottom, Pissing Puddle and the Paps. The names of home. Presumably Italy has them, too, but in Rome you are cut off from them. Certainly when I arrived there I found neither the opportunity nor the desire to make a den next to a stream and name it Nixie Hollow. But here it was, my little refuge close to the track, just as I'd left it. Which is to say, just as I'd found it in the first place.

Now the memories were rising up like startled ducks, of a carefree boyhood spent as much a local urchin as a king's son, where my constant companion was a dog and my friends were as likely to be an elm or a linden tree as another boy, where I knew the birds and their song, could whistle at a robin and get a reply. I would loiter at the forge with the smiths hammering iron, or the bronze-caster pouring molten metals into clay moulds — old Gofannon making me a horse in bronze based on the Albios Horse when I was just four.

Why so miserable, lad?

I want a horse.

A boy like you should have a horse. Here, watch me make you one out of fire and metal.

I would sit with the women in the weaving hut, listening to their stories and songs, the tales of our ancestors as much a part of the cloth as the wool. Bello and I would help a local farmer bring in sheep for shearing or herd his geese. A lonely child? Perhaps, until Katuaros arrived. I was certainly a free child who had escaped his half-brothers or his father for a morning. The world of leaves and wool, earth and fungi, streams and flowers, was my world, my refuge. Everyone in the oppidum colluded, shielding me from the King's bodyguard when they were sent out to find me. The dairymaids, the bee-keepers, the market stall holders, the goose-girls, the tanners, potters and basket-weavers, all knew the boy called Delfos and hid him from those calling for Togidubnos.

When Katuaros arrived, he shared my life in the woods, and I shared his life of training in arms, learning to ride and to steer a chariot over rough terrain, bending my knees at each bounce so that nothing jarred. It was exhilarating, I do not deny it. If I had avoided my half-brothers it was not because they were warriors but because they were only warriors. I did not share their love of leisure after the fight, their satisfaction with a night of drinking, their lusts and appetites. It all seemed so much less than could be had. Katuaros was more. He came with me to sit with the druids, who were still with us then and whose company I preferred, enjoying the far horizons of their thoughts, the grand elevation. For them, nature was wealth; for the warriors the only enrichment was stolen goods, raided horses, weapons torn from a dead man, his scalp. Katuaros claimed he was as interested in the cosmos as I was, but perhaps he was only trying to be.

According to Mandred, as we came within the scent of Calleva I suddenly said *Ithaca!* as if I had come home. I halted our party with a raised hand and told my companions, 'I'm going to go home like Odysseus.' Only Mandred understood what I was talking about.

'Who's O'Dissus?' asked a startled Katuaros.

'He was a hero of Troy who was away for twenty years,' I explained as I made a hooded wrap out of the mantle. 'When he finally got home, he approached like a beggar. Only his dog recognized him.' I sighed. Bello had died in my absence and had been put into the burial place of dogs we had at Calleva. His pitiful whining and furious yaps as I'd left had almost undone me.

Katuaros stared at me wildly. 'Are you mad?'

'We need to find out where Caratacos is.'

'Then I will come with you.'

'No point in both of us getting slaughtered,' I said, removing my sandals. Bidding him and the others to wait for me concealed in the woods, I mussed up my hair with handfuls of forest litter, dirtied my face, scratched myself with briar. Then I walked through the trees on an old, familiar track and into Calleva by the open western gate, to be caught up like a leaf in a whirlwind of memories and the madness of loss. If I stumbled along, wildly staring about and talking to myself, it wasn't all an act.

No dog ran to me in greeting but plenty yapped at this stranger. I crossed the oppidum on the main dirt road, bordered by the wattle fences of the various compounds. There were taverns and shops, forges and carpentry sheds, all of them occupied by my own people. For only the warriors and the king's retinue had escaped south with Verica; the rest had stayed and had taken on the new masters like a new mantle, wriggling inside it until they were used to it, and then carrying on as before. I recognized many of them; none recognized me, nor took any notice. Just an itinerant passing through. I stopped to speak to anyone willing to talk to a madman, which were few, but I learnt that Caratacos was indeed at Verlamio with his brother — 'keeping a foot in the east and a foot in the south' — ready to spring whichever way he needed to.

'Where are you headed?' one of them asked.

'East. I'm going to see the Romans land.'

'We've heard they're not coming.'

'It's true,' I said. 'They are not coming, but if they are coming, they will land in the east.' And out of the east gate I passed, knowing I was leaving behind a strong and, I hoped, contagious rumour of a warning by a mad beggar of imminent invasion.

24

AT CUMA'S HILL

Thames river snakes across the country in broad meanders from its source in the west to the sea in the east. The Catuvellauni controlled the beech-woods of the hill country north of the river and the Atrebates controlled the rolling chalk downs on the south, or had done so until we lost Calleva.

We came to Thames river at the foot of an old Atrebatic dun, abandoned now. A small tribe of river people lived in huts on higher ground but spent their days amongst the piles and shambles of raised sheds where they built boats. Leaving the fianna to take the horses upstream on a track across hills, we hired a broad, shallow boat with six oarsmen and a pilot who could navigate tricky currents, changes of level and the drowned forests of sodden yews which catch the oars of the unwary and suck their boats down into the Otherworld.

At a great loop in the river was an imposing fortified dun of the Catuvellauni on the far bank, on our side a handsome pair of matching hills standing proud and curvaceous in the river plain. The place was known to its inhabitants as Sino Dun but the Catuvellauni called it 'Old Mother's Buttocks'. One hill was a place of temples and shrines with a dark and mighty grove of yews; the other was the camp of the Ravens, once governed by us, now by Catuvellauni. They were a taciturn tribe, blessed with the habit of asking no questions of those who passed through or lodged with them. They could tell by our dialect which side of the river we were from (their side) and said nothing of it.

Reunited there with the fianna, we discussed the next day's journey. 'Avoid the river. Avoid the confluence,' a Raven uncle said. 'Flooded. And avoid the Sanctuary of the Wheel. Broken. Derelict. Not a healthy place. Go to Cuma and make your offering from the south bank of Tamessa.' Cuma's hill, the northern-most settlement of the Belgic territory, was still in our possession. 'Go across country,' the uncle said, but I was determined to make the approach by river. On one hand it was useful to get views of the north bank and see what activity there was in the Catuvellauni camps; on the other... There was something deep within me, a memory of a story perhaps, or lines from a song, which told me that the proper approach to the Sanctuary of the Wheel is to go upstream on Thames river. I sent the fianna off with the horses again on an arduous journey over wooded hills and vales, and we got back into the boat.

The water stretched across the land north and south, but the pilot could tell by the currents where the river ran amidst the flood and used a long pole to establish depth. By the end of a day navigating the broad loopings of Thames river, we came to a dark place where the water was shadowed by overhanging trees. Just as I noticed another river joining ours, the pilot pointed at the turbulence where the waters were greeting each other. 'There!' he said. 'The union of the goddesses, Tamessa and Charwelle.' To the right, still-naked alders standing in the water marked Charwelle's course, to the left, willows in that gentle haze of colour which is bud-break marked the course of Thames. Throughout the trees votive images hung and wooden carvings sat in branches like crows, sanctifying the place of confluence, not just of rivers, but of worlds. Here was the place Verica had stipulated for his remains to be offered to the gods. On the overgrown bank of the land that the two rivers embraced I thought I could discern the ancient entry into the Sanctuary.

'I'm not landing there,' said the pilot. 'It's bad luck. Do as you were advised and go to Cuma's hill, there to make sacrifice, purify yourselves, do everything you can to propitiate the gods.' He kept his eyes on the water. 'I don't know who you are or what you want, but since we have come within sight of this place, my blood runs cold to look at you. Perform the proper rituals or you will be cast out.' He reached down into the river, took some water and splashed it on his face as a protection. 'Go to Cuma. Perform your rite from the south bank. Do not enter the Sanctuary,' he said. 'Empty now these twenty years, it is the realm of those spirits who can alter the fate of a man, spirits over which even the gods have no power.'

'There is nothing over which the gods have no power.'

'Oh, believe me, there is.'

Katuaros, twitching like the cat's whiskers, agreed and ordered the pilot to continue upstream. 'Let's get back into the light, man,' he said.

'Such as it is at this hour,' grumbled the pilot. His men began rowing again. Coming out of the overhang of trees we entered into clear land and the last hour of daylight. To our left the flood and out of it rising the hill of Cuma; to our right, the flood and out of it rising that spur of land on which is the Sanctuary of the Wheel.

Gelder and Ten Horns were waiting for us with the chariot and horses at Cuma's jetty.

'Am I glad to see you,' said Katuaros, readying himself to jump out of the boat to join them, but something darting past like sling shot caused him to lose his footing. He slammed against the jetty with a mighty crack and fell awkwardly into the green water. I shed all my loose clothes and jumped in after him but at once something tangled round my legs and tried to pull me under. I thrashed about, too busy saving myself to help Katuaros, and it was Ten Horns who dragged him out. The pilot rammed his pole into the water beside me; I caught hold of it and pulled myself back on to the boat with his help.

'What was pulling you under?' he asked.

I had no idea. 'If it was weeds, they have a will of their own and wanted me dead.'

The pilot shuddered.

Katuaros kneeling on the shore was passing in and out of consciousness and could neither stand, walk nor ride. We sat him on the back of the chariot. 'Where's my mantle?' he moaned, as if it were dearer to him than his life. 'Is it alright?' One of the oarsmen fished it out of the river and we assured him it would be fine once it was dry. Meanwhile I gave him mine and noticed the strange shape of his back as I draped it over his shoulders. I invited the pilot and his crew to stop overnight but he said he'd rather camp downstream at Sino Dun, for this place, he said, was cursed.

At the top of the hill, old men, women and children were on the ramparts, watching the sun set as they waited for us. Watching the sun set... When this camp had first been established, it had been aligned to the sun's rising. The Cuma people had looked out over the vale, its two rivers embracing the Sanctuary, guardians of the place. Now they had their backs to it. The eastern gate had been closed off, the ramparts heightened. They faced west.

'Ai, ai, ai!' they cried, as we came out of the darkness and into the light of the flaring torches that illuminated the gate. They hurried down to greet the chief of their federation, who was groaning with pain. A branch of the Morini tribe of Belgica, they spoke in an old dialect that was closer to Draumur's German than to my Gallic. From what I could gather, however, they had that day sent their fighting men to join Caratacos at Verlamio.

Katuaros was livid. 'Without my permission?' What should have been a thunderous protest came out like a whimper.

'If we didn't send them, he'd have come and got them, and left none of the rest of us alive.'

'Which way did they go?'

'East. The Romans are landing in the east.'

I exchanged a glance with Katuaros who managed a wan smile.

'We were told to expect them in the south but now suddenly it's the east.'

'And where are they at this moment, the Romans?'

No one knew. 'At sea?'

'Oh, who isn't?' Katuaros tried to hide his agony as he was set down and his men helped him stand. 'I'm alright, I'm alright,' he said, but clearly he wasn't. I could see by the light of kilns that one of his shoulder blades was standing out at right angles to his back. 'I've just taken a fall. Into the river.'

'You?'

'Hard to believe, I know. I was getting out of the boat and something flew into my face.'

'A kingfisher,' I said.

'So you think.'

I don't know how he walked but he seemed to be all stitched up with the pretence of nothing being much wrong. We were taken to the communal hearth at the centre of the dun to be given a change of clothes. One of the elders took my mantle off Katuaros, held it up to look at it by the light of the fire and demanded to know why he was wearing 'this Atrebatic filth.' I was about to claim it as mine, but Katuaros stilled me with a fierce glance of warning.

'You are part of the Atrebatic federation,' he reminded the elders of Cuma. 'What, would you rather be Catuvellauni?'

'We are Morini. We are Belgae, like you. We are happy to be governed by the chief of the Ford of the Alders. But we renounce the Atrebates and their crooked king.'

'Who is now dead,' Katuaros told them, 'so be careful of what you say.'

I expected him to tell the people of our purpose but he kept quiet, said nothing about the yew bucket, and nothing about me, other than that we had come to make an offering at the confluence, but the chief of the elders was sharp-witted, saw the Alders mantle laid out by a kiln and realised that the mantle Katuaros was wearing, this piece of 'Atrebatic filth', must be mine. He looked to me as he asked Katuaros, 'Who is this, your companion? Your kinsman?'

'My foster brother, Delfos.'

'There is no point,' the chief said to him, 'in your hiding this man's identity. We know who he is. The wind sighs and the leaves tremble. We know who, we know what he is. The lambs bleat and the dogs moan.'

'Togidubnos,' I confessed, 'Togidubnos ap Verica.' But that wasn't who they recognized. What they saw was the fruit of the rape that had destroyed their sanctuary and they rustled like trees before a storm. Katuaros distracted them by shouting out in pain. 'Get me help!' he cried. 'Get your medicine woman!' It worked, deflecting their attention.

There was no medicine woman in the tribe but a young midwife, a widow-woman who knew her herbs, examined Katuaros's shoulder. Having moved his arms until he shouted out, cursed her for a witch and called on Cuma to strike her down, she bade him sit on a log and gave him a piece of willow bark to chew on. Knowing what was to come, Katuaros tried to maintain his dignity while beads of cold sweat formed on his brow. The woman went round behind him and, with the grip of a wrestler, hooked one arm round his neck and the other under his armpit and with one expert yank put his shoulder back in its right place. The loud click of bone was accompanied by a sob from the great warrior.

The woman stood up and rearranged her mantle of yarrow-green and burdock-yellow. 'Out of joint like a slipped axel,' she announced. 'All well now, but he will need to rest for at least a moon.'

'I don't have a moon.' Katuaros stood up resolutely, turned the colour of an oyster and sat down again. A moment later he was vomiting. Mouse Ears and Cow Crippler helped him into the woman's deep-thatch where she cut down bunches of dried comfrey and horsetail from the rafters to make poultices. The elders commanded me to go with him, saying that they wanted to deliberate my fate amongst themselves. I stood up. 'I am the chief of your chief,' I said in resounding tones, a great utterance of authority. Like pesky bullocks being challenged by a man, most of them stepped back, but one came forward.

'You are the son of Verica and Innogen,' the chief of the elders said. 'You are the Fruit of the Sin. There must be atonement.'

'And there will be,' I said, 'but it is for the gods to command it, not you.'

I went inside the midwife's house. Midwife she might be, but she had no husband and no children of her own. Nevertheless her house was full of little ones who called her mother, neighbours' children who peeped out from under bedding to see the strangers. Against the wall of the house was a tanned hide stretched taut across a frame on which something had been drawn with a burnt stick. I asked what it was and one young lad told me it was a picture of the Mother. This did not satisfy me: it was just some irregular lines meeting in a V with a spot in the middle. Katuaros looked sideways without moving his head. 'It's the Sanctuary,' he said.

'Hush!' said the midwife. 'Children! Go to your own hearths! Now!'

'But it is,' Katuaros insisted.

'We don't speak of it these days, not since the Sin. I found that old hide and thought I'd stretch it for a new scraping, get it clean for new use, that's all.'

'Do you know what form my atonement should take?' I asked her.

She was bold enough to look me in the eye and say that, for being the fruit of that particular sin, the only possible atonement must be my own sacrifice. 'By fire and by water,' she announced.

Katuaros intervened. 'Some are born kind, some cruel. This man is the most gentle I have ever met. He carries no arms, bears no ill will, is kind and generous. Ask his slave. If the people of Cuma were to sacrifice him, the gods would be so full of wrath that the dun and all who live here would be destroyed. Go and tell that to the elders, to aid their deliberations.'

He watched her leave. 'Spirited woman,' he said, appreciatively. 'Good hips.' He turned back to the map. 'It shows the confluence, the two rivers meeting. And there, the navel. The Wheel… They say it is the centre of Britain, or used to be.'

The omphalos. The navel of the nation. 'It moved to Venonis?' I asked.

'No, no. There are many centres. This one died. After Verica's sacrilege the ring of stones they had restored and maintained were thrown to the ground, who knows by what agency. Some say the druids did it, others… Well. It was destroyed. The Pole of the Nation,' he said, pointing to a dot in the circle on the hide map. 'The Pole of Britain. They say that the fixed star beams upon the land at that point. It is the axis of the world. Or was…'

As the gravity of Verica's act of lust became ever clearer, I was becoming breathless. The omphalos. Not the public one, which is at Venonis, where all the tribes gather for administration. No, the secret one, the hidden one, the true one. I sat down to contemplate the map, wondering how there could be so many centres in the world. What are they centres of? 'What is that line of dots close to the Wheel?'

Katuaros did not reply.

'The tombs of the ancestors,' said the midwife, returning. 'A line of barrows.'

'Enough!' said Katuaros. 'We do not speak of them.'

'The elders want to see you,' she told me.

I went back out to the communal fire that was sending sparks up into the night. At the far reaches of the dun, close to the palisades, the pottery kilns glowed in the dark and the penned cattle were lowing. Katuaros joined me, eager to hear what the verdict was.

'In one moon it will be Beltane,' the chief of the elders told me. 'Once that would have been celebrated in the Sanctuary with giant fires but now we have to make the long drove to the Hill of the Albios Horse.' He took from the fire some glowing sticks and smudged the air with them, flicking their sparks into the darkness. 'The law says there is only one way for you to atone and that is sacrifice. But you are the chief of our chief, and it is not for us to say what form that sacrifice will take. To find out, you must enter the Sanctuary.'

'Every man who tries to do that has been repelled,' said Katuaros.

'He will not be repelled. He was born of the Wheel's destruction. The Wheel may choose to destroy him, but he will not be repelled. Do you have the mettle to undertake this ordeal?' he asked me.

I said that I had, that I would lay myself down before the will of the gods if it would purge me of the sins of my father.

Katuaros grew irritable. 'Listen,' he said. 'The times are perilous and we need every good man. Caratacos has passed beyond the bounds of what is fit; he is out of control; the people are starving. The Romans are on their way to put things right again and Togidubnos has come in advance to persuade everyone not to resist.'

The chief, with his eyes closed, was rocking back and forth on his heels. 'The Romans will cause as much harm as Caratacos, perhaps more. You don't burn the forest to rid the tree of canker.'

'I assure you,' I said, 'they will not. I know the Princeps, I know the generals. They are self-interested, yes, of course, but it is not in their interest for Britain to suffer. Prosperity, that is what is in their interest, and the Britons will take their due share of it.'

'Listen to him,' said Katuaros, 'and trust him.'

The chief grunted and opened his eyes a little. 'Perform what the gods ask of you,' he told me, 'and we shall trust you with our lives.'

'But you will not have the company of Katuaros,' said the midwife firmly. 'He needs to rest.'

'I will take the risk,' I said.

'But will you risk your soul?' the chief asked.

'Risk my soul? What is there to be frightened of? A dragon? A ghost? Some other monster out of the cauldron of stories?'

'Spirits of the dead?' Mandred asked.

They gazed at him, this slave who dared to speak, and a Durotrigan at that, but they condescended to answer him. 'Spirits of the place. Unchecked now in their powers, and furious with men.'

'Tell the truth,' said Katuaros, but the elders seemed unable to form the word on their lips.

'It's Shee,' said Katuaros, and the name soughed in the circle squatting round the fire. The sound of a menacing whisper or a cold draught, the sound of water hitting flame. *Sheeeeeee*. The pale ones who can suck the substance out of a human soul, turn it into a cobweb of gossamer threads. I remembered the face my grandmother used to pull, as if her teeth were tugging on raw meat, when she described Shee gorging themselves on human souls. 'They really are here?' I asked uncertainly.

'Of course, they have always been here. Barrow wights.' The chief of the tribe waved his feathered staff at me and challenged me to meet my fate. 'If you truly wish to make amends on behalf of your father, the Shee may allow it. Who can tell? They are capricious and unpredictable. But if it is your fate, then you must go to meet it.'

I remembered what Seneca had taught me, that Fate will strike you ten times harder if you try to avoid her. Katuaros, who was clearly enjoying the attentions of the handsome midwife, pretended to be reluctant to have to stay behind. 'But at least I can keep watch, send a message if needs be,' he said.

'Do you want to stay with him?' I asked the fianna. To a man they did.

'Do you want to stay?' I asked Mandred.

'Of course!' he said. 'But I'll come with you.'

I turned to Draumur. He was chewing on a wisp of his own hair and staring at me crossly as if insulted even to be asked. I nodded in gratitude and felt peculiarly safe to be going to the Sanctuary with him and Mandred as my only companions.

25

THE SANCTUARY OF THE WHEEL

We rowed a boat across Thames river, from the jetty to some timber planks of an ancient causeway dark with age. Between the river and the raised spur of land that was the Sanctuary lies a vast and flooded pasture occupied by wild horses and water birds. The bluebell sky arched over the lime green pasture, sunlight glinting on a multitude of puddles, ponds and small lakes being left as the flood waters receded. Wild horses and geese. Swans throbbing across the sky, necks outstretched. The green and the blue. No, not the green and the blue but *that* green and *that* blue. I felt a stab of recognition that was not of the mind, as if the heart were a small, closed space but, once its door was forced open, a summerland of green meadows and blue sky. This was my place. The place of my soul. They say souls choose the moment and place of their conception. Had I inspired Verica to snatch Innogen? Was I, then, the cause of the Sanctuary's abandonment, its destruction, its desolation? It was a momentary but incandescent revelation of grief, loss, and guilt.

We climbed the gentle rise of land to where we had an uninterrupted view across the broad vale to the horizon in all directions. The track led us to a small square temple of which nothing remained but its walls made of planks; nothing inside but tidy dumps of swan droppings and horse dung amongst last year's dead thistles. As if in a dream, however, I could see the temple divided into several rooms, one of them full of girls studying medicine and, teaching them, Innogen. I fell down deep into the well of understanding and watched, as if I were seeing it happen in the mirror-waters, the Atrebates sweep down on this sacred land that belonged to everyone and to no one. Innogen coming out of the teaching temple to challenge them. Their king lassoing her like a horse and dragging her along the ground, into the Wheel, to rid her of her pride. And then the mounting, taking her from behind like a horse. Sacrilege of the worst kind: an offence to all the gods. An offence to Ana, the Mother, herself.

The Wheel itself was further on, close to a crossing of tracks. Nothing could be seen of it but a high bank of earth and two standing portal stones embedded in each side of an entrance. The Sanctuary of the Wheel was a place that had been put in my heart by my mother; a place I had grown up knowing about; a place which, in my imagination, was a thriving land of spirits, gods and wise men, a portal to Annwn. I was shocked by the emptiness of it.

At the cross-way, Draumur stood with his back to the sun and arms outstretched. He pronounced the line as north-south, being crossed by the east-west track we had come on. He was impressed by the simplicity of the alignment and asked to go into the Wheel but I said we should make the offering first. We followed the track running south, straight to the landing place at the confluence where there was a shrine to Tamessa and Chara. 'Offer me to the Thames where the two rivers meet.' That had been Verica's wish. I stepped on to the jetty. Suddenly a wind blew up, so brutal that I fell to my knees, seeing double. I struggled to concentrate as I tried to offer my father's ashes. Unable to stand, and robbing the occasion of all dignity, I pushed rather than lowered the bucket into the river, saying a prayer to both goddesses as I did so. It bobbed and floated but would not sink, so I took it out. The winds abated and a gloomy darkness came down in which the waters shone like silver. Leaning out to gaze on the water's surface I looked into my own reflection, but my face was changing, becoming older, more feminine. Her hair was longer, thicker, fairer than mine, but the line of her jaw much the same. She mirrored me.

'Mother!'

'My son.'

That's what I saw: Innogen. Soft bare arms, golden arm rings, just as I remembered. Her round, open face and loving eyes. Innogen.

'I have been calling and calling you home,' she said. 'Why did you tarry?'

'Forgive me.'

'Did you not hear me in Delphi? There I spoke through Pythia. At Eleusis I spoke through Demeter. And yet you tarried, fond as you are of your Roman life.'

'Forgive me. It was cowardice.'

'It took your father to bring you home! Shame upon you!'

I hung my head. 'I do not understand what the Oracle said. How can I see you and Verica married? You are both gone from this world into the next. Where does your body lie, Mother?'

'Truly royal, I am barrow-buried — or I should be — in my Dobunnic homeland, on the rim of the Cauldron. Go there. See the job done.'

I promised her that I would. 'What did the Oracle mean?' I asked.

'Why do you consort with the Romans?'

'They offer peace.'

'The peace of the body, an easy life of indulgence. Are you prepared to murder your soul for it?'

I swayed under the impact of her words.

'The fate of Britain lies with you,' she said. 'Favour neither side. Marry them. Make something new.'

The vision of her turned into rippling water. But I could still hear her. 'Take his accursed ash to the Wheel,' she said.

As we turned from the confluence, I noticed that the alders were in leaf yet when we had approached the day before by boat, they only had catkins. What magic was this? The moment I set my foot on the track back to the Wheel, time tipped like snow sliding off a deep-thatch; the land also tipped: the horizon was slanting, or was it me?

'Cuma, Tamessa, Chara,' Mandred chanted softly, calling on gods of hill and river. 'Help us.'

The closer we came to the Wheel, the harder it got to move. A sharp easterly whipped our faces and snatched our breath. The waters on the pasture receded more swiftly than is possible, as if they were pouring down hidden cracks and gullies, leaving behind only puddles caught by dips in the land. It was as if the enormity of my father's crime had tipped reality sideways. And that's as much as I remember in the way a sane man remembers anything. I walked in the Sanctuary trying to get to the Wheel and lost touch with what I've always believed to be reality. Looking into puddles was to see clouds flowing over agitated mirrors. In one I saw a horse staring back at me; in another a small group of geese doubled, joined to their reflections at their webbed feet. Upper goose and lower goose. Was I looking into Annwn, the Otherworld, or was I looking out of it? That cutting wind blew and the sky flashed light and dark in rapid alternation, and in the dark part the moon moved from full to last quarter. Mandred fell to his knees retching. 'I am thirsty,' he said. 'And hungry, so hungry.' Somehow, somewhere, he had lost his red neckerchief and the lump stood out like a goitre. Draumur had gone off alone to play his harp to the long-maned horses. Once we heard a beautiful voice singing which we simultaneously knew to be Draumur and yet not Draumur, for our harpist was a man of few words and none of them sung.

Repelled by the Wheel, we went to the square temple to get out of the wind. Hanging from a thorn bush was the red neckerchief, which Mandred shook clean and put back on. Out of the wind, the passing of time slowed to something close to normal. We could still hear Draumur playing one of those lengthy songs he made up in the moment, the dance of his fingers over the strings and the click of beads.

'Who is he?' Mandred asked me.

'I know so little. Katuaros thinks he's a deserter from the Roman army. I presume there has been tragedy in his life.'

Draumur's harp seemed to calm the wind. The fire in his eyes, I thought as I fell asleep, is the light of a burning forest. Mandred woke me the following morning to breakfast on a salad of fat hen and mint he had picked. 'And this...' he held out a bowl full of cold stew he'd found at the door to the temple.

'I seem to remember seeing this yesterday,' I said. 'I think it was yesterday.'

Mandred agreed it was familiar. 'Do we dare eat it? No fox or bird has bothered with it. Perhaps...'

'Give it here,' I said, too hungry to worry about enchanted food. 'Has the wind dropped?'

He said it had. He reached out and tugged my beard. I frowned, realising groggily that I'd been watching Mandred's face grow increasingly hairy. 'What magic is this? Have we been here a year and a day?'

We left the temple to find that we still could not make our way to the Wheel, as if our feet had been nailed to the ground. 'It's our guilt that stays us,' I said.

Mandred looked at me with haunted eyes. 'Whose guilt?'

'Mine.'

'Guilt may be atoned,' said a voice beside me. I turned, startled, and found myself staring into sadness. It had the form of an old man with long hair, just as you would expect a druid to look. He said he had remained here when the druids left. 'It is my duty to look after the birds and the horses.'

Mandred looked at me askance but I ignored him.

'What is your name?' the old druid asked.

'Delfos. A name given to me by my mother, Innogen of the Dobunni, who thought my paternal name unmusical.'

A glance of a smile on the stern druid face. 'She was right, as always.'

'You knew her?'

'She taught here for a while, before your father dragged her off to be his queen. And I mean dragged.' He looked at me balefully. 'That act of desecration put the land out of balance. That is why you cannot find your feet. The land sickens with your presence, wishes to disgorge you, O son of Verica.'

'Please,' I cried. 'Tell me how to make it right!'

Mandred tried to pull me away. 'It's Shee,' he breathed. 'You're having a Shee dream. You're talking to no one.'

The Shee... I stared at the old druid and could tell by his smile that druid he was not.

'I wish to enter the Wheel but I am prevented,' I said. 'Tell me what is there.'

'The great Pole of the Nation lies in pieces on the ground.'

'Nation or nations?'

'Set up before there were tribes.'

'Before there were men?'

'No, before there were tribes, when all people of Britain and the Isles were one people. The festivals are a vestige. Now you treat them as horse markets; once they were the mingling of families, renewing old ties, making new ones. The Pole, made of an oak thousands of years old when it died, was carved with two dragons, one coming up from the earth, one coming down from the sky, to meet in a snarling knot.'

'Representing good and evil?"

'Good and evil, no. There is no such division of things. It is all to do with balance. They hold each other in check but when that changes... This is the place which holds the balance of the nation, or nations as you would have it now. The balance is always being lost and restored. When your forefathers came, they overwhelmed the nation and, with their cantankerous cattle-raiding and assaults on rival tribes, put everything out of kilter. Balance was restored by the druids. Then your father desecrated the place, upset it again, fatally weakened his own tribe and allowed for the ascendency of Caratacos.'

'Must I kill him?' I asked dubiously. 'Must I kill Caratacos?'

'He must be stopped, but not by death at your hand. You are a man of peace: that requires more strength than being a man of war.' He ran a sharp finger down my spine so that I involuntarily straightened. 'Remember it. Never react to his provocations. You are stronger than he is.'

I looked over to the ditch and bank of the great Wheel. 'I wish to make things right, restore this place once again. Is this our Delphi?'

'It was greater than Delphi once. Here they took the offerings of kings and did not hoard them in priestly treasuries but adorned the gods with them, buried the wealth in the sacred earth, placed it in the sacred water. True sacrifice.'

'What can I do to make things right?'

'Listen and obey the spirits of place, the genii. Here they ask only to remain hidden.'

I looked at him astonished. 'Are you not that? A spirit of the place? I thought that's what the Shee were.'

'We favour certain spots but we are not bound to place, not like the dryads, the nixies, the hooded spirits and the rest.'

'What is your purpose?'

He laughed. 'Our purpose? What is yours, human?'

I saw his point and laughed with him, but he stopped abruptly and said, despite all appearances, mankind does have purpose, which is to serve the gods. As for the Shee: 'We are disruptors. We are the feeling of unease that keeps you on your guard; the doubt that gnaws at belief; the magic that does not obey your natural law. We are your dreams and your groundless fears, the growl in the night, the groaning in the roof timbers.'

'Did you bring down Verica's house?'

He just shrugged as if to say, Why not?

'Was it you, running through Noviomagos, looking like my mother dishevelled and starving?'

'That was her ghost.'

'Did she bring the house down? Did she kill Verica?'

He shrugged again. 'We heard that, against all the laws, he killed himself.'

I looked about, at rooks in the elms and gulls wheeling in the sky above, and shivered, for here, being revealed to me, was the thriving land of spirits I had imagined. We think there is a nymph here at the well, a dryad there in the tree, that every flower has its spirit but we humans are lumbering beasts in a world filled with moving, breathing Spirit. One Spirit in countless forms. Some forms rooted; some walking; some swimming; some flying. And we men rolling about like seals asleep underwater, at the mercy of tides.

'The Sanctuary of the Wheel needs to be kept hidden for now,' he said. 'When the druids left, we took over, but our powers are not great. All we can do is to keep men away through fear. But here you are...'

'I am not afraid of you,' I said. 'I have drunk the blood of boar.'

'And you have survived the vision of Persephone.'

Now I knew he was supernatural, for this was a fact of my initiation at Eleusis I had shared with no one.

'You have no cause to fear us, Togidubnos,' he said. 'It is we who need the help, your help.'

I laughed at this. 'How can I possibly be of service to your ancient race?'

'You already are, keeping this Sanctuary hidden from the Romans.'

'It was Verica who did that, at the planning meetings in Rome. He said it was just bog, best avoided.'

'Continue that work. Confound and confuse them, for they will destroy us.'

'How? Can the Shee be pierced by a sword? Killed by a stone?'

'The Great Spirit provides enough for all, but the Romans are rapacious and with greed comes poverty. They will use the land. Use it. They will enslave the Mother to satisfy their desires. They will poison our waters, deplete our soils, mine our hills. We shall die for want of refuge. Help us.'

'How?'

'We shall be with you on the way. Learn to recognize us. Learn to obey us. Set up shrines where you can, temples, reawaken sleeping Sanctuaries. That is your real work. Where is your destination?'

'Venonis and the Midsummer Assembly.'

'A king would go to Kyronion.'

'Since I am no king, that means nothing.'

'Because of this reluctance to assume your duty, you will be deflected many times by local gods. We shall help you find your way. Look for us....'

Two swans were gliding by on a stream that was little more than a ditch in the pastureland. The Shee-druid raised his staff and roared. The birds took fright and, with a great beating of wings, rose into the air and flew off in different directions. 'You may go,' he said. 'You may pass into the inner sanctuary.'

I became aware of Mandred tugging at me. 'Please, please. It's Shee. We must go or we'll be lost here forever.'

'Did you see those swans?'

'What swans?'

'The ones who flew off in different directions.'

'Swans never do that.'

'I know.'

'Come with me now, Delfos,' Mandred pleaded. 'It's time to wake up.'

'Not quite,' I replied. I led the way, passing easily now between the two sentinel stones into the great circle overgrown with grass, thistles, sapling trees, in which lay a jumble of fallen stones attended by dancing clouds of butterflies. It seemed like a rape in itself, the way the stones had been cast down, but it was still possible to make out the original pattern, the wheel drawn on the land. The pattern of Eleusis, here in my own country.

Draumur joined us, coming from wherever he had been, and walked the circle on top of the bank, looking out to the surrounding hills to see what the Wheel had once shown: landmarks or notches between hills that marked the places of sunrise and sunset at midwinter and midsummer, the solstice lines, crossed by the east-west line of the equinoxes. A six-spoked circle until you added north-south. He said it was a wheel of Whereness. He pointed north to show us where Venonis lay, then turned to point south to Ford of the Alders, all on a line. Pointing east, he pointed to Verlamio; to the west, to Kyronion, all on a line. 'According to the druids, this is the ancient centre,' he said. 'The true omphalos of Britain.'

As well as Whereness, it showed Whenness. 'If you can read the Wheel, you know when to sow and when to reap, when to put the cattle out to pasture and when to bring them in again, when the lambing and when the slaughter.' It also told when to visit this or other Sanctuaries for the great festivals and gatherings. Draumur walked the circle, studied the fallen stones and their markings; in his imagination, he set them all up again and grew radiant at the picture he could see.

In the centre was a deep shaft where the Pole of the Nation had once stood. Now it lay in pieces, breaking down with decay, but you could still see the carved dragons. She had told me about what happened, Innogen, more than I had admitted to Verica. She had described lying on her face after the defilement, robbed forever of her ambition to become a priestess, then turning over on to her back to stare up at the *bilios*, the great oaken pole as the circle was wide. The *bilios*, the Tree that links the worlds, its canopy the sky, its roots the Otherworld, and the two dragons striving for control. Innogen had told me none of the details of the rape, only the vision she'd had during the course of it, of one of the dragons devouring the other one. 'If the centre is lost, the nation is lost,' she once told me. 'Whoever holds the Wheel holds the balance of the earth. Let it be druid always.'

I looked at the pattern of the wheel on my forearm that she had given me. I had always been bothered by its apparently arbitrary alignment, thinking that it should have been set to the line of my arm instead of being at angles to it. And then there was the blob of soot that looked like a mistake. 'Show me east-west,' I said to Draumur and, when he did so, holding out his arms, I turned so that the east-west line on my arm matched his and I looked to where that spot pointed. Then I knew what I was facing as surely as if there had been some physical sign. I walked across to the fallen stone that surely marked the place of my violent conception, beneath the shadow of the pole on the line of the midsummer sunrise, and fell to my knees. With my forehead on the ground among cowslips, I intoned prayers to the Mother, begged forgiveness for anything I had done inadvertently to hurt this place, begged to be allowed to help it heal. It was here that Britain's decline began; it was up to me to change her fate. But how? Where to start?

Something wet and snuffly pushed against my face. One of the wild horses nudging me so hard that I fell sideways. Before I could get up, she did the same herself, falling sideways and rolling over from side to side, rolling in mud and kicking her legs in the air. I lay there, staring at her, trying to understand. Was she just scratching her back or trying to tell me something?

They say the Shee can take any form. I had not expected it to be so real. I could smell the familiar smell of horse, feel the wet mud caking her shaggy silver hide. She was the image of Verica's horse Amabel. If she was real, she was of the line of the stallion Tiberius. She rolled over again and whinnied.

'Fetch the pail,' I said to Mandred, who brought it to me. 'Can you see the horse?' I asked.

'Of course,' he said, looking at me as if I had lost my senses.

I set the yew bucket down on the ground and the horse got to her feet with a snort. She stood there, watching me. I did nothing. She pawed the muddy puddle she had been rolling in, raising and lowering her head. I understood. Taking off my clothes, I rolled in it, too, until I was caked. As I stood up, the horse walked over to the bucket, nudged the lid off it and knocked it over, spilling the contents on the ground. My two companions were dismayed, for the body of a king must be given to the water. But I put my trust in the horse and spread the ash on the place of my conception then laid down in it.

Mandred cried out, shocked. 'That is Verica!'

I rolled right over and back again to cover myself in the ash which is not ash, which is bone pulverised by heat, brittle and scratchy. Here and there bits of bone, a tooth. I rolled in my father. I took the substance of him on to me and then, as if burning, I jumped up on the horse, who carried me down to the landing place and into the confluence of rivers. Head down as she jumped, she carried us into the deeps, down, down below the surface. I clung to her mane in trust, expecting her to rise up to the air again, but she did not. So I let go and gave myself to the water to carry me back to my world.

I returned to the upper air alone. All vestiges of the king left me, washed away with the ash. His sin left me. His mannerisms, anything I had inherited, left me. I knew that the act had also freed Verica of the sin. 'I am Delfos,' I said to the willows and the water, as I drew myself up out of the river. The sun came out from behind a cloud and blessed me with its warmth. I greeted it with my arms wide. 'I am mine alone. I am mine to give. I give myself to you, O Light, O Belenos-Apollo.'

There was nothing on the river but the agitation of the confluence. Then a line of bubbles broke the surface where I had emerged. A fish, probably. Or the sign of a spirit horse returning to Annwn.

26

CARATACOS

It felt like only a day, two at the most, but Katuaros said we had been gone twenty-four days.

'How long?' I yelped.

'Nearly a moon.' He handed me the notched stick he'd kept to prove it. He had set up home with the midwife, who was called Debonia, and she showed me my image in her mirror: I looked like the wild man from the woods.

Katuaros tugged my beard. 'Where's the Roman now?'

'Do I look British? Am I that filthy and bedraggled?'

'You still think like a Roman.'

'Speaking of whom…'

'No word of them.'

There were no Romans, no fleet, no landings either east nor south. 'We think they've gone home,' he said.

I did a quick calculation and found that thirty-seven days had passed since the expected landing date after the equinox. I paced about in agitation. Had the mutiny been successful? What if they were not coming? Had the German cohort sailed back to Gaul? Where was Caratacos? Was I cut off from the coast?

'The Britons waited in vain on the shores and headlands,' Katuaros told me. There's only so long you can keep your war paint on and your hair limed. They've been disbanded and are returning to their farms. The men of Cuma came back yesterday.'

After a meal, Debonia made me sit still while she creamed my face with goose fat and began scraping an iron razor over my skin. I felt like a piece of wood being planed. 'Don't flinch,' said Katuaros.

Mandred, who usually did my barbering, looked on critically and every now and again winced and said, 'Ouch!', as if he were the one under the razor. The midwife sent him away to fetch an ointment made of spiders' webs and continued to snip, tweak, pluck and trim me with what she considered to be consummate skill. The salves soothed my skin but did little for my agitation. Mandred went to help Draumur who was having difficulty getting a comb through his hair.

'So, what happened?' asked Katuaros, oblivious of my mood.

'Not hard to tell,' I replied, with a certain bitterness.

'They say that men have been down there who didn't come back for years. Some have yet to return. If it hadn't been for me, they would not have let you back into Cuma dun, but would have taken you for .... one of them.'

'It's a wonder we didn't starve,' I grumbled.

'Would I let you starve? There's an idiot boy, a changeling they say, who is master of the coracle. I sent him across every evening with food which he took to the temple. He always brought back the dish from the day before that he'd found empty, so we knew you were eating; either that or it was them. Or it could be foxes, I suppose.'

'You didn't think to send the fianna?'

'They threatened to desert if I made them go there.'

'The brave fianna.'

'Yes, the brave fianna.' He looked across to where his men were passing the afternoon with the warriors of Cuma training young boys in the use of the sling. 'They are fighters, Delfos. Warriors can't fight water, air, fire. Or fairies.' He sighed deeply and apologised. 'We read the omens every evening and they were always favourable. Had they not been, or if the idiot boy had brought back a full dish, or any story of distress, I would have come down, on my own if necessary.'

He sat combing his fingers through his own shining hair

while he watched Mandred work on a felted lump of knots on the crown of Draumur's head. I, too, watched, because it was becoming a grooming session that could have been the thirteenth labour of Hercules. After spending considerable time on the matted tangle Mandred had freed only a few hairs. 'I can't go on,' he complained. 'You have to,' said Draumur, studying his head in a bronze mirror. Mandred tugged harder on the knotted lump and got a curse for his efforts. 'There is only one way,' he said at last, reaching for the shears.

'No!' cried Draumur. 'Don't you dare! Patience! Try patience! It is the only way!'

Katuaros was astonished. 'I've never heard him say so much at one time.'

'Desperation on his part, I should think.' I said nothing about Draumur's voice having been restored by the Shee.

With the cattle departing on the long drove to the Hill of the Albios Horse, Cuma was quiet, almost deserted. Katuaros, he who wished for a vast parcel of land, seemed oddly at home in this small settlement. How to tell the tale of enchantment? I told him what had happened as best I could without calling my sanity into question. 'There is no sense of time down there,' I said. Regarding Verica, I related that his ashes had been given to the confluence of the two rivers without saying anything about my rolling in them on the instruction of a spirit horse. 'The Sanctuary itself is little more than a vast pastureland, inhabited by wild horses and geese. That is what Verica himself told the Romans, deliberately turning their attention from the place. He knew it was sacred; he knew the depth of his own sin. I believe he is free of it now.'

'I am glad of it. But how come you were so long there?'

I shrugged irritably. 'As I said, it's easy to lose track of time, that's all.'

'It's a lot of time to lose track of.'

'What do you want me to say? That I was captured by the Shee and held in a mound for nearly a moon?'

'If that is what's true,' he said with a grimace.

I felt unable to tell him about the crossings between worlds, of those I'd met and the messages given. He was my brother, my friend. Why did I feel so sour? Mandred, still tugging in vain on Draumur's knots, was beginning to whine with the effort. In one swift action I drew my knife, crossed to my harpist, pulled up the offending lump of hair and sliced it off close to the root.

Draumur shouted with such rage that those in the vicinity thought for a moment I had scalped him. I gave him the bundle of knotted hair and told him to comb it out himself.

'Why couldn't you just leave things be?' he stormed. 'What did a few knots matter?'

'I think I preferred you silent,' I growled.

I went off to walk alone. The vividness of new leaf and the rich scent of spring calmed me down for I was annoyed with Katuaros, but soon I realised that, had he come to the Sanctuary to find us, things would have turned out differently. As it was, all was well, apart from the tardiness of the Romans... I came to a clearing in the woods that gave a view through the trees to the river below, the pasture, the rise of land and the Wheel. I stood there wishing I had the power to get the Sanctuary revivified, re-consecrated; I wanted the people of Cuma to turn around and face east again. The sun was setting behind me. Mist from the two rivers seethed over the plain, met and mingled in the middle. A tremendous honking filled the sky as a vast skein of geese flew over, east to west as if following the dying sun. I had never seen so large a flock, and all perfectly arranged in the V-shape that is the wake of the leading bird. Honking, honking to the beat of their wings. One-two; one-two. East to west... I stopped seeing the birds as birds and began to read the writing of the gods.

I went back into the dun and told Katuaros we had to leave in the morning.

'Do you want to go back to Noviomagos?'

'No,' I said, with a confidence that surprised both of us. 'We press on. It's imperative that I find Esius. Do we know where he might be?'

'But if the Romans aren't coming...'

'Where might Esius be?'

'Could be anywhere in his territory, from Clevo to the hot springs.'

I remembered what the Shee-druid had said. 'A king would go to Kyronion.' Perhaps he had not meant me. 'Could he be at Kyronion?'

'I believe he favours the place as a retreat.'

'So, we go west,' I said.

'But Venonis... It's due north from here, not west.'

'Due north as the bird flies,' said Draumur, 'but between here and there are badlands — marsh, rock, river. The only tracks are those made by animals. If we go west, however, we can pick up the Albios Way at Kyronion and that will give us a good road to Venonis.'

'So,' I said, 'we leave in the morning.'

'No, not tomorrow,' said Katuaros. 'The dark days begin tonight.'

'I cannot let these superstitions govern my every action. I've lost too much time!'

'Katuaros needs another week here at least,' said Debonia firmly, standing between us. 'Insist he ride with you now and you will make an invalid of him.'

I stared at her doubtfully, and she stared right back. In that particular battle of wills, she won and I left Katuaros behind, the fianna with him, telling myself that it was better that way, that to travel with an escort would draw attention. I also left the chariot for Katuaros's use, telling him to catch us up as soon as he could. I set off the following morning, accompanied only by Mandred and Draumur.

238

On the far side of Cuma Hill we took the ancient track, which ran from the Wheel to the Horse, intending to follow it until we came to the first cross-track leading west. Streams of people and kine coming from their steads over the land were converging and, as they joined the river of pilgrims, there were halloos between families and insults shouted between tribes. Cattle and people were alike all dressed and garlanded to greet the start of summer at the Hill of the Albios Horse. No one here seemed to worry about travelling on dark days. Songs vied and became one song, a walking song, a Beltane song. The Dobunni patrols protecting the pilgrims from bandits moved with us and sang along with the rest. When eventually we came to the cross track, I decided to stay with the pilgrims. 'If we left this current to strike off to the west, we'd draw far too much attention to ourselves,' I explained to my companions. 'Let us dismount and walk with the crowd.'

'Admit it,' said Mandred, 'you want to see the Horse.'

'As you know,' I said haughtily, 'my business is momentous and is concerned with the fate of these people. Even if I did want to see the Horse, I would not let it interfere with my purpose. Perhaps we should take refuge for a few days until the crowd has passed, then we can go west.'

Truth be told, I not only wanted to see the Horse, I wanted to skip along with the throng, singing and dancing in the Season of the Ever-Young, at one with all. The Dobunni patrols went with the stream. Against the stream, like the Severn bore, came the Catuvellauni. We heard the carnyxes first, blaring and bellicose, cutting down the songs like blades. We could see the chariots in the distance, coming our way, and soon we could distinguish the wheat sheaf on the flying standards. The people leapt from the path and the frightened herds began to stampede. I wanted to step out in front of the leading chariot and its retinue of warriors, to stop it in its tracks as some druids are able to do, but common sense prevailed and I leapt off the track with the rest.

Clearing the path were the carnyx-players carrying their mighty trumpets, as tall as a man and as upright. Blown at random, they created a cacophony to frighten man and beast. I had once tried to blow a carnyx but my breath had only got half way up the tube before it fell back down again to choke me. Laughing, my mother had taken the instrument, held it straight and tall and blew up it to shake the clapper in the mouth of the boar at the top.

Through the blaring came the sound of surging excitement as people recognized the driver of the chariot, standing not sitting, proud in his chainmail and tunic, a golden torc round his neck. 'Caratacos!' came the shout up the line of onlookers. They bowed their heads as he passed; some fell to their knees. You'd have thought that here was the High King.

'To war! To war!' shouted Caratacos.

It was a rupture of joy, a transition that ripped them from happiness to ecstasy. The people held their arms up to the sky and shouted the name of Camulos, the god of war.

'The Romans are coming!' Caratacos cried. 'We have had word from Gaul! They are going to their ships! Gather, O Britons. If you would be free, never let them land. They abuse our sacred soil and our sacred festival. Gather, O Britons, and never let them land. All men of fighting age. Women, too, if you have the muscle for battle. Come to the mustering ground. Prepare yourselves for war!' He had the bellow of a bull; his voice could surely be heard on all the surrounding hills.

Sensing the danger we were in, I gave Scipio to Draumur and told him to get back to Cuma. He left at once, leading my horse against the flow, moving quietly, creating no disturbance. In response to the calls of Caratacos, the crowd began to separate like oil from water with those fit to fight stepping apart from the rest. One of the Catuvellauni caught me round the neck with a shepherd's crook and pulled me out from among the halt, the infirm, the old men and the children.

'Druid,' I said, for druids never bear arms.

I was taken to Caratacos, who squinted at me. He reached out with his furled whip and pushed back my sleeve to reveal the wheel tattoo. 'Ha,' he said, 'so it is you. I heard you were home. Druid indeed. Arrest this man!' he shouted. 'Arrest him as a coward who refuses to fight!'

As I was dragged off in chains, Mandred bound with me, I was spat upon by people who, for the most part, were of the Atrebates. Caratacos, the boy who had had the power to command his own family, now commanded all men. He had called up their lust for battle and all thoughts of song, flowers and Beltane love-making vanished. The cattle were left to wander as they would.

It was no way to see the Albios Horse of Belenos, being driven along in a growing herd of captive cowards. And yet I looked up and still felt wonder to see the ridgeway rising up like a green wave in the land, high and dramatic beyond the flat vale. Despite my plight, my heart leapt for it was on those chalk hills that I had learnt to ride and drive a chariot, bouncing over turf so soft you could fall and not break a bone. It was here, at the Hill of the Albios Horse, that I'd received those tattoos that had marked me indelibly as barbarian. It was here that, at any of the Fire Festivals, I had run wild with boys from other tribes, my Dobunni cousins, more distant relations from the Trinovantes, and the sons of Cymbelinus. We were competitive, of course, but not viciously so. We jumped the fires together, rolled burning chariot wheels down the hillsides, joined the tribes to scrub the Horse and reveal the chalk.

The Horse... the White Horse, the Celestial Horse... A muttering made us look up and suddenly I had a vision of the horse that is not available anywhere except from two places, one of them being here in the middle of the vale, for the Albios Horse rides the ridge for the pleasure of the gods, not men, and hard indeed it is to see it from our mortal point of view. The sun was beginning to sink and although the approaching crowd was now but a remnant, it was still Beltane eve, the night of the fires. The dun on the ridge was in sight now, standing out above the Horse, its white palisades turning rosy in the dying light. When the Atrebates had won the territory from the Dobunni, we respected the ancient traditions of neutrality that protect the Sanctuary of the Horse as they protect the Sanctuary of the Wheel. This is sacred land and not a market, although at festival times the merchant stalls are everywhere; but it is only at festival times; the rest of the year, the dun is deserted except for guardians. The Horse presides over a no man's land between tribes. Or it did. Now Dobunni and Catuvellauni banners and emblems were everywhere, the standards of possession.

Those sinuous lines of chalk were like a forgotten song heard again. The same lines that are engraved on our coins. The same lines of the mould that Gofannon used when he cast a horse for me at Calleva. I had watched the magical operation, from liquid fire through to cooling bronze. He had given me an awl to divide the soft metal to make a mouth, and a point to make an eye and to indicate a mane. It was my Horse, the spirit of my ancestors caught in bronze. And I'd lost it here, at the Hill one Beltane. I'd put it aside for safe-keeping while I went fire-jumping and when I got back it had gone. One of my companions, who I've always presumed was the thief himself, said the Shee had taken it.

We emerged from the marshy vale at Dragon Hill, a tall mound with a blood-soaked altar on its summit and a shadow pole that marks the cycle of the year, and were led along the sheep track that winds up above the place they call 'the Manger', the great runnelled hollow in the chalk escarpment — claw marks made by a dying dragon, they say — that embraces Dragon Hill. The higher we went, the more the view opened up. The sky was marbled with clouds of different colours, white, grey, blue, black, and the dying sun sent up shafts of glory. Most of the captive cowards were penned, some chosen few to be sacrificed on the morrow, the rest to be persuaded one way or another to fight. But I was singled out to attend on Caratacos.

The other vantage point for a view of the Horse is from the deep-thatch on the hillside called 'the King's Place.' As we made our way across to it, the reddened shield rim of the sun finally sank below the horizon and a piercing, haunting note sounded across the landscape, to be repeated several times. At first I thought it was a carnyx, but then I remembered... the Blowing Stone, announcing Beltane and the new moon. A sacred standing stone with a hole in it, being blown by a chosen boy on the eve of becoming a man. I remembered the effort required to make it, and the imperative not to fail. I had been chosen that year above Caratacos, a fact I recalled with a shudder, for that would surely be part of his reckoning with me.

As the last notes of the Blowing Stone died away, the first fire was ignited and its flames leapt for the sky. At once a neighbouring fire caught, and then beacon fires all across the country blazed on hilltops. Beltane had begun. The cattle that had arrived of their own volition were penned up in numerous compounds; they lowed plaintively as if they knew the trials that were coming on the morrow.

'There,' I said to Mandred, nodding towards the dun above us on the ridge, 'is where I had my Rite of Becoming. Katuaros and I together. He never flinched.'

'And you?'

'I flinched.' I shrugged inside my tunic as if it were itchy, remembering the agony of tattooing, the impassivity of Verica as he inflicted the pain, the absolute requirement not to cry. Katuaros was being done at the same time, he by the priest, and he watched me with his bright eyes as if nothing were happening. When my face suddenly crumpled with the pain, Katuaros began to cry out as if in agony himself, but it was just to deflect attention from me. Boys waiting outside began to jeer but Katuaros withstood that as he had withstood the pain. We emerged from the tattooing tent at last, both of us with the sacred symbol of the triple-tailed horse on our left shoulders. I also had the goosefoot on my right shoulder. 'These three lines,' Innogen told me, 'represent the flow of the spirit and balance between two opposing forces. It is your fate.' The eight-spoked wheel came later. By the blood of the boar and the pain of tattoos, I could withstand anything, so I told myself as I was dragged by the halter towards the King's Place.

Caratacos pushed his way out through the hides hanging over the doorway of the large, circular house. He was just as a Briton is supposed to be, according to Roman writers (in truth Britons are varied in height, build and colour). He was tall, massive across the shoulders, with hair the colour of oats falling in coarse waves. His moustaches were long and tapering, his eyes as bright as a buzzard's and as blue as the sky. His fine plaid cloak of oak brown and nettle green was fastened with a heavy silver brooch and around the reddened skin of his neck he had added two bronze torcs to the gold one, three torcs, as if to prove his mettle by the very weight of his ornament. By his bearing alone Caratacos would look the king even if he were naked. And yet he was but the younger brother of King Togodumnos.

'Take the chains off this man,' he commanded. It sounded magnanimous but I understood that my freedom was only to be freedom from the bonds. I was still his prisoner.

'By the laws of hospitality, you are my guest,' he said, this man who had taken Calleva, who had taken our horses, driven my father into the sea, our people into poverty. 'You will spend the night here.' He slapped me so hard on the back that I stumbled inside the house.

'This is my wife,' he said, beckoning forward from the shadows a tall woman gravid with child. 'Carrying my first son.'

How did he know it would be a boy? Except that Nature, like all the gods, was subservient to his will. I took both the hands of Dryadia in mine in greeting. She was large, strong in limb, a warrior woman. Her hair, the colour of primroses, was so thick that it could not be plaited but must be bound. Tendrils in tight coils like those of pea plants escaped in every direction. This woman must have been born of a goddess, expressly to be the wife of Caratacos.

'This is Togidubnos ap Verica,' Caratacos told her. 'Home from Rome and here, presumably, to spy for the Romans.'

She drew her hands from mine in distaste and returned to the fire where, gathered amongst the chief warriors, were the elders of the Catuvellauni tribes and the extended family of Caratacos.

'Why have you brought him in here?' one of them asked. 'He should be with the pigs.'

'Our fathers were foster brothers. It is the law of hospitality.'

They grumbled but agreed and looked on their young leader with pride and approval. Although the child in Dryadia's womb was Caratacos's first, there were children scampering everywhere in Beltane excitement, nephews and fosterlings. At the fire was another woman, who, though she looked at me with disdain, had a face beautiful beyond any I have seen in this world.

'What's a Roman doing here?' she asked and spat into her hands.

'Theana, it's that puny runt of Verica. Don't you recognize him? Why sister, I do believe you were sweet on him once. Eh?' Caratacos guffawed. If she was embarrassed, she did not show it. Theana. I remembered her name but not half so well as I remembered her body, glistening like a salmon as she bathed in the pond, five years older than me and budding into womanhood. Theana had had a liking for me? Could that be possible?

It had been at the midsummer gathering when I was nine. Innogen was the guest of the archdruid along with the wife of Cymbelinus and her large brood. Katuaros was spending the day with his family and I was out in the woods, playing on my own, pretending to stalk prey. Coming to a pond in a clearing, I thought I saw a young doe amongst the reeds. I crept closer stealthily, the great hunter with his handmade ash spear, but when I saw who it was, I ducked down hardly daring to breathe.

I knew her, the sister of that brat Caratacos who had to win all the prizes, had to get himself heard above the rest, but I'd never spoken to her. She was the eldest of the litter of King Cymbelinus; Caratacos was the second youngest but all his brothers and sisters were in his court, sometimes affably so, in the way of siblings who love their younger ones, sometimes not so affably. Togodumnos, the eldest boy, would suddenly blare at his brother when he became too annoying. Theana merely went for solitary walks. She was angry, continually, consistently angry, that she would never be queen while a brother lived. She had discovered that the best way to make her power felt was to work with the gods and she had arranged that, when the family returned to their capital at Verlamio, she would remain behind to study with the druids at Vernemeton, the grove of groves, greatest of them all, north of Venonis.

I watched her from a clump of rushes, naked in the pond and repeatedly dunking herself, crouching down until the water covered her shoulders, then rising, so that it poured off her, leaving her dripping with pond weed. There was a crossing-point, a threshold. For a moment I hung in the balance, where I could see her for what she was, just a girl of thirteen in a ritual ablution or... I could see water droplets on goose-bumps, the slenderness of her arms, the length of her neck, the line of her spine down to the water. The balance tipped suddenly, pitching me into that world where the senses are exquisite, where nothing matters apart from the object of your adoration. Suddenly my breathing became jagged, a kind of feral panting, and she turned. She looked at me and saw a pale boy half-concealed among the bulrushes and for a moment she, too, had a choice: whether to be angry and chase me off, threatening me with dire retribution from men and gods, or to be friendly. Theana? Friendly? She had never shown that side of herself — until now. With a generous smile, she beckoned me into the water and I waded towards her, my feet sinking in mud. When I got to her, wide-eyed in gratitude, she reached out as if to help me. There was a moment when I was on the brink of everything, of standing on the horizon of the sky and seeing all the planets in their dance, but then, like a black cloud scudding over the moon, malice rolled over her face.

'Teutates!' she called on her god, 'I offer you this boy as my gift.' And she pushed on my head until I was under the water and scrabbling. The pressure on my head got worse and worse until I came to another point in that day of thresholds, the point where it is reasonable to give up. I stopped flailing and surrendered to inexorable fate. Then her hands cupped my head and she was pulling me up, out of the water, as if birthing me. She waited until I had stopped spluttering and gasping then brought her face close to mine. 'You will come to me when I want you, and not before.'

And now here she was, a chaste priestess. She had become what my mother had longed to be. 'I'm not sleeping under the same thatch as him!' she said, rising up. She was almost as tall as her brother and her black gown trailed over the chalk floor in a whisper.

I tried not to inhale the scent of her as she brushed past to leave for the dun at the top of the ridge. It reminded me too much of near-drowning. She stopped at the doorway and turned. 'Is he to be one of the four in the morning?'

'Do you want him to be?' Caratacos asked.

Theana shrugged. 'As you and the gods will it.'

'It's tempting,' Caratacos said, staring at me through narrowed eyes. He followed his sister to the door to watch her striding up to the ridge, bearing a flaming torch that guttered in the wind, as elemental herself as fire and air. And water. Theana. If it turned out to be my fate that I be sacrificed by Caratacos on the altar of Theana, at dawn of the day when the sun rode in the chariot of the celestial horse, it seemed right, somehow. Fitting.

'Yes!' Caratacos shouted after her. 'Let it be!'

27

BELTANE

'Where is Katuaros?' Caratacos asked.

'At Cuma's Hill.'

'Why?'

'He took a fall and needs to rest.'

'We've been watching you. You were a long while at Cuma.'

'It was a bad fall.'

Caratacos ignored me. 'You were in the Sanctuary of the Wheel for nearly a moon. What happened?'

'I got lost in time.'

'Good way of putting it. Shee?'

I nodded.

'You must be blessed to get out of there with your wits intact. What did they have to say?'

I shrugged. 'Nothing intelligible.'

'Did they tell you the Roman army has mutinied?'

I strove to remain expressionless. 'But you're mustering. You said they were on their way.' I had had a mad hope that they had already landed and would rescue me before dawn.

'Ah,' he said, 'so they are. Yes. Some slave came to Gesoriacum from Rome and put mettle into those cowards.'

'Slave?'

'Someone called Narcissus.'

'He's a freedman, not a slave, and the chief adviser of the Princeps.'

'Once a slave always a slave. If I were Plautius, I'd have fallen on my sword. Isn't that what humiliated Romans do? But over the past few days there have been omens. I myself saw a star shooting from east to west.'

I remembered my skein of geese.

'According to the priests,' said Caratacos, 'this sign tells us the Romans are on the move, making for the ships.'

'So why are you not rushing to the coast?' I asked.

'And which coast do you suppose that to be?'

'The east one, of course! If the star went from east to west, from Gaul to Britain, it stands to reason.'

He stared at me through slitted eyes. 'When I was a boy, you'd have caught me with that one, but I have grown up, you jackass. Not so easily tricked now.'

As his retainers were looking bemused, Caratacos scratched lines on the dirt floor to show them how, to reach the east coast of Britain, a fleet must sail north from Gesoriacum. East to west meant sailing along our — my — southern coast. It would be a south coast landing. At least, according to the omens of stars and geese it would be.

'South coast, so they'll be a few days yet. It's Beltane and I'm not going to miss seeing the Chariot of the Sun for a bunch of poxy Italians with bare legs and no breeches. There's no point. They know, I know, all our ancestors know, the Britons will never be beaten. Claudius will come and Claudius will go, like Julius Caesar. We are Beyond Ocean. We are Dis. We will never be subject to that stewpot city that wants to lord it over the world. So,' he said, 'it's a coincidence, is it, that you return, as it were, in advance of them?'

'I was due to come home anyway; why should I not return with my father?'

He fingered his tapering moustaches. 'You were always devious. While the rest of us flexed our muscles for contest, you were a brain on legs running rings around us. Do you still wrestle?'

'I do.'

'Hmmm... Well, I'll take your word for it. I'm in no mood

for being winded by one of your surprise moves. Not tonight. Too much mead in my veins. Perhaps tomorrow; or, there again, perhaps not. I never could understand why you lost at Black Raven. That's a puzzle.'

It was true. While I could easily anticipate moves in a fight, I was befuddled by a board game. 'It's cold,' I observed.

'It's very cold,' he agreed.

'Could my man not be given shelter?'

He snapped his fingers at a slave. 'Fetch him in, the cripple, for the night is a cold one. And fetch the dogs in, too.'

Mandred was hauled inside the deep-thatch, his teeth chattering.

'Chief, look...', a bondsman said, dragging the red neckerchief off him. Caratacos examined the inflamed lump the sore had become. 'This man bears the mark,' he declared. Catuvellauni elders gathered round to look.

The mark! I remembered my childhood fears of finding or developing any deformity — the mole behind my right knee, the time I sprained my ankle but never limped in public, the illness I caught that blinded me until my grandmother made a compress of herbs for my eyes — the fear of being singled out for sacrifice. If a British boy does not wish to be offered up to the gods, he must never be abnormal.

'Mark?' I said. 'The only thing it marks is where the neck iron chaffed him!'

'Where is your tribe?' Caratacos demanded of Mandred.

'Yew River.'

'Durotriges? What are you doing, enslaved to another Briton?'

'Delfos bought me in a Roman market.'

'How long have you had this deformity?'

'Since I arrived in Rome.'

'And this is your slave?' he asked me. 'You bought him deformed?'

'He is not deformed. It's a mark only of mistreatment.'

251

'Ah well,' he said, subsiding. 'Perhaps so. In which case I shall let him live. After all, someone needs to tell of your death and the sacrifice of a king.'

'I am not king. I have renounced the title.'

'Then who will be in charge of your people?'

'Rome, if all goes according to plan.'

Caratacos laughed, so hard that all the kine in the back stalls bellowed. 'And if it doesn't? What if everything goes according to *my* plans?' He took from Dryadia a bowl which she had filled with a liquid brew from a steaming cauldron. It smelt like rotting stable hay. 'Drink!' he said. 'It will help.' I remembered — will never forget — that time as a boy when I drank from the forbidden Dreaming Cup and found myself alone with the gods, or so it had seemed to an impressionable child. I shook my head. 'If I'm about to die, I want to keep my wits.'

'Believe me,' said Caratacos, 'you don't. Take it.'

A man who has drunk kykeion at Eleusis does not drink elixirs for mere oblivion or for intoxication. I shook my head, keeping my lips sealed. While the women sat and watched, the bowl was passed round the men. A druid of bardic degree began to sing the song of the tribe. One by one each man entered his own dream, eyes glazed over; some danced, two of them rutted like a pair of antlered stags, one stood with his face to the cattle stalls in silence but his right foot tapping hard. The women withdrew into their own house and their own dream. The fire crackled in the hearth, sounding lonely.

Caratacos bade me sit beside him. His large eyes, framed by sandy lashes, were eyes that could be merry or cruel. Eyes of love and war. Here, now, looking on me, they were hard. 'So, you've come back, but why if not for the kingship? I would have thought Rome suited you very well. Were you not the house-guest of the man who is now princeps? Your life must have been pampered and sweet. You lived in the house of Claudius and now he is princeps. Verica runs to him for help in defeating me and suddenly you're both home with the Roman army not far behind. Do not take me for a fool as you did when we were boys, tying me in knots with your logical puzzles and druidic riddles. Any agility I lack in the mind I more than make up for in my sword arm. So riddle me no more. If you tell me the truth I won't pass you over to the priests for the three-day death.'

He reminded me in gruesome detail what to expect in that sacrifice devised to free a soul from the cycle of birth and death. Somehow I kept my nerve. Seneca had once advised, 'when frightened, keep your attention on a detail' and I noticed the redness of the neck of Caratacos beneath the torcs. 'You should be careful,' I said, 'or you will form a lump yourself from all that weight you carry on your neck.'

He slapped me to get my attention back to what he was saying.

'What's the difference between a torc and a slave collar?' I persisted.

He slapped me again, harder, and my nose began to bleed.

'When you finally die, they will flense your skull and make a drinking cup of it,' he growled.

I might have won our battle of wills except at that very moment I saw Dryadia stirring a skull-cup and that was a detail I shouldn't have focussed on. I could feel the fear like poison in my veins, but I still had enough wit to remind him that he did not have three days. 'The Romans are coming.'

'I hear they're sending four legions,' Caratacos said.

'And as many auxiliaries.'

'How many does that add up to?'

'Eighty thousand.'

'That seems a lot. Do they have to make up for lack of bravery with superiority in numbers?'

'They are coming to stay. They will be building forts, and each one will be maintained by a garrison. As a legion moves, so it shrinks, but never, ever suppose a Roman soldier lacks bravery. The difference between them and you is that they fight together, as one. You think of battle as a charge of chariots;

253

of fighting as hand-to-hand combat. They fight in solid formation, not for glory but for a pension. The Roman soldier surrenders himself as an individual and fights as part of a cohort. He is trained to mow you down and has siege engines, catapults and crossbows, cruel mechanisms for killing anyone in the way, because what they want even more than glory and fame is land and all its resources.'

'I'll wager they don't have brain balls,' he said.

I smiled despite myself, remembering Claudius hearing about our most potent weapon with a mixture of horror and fascination. 'No, they don't have brain balls. They have ballistas, bolt-throwers that can bring down a house. Scorpions that sting with lethal darts. Onagers, catapults that can punch holes in palisades. All these they can fire from a distance: they don't have to engage with you at all. Caratacos, the only way to win against the Romans is not to resist. Remember what happened in Gaul. Remember Vercingetorix and the siege of Alesia. He ended up being dragged to Rome to be garrotted in public. Do you want that? Let the Romans in. Do not resist.'

'What do you take me for?' He brought his face so close to mine that I could smell the wax in his moustaches. 'If I were you,' he snarled, 'I'd not drag up the past. Who was it who betrayed the father of my tribe? Who gave Cassivellaunos up to the Romans? Kommios.' Now I began to feel the weight of his objections; began to understand his hatred of the Atrebates. It was not just about land; it was about history; it was about honour. 'Why are you here?' Caratacos demanded.

'To persuade the Britons to resist.'

His eyes widened. 'What? To resist? But...'

'Yes, to resist. Not the Romans. To resist you.'

He pulled my hair back hard. 'Who was that bedraggled messenger who hobbled into Calleva, told us lies and hobbled out again? Who was the Lord of Misinformation who sent our forces on the wrong track? It was you. At least four people swear it was you. Grown tall. Grown brown. But still Togidubnos. You traitor. You betray your own people! And for what? Oh, you son of vipers!'

The Dream was calling him and, rising up, he signalled to a servant to bind me and Mandred to a post. 'The three-day death. If only I could make that five but no one can live in such agony...' He went to his stall. 'You bastard, Togidubnos!' he shouted across the house. 'You slimy maggot-ridden toad! I always hated you!'

'Maggot-ridden toad,' echoed those of his men still awake, as if it were a refrain in a song.

'You Atrebatic shit!' Caratacos slammed the gate to the stall behind him and in a moment was lost to the Dream amongst the warm cows.

His fianna slept in a tangled mess of hides, mantles and men. I thought of the soldiers who sleep in barracks as neatly filed in their sleeping as in their marching, line after line of them, and here the enemy in an intoxicated heap. All the warrior wants and needs to attain Annwn — the Land of the Ever-Young — is to die in battle with honour untarnished. Those Roman soldiers: what they dreamt of in their regiment of beds was twenty-five years staying alive so as to attain their pay-off. I stared up at the dusky thatch, steeling myself by recalling every tenet of wisdom I'd memorised to overcome my fear of what the morning might bring. I knew he was bluffing, just trying to terrify me, but in the night hours I kept thinking about the three-day sacrifice where the priests keep the victim at the point of death not in an act of cruelty or punishment but to release the soul from all attachment to worldly things. I don't know what happens after that but presumably you go neither to Annwn nor Dis. However intriguing to the philosopher, this place beyond death and rebirth, I had no wish to experience the access to it. But even if it was a bluff, and impractical in this situation, there was still to be a sacrifice of cowards in the morning and it wasn't beyond Caratacos to add me to the pile of corpses. Bound to the same post as Mandred

I could feel his absolute calm. If he shivered it was only from the cold.

The lamps were guttering. A fox barked in the distance. It was late: ember hour. Caratacos came out of his stall, picked up a bear skin from a pile of hides and brought it to me. 'Your chattering teeth are keeping me awake,' he said, throwing the heavy, coarse hide down on my legs. It didn't help. I began to doubt I would ever get warm again. 'I need to move,' I said.

'Too bad.'

'Perhaps it would be better to freeze to death than be sacrificed,' I said.

Caratacos humphed, undid me from the post and took me in to the cow stall he was sleeping in. Bound by a short leash to another post, I was able to lie on a pile of straw and lean against the hairy warm flank of an animal whose breath steamed in the cold air. The Dreaming Cup had mellowed him. 'Things have changed since you went away,' he said, in a tone of collusion I had never heard from him before, as if our shared history made us friends, which it did not. Kinsmen through fosterage, that was all, and yet he spoke to me as his equal. 'The tribes have divided between those who support Rome and those who do not — empire-lovers versus those who would remain free. The Britons need a leader, a Vercingetorix, a High King...'

'Who would be...?'

'According to the prophecies, to the stars, to the flight of birds, yes, me. Who else? Relax,' he said, 'if you wish to avoid death in the morning, you need only to co-operate. I have a proposition. Join me. I need your intelligence. You need my protection. Together we can make this one nation again. As one, we really shall be invincible. I have all the south-east. Next I'll take Noviomagos, then move to take the Durotriges. The Dobunni I have already by treaty, not that treaties are anything to rely on, but it will do. I am related to the Silurians by my marriage to Dryadia. That leaves the north, the Ordovices,

Corieltauvi and Iceni, the far north, the Brigantes and, beyond them, the Caledonians. I will gain all these lands in time, and not by any poxy treaty. Possession. It's the only way.'

Was he still in the Dream?

'I have lived under Tiberius, Caligula and now Claudius,' I said. 'I have experienced government by insane autocrats and loathed it. But there is something there, something in the heart of that civilization, perhaps at the root of it, which is good. Why would I want to deny my people all that empire can give? — peace under one law, art and learning, prosperity, improvements in agriculture, mineral wealth, an easier life with a fuller belly. Not looking over your shoulder all the time for the next murderous raiding party from the neighbours. Not worrying about your wife and children whenever you are away from home. This freedom of yours is no freedom at all.'

'Peace, plenty — such luxuries turn men into slaves. Everything would be lost: our traditions, the warrior-way, our gods, our land. But why argue about it? The outcome is known to us. When Claudius comes he will meet the invincible British and turn tail like all before him. Rome may rule the world, it will never rule Britain. We are Beyond Ocean. We are the portal to the world of the gods. We are the gatekeepers. We are invincible.'

Sleep came over him like a wave and he slumped beside me.

After long hours of wakefulness, towards dawn I nudged him and told him I had decided to accept his offer.

28

CHARIOT OF THE SUN

I cannot say that Caratacos was easily fooled but he did believe that the gruesome details of the three-day death he'd told me had done the job. He was also in the dregs of the Dreaming Cup, which levies a charge for the ecstasy of the night. 'You will co-operate? Good. It's for the best, though I trust you not at all. Do not try any of your tricks, Togidubnos. What do you know of the Roman's plans?'

'Everything.'

His eyes glittered like a magpie's. 'Tell me.'

'Having landed in my harbours, they plan to move on Calleva. There's no point sending your warriors all the way south to meet them. Lure them in. Leave your main force in Calleva and use the rest to harry the Romans along the way.'

'Why? Where's the glory?' Caratacos asked.

'In ultimate victory. Meet them at the coast and your battle will be short, soon over. Let them land unopposed. Lull them and lure them in. Harry them along the way so that they maintain their belief that Britons are little more than war bands on shaggy horses. Divide the main force into three, keep the flanks hidden, lull them and lure them in. Clasp them to the British bosom at Calleva and squeeze them to death.'

You might think I was betraying the Romans. Instead I was ensuring an unopposed landing and saving Noviomagos from becoming a battlefield. I thought I should send word to the Romans, if and when I could, but they needed no warning. I had seen Caratacos's forces and they offered little threat especially if as, on my advice, they tried fighting in the Roman style of battle lines and flanks.

Caratacos smiled. 'I always thought we should have been brothers, fostered as our fathers were. I have the strength, you the brains.' He stretched, reached behind him, scratched his bovine pillow on the back by way of thanking her for her warmth and stood up. He jumped about rubbing his arms. 'Ai, it's a cold dawn but, ah, I feel good. I did not want to kill you. Truly I did not. '

'But you will,' I thought, 'as soon as you have all the information out of me.' I rose up with a smile and he slapped me on the back. A solitary horn sounded, soon joined by others.

'Come on. It's Beltane. Up and out before the Chariot!' He left the stall and woke his men with the same call. 'Up and out before the Chariot! Beltane! Beltane!'

No matter what state or condition each man was in, thick-headed or nauseous, every one of them jumped up like boys. It was still dark and the birds had only just begun to sing. Slowly out of the dawn gloaming the interior of the deep-thatch appeared, slaves bending over the glowing heart of embers to stoke the fire back into flame, their shadows dancing over the chalk floor and flitting over the livestock stalls. The doe skin covering the door lifted and Theana came in, bringing the chill of the dawn with her. 'The hillside is white with frost,' she said. 'We will not be able to see the Horse, white on white.'

'Frost? At Beltane?' Caratacos asked, concerned. 'What does that portend?'

'Annihilation,' I thought.

Theana went to the cupboard by the door and drew out various vessels and tools. 'Is he to be sacrificed this morning?'

'No,' said Caratacos. 'I decided against it.'

'Is that wise?' she asked. I glared at her but she ignored me, concentrating on pounding something up in a small mortar. I worried stupidly about magic but when she crossed to her brother it was with some blue pigment she had put together with a binder, all in a secret recipe passed down through the generations. She began to paint his face with flames and feathers. Her artistry was fine and to watch her was to see nothing of the spiteful, spitting wildcat. Caratacos sat with his eyes closed, back in a dreaming place while his sister decorated his skin. When she had finished, she changed bowls and with a lime mix ran her fingers through his bushy hair, pulling it back from the forehead to the nape of his neck so that, heavy and coarse, it looked like a horse's mane. Before my eyes, Caratacos turned from a man into something from a child's nightmare.

'You must reconsider the sacrifice,' Theana said to him, just as I was beginning to fall in love with her again. And that is how it was with Theana, any ardour soon doused by pain and fear. 'The gods must be fed.'

'Not with kings,' Caratacos replied.

Theana's eyes flashed.

'Verica is dead. Our prisoner is the King of the Atrebates.'

'You are right,' she said. 'We cannot sacrifice a king, not without long preparation.'

'The only thing worthy of sacrifice,' I said to her, 'is your pride.'

Theana came at me, one-eyed. That is, she had one eye closed and the other peering, as witches do, examining my soul. 'Are you godless?'

I quivered under her gaze. Was I? After spending so much time with the philosophers, I was certainly sceptical, but then the Sanctuary of the Wheel had reintroduced me to the Otherworld. 'I lived in Rome nearly ten years,' I replied lamely.

'They don't sacrifice there?'

'Yes, of course they do, but I spent feast days listening to philosophers expounding. Among them there are many who question the need for sacrifice, especially human sacrifice, which has been banned for a generation at least in Rome.'

'So how do they deal with criminals?'

I sensed more than saw Mandred's smile at my discomfiture. 'They crucify them.'

'And that is not human sacrifice?'

'It's not an offering to the gods.'

'Perhaps it should be,' she said, washing her hands in a bucket of water kept by the hearth. 'Brother, I am not happy to have an unbeliever at our ceremony of the Sun.'

'I have never seen the Chariot bearing the Sun,' I said, suddenly fretful. 'Each year I came here as a child, the weather was bad. That's my memory of Beltane, greyness, clouds, crushing disappointment. If it is frosty outside, as you say, then the sun will rise today, gloriously. Do not take it as a bad omen, but as a sign and a law. And please let me see it!'

Theana and Caratacos glanced at each other. Caratacos nodded. They seemed to rule together here. 'In honour of our guest, who like his grandfather has changed sides,' he told her, 'limit yourself to the four cowards.'

He went to the entrance and lifted the hide. 'You can see the Horse, look there: a chalky streak in a sparkling sea.' He stood at the doorway looking out with eyes full of wonder. I had to remind myself that this was the man who had driven my tribe off our lands, who had taken Calleva, who had killed my half-brother Marcomaros. He it was who had caused the disunity he was promising to cure. He was the enemy of all Britain and had to be dealt with, harshly, as soon as possible. But that moment burned itself into my soul, like seeing beauty in the eye of the wolf, that moment when Caratacos stood looking out at the frost on the hill of the Albios Horse.

Our feet crunched on tussocky grass as we walked the few steps to the vantage place but even in the pale light of dawn we could see that the 'frost' was little more than a frozen, brittle dew and would soon be gone. We were on a level with the flat top of Dragon Hill so anything that happened there was in clear view. Just above us were the sweeping, fluent lines of the Horse, first carved by men long, long ago, men who were not our ancestors, although the druids claimed them as theirs. Below us, in the watery vale we had crossed the day before, were the mustering camps where warriors were rising to watch the spectacle. Mandred was led out, bound to a leather-clad bondsman, and looked wide-eyed at my standing freely beside my enemy. Transfixed by the beauty of the frosty hill and the raspings of distant partridges, I did not notice my hosts, Theana and Caratacos, slipping away.

The people, a much thinner crowd than usual, had been gathering on the slopes since before dawn. They fell into an awed hush as the sun's rim began to pulse on the horizon, just above Dragon Hill. British weather does not allow for too many cosmic wonders: every eclipse is obscured by cloud, and sunrise at midsummer or sunset at midwinter are often curtained off by rain. It's what makes the British morose. But here, this year at Beltane, the cross-quarter day between solstice and equinox that marks the beginning of summer, it was happening, and we were witnessing the Chariot of the Sun. Just for a moment we could see it, the Sun trembling on the summit of its chariot, which was Dragon Hill, and being pulled skyward by the Albios Horse. The gathering of people scattered over the hill gasped and moaned. Everyone knelt and touched the ground with their foreheads, for truly we were in the presence of Apollo, which is to say, Belenos. Theana was wrong: I had not become godless.

When I rose up again from my prostration, a shape stood out against the now risen sun on the top of Dragon Hill. Caratocos, arms outstretched, standing on his own elaborate chariot with his back to the sun, his shadow so long it almost reached us. We were blinded if we tried to look at him.

'We have seen Belenos riding in his Chariot,' he cried to the hillsides. His voice boomed in what is a natural amphitheatre, with Dragon Hill its stage. 'It bodes well! I have taken captive Togidubnos of the Atrebates who, on this sacred night, has deserted his Roman masters and joined our cause.'

I heard Mandred gasp behind me.

'The Roman are on their way and will land in the south very soon. Let them come! They will sink into the bogs and drown! Britain will live! Belenos has spoken!'

The people thundered on the ground with their feet, hollering and ululating. He stilled them by holding out his hands, palms down. 'When they land — if those cowards dare to land — they will make their way to Calleva. We shall appear to offer no resistance.' His voice was rising; you'd have thought he'd trained in oratory. 'Listen for the call!' he stormed. 'As soon as you hear the carnyxes, fetch arms and ride for Calleva!'

With everyone stirred into battle fury, the rites of Beltane continued. Up on the brow of the ridge, between the head of the Albios Horse and the gateway to the palisaded dun, two great bonfires were flaring up in the still air and crackling. The passage between them was narrow. As the flames began to reach for the sky, the gates to the dun opened and across the bridge over the deep ditch that surrounded the fortification were driven those cattle that had been penned inside. Brindled cows, their horned heads lolling, trotted forward under the lash of willow wands.

From a distance, the expert drovers looked like gods; wild on herbs, their heads antlered, they performed the impossible task of driving cows towards fire. Then a woman sitting sideways on a milk-white mare, her face painted black, rode out of the gateway in the ramparts, her arms outstretched and her head back as if she were suckling milk from the sky. Her torc and bracelets of twisted gold wire shone red in the light of the sun. Theana, I was sure of it, dressed as the Baive, goddess of war. While our attention had been captured by her, a pyre had been lit on Dragon Hill. What Caratacos sacrificed on that morning was his own chariot, along with its rich ornament and fittings. He gave what he held so precious to the god.

The cows were driven towards the fires. They bellowed and seethed, seeking any other path, but were switched hard on the haunches. A slingshot to the rump of the leading beast started a small stampede and the cattle suddenly pushed through between the fires bellowing in fright. The flames licked their hides. As the smell of singed hide floated down the escarpment to the vale, the people cried out in ecstasy.

Although the crowd was much diminished by the mustering, and games and dancing were abandoned, there was still work to be done, marriages to broker, territorial disputes to be settled, and the Horse to be scoured, all on this Beltane blessed by clear skies. But first, the execution.

The four chosen cowards were led naked to the summit of Dragon Hill and made to kneel in front of the charred and smoking sticks which remained from the chariot. They were trussed like animals for the spit, hands to ankles, leaving their heads down and their buttocks in the air. The frost was vanishing fast but it was still spitefully cold and Caratacos did not linger or prolong their agony. They had been placed with the head of each facing one of the Four Quarters and while a priest sang prayers to the god of each quarter, Caratacos cleanly beheaded the poor wretches. Their heads were taken up, impaled on lances and carried off ceremoniously to be displayed in the mustering camp, there to inspire greater valour in the warriors.

I turned and looked at Mandred who, still shackled, gazed at me with wide eyes. Had I changed sides? Did I approve of this sadistic sacrifice? I shook my head at these unasked questions.

'Does my slave have to remain bound?' I asked his keeper.

'By the will of Caratacos, yes,' he said.

I understood. Caratacos knew I would not leave without Mandred, would not slip away while all attention was on the rites and the festival.

29

ESCAPE

Although the Beltane festival had the shadow of Rome over it, the day was still spent in men seeking horses and girls seeking men. Caratacos was keeping court, sitting as the chief of the elders and listening to various cases requiring judgement. This was the work of a king or a druid and yet he took it upon himself. He introduced me proudly as his comrade, a Romey who had come to his senses, and often colluded with me on a judgement. As the night came on at last, fire beacons in each of the four directions glowed brighter and brighter.

Horns were blown monotonously to give a background sound to a thousand percussive instruments, antlers, bones, tree-drums, skulls, and the singing which was more like moaning, a drawing up of sound from the earth and letting it fly to heaven. In the fire-light, the sharp and threatening outlines of horned creatures, half-men, half-beast, dancing in circles. Fringed mantles of soft leather; cloaks of feather. Glinting arm bands of gold, bracelets, circlets. Faces painted with sacred signs. Young braves jumped the fires in an enactment of the annual war of dualities, the moment when winter loses to summer. At dawn, everything would be floral and lovely; now, in the middle of the night, the Winter God was in his death throes and groaning.

As the percussion rose to a frenzy, Theana danced the Horse Dance on the sacred hillside. In the height of her trance, she neighed with such a piercing sound that you knew it was the call of the Albios Horse itself, whose sinuous white curves she danced upon in bare feet. There was not a man there who was not robbed of speech and sinew by this vision. Even Caratacos had to clear his throat after silence descended. He ushered us back into the royal house.

'Forgive me,' he said, as he had me bound again with strong rope, back to back with Mandred against a post. 'I am too wise to trust you. Your turnabout has been too quick, too easy. I need to be more certain of you before I leave you untethered for a whole night. Especially this night.'

Outside in the moonlight the squealing began. All over the hill, all over Britain, maids and swains were coupling by the light of giant fires in full view of the gods. Caratacos grunted. 'My favourite night of the year...' he glanced at Dryadia, who was watching him, one eyebrow raised. He held out his arms to her and she came to sit on his lap. He unbound her hair and buried his face in clouds of wheaten curls.

The warriors round the fire made music on bones and flutes. They would have their night of passion, but not yet. They needed fuel first. Theana was serving mead and Dryadia, who with her hair loose was a walking hay-stook, left her husband to help with the serving of wine. Theana's eyes flashed at any man who reached out at her, silently reminding him that he did not want to lose his hand to some mysterious withering. Stories abounded about her, stories of Theana the Witch, who lay spread-eagled at full moon and let Father Sky come down on her, or Theana the lady of the beasts who coupled with bears, or Theana, the priestess who rode her horse naked, skin to skin.

After that episode in the pond when I was a child, I could never hear stories about sirens drawing men to a watery death without having to leave the hearth to go outside and retch. I had thought of her often over the years but I had never wished for a time when she might want me.

'Not married yourself, then?' asked Caratacos, settling himself close by. 'I hear a night with my sister can ruin a man for life.'

'I wouldn't know.'

'No, it wasn't a night, was it? Just a few minutes' fumbling by a boy about to become a man of a girl already a woman.'

Fumbling? All I remembered was desire being doused by water. 'I'm surprised you know about it.'

'Oh, she had us laughing until the tears ran, telling us how you lost your innocence in a pond and nearly drowned.'

A bard was singing the song of origins of the Catuvellauni, all made up in my opinion, a story for children of gods and heroes. One moment Caratacos was sitting beside me like a kinsman, but the next...

'I do believe,' he said, holding his knife to my throat, 'that you bought your life this morning with the betrayal of the Romans, but there's always tomorrow.'

'Is that how you treat partners? Kill them on a whim?'

'It's how I treat anyone who takes me for a fool, especially if that one is disloyal not only to the enemy but to his own. You are despicable. The day of sacrifice is past, but there's nothing to stop me taking your head anyway. Or I could hold you to ransom. Presumably the Atrebates want you back? If not, then I could sell you into slavery. You'd fetch a good price in Rome as a grammar teacher, even higher price if I were to geld you. Hmmm.' Keeping the knife against my flesh, he held out his bowl to be refilled. 'What do you think, Theana?' he asked as she came to him. 'What is the fate of Togidubnos to be? A eunuch, a slave, a dead man or a free one?'

She shrugged. 'What is it to me? Anything so long as he's out of here soon.' She went to the cupboard of the vessels.

Caratacos frowned. 'My sister loves no one, but you she hates. Why is that? Most men complain about her indifference, so you must be special. Why?'

Theana returned with a bronze bowl filled with water and a rag and proceeded to wipe the paint from her brother's skin. She complained that I was watching her and that if I didn't want my eyes to turn into milky white oysters, I should desist.

Bellowing with laughter, Caratacos ordered me and my slave to be moved to a place out of view. We were taken and bound to a more distant post in the shadows but I could still see her, Theana, going round the company repeatedly with a Greek krater, from which everyone drank to aid their fertility. She even gave some to the dogs, I noticed, but she gave us none. What she brought to us was a skull. She knelt down, lifted the cranium as if it were a lid and took out some moss which she then pressed to Mandred's neck. She said nothing, no soothing word, nothing of explanation.

'Is it a cure?' I asked.

'That's what I'd like to find out,' she said as she moved behind us into the shadows of the stall and began to undo the binding cords. I turned my head to gaze at her in gratitude. 'Keep your eyes to yourself!' she snapped. 'He needs to have one hand free to hold the poultice, that's all. No funny business.' She had loosened both of us but only Mandred had a hand free. She ordered him to press the poultice to his neck until told otherwise and went off to take the krater round again. When she returned she took the moss off and poked at the lump.

'Ow!' said Mandred.

'It may take all night to have effect,' she said. 'Hold it there. All night if necessary.' I knew then for certain that she was helping us to escape.

'What is this remedy?' I asked.

'The pus of a thousand boils. It's a principle of sacred medicine, to give the patient a little of what he's already got.'

'Show me!' I said, and she held the open skull so that I could see into it, and the thousand crushed and weeping white berries it contained. 'I thought you had to drink that.'

'Pus?' Mandred whimpered. 'Of a thousand boils?'

'It's mistletoe berries,' I said. 'Pickled in vinegar.'

'I recently learned that it can be usefully applied in a moss poultice,' said Theana, 'and thought I would try it on your slave.' She put the moss back into the skull, lifted it deferentially and carried it back to the cupboard of vessels. No one in their Beltane stupor noticed that she failed to tie Mandred up again.

He picked away at the bonds but couldn't get my hands free without making a noise. We waited for the snoring but the warriors had little appetite for sleep on this Beltane night. After some young women had run into the house giggling the place now had the air of a brothel in a Roman back street. Distracted the men might be, but they were awake, and we waited our moment. I must have slumbered for I dreamt that someone kissed me, so hard I couldn't breathe. I struggled back to wakefulness, to an uncanny peace reigning over the royal house, broken only by the rustle of rats and the hooting of owls. Mandred was already awake. There was a movement at the doorway and I watched, breath held, as the soft hide curtain lifted and someone came in. The moon projected his shadow on to the wall and I saw the outline of a one-armed man — that is, a man with one arm in a sling. I quietly cleared my throat and Katuaros turned towards the stalls. He stooped to finish off the work of untying us; we got up as silently as we could, without even disturbing the dogs, and picked our way over prone bodies to the doorway where we ducked out under the drape of skins. The warriors were so heavy in their sleep they could have been dead, but the eyes of a witch watched us in silence. We crept from the house, out into the cold yet gentle night and its ocean of stars on which sailed the waxing moon.

'Come now, quickly,' said Katuaros. 'I have put a restraining spell on the dun but I don't know how strong it is.'

I was used to his empty boasts about having magical powers, yet it did seem that all living things were asleep. That occasion is still remembered as 'The Silent Beltane'. Caratacos and his companions slept without stirring for a night, a day and a night, whether from a restraining spell or from what Theana had served them, I shall never know, but it has to be said that even the dogs slept. We slithered down the steep escarpment they call the Manger and found Draumur below, waiting with our chariot and horses. Scipio bent his head to greet me with an affectionate nudge.

Katuaros had sent the fianna on to Kyronion but I was worried about going there, thinking it would be an obvious place for Caratacos to look for us.

'We could take a circuitous route,' said Katuaros. 'He won't expect us to go south. If we follow the ridgeway, we'll come under the protection of the Belgae. It's a longer but safer way to Kyronion.'

'I know it,' said Mandred.

'Way-finding is my skill,' said Draumur.

Making a bitter sound, half laugh, half sneer, Mandred took his place as shield-bearer on the chariot, leaving Draumur to mount Scipio and lead us up the hill west of the dun and along the ridge. I looked back just once, telling myself I was checking to see whether we were being pursued, but, truth be told, I was wanting one more glimpse of her, the woman who had ruined me for love. We passed an ancient tomb, a long hump in a grove of trees, its entrance guarded by six stones standing as tall as a man. 'Move on,' said Katuaros. 'Pass it by, eyes averted.'

Just a month before I would have laughed at his fear of the Shee. Now I looked boldly towards the tomb and sensed that I was being smiled at in the dark. A subtle acknowledgement, a nod. We had taken the right road.

'This ridge path is good — the ground is dry and we leave no tracks,' said Draumur, his long, thin hair whipping in the wind around his all-but-bald patch, his harp hanging across his back where another might carry his shield. His tail of matted hair hung from it like a trophy. The sun rose behind us and illuminated a land unfolding in wave after wave of low hills. Their beauty, as the sun chases shadows across them, catches you in the chest. In Italy and in Gaul there are different shades of green: light, medium and dark. Here in Britain there are as many greens as there are blades of grass. Turquoise green, lime green, yew green, tired old summer green, barley green, green as translucent as glass that the sun shines through, and one thing can be all of these depending on the light. As the sun goes behind cloud, the land flattens into opaque, chalky shades; as it comes out, there is a glimmering iridescence, as glancing as a kingfisher's wing. It is the colour of life. This is the land of Ana the Mother, laid out with a hip there, a breast there, a long thigh, an ankle. Mother, our Mother — it would be easy to forget the danger, but we stayed on our guard and kept going.

Katuaros, who was driving the chariot, was whistling, but there was another air to him, one that I had marked first thing, the air of a man who has engaged in long exercise, or battle, and is now relaxed. Long exercise, battle, or sex. I rode up next to him. 'So, you enjoyed Beltane while I was bound to a post?'

'I did.' He smiled, unapologetic.

'You chased some poor girl down the hill and rutted with her like a beast.'

'What, trussed up in a sling like this? I had to let her come to me.'

If Katuaros had any power of spells, it was those he cast on women and I had taught myself never to envy him for it. You might as well envy a deer for speed, or a boar for strength, or a spider for tenacity. Katuaros was born to rut. No, more than that. For his magic worked just as well on crones. Any woman was prey to his charm. And any woman was fair game to him. He didn't want to bed them all, especially not the crones. What he wanted was for all women to love him, and most of them did.

'Who was it?' I asked, suddenly curious.

He shrugged. 'It would not be fair to say.'

'Well, I can be certain it wasn't Theana. Or Dryadia. Was it you who arranged for them to drug the mead? Why would they help us?'

'What makes you so certain it wasn't Theana?' he asked, aggrieved.

And then I felt stabbed in my innards, envying Katuaros not for sleeping with Theana so much as being always free while I was always bound.

'So...' I said, eventually, when my breathing had steadied. 'What is it like with Theana? I thought she slept with no man. What's the secret of your success?'

'Kindness,' he replied.

30

THE DIVIDED WAY

We rode across a land that swept away to a far horizon, a vista of low hills under an ardent sky. There was silence but for the song of the wind and the larks, the rustle and burr of insects in the grass. 'This is a good parcel of land...' Katuaros observed. He'd removed the sling and was trying to get some life back into his arm and shoulder, doing exercises in the back of the chariot while I did the driving. We were now deep in Belgic country. The Belgae are a jumble of tribes descended from the Morini, the Ambiani and the Suessiones of northern Gaul. Like the Atrebates, to whom they are related by a thousand marriages and countless fosterings, they were transplanted here by Kommios. All along the ridge were the ruins of ancient duns that, under the Belgae, had been left to decay; with their palisades and defences gone, the duns were like gums without teeth. At the height of our powers, these lands were productive farms guarded by warriors at the borders. There was no need for local defence. In the time of Biccos, even more so in the time of Biccos's own father, it had been a proud parcel of land and breeding ground for both the best horses and the best warriors in Britain. Now all we met were shepherds, herdsmen, children collecting fresh leaves for green broth. The warriors were away, protecting the oppida, leaving it an empty parcel of land.

'Be here my darling, my lovely,' said Katuaros to the land, 'when I come back, your lord and king.'

I reminded him that for two generations the Belgae had been

confederated with the Atrebates, all together under an Atrebatic king.

'Given that there is no king of the Atrebates now, with Verica dead and you intent on renouncing the title, things will inevitably change. Slip back to how they were...'

The Romans, it seemed to me, had sole possession of the future and there was no point in arguing about it. I left Katuaros to rotate his shoulder and dream about returning his parcel to its former glory.

Some duns showed signs of restoration, whether against the Catuvellauni or the coming Romans, we could not tell. Whenever he saw one, Katuaros became angry, wanted to storm the gates and demand by whose authority the ramparts were being built up again. I had to remind him that we were a small party trying not to be recognized and, besides, he was in no condition to storm anything. So we avoided these duns and their teams of ditch-diggers and took shelter in abandoned places.

On the first night we camped in a broken dun, choosing the sturdiest of the deep-thatches still standing. Inside it seemed as if someone had just left. There was a cauldron hanging over the hearth and grain and spring water stored in tall jars. Draumur felt the ash in the hearth and said it was cold.

'So who leaves such things?' I asked.

'Shepherds,' said Katuaros.

'Druids,' said Draumur.

'The Shee,' said Mandred. 'We leave it as we found it and add to the stores if we can.' He set to making a fire so that we could make ourselves a porridge of what was available.

That night I was awoken by what sounded like the wind snuffling round the house, seeking entry. Mandred was sitting by the fire, hugging his knees and staring into the embers. I wanted to speak to him but did not wish to disturb the others, so turned over and went back to my dreams, troubled though they were by Catuvellauni tortures.

Returning to the track in the morning, we continued south seeking a path going west, but could not find one, the track bending and bending again until we were going north, then north-west, and then west. Just as we were cheering, it swung south with renewed determination.

'By Nodens,' Katuaros muttered. 'It is an enchanted path.' Draumur rode ahead, the harp across his back twanging softly. Every time there was a choice of path, he and Mandred bickered. 'You're wrong.' 'That's not right.' 'It's a mistake.' 'Listen, Baldy...'

Draumur had what my grandmother used to call 'the nose'. He could sense direction, name the stars and predict exactly where and when the moon would rise. I knew these things by my studies, but he knew them instinctively. Blindfold him and spin him until he was giddy, he would always know, once freed, which way was north-east, the direction for him of home. Draumur's self-assuredness in what was merely intuition was grinding Mandred's patience. My slave could read the language of the land, using trees as his guides, noting on which side the whiskery lichen grew, and which side the branches preferred to be, which side of the track puddles were on, the direction indicated by a clump of wind-harassed thorns on a far hill. He had his own pride and it was in the wisdom of ages passed to him by his forefathers. Everyone knew which way was south, but Draumur would lift his nose to the wind and insist it was in the opposite direction. Because of the bends in the track, more often than not he was right. Katuaros kept laughing at our way-finders, which did not help anyone's temper.

The further south we went in our efforts to go west, the more distressed Mandred was becoming, but I soon realised there was a deeper cause to his tetchiness than any self-regarding German know-it-all. We had many miles of Belgic lands still to cross but the track, for all its bendings, was leading us inexorably towards the Durotriges.

'There it is!' Draumur called. 'The road west!' We were standing on high ground above where the track dipped and rose again. In the dip, a cross-track. As we rode down to it, the sky it led towards frayed and fell to the earth in grey strands. A rain squall rushed across the hills towards us, seeming to seek us out, to darken our way and pelt us with hail. We peered into the murk and saw three hunched figures coming towards us, swathed in doe skin cloaks, hooded heads down against the biting rain. Katuaros clutched the amulet he wore round his neck, worried they were Shee.

'Good fellows!' I hailed them. 'From which way do you come?'

'Where do you want?' asked one of them, in the Belgic dialect.

'The road west to Kyronion.'

'That way,' he said, pointing to the south, on the very track we were on.

'Ha!' said Draumur.

'That leads to Kennett, surely,' Mandred said.

'It certainly leads somewhere,' said the second of the three hooded figures.

'But where have you come from?' I asked, since by my sense of direction they had come from the west.

'There's nothing that way,' said the third. 'Just folds and combes and paths leading nowhere.'

'Rough weather to be out,' I said.

''Tis indeed, although it wasn't when we started, and probably won't be when we finish.'

'Just folds and combes and barrows,' repeated the third, 'and Catuvellauni patrols searching for strangers.' He peered at me from within the shadows of his cape to see if I'd understood.

'We continue south,' I said, giving my informants a brief nod and thanking them. They turned and went back the way they had come, taking the rain with them.

'Why listen to those old duffers?' Katuaros asked when we resumed on the track south. 'Why ignore the sound knowledge of Mandred? Even the instinct of Draumur is preferable to those brainless riddles.'

'Did you not recognize them?'

'Yes, of course I did. Three local peasants who are clearly inbred.'

He hadn't recognized them, had not seen the three attendant spirits of the Mother; nor did he know how the gods move amongst us, shape-shifting, taking forms at will. Did it take a Roman education to know such things? Or had I indeed been dropped on my head as a baby, as Verica used to claim?

I rode alongside Mandred and let some distance grow between us and the others. 'Strange,' I said, 'that Katuaros sees the Shee everywhere and the gods nowhere.'

Mandred looked at me askance. 'You recognized them?'

'Didn't you?'

He nodded.

'Do you think this way will lead to the west?' I asked.

'We'll come to another cross track in time, and it will be a better route,' he said. 'I think this way leads us where the gods want us to go.'

'But it's not the way you want to go. For you it's the way home.'

He shuddered. 'Home no longer.'

'You need to tell me what happened,' I said to him. 'How dangerous would it be for you to be recognized by any Durotrigan?'

'I would be arrested. Taken for trial. At best, excommunicated, at worst... At worst... '

'Death?'

'It's not death that scares me, but the manner of it.'

This I could understand after the mental torture Caratacos had subjected me to.

'Speak it out, my friend. I will not think the less of you.'

'I am druid, born of druid parents — my father was Bethryn of the temple of Belenos — and I was educated at the college of priests close to Mai Dun. Druids are born, not made, as you know, but I felt I had been born to the wrong family. I did not want to be a priest; I wanted to be a charioteer.'

I laughed. 'What boy does not?'

He kept his head down, hiding his face. 'Boyhood had long passed but the desire had not. I had no taste for the priesthood, none... They knew it so they tested me... You know as I do that if you fail in a sacrifice you become the victim...'

'That's the old way. It's usually commuted these days.'

'Not at Mai Dun. It was a... a... pig, that's all, a squealing pig. The pig or me. Why did I make a botch of that? But when something is wrong, when you feel in your bones it is wrong, then to do it is a gross profanity.'

'So what was the punishment to be? Not death, surely?'

'I didn't stay to find out. Stole a chariot. Escaped into the forest. Lived there about a year until my camp was discovered by the people of the Yew River. They sold me to a galley master at Bol harbour, and then I realised that death would have been preferable.'

I remembered the broken man I had found behind a pile of furniture at the Tiber market. 'The rest I know,' I said.

'The rest you know, except this. Yours was the first act of kindness I had experienced since my banishment.'

'There is no need for you to be concerned about what we might meet. No one can arrest the slave of a visiting king.'

'King now, are we?' he asked, his usual mocking tone returning.

'It has its uses.'

As night came on we saw an ancient dun ahead, its broken palisades standing out against the wide sky, obviously abandoned long ago.

'Barbryth,' said Mandred. 'Once a major border camp.'

As the sun dipped, a pale yellow stain on a grey blanket, we rode up a track that crossed two simple ditches. The entrance had lost its gates and inside we found nothing but a few deep-thatches gone grey with age and mould. Perhaps the only enemy here had been time.

Mandred made a tinder bundle, struck a spark from his steel and flint and, softly blowing, got a flame for a pile of kindling while Draumur made a broth from nettles, singing in his new voice a tale to the fire, an ancient lay of love between a warrior and the queen of the Shee. Rain came and crackled on the ground all around the house but the thick thatch made not a sound under the onslaught and the walls did not move. The only draughts came in through the doorway which we covered with extra hides. It is at such times as these that I enjoy deep-thatch life. Where else could you hear such stories as ours? While their poets sing, Romans eat and, worse, talk to each other. Here stories, stories of the hour and stories ancestral, are for listening to with rapt attention.

And so we told each other stories but when it came to Draumur's turn next, he picked up his harp. It was carved with a pattern of dragons and hung not only with a long knot of tangled hair but also with a small bunch of feathers, some finger bones and a dried teasel. He began to play but we did not know what. The music had no tune, apparently had not been heard before and would never be heard again. It was of the moment and drew on the elements. It was rain music, chilly night music, spring music, smoky fire music. It was music of Annwn, driven by the emotions and revealing the depth of passion in this otherwise reserved man. It grew louder and faster, his tattooed fingers flying over the strings, plucking at them beyond what, one would have thought, they could endure, but the strings held, sounded, reverberated under their lover's demands. Draumur's shale and bone armlets rattled in accompaniment. He put back his head, closed his eyes as if in agony and became oblivious to everything except the music now playing through him as much as through the harp. At the end, he laid his harp down and stroked it as if to calm it.

The only one who really understood the song was Mandred, who turned, twisted and bent double, crying, 'I cannot bear so much loss!'

The music disturbed memories. A burning forest, a spirited resistance, I remembered it now, the story I'd heard from Claudius of the exploits of his father and, subsequently, his brother, in subduing the German tribes, to avenge the destruction of three Roman legions led by Varus.

'Were you there?' I asked Draumur gently. 'At the battle of the Teutoburg forest?'

He said, 'I was six at the time. I barely remember.' Six years old, on the run from whoever it was who butchered his family, on the run through the burning forest littered with the slain, picking up the harp of a dead man somewhere along the way. He had looked after himself until he'd been recruited into the auxiliary cavalry attached to Legio Germanica as a groom. How he left the army and came into my father's life as a slave, I never found out. He said that this life, in this world, was hardly worth the telling. One should save one's breath. Another time he said, 'If you want to know me, listen to my songs.'

31

THE KEEPER OF KENNET SANCTUARY

After three days on the serpentine track we came to a hill called the Head of the Snake. On the summit was a sacred circle of concentric rings from which was an extensive view of a land swelling here and there into hills. Everywhere barrows and those scatters of large grey stones easily mistaken in the distance for sheep. The horizon-seeking eye, however, was caught by a vast mound emerging above the trees, stepped in outline and with a chalk path ascending in a spiral. I knew where we were, had heard stories from my mother about shape-shiftings and hauntings set in this place: the Sanctuary of Kennet and the Albios Hill.

This vast sanctuary was overgrown now. There had been some clearance for farms but the secrets of the place had been lost to the wild wood. The land wheeled about us and the vast sky wheeled about the land. We were insignificant, the poor remnant of something once mighty, something that could never be known again.

'It's an omphalos,' I said, 'from an age far beyond ours, an age with different centres. The time of the star-gazers.'

Katuaros did not want to hear about an ancient temple hidden in the woods, so large that giants could get lost in it. 'Look,' he said, pointing down to the vale. 'A sturdy track running east-west.'

'But we can't come this close without looking for it,' I protested.

'The temple is lost to the trees now,' said Mandred, 'and no one but an idiot goes to find it. It's a place of the dead. Best leave them in peace.'

'You lost nearly a moon at the Sanctuary of the Wheel,' said Katuaros, 'and you've lost days to the Catuvellauni, and now you want to look for a lost temple? Leave it! Let's go on. See, there's our road west, down there, clear as the serpent on my arm!'

I struggled to master opposing desires but eventually, admitting they were both right, chose to continue the road west rather than linger. The mission I had been given by Claudius did not involve satisfying my curiosity about the temples of men long gone. With a sigh I led the way back down the hill to set off westward. The track was accompanied by a stream flowing past us which I thought must be the beginnings of Kennet river. Shrines on both sides of the track revealed it as a processional way, but then all our major tracks had that function before the coming of the Romans. Draumur said it would lead us eventually to the Hot Springs of Sulis.

'We could cut across country for Kyronion,' said Katuaros but Draumur thought this inadvisable. 'Better to go to the Hot Springs,' he said, 'and pick up the Albios Way there. Longer in miles but quicker in days.' Even as he spoke, we passed a large circle of tall posts that enclosed and hid the Kennet at what must have been its source. Within the posts it seemed to be scrubby woodland. It was dark in there, that entrance to the Otherworld and Katuaros called for us to press on.

Just beyond the wooden circle, the track bridged a stream (same stream? another stream?). I paused the party to take off our mantles for it was becoming the first hot day of the year and it felt good to get the sun on my skin again. Draumur squinted into the distance and said the stream seemed to be flowing from the sacred mound. 'It's a different stream,' he decided, 'but it seems to flow to join the other one.' There seemed nothing remarkable in that until he pointed out that, while the first stream had clearly been flowing from its source, this one was flowing towards its source.

'That's not possible,' said Mandred, and the two of them bickered about east-flowing and south-flowing streams until Katuaros said sharply, 'So what? It's just a place of many streams...'

I had a vague memory of something Innogen had told me about the source of Kennet river. We had been playing in the river where it flowed near Calleva, she teaching me to swim 'like a dolphin'. As we dabbled more like ducks than dolphins, I asked her where the river came from. 'It has two heads and comes from the Mother,' she had told me, 'at the Well of Swale near the Albios Hill.'

The Albios Hill, that great mound ahead of us, was grassed-over now but would have been pure white chalk on its building. I took a votive image from my bag and laid it in the stream for the Spirit of Kennet. Two heads, two streams. Just as the Sanctuary of the Wheel was embraced by two rivers, so the Sanctuary of Kennet was the source of two streams. While I was pondering these things, four men appeared as if four trees had just come to life. They bore no weapons other than voice and compelled us to dismount simply by telling us to. 'Togidubnos of the Atrebates,' said their leader, a tall, slender man with fiery hair. 'We've been waiting for you.'

My companions rustled with shock but I kept my head. 'And you are?'

'Apnodens, master of bards and keeper of Kennet Sanctuary.' There was a power in his utterance that all the orators of Rome have sought in vain to acquire. It was a voice to take you by the ears. All he was doing was telling me his name and I felt a chill on my spine.

'How do you know who I am?

'We've been watching you since you landed.'

'For what purpose?'

'To discover your purpose.'

It felt like being blocked on the Black Raven board.

'If you've watched me carefully,' I said, 'you will be suspecting I have no purpose at all.'

He smiled, genuinely amused. 'When you want a bug to walk in a particular direction, you put obstacles in its way.'

'A bug...'

'And here you are.' He gestured for us to dismount and none of us had any choice but to obey. Mandred, keeping his head down so that his hair covered his face, looked the very image of the cowed and mistreated slave. Apnodens took hold of my right arm to study the tattoo of the wheel. He himself wore the same symbol, a wheel with eight spokes, as a brooch fastening his mantle. Was he Eleusinian? Clearly not. What stood before me was a druid. Although he and his companions were unarmed, dressed simply and walking barefoot, yet we felt constrained to go with them into the circle of posts and the woods it embraced. I learned later that the circle defined the College of Bards.

We took the chariot into the trees as far as we could and concealed it with branches. Although I kept a look-out for a way of escape, at the same time, I did not wish to find one, for I would be escaping into a world of uncertainty from a world as familiar as the womb. That sense of having been somewhere before... I had never been here, and yet everything was known to me. Accompanying our path through the trees was the stream from the bridge, brimming with life: ducks followed by ducklings, water voles keeping to the shadows of the bank, fish clearly visible in the clear water, the whole course lined by iridescent green grasses and yellow flowers.

'It leads us to the source,' said Apnodens.

'How can it? It flows with us.'

He smiled enigmatically and walked on, leading us into a small grove of gnarled trunks and generous branches, a place where new leaves drooped, a place of Annwn, another one of those thin places where you can inhabit both worlds at once.

The stream ran into the grove and turned sharply left. At that place, in the crook of its arm, as it were, was the chalky basin of a spring. As the water overflowed from the basin, it joined the weak stream and turned it into the source of Kennet river. My river... the clear waters that flowed sedately past Calleva where I had learned to swim.

'The Well of Sulis,' said Apnodens, introducing me to the spring, 'although here we call her "Swale".'

I knelt and, reaching into the water, wetted my hand and put it to my lips, as if to kiss the spirit. Approving of my gesture, Apnodens took up some water in a wooden cup and invited me to drink. At the taste of it, my heart ached with longing for something just out of reach, some eternal place. I began to understand Mandred's agony of loss brought on by Draumur's song. There is loss of what you once had, and the greater loss, of that which you never possessed. I could feel the water running inside my body like an underground spring, down the throat to the heart. Draumur gently laid down his harp and his sword as if in a holy place.

A rustling amidst the trees alerted us to others who were present, who had hidden at our approach, and a group of student bards emerged tentatively like curious fawns. Apnodens sternly ordered them back to their studies.

'Son of Biccos,' he said to Katuaros as he gestured for us to sit with him, 'please remove your sword in this holy place.' Grudgingly, Katuaros drew Firebreath from her sheath but kept her close to hand. Apnodens glanced at the sword with disapproval but said nothing. Felled trees, crudely hewn, provided our seating around the hearth. Some of the living trees had been carved with the images of wood spirits, offerings were tucked into holes amongst the roots and the branches fluttered with votive rags.

'Are we prisoners?' I asked.

'Guests,' he said, 'but we need you to stay awhile.'

I shifted impatiently.

'Is there something you would prefer to be doing?'

'I am headed for Venonis,' I said, 'but we lost our way on the ridgeway track and ended up here. Which is to say, we were guided here like bugs, but I am losing precious time.'

He leant forward, took some ash on his finger and drew a line down my brow. 'A man marked with the wheel should not lie. Truth telling,' he commanded. I swear the leaves on the trees trembled at the tone of his voice. 'What are you doing back in Britain?'

The ash was warm but it grew hotter and I broke into a sweat.

'Come,' he said. 'Is it so hard to speak the truth?'

'The Romans...'

'Yes.'

'I've lived in Rome ten years. Verica came, asking the emperor for help to regain his territory from the Catuvellauni, from Caratacos. His request was granted and he and I were sent home in advance of the army...'

'For what purpose?'

'It would be madness,' I blurted out, 'to try and resist what is coming. The Divine Claudius assures me, and wants me to assure the Britons, that if you do not resist you shall be treated as allies of Rome. But if you do resist...'

'Let's not list out the consequences of that. But do these assurances extend to druids?'

I had no answer to that and began to wonder myself if Claudius had different intentions for druids. I rubbed at my forehead which had become hot and dry.

'Why do you want to go to Venonis?' Apnodens asked.

'I thought if I could get there for midsummer — which seemed an easy proposition when I set out — then I could speak to the gathered kings and chieftains all together. But on the way I need to find and speak to Esius, King of the Dobunni, a kinsman of my mother. His allegiance is vital to the Romans.'

'Do you know the plan of invasion?'

'I do. They will land in my harbours and march north to regain Calleva for the Atrebates.'

'And then?'

'The legions will split up. One goes north to Venonis, two east to Camulodunon and one west.'

'How far west?'

'To the Albios Way,' I muttered. My voice was getting softer and softer; more than once he had to ask me to repeat what I had just said and each time his companions grew paler. Now he picked up a stick and prodded me with it. 'The Albios Way,' I repeated.

'For what purpose?'

I sat mouthing air. He prodded me again. 'It will be the new frontier,' I mumbled.

'What? Speak up!'

'The Albios Way. It will be the northern boundary of the Roman Empire.'

With a yelp, one of the druids jumped up and walked off, but Apnodens remained impassive, more stoical than a Stoic. He was silent for a long while, until I broke into his reflections with a question of my own.

'The Romans...' I said. 'Have you heard anything of them?'

'The fleet has embarked from Gesoriacum.'

I had waited to hear that for so long, but now my feelings were mixed. I was beginning to worry about any druids the Romans found in their path. What would happen to them?

'Why are they expending so much energy and expense on Britain?' Apnodens asked. 'For our gold? Our silver?'

'They are running out of lead.'

'*Lead?* The only value of lead is the silver it contains.'

'Lead itself is the stuff of civilization. Soft and malleable, it is good for making things such as cisterns, plates, pipes and drains.'

'And for that they are moving thousands of soldiers over Ocean and beyond the known world?'

'Not only that, no. As I said, they want to restore to the Atrebates the territories snatched by Caratacos. And Claudius needs a triumph.'

'What is a triumph?'

'A spectacular parade through the streets of Rome, lasting several days, accorded only to those who have extended the Empire. If it impresses itself sufficiently on the minds of the citizens, it assures a man everlasting fame. Most men want a triumph because of vanity; Claudius needs one to seal his authority over Senate and people.'

Apnodens rose to pace about, as self-absorbed and leggy as a heron.

'Their forces are so far superior to the British,' I said, 'there can only be one outcome.'

'They lost whole legions in their fight for Germania and Gaul.'

'But they got possession in the end, and it was far bloodier than it would otherwise have been. Why protract the inevitable? The choice is simple,' I said. 'Resist and die or submit and live.'

He sat down next to me on my log. 'It's because of that kind of mistaken thinking that I've been told to keep you here.'

'Who by?'

'The archdruid. We can't have you travelling about infecting everyone with Roman thinking. Submit and live? The choice in truth is this, resist and die or bend your abject knee to new rulers. For a druid this is a choice between death of the body and death of the soul.'

I understood what he was saying and blanched at my temerity. Had I really thought I could go about negotiating with kings? What had seemed possible in Rome was proving impossible in Britain.

'Is there no middle course?'

'There is,' he said, sitting down again. 'There is. It is to melt away. Isn't that what the druids did in Gaul? Many came here, but others remained and just disappeared into the forests.'

As if being bitten by ants, he got up and continued his pacing. 'If you knew me, you'd know that what I am about to say is highly unusual, but I just don't know what to do.'

'Master,' one of the druid tutors reminded him softly. 'You can do nothing without authority.'

'That's true, that's true. I need to call to my father.'

When I discovered that his father was not only the archdruid but resident north of Venonis, I was astonished, but then a calling made by a master of bards was not one of the usual *halloos* that go from hill to hill.

'O son of Biccos,' he said to Katuaros. 'I hear there was a holding spell put on the Catuvellauni at Beltane, they say by you. That was just a sprinkle of some herb in the mead, wasn't it? This is what a real one feels like.' He clicked his tongue twice against his palate and Katuaros was glued to the log, his eyes bulging with the strain of trying to move. Apnodens stepped forwards and took away his sword and dagger. 'And this is half-strength,' he said. Making another click, he limited Katuaros's immobility to his feet; suddenly I realised that I, too, could not move. We were left thus in the grove while Apnodens and a senior tutor of the bardic college went back the way we had come, over the bridge to ascend the sacred mound, the Albios Hill.

About an hour later, we heard the calling. It began like the cry of a wolf but the reach and volume of the sound went far beyond anything a wolf can make. One of the tutors guarding us sat with his head cocked, reading the message that was now rolling through the air like thunder.

'What does it say?' I asked him.

'Not for you to know.'

'Will it reach all the way to Vernemeton?'

The man laughed at my ignorance. 'Of course not! It will reach Kyronion, though, and be passed on from there, from dun to dun along the Albios Way.'

'When will you get a reply?'

'Tomorrow, or perhaps the day after.'

When Apnodens returned he came with a basket of food that had been left for the college at the bridge. Unshackled now, we ate with our captors in the grove but of the students there was no sign. Throughout the afternoon, however, we heard them chanting deep in the woods, practising their Song of Origins.

There are no books in druid colleges: everything is done by voice. And if that is true of all druids, it is even more so for the bards who are students of sound. The constant drone of their voices, the stopping, the starting, the repetitions, were oddly soothing and reminded me that a Stoic would not sit hunched in despair but would patiently accept the unfolding of Fate. I breathed in — the air smelt strongly of wild garlic and blue-bells — and straightened up to listen properly. A strange peace began to unfold inside me that had nothing to do with our circumstances or the onset of war.

Night came on. The students were quiet now but still had not returned to the hearth. I looked around, wondering where we were going to sleep. The druids lived so simply: food was brought to them by local farmers. Were we to bed down with the beetles and ants of the woodland floor? But when the moon rose, Apnodens had us each take up a tallow torch and led us along a field track to a great long barrow, about a mile south of the spring and standing out against the sky on the horizon.

'If you have been watching me since I arrived back,' I said as we walked, our shadows dancing under the flaring lights, 'you were at the Sanctuary of the Wheel?'

'Not personally. There is a college of medicine hidden close by. Not difficult for them to get you hallucinating.' Apnoden's laugh was like the bark of a fox, sudden and short.

'You were delaying me! Every delay I've suffered — druid work!'

'Either us or the Shee. We work together.'

'The Shee have been helping me.'

'Helping you to find me, that is all.'

290

'And now that I have found you?'

'We must wait. Not long. My father's reply will come soon and, meanwhile, we shall seek the advice of the gods.' We were approaching now the long barrow that, in the gathering dark, looked menacing. 'Tonight,' Apnodens said, 'with the help of the gods I may hear what I need to know from Annwn.'

32

THE TEMPLE OF ANA

The barrow stood out against the darkening sky, ancient and forbidding. The closer we came the more Katuaros held back, certain that he was being led to a mighty abode of the Shee. Mandred, too, was greatly reluctant to go towards those standing stones that stood up like broken teeth at the mouth of the barrow's entrance.

'Must I put ropes on and pull you like donkeys?' Apnodens asked. Pride got the better of both warrior and slave; they steeled themselves with resolve and walked on. When we arrived at those terrible stone sentinels, we planted our torches in a circle and lit a fire. It gave some cheer, though Katuaros sat quietly invoking the gods for protection. 'Come,' Apnodens beckoned me to rise and took me along the side of the barrow. It stretched back a great distance, tapering to its end, its long spine providing a false horizon of the expansive sky. Along the hump ox skulls had been placed to mark the risings and settings of certain stars. 'We can only wonder at what the star-gazers knew,' he said, stepping down into the ditch that, running the length of the barrow, gave him the eye-line of the horizon.

I joined him there and looked up into the soft sky and the half-moon now rising. Apnodens put up an antler tine to show the place. As we stood there watching the moon rise, unable to detect any movement except in comparison to the marker, I told him about my travels in Greece, the temples I had seen, about Delphi and Eleusis. He said that our star-people and their star-people had once known each other and that it had been possible to visit foreign temples and feel at home. With Apnodens I was having the kind of conversation I'd not enjoyed since I'd parted from Seneca. He was educated, he was curious, he was intelligent and, although he was holding me against my will, I was already beginning to regard him as a friend. In his company, time seemed as immense as the celestial vault we think of as an upturned cauldron. All encompassing. All embracing.

'I was here ten nights ago, watching the stars,' he said. 'Close to dawn I saw a ball of fire with a shimmering tail plummeting into the west. The line of light followed the profile of this barrow, drew its shape in the sky.'

'Many saw it. I saw only geese.'

'Geese?' he asked, abstracted by his own memory. 'I saw it close to dawn. By midday a calling had come from the Canti territory that the fleet had been sighted and was heading along the south coat. East to west.'

'So the shooting star was an omen of something that was already happening?' I intended this as wry humour, but it was not taken that way. Instead, Apnodens looked at me with a puzzled frown.

'You are right...,' he said at last. 'Why would the gods give sign of the obvious? Did I misread it?'

'What else could it mean?'

'I am not yet sure. Perhaps after tonight...' He guided me back to the fire at the entrance which was now sinking into embers. These he arranged in a circle with lines of charcoal dividing the circle into three. The Hearth of the Three Mothers of Light. As Apnodens began to chant I was suddenly a boy again, watching my mother perform the evening rite.

To the Three Mothers,
Save, shield and surround us.
This is the hearth of the Great Mother's house.
On this night and every night, protect us.

'Protect us,' muttered Katuaros.

Apnodens subdued the embers with a light covering of ash. Down by the river, all was quiet, all fires similarly smoored. 'Do the young ones sleep in the grove?' I asked.

'Not at night. They sleep with the sun and rise with the moon.'

The young bards, having spent the late afternoon and evening hours rehearsing songs or chants, would now be lying on the hard ground with a heavy stone on the chest to keep them awake while they memorised what they had learnt. I felt grateful not to be among them, before, that is, Apnodens ushered us into the long barrow. Katuaros hung back, whispering *Oh no, oh no, oh no* ... until I pushed him in. And now Mandred was hanging back. He had no fear of the Shee, but the spirits of the dead drained him of courage. Momentarily he forgot to keep his head down in that beaten-dog way he'd adopted since we came to this sanctuary and Apnodens, as if noticing him for the first time, peered into his face, causing him to stumble. Draumur broke Mandred's fall and pulled him into the tomb.

By the light of the waxing moon and one now feeble torch, we could see that the interior comprised stone chambers in five lobes off a central passage. From the great extent of the barrow seen from the outside, I'd expected something similar on the inside, but the chambers clustered behind the entrance and did not run the length. In them were earthen shelves bearing skeletons curled up like babies, some missing their skulls.

We were each given a shelf as a bed to share with an ancient and any restlessness we might have suffered was dealt with by Apnodens clicking his tongue on his palate. The lamp was extinguished, the darkness absolute. I had been through this before. As someone who had spent a night being initiated into the Mysteries, the prospect of a night in a barrow did not concern me. Even the discomfort of the hard 'bed' was easily endured, thanks to the practice Seneca had given me in sleeping on floors. I lay there listening to the troubled breathing of sleepless Katuaros, the whispering hymns of Draumur and the whimpering of Mandred.

Then began a sound which threatened to dissolve my bones. A low resonating hum, which I took to be from a man's throat, that of Apnodens? And soon it was joined by others, this hum like bees in a hive. But it grew in volume and, as it did, it began to echo back from the chamber itself, as if other beings had taken up the wordless chant and were reflecting it back, amplified. 'Oh no, oh no, oh no...' Katuaros moaned, struggling against the spell. Waves of sound began to wash over us. The gates of my mind suddenly flew open and out from some hidden place as bats from a cave came the bad memories, the regrets, the fears. This part was familiar: I had experienced it at Eleusis. I knew what to do and kept my thoughts firmly on an image of light. At some point in the middle of the night the vibrating hum began to diminish and I fell asleep, to dream of oars splashing on water, of armed men shouting, a woman screaming. I awoke with a start, the rising sun fingering into the barrow; I lay there, listening to a fading lament, a woman, no, the Mother herself, crying...

Then I became aware of a one-sided conversation. Apnodens was whispering, to himself or another I could not tell. All I heard him say was, 'Was the omen of the star meant *for us*?' And then, as if in response to a reply, 'What will they do to us if we stay?' Another pause and, 'Are we directly in their path?' Finally, 'Yes, of course, I can do nothing without his authority.'

The next thing I knew, Apnodens was waking me up as if pulling me out of the deepest well and helping me to rise up. I was as stiff as the dead. 'Sleep well?' he asked with an affable smile.

I told him of the visions that had haunted me.

'You are, as I've suspected all along, a son of the Mother,' he said. It was dawn and the standing stones at the entrance gradually emerged from darkness, giving that sense to be had every day if only we were alert enough, that sense not so much of a new beginning as the return of illusion, as if the truth is in the dark. Perhaps that's why my people are a lunar culture who begin the day at sunset. A little while later, the sun is up and all hope of reflection lost while we stand bedazzled by the world.

We all stumbled out into a grey dawn alive with birdsong. Katuaros, stunned by insomnia, claimed he'd heard nothing during the night. Draumur had heard faint and very beautiful music and followed it into Annwn. Mandred said he had not slept at all for the deafening sound of bees.

Apnodens laid his hand on my slave's trembling arm. 'Don't I know you?'

Mandred hung his head and denied it.

'He's just a slave,' I said. 'Got him cheap in a Roman flea market. Ignore him.'

'But Durotriges?'

'Ignore him,' I repeated. 'He's my property, nothing more.'

'What's wrong with his legs?'

'Lamed by a long sea voyage in shackles.'

Apnodens took Mandred by the chin and turned his head so that he could see better the lump on his neck by the gathering light of day.

'Made by the chafing of the neck iron,' I explained.

'So all your sufferings have been inflicted by others?' Apnodens asked Mandred directly.

'On the contrary. I only have myself to blame.'

Apnodens nodded. 'I think we have met. At a festival gathering, perhaps?'

'I certainly recognize you,' Mandred muttered. 'Son of the archdruid.'

'We'll have a look at that lump later,' Apnodens said.

'What was the point of a night in the tomb?' I asked him as we walked together back to the spring.

'It reveals.'

'Reveals what?'

'The nature of men. It showed, for instance, that a philosopher can have more courage than a warrior. Your lame slave remains obscure to me, however. His face is familiar and yet not familiar, as if it were the shadow of his true face. We druids know how to shield our souls, and his shield is impenetrable. What do you know of his story?'

'Very little. He was a druid, it's true.'

Apnodens nodded as if remembering something. 'Ah, yes, I think I recall him now. Mai Dun? Yes, Mai Dun. Son of Bethryn. Yes... So, he's back.'

'Is he in danger here?'

'Here? No. This is sanctuary.'

'I only know he failed to perform the sacrifice of a pig.'

'A pig?'

'And he stole a chariot.'

'Ah, yes, the chariot.'

'He says, although born to be a priest, he is better fitted by nature to be a charioteer.'

'That is true of many of us, that our desires go against the grain of our duty.'

The way he said it, with a tone of regret, caused me to glance at him sideways, but he deftly changed the subject. 'He will tell the full story when he is ready to reveal himself.'

'He hasn't told it yet?'

'Not yet, no. It was more than a pig. Everyone accused him of cowardice when he ran, but I always suspected it was something else.'

'What would happen to him if he were caught by the Durotrigans?'

'He would be tried in the druid court. The Durotrigan druid court, an uncompromising, merciless seat of judgement. Best avoided.'

'And you, what did you learn?' I was longing to know the other half of the conversation I'd overheard. He gave no answer but stood with his back to the tomb, facing the rising sun with his arms raised and his eyes closed, as if in thanks.

Back at the spring we found the young bards cooking breakfast at the fire while competing with each other in cross harmonies, each one outdoing the rest in tongue-twisting metrics. They fell silent when we appeared and looked at me and my companions nervously, as if their world must consist entirely of poetry or else be a threatening place. Apnodens soothed them as a shepherd his sheep and introduced me to them not as a king but as Delfos, son of Innogen. One who had been trying to outdo the others in the most inventive and eloquent curses glanced up at Innogen's name but, catching my eye, became sullen and stared crossly into the fire. I realised with an odd jarring sensation that it was a girl of about ten years. She wore her hair long and untied like a boy; it was the sullen-ness that betrayed her. Girls have a way of looking as brown as a bog when they don't like you.

After they had eaten, they went off to their huts to sleep for the day. I asked Apnodens what he could tell me about the temple which, to him, surely was not so much lost as hidden.

'Thousands of years ago,' he replied, 'the land was clear and the Sanctuary of Kennet, the greatest in the world, was laid out over many miles. The temple is the heart of Great Mother Ana — we slept in her womb last night — but the great stone circle is her heart.'

'I would like to visit it.'

'I may permit that, but only you. Your companions must remain here.' A sound began deep within him, rose through his chest and came out a prolonged, vibrating hum. He held me tight by the wrist, protecting me from the sound which wreathed around my companions like smoke and put them all into a doze. So, it had been Apnodens making the sound of bees...

On the promise that I would not try to escape, we set off following a stream that came from the north to feed into the sacred spring. I realised for the first time that everything was in a line running from south to north: long barrow, sacred spring, sacred mound and on to the temple hidden in the forest.

'Who built the Albios Hill?' I asked.

Apnodens told me what he knew of it, that it had been created by men, that there was an ancient altar on the summit, close to the gods, from where they made and received their callings. 'It is the pregnant belly of the Mother, whose body now is hidden by the trees. You call it the Albios Hill and, certainly, it once was white. When the surrounding ditch is flooded, it is a beautiful thing, but when it was white... it must have brought proud men to their knees. Now, however, it is known as the Hill of Sovereignty for it is where new kings are blessed.'

He gave me one of the two sickles he'd brought with him and together we cleared the way of cow parsley and nettles. 'It is the duty of the keepers of the sanctuary to keep the paths clear; at the same time we are enjoined to keep the temple hidden. It's a riddle we try daily to solve.'

He told me that there were two avenues, lined by those grey sheep-stones which our ancestors had set up on end to mark the way. According to ancient legends they were routes of procession, one male, the other female, leading to two circles in the centre of the Temple of Ana. 'It was a place of mass marriage between the tribes, a rite held at Beltane.'

Eventually the avenue led us into dense woods bright green with fresh leaves. While last year's beech leaves crackled, still on the boughs, the new leaves of birch, aspen and poplar made a song of sighs in the breeze. At last we came to a bank rising like a tidal wave above our heads, made of chalk but grassed over now and with trees growing out of it, their gnarled roots exposed, and here and there scars of white to show the chalk beneath. The path cut through the bank and crossed a ditch now almost filled with scrub and bramble, so there was no way of discovering its depth; once we were across, however, I could see the extent of the area of the temple and it was truly gigantic. The ground within the bank and ditch was kept clear by horned sheep gently munching grass within and without a vast circle of mighty stones of curious shapes. I could see in the far distance another 'gate' in the bank, directly opposite, and then other openings at what I supposed to be east and west but Apnodens said they were not the four cardinal directions. He undid his wheel brooch and held it out, aligned it due north against a marker he had put up himself on the rim of the bank and showed how the paths were closer to the cross-quarter spokes. 'Almost solstice lines but not quite. We don't know what they aligned to in those days: some say it was the stars and not the sun. Sometimes I come here at night to study it but the key eludes me. Perhaps it is enough just to wonder.'

He led me round the stones, some like dancers balancing on one foot, others more solid and square. Within their vast compass were more stones, in a pattern I could not discern but which he explained were the remains of several structures, including two large inner circles set side by side. I began to feel strange, as if something were happening to my eyes, as if I could see but not see. These queer stones looked as if they were desperate to tell me something.

'The stones are male and female, had you not noticed?' he asked.

I had not, but now I could perceive that some were rounded, some straight-edged.

'Mass marriage? Was there any element of choice?'

'Only by the druid elders. Your wife is near,' Apnodens said gently.

'What?' I looked around the vast arena and its stones in alarm, wondering if one of them was about to move towards me. Some of the stones had faces, etched into the rock by nature and not by men, and all were facing east.

'What does the word "wife" mean to you?' he asked.

What indeed? For sure the word did not summon up images of naked Messalinas; instead, and oddly, I found myself thinking of Seneca's Cornelia, who brought order to the house and peace to her husband's life. He loved her to a degree that conflicted with his stoic principles. Someone once asked him if a wife was an 'indifferent' and he explained that some 'indifferents' were to be preferred, since they run in accordance with nature. I remembered Cornelia as a woman solicitous of her husband's health while her own health was poor. She died, I heard, from a broken heart. I answered Apnoden's strange question with a shrug.

He rolled his eyes and used my youth as an excuse for my ignorance. He went to a stone that was like a giant's head, rested his hands on its craggy surface and gazed up its height to the sky. Then he spread his arms wide across the face of the stone and pressed his ear against it. He began to look like a sleeping child listening to its dreams. In a whisper, he asked a question of the stone which I could not hear. The answer furrowed his brow with deep concern. He turned and rested his back against the stone, staring at the sky.

'What is it?' I asked him.

But he slid down the stone until he was sitting on the ground, pressing his face into his drawn-up knees. 'I don't know what to do...' he said, and his voice was wretched. I crouched next to him to see if I could help.

'You say the Romans will take Calleva and then split the army,' he said. 'A legion will come west?'

'Yes.'

'They will follow that track you were on, passing close to our grove?'

'Presumably.'

'What must I do?'

'What do the spirits say?'

'They are divided! Even Annwn is divided! How can I act when even the gods cannot agree? The Shee say the

301

druids must melt away like mist and leave it all to them. The Mother says I must defend her at the cost of my own life if necessary. Swale of the spring, she begs me not to leave her. But the gods, they say go west. Tell me the truth, what would happen if my college found itself in the path of the Roman army?'

I told him that the legate in charge of the Second Legion was a just man not given to cruelty. 'He will probably offer you a choice: give up your druid ways or migrate.'

'Give up our druid ways? A thousand years of tradition is what you're asking of us. A hundred thousand years. Our ways go back to the beginning. Ways that have been lost in Gaul since the Romans took over. Britain is the last refuge. Delfos, you have gone from place to place, identifying certain sites as sacred, but the whole land is sacred. It is all sanctuary. All the Temple of Brit-Ana, not just here. The Romans promise peace, but they will desecrate the sacred land. They will tramp over it, build chains of forts, mine it, foul its waters. How can we allow that to happen?'

'How can you stop it?'

Now it was his turn for truth-speaking, and he needed no hearth ash. He rose up and brushed the dust off. 'I can lend what I have to the cause of Caratacos.'

'What?'

'Whatever you say to King Esius to persuade him to ally with the Romans, I will unsay. He will listen to me. I will move my college to wherever Caratacos suggests and give my full weight to the fight for the liberty of Britain.'

It was my turn to blanch. 'That would make us utterly opposed.'

He nodded. 'I could do these things,' he said, 'except that I can do nothing without the authority of my father, and I know his mind already. Regalis says we are doomed to extinction, it is our end of days, but if we work with the Romans, something may be saved of our traditions and teachings.'

I began to breathe again. 'So, then, that is the choice: fight to the death with Caratacos and lose everything in the process, or submit to the Romans and preserve the traditions.'

He smiled at how simple I made it sound. 'Or there is the third way. Go beyond the frontier. Melt away west. But that is for my father to say.'

On our way back to the grove, we took the chalk path that ascended the Hill of Sovereignty on a spiral's curve to speak to the man on watch and find what messages had been received. 'It's all a babble,' he said. 'And some of it out of date. There are still calls that the Romans are not coming even though they've been sighted on the sea. But mostly it's Caratacos calling men to Calleva.'

'And nothing from my father?'

'Not yet, no.'

IV

THE ALBIOS WAY

33

THE SCHOOL OF VOCOS

The name of the girl bard was Branwen, though everyone called her Little Sister. Each morning she spent time alone with Apnodens in a clearing in the woods where they sat cross-legged and facing each other while Apnodens patiently instructed her in a long invocation. Their sound drew me towards them, although I kept myself hidden in the trees. I swear the animals of the woods used to come to the edge of the glade to listen to their chanting. It was the sound of eternity, as if these hymns had been sung forever, each of them passed from tutor to pupil just as was happening here. If Apnodens singled her out for special instruction, it was for two reasons: her time in the college would be short, and she was the best of them all. He sang to her as if he would give her all that he knew, and she sang it back to him.

Apnodens told Little Sister to try the waters of Swale as a cure for the sore on Mandred's neck. She went to the well, knelt down, took the wooden cup that was always kept there and, intoning a spell, drew out water, scooping eastwards in the direction of the stream's flow. She carried the cup back to Mandred, whom Apnodens commanded to drink. Three times this rite of cure was performed, a rite which could only be performed by a virgin at an east-flowing spring. I asked if it would also help Katuaros who, I knew, was pretending to have recovered from the injury to his shoulder: the long ride had undone all the good healing he'd had at Cuma's Hill. Branwen duly filled the cup and poured it slowly over him, not the shoulder as I'd expected, but nape of neck and spine. When I asked why, she shrugged and said it was as Swale directed, and she trusted Swale.

It was as Katuaros shivered under the trickle of cold, healing water that we heard the first calls of the carnyxes, followed by shouts from hill to hill where the flames of beacons sprang up: the Romans were landing. The students grew agitated but Apnodens assured them that the Romans were not coming to Kennet. 'They are going to Calleva. We shall be safe.'

'For now,' he muttered, brushing past me.

Apnodens took me with him to keep night-watch on the Hill of Sovereignty where I heard the calls myself and their confusion. 'It's like trying to hear a cuckoo in a rookery,' he complained. 'I can no longer distinguish one voice from another.' At any other time, keeping watch on this breast of the goddess, sitting close to its altar to the celestial gods, must surely have been an experience of profound peace. Apnodens had a theory that the mound had been built as a spoked-wheel in plan, for the sides were flatter than they appeared from a distance. 'Eight spokes?' I asked excitedly. 'Nine,' he said, and smiled at my disappointment. 'Wouldn't it be satisfying if it were eight? But the patterns of the past never quite fit with those of the present. Otherwise we would understand everything...' He gazed out over the land. By the light of the waxing moon we could see the entire sanctuary as shapes of darkness against the sky, all encircled by the horizon and its many barrows. The place of king-making... To this broad audience of the ancestors, a man would take on the robe of the sky to marry the sovereign goddess, the land. As the night wore on the callings petered out but, before we could enjoy pure silence, the chorus of birds began and we were relieved from the watch by the next man on duty.

On the way back to the grove, we crossed the bridge made of sheep-stones and planks which was dedicated to the horned god Cernunnos. He found a basket of bread and cheese the locals had left us and put a little of it on the god's altar.

'When we met,' he said, 'you were looking baffled by the flow of the stream.'

'We had followed it from the Hill of the Serpent's Head, walking against its flow, but we lost sight of it in the great circle of wooden poles that is your grove. Next thing, we were about to cross this stream here at this bridge, heading in the same direction, flowing *to* the source. Before we could work it out, four tree wizards materialised.'

Apnodens smiled. He confirmed that Kennet has two heads. 'This stream flows around the sanctuary and through the wood circle before it arrives at Swale's well. We call Swale the Nursing Mother, in that she feeds this stream and turns it into a river.'

It was not only Kennet river that had two heads. In the old days the druids had been governed by the priests, and they still were, but in the last few generations a hybrid caste had arisen, that of the druid kings. Over the days we spent together, Apnodens did his best to explain it to me. As I might by now have expected, even the druid kings had two beginnings. When the Romans had invaded Gaul, some younger priests, angry at the submissiveness of their elders, became militant and began to go about armed and even, as in the case of Vercingetorix, to fight back. Around the same time but for different reasons, tribal kings began to send their youngest sons to druid college. It had been suggested at an annual gathering, and agreed upon, as a means to stop the division of lands and the fratricide. In that respect, it had worked. That my own father had killed his brother was within living memory and yet seemed archaic. However, there were some young men who combined druid power with kingly ambition and they went about raiding the countryside and forming territories from stolen lands. Needless to say, Caratacos was one of them. Indeed, he was the chief of them.

'This is what your father was up against,' Apnodens said. 'Caratacos is no ordinary chieftain. He has the voice.'

'I've heard it.'

'So you understand that the pull to join him is a strong one?'

'Not as strong as the pull to peace, I think.' Although, thinking back to Beltane, I was not as certain of that as I would have liked to have been. I had been so close to being drawn into Caratacos's party. Closer than I had realised, although Caratacos would have known it. It took Apnodens to point out the obvious to me: had I remained in Britain, I would have been sent to druid college as the youngest son of a king. I could well have become a druid king myself.

'Although I think,' he said kindly, 'that it would not have been in your nature. You would have been more likely to have ended up in my grove than the court of Caratacos.'

Nevertheless, I was left to ponder and to remember the heated rows between Verica and Innogen, she insisting I study in a college, he shouting that I would go to Rome and that was that.

'Your father,' Apnodens said, 'saved you from your brothers. He was not a bad man.'

'How can you say so! He expelled the druids from our territories!'

'Men of rock, not of water, who were trying to persuade him to break with Rome.'

I learned from Apnodens that the daughters of kings were sometimes sent to druid college also, especially when they required discipline.

'Theana?' I asked, trying to sound disinterested.

He nodded. 'She trained at the same time as Caratacos at Camulodunon.'

Branwen, he told me, was the daughter of King Esius. That explained much, for Esius was a cousin of Innogen and thus, although Branwen did not look like my mother, she reminded me of her in her spirit. She had entered the bardic college only two years before and would stay until she was fifteen. 'With the girls,' Apnodens said, 'the course of study is short and prepares them for royal marriage. Usually. Esius found Branwen impossible to control after her mother died and sent her here simply to be rid of her. None of us knew she could sing until the first lesson of the first day. I'm hoping to keep her beyond fifteen. Losing her to marriage would be a great waste.'

'Yes,' I agreed, 'a great waste.'

As the days passed, the aerial hubbub continued and Apnodens began to despair of hearing from Regalis. The night of the full moon approached and he arranged a gathering on the summit of the Hill of Sovereignty.

The students were subdued. Usually on such a night, let off from their studies, they would entertain each other with songs that were not of any formal tradition, were not metrically exact but involved a lot of clapping and thigh slapping. In raucous voices they would tell tales of singing heads, screaming stones and the Battle of the Trees. On this night, however, they walked solemnly up the chalk path as if to their execution. When we got to the top, we had some time before the moon rose and Apnodens tried to lift the mood by telling the tale of the Golden God. 'Once,' he said, his voice booming, 'the Silver Maiden was picking ransoms in the wood when she saw the Golden God ride past in all his glory. She stared at him with HUGE eyes and followed his trail through the forest. For fourteen days she followed his trail and then, suddenly, he was coming back towards her. He passed her by—'

'In all his glory!' cried the young bards.

'—and she hid her face in sorrow and despair, for the sun god took no notice of her. He was so in love with himself that he did not even know she existed. She waited fourteen days and

LIT UP when she saw him again, but fourteen days later, she hid her face in sorrow and despair.'

'Sorrow and despair,' echoed his students.

'And so it went on for all time and a day, except...' The storyteller lifted a long, tapering finger. 'Every now and again, it's the Golden God who hides his face in sorrow and despair, and no-one knows why, but they say the Silver Maiden has something to do with it.'

'The sun, the moon and eclipses!' cried one of the younger ones, solving the riddle.

The night was quiet. All war calls had ceased. At the moment of the moon's rising, Apnodens stood and, raising his arms to the south, began his invocation to peace for the four quarters. 'May there be peace in the south!' He turned ninety degrees. 'May there be peace in the west!' He turned again. 'May there be peace in the north!' and, 'May there be peace in the east.' Finally he held his arms open to the sky. 'May there be peace throughout the land. May the gods help us.'

'May the gods help us,' echoed the college.

The moon was half way above the horizon when the Call of the Full Moon began to resound throughout the land. Apnodens again faced the south, and sent his call to the Great Stone Temple, then west of the Hot Springs of Sulis, north to Kyronion and east to Calleva. Such was the volume and depth of resonance in his voice that it was easy to believe he could be heard in those places. All over the land the druids of the four quarters connected with each other by beacons and voice, every holy hill joining in the chorus for peace on this night of reaching out and touching. Apnodens stood and held his arms out at the sides; an acolyte came with the Bardic Cloak which he arranged on the shoulders of his master. Made of feathers, the lower half of swan, the upper part of iridescent mallard, it glowed in the light of our fire beacon.

Around this vision of a great bird, the students performed the swan dance, pacing the circle to the beat of the drums, waving wing feathers, stopping every nineteenth pace to turn, face each other and raise their arms in the shape of swans. When the dance was completed, one of the young bards rose to sing the Song of Origins. Katuaros can trace his ancestral line back five generations, some old men can go further into Gaulish ancestry and there is one old druid who, between nightfall and dawn at midsummer, can chant the names of one hundred generations ending with the name of the god who begat his line. But this one was not like any Song of Origins I'd ever heard.

In the beginning was the One
The Monad beyond all created things
From which all created things have their being.
And the One became Two
To begin the spin of the worlds
Woman was born for Man. Strife began.

The singer was accompanied by Branwen, whose fingers plucked at the harp like small birds pecking seed. Epic in length, the song told of the world freezing over and a people moving south and south and south, over the seas and south, and who, many generations later, returned as the ice withdrew, coming back across the seas to this group of islands they called 'The Poetic Isles' north and north and north, over the seas and north. The first bards. They learnt spells to keep the wolves and bears away and by the gods were given the knowledge of how to tame the horse and breed cattle. At one point Branwen took the song, laying down her harp to hug her drawn-up knees as she sang. The voice that came from her was deep, rich, vibrant — the voice of someone at least twice her age. Only when the song had finished did she become a girl again.

The celebration of the moon ended when Apnodens held out his arms to have the Bardic Cloak removed and sent the students back to the grove and their beds. I stayed with him on night watch. The air returned to silence and there were neither peace calls nor war calls to disturb anything.

'Five days I have waited and there has been nothing,' Apnodens said, 'not even tonight. Nothing from Vernemeton.'

'Why must you wait?' I asked. 'Can you not act by your own authority? You are very obedient.'

He laughed shortly. 'You don't understand. I am a master of a bardic college, but I am a student of a priestly one and my course is nineteen years. To act by my own volition would be to break my oath, and I have two years left to go.'

'Is Regalis your only authority?'

'He is the archdruid and my father.'

'But is there no one else?'

'My master is Cynefin of the Temple of Sulis, two or three days from here. I have been calling to him as well but, again, no specific reply is audible. I could send a messenger but would prefer to speak to him in person yet cannot leave the others alone.'

'Could you not take them with you?'

'Move the whole college?'

'Apnodens,' I said gently, touching his bony arm. 'Whatever happens, I don't think you will have those two years to complete your course, not if you remain here.'

'What would you do?' he asked.

'I would set off at first light.'

'You make everything sound so simple!'

'It is simple. We take the college to the Temple of Sulis and leave everyone in the care of Cynefin while you come with me to Venonis to speak to the archdruid in person. With Cynefin's permission of course.'

Sometimes, perhaps always, the only way to know if a plan is a good one is seeing how everything falls into place once it has been decided.

'You will come with me, then?' he asked.

I said I would.

'If nothing else, Cynefin, who is a master healer, would be able to cure Mandred, in the legs as well as the neck. It would only take a few days,' he said.

Only a few days... It was yet further delay but I agreed. I was coming more and more to trust the subtle forces of the land. I could force a route like a Roman, cutting through hills, overcoming all obstacles, but it seemed that only when I let the land and its spirits carry me did I arrive at places I should be. It is the better way. How did Apnodens put it? The way of water and not of rock.

The next morning, he called the students and tutors to him. He was wearing the golden torc of truth-telling. Should he say anything untrue, it would tighten round his throat. 'These, our visitors,' he told the college, 'are Roman spies.' Everyone stared at him like owls. He introduced me for the first time as Togidubnos of the Atrebates and told them they could trust me and my companions. 'As you know, the invasion of Britain has begun,' he said. 'Rome wants nothing less than to make us a province of the Empire. I have thought about it in great depth and I have consulted the spirits and gods. Today we pack up and leave to go west to Sulis.'

Branwen leapt to her feet, crying out in agony. 'We cannot leave Swale! The birds! The trees! The sanctuary! This is our place, our duty!' She threw herself at her master, beating him with her little fists, fighting with the spirit of a small bird defending its nest. Apnodens caught hold of her arms and she hung sobbing in his grasp. She had so many friends here. Apart from Swale, there was a holly tree, always green, in the middle of a dense tangle of briar; a mossy stone under which lived her newts; a coot which she fed every day; a bat she had found injured that, after it had been healed, refused to leave her but spent its days roosting in her hair. Her grief was terrible. It was bereavement. She was so limp; Apnodens picked her up like a child and passed her over to me. I was startled at his choice but knowing what to do came instinctively and I rocked her like a baby. She was too lost to grief to realise she was being comforted by a bellwether of the Roman army.

'This is cowardice!' one tutor protested. 'Only cowards run away.'

'The desire to avoid war is not cowardice,' I said. 'War causes so much suffering, not only to men but to animals, trees, the land itself. This living, breathing, water-dappled land of the gods. Do you wish to fertilise it with your blood?'

'What of the sanctuary? Do we abandon it to be defiled?' another asked.

'If we walk away,' said Apnodens, 'yes, we abandon the sanctuary, but we take the knowledge with us and keep the learning alive.' He was struggling to stay resolute. 'Listen,' he said, 'we shall hide what we can and call upon the aid of the Shee. Like the Sanctuary of the Wheel, Kennet will pass into Annwn, there to rest until some future time when we can bring it back.'

As a gift to the sanctuary, he performed his own *vocos*, the only time he had done it complete before anyone. He sat cross-legged on the ground, closed his eyes, drew in his breath. At first we took it that a bird was singing close to him until we realised the song was coming from his own mouth, first one bird, then another, followed by the rustlings of squirrels and the grunts of badgers. His cheeks filled with air and emptied again as he gave us the song of the forest with all its flutterings, whistlings, beatings and soughings and the occasional squeal of something dying. As he sang, the creatures came forth to see this Orpheus. Towards the end, his voice became human and his own, as if he were singing under a waterfall; then, at the very end, came another voice: Branwen's. All this while, Branwen had been in another place; not sleep, but a place of oblivion beyond pain. Now she came out of her faint, awoken by her own sound coming from her tutor's throat, rising and rising to a note surely not possible for a man. Then we all knew, if ever there had been any doubt, that Apnodens was truly a master.

316

We set to work. Naturally we could not hide the Hill of Sovereignty, but while the students piled brash over Swale's well, the rest of us worked to obscure all paths, including those to the temple. Apnodens summoned up the help of the Shee to put bad luck on the place, cold draughts to spook horses, sudden floods to soak the feet of infantry, but it wasn't Shee who were acting when, as we left the following morning, the road behind us began to fill with water. The brash had dammed the spring and sent it back on itself. Branwen wept uncontrollably for Swale, whom she had served for half her life, as she walked away hand-in-hand with her master.

We had loaded our chariot with druid treasures, the sacred cauldron, the cups, the sceptre, crowns, drums, flutes and the Bardic Cloak; Mandred drove it alone. Katuaros wanted to go direct to Kyronion, concerned to meet up again with his fianna, but Apnodens said another long ride would undo all the good he'd received from Swale's healing. He was to come with us and, like us, walk. Apnodens set the pace, striding out with his staff, Branwen half-running to keep up, the bat roosting upside down in her hair finding it difficult to sleep.

Strange little Branwen. Since I had discovered we were related, I had tried often to speak to her but was always rebuffed as a Romey. Once, tired of seeing only the top of her head, I bade her raise her eyes and look at me: when she did, I felt as if I had destroyed her world.

34

THE HOT SPRINGS OF SULIS

After we had passed the Hill of Sovereignty, Apnodens turned on the road and held his arms out to the land he was leaving behind. 'Forgive me,' he said, and tears on his cheeks glistened in the sun. 'O Shee of the barrows and the stone circles, protect Swale!'

'Do you think they will succeed?' I asked.

'I do. They can conjure fogs and visions, make men lose their way, make men lose everything, including their wits. Mere stories about them can turn even the bravest warriors soft with fear. Look at your Katuaros! But it is the Shee who compose the stories in the first place. All that chanting at looms: do you think the women make the stories? Shee-thoughts are woven into the very fabric of our clothes. But they need the druids to protect their shrines and locations. Without us... They will do what they can. But, oh, Swale...' He sighed as if he were leaving his lover behind as he turned to continue the journey.

As we travelled along the westward track, we passed warriors riding down from the duns to hurry east to Calleva. Foot soldiers coming from the farms joined them on the road. Walking slowly, sedately even, against the shove of warriors it took us three days to reach the Hot Springs. The easiest way into the Sanctuary of Sulis was by the olive-green river that ran through a narrow valley between hills. I put the chariot and horses into the care of two of the druid tutors, arranging to meet them on the morrow at the Hot Springs. The rest of us took to coracles and paddled along the river to a ravishing chorus of songbirds. At one point of fast water, Branwen suddenly lost control and spun away from us. With no thought of the risk to my own stability, I held out my paddle to her. Her pride and defiance melted as she pulled herself back from danger. For a moment as brief as sunshine in winter, she looked at me with the door to her soul open. Her eyes... They reminded me of Innogen and suddenly I felt the ties of kinship in a physical way. A distant cousin, perhaps, but also my Little Sister.

The river slowed and became tranquil as we paddled between hills that were sentinels at the gateway into the Sanctuary of Sulis. Apnodens sang a prayer of thanksgiving to the river for having carried us safely. 'Be careful,' he advised as he helped us from our hide-covered wickerwork shells. 'There is only one route to the temple. Follow me carefully and do not stray. The springs are hot, but the spirits are hotter.'

From the crude jetty a causeway led through a land of streams that tumbled over rocks to form pools. There was the sound of water everywhere, trickling, dripping, plopping, every now and again belching. The gravelled causeway, lined with wooden stakes, meandered past three knolls from whence flowed the hot springs. The steaming water was orange; I touched it cautiously and found that, like a caldarium in a bath house, it was above skin temperature but not scalding.

Humming with ever-deepening pleasure, Apnodens strode ahead on his long, thin legs, aided by the staff he had whittled himself into a pair of entwined serpents. On a rickety bridge where the very air rippled with water reflections he whistled and an old man came out from amongst the trees. His plaids were as orange as the water, his breeches as brown as oak bark. His head was shaven from ear to ear and his forehead as bald as the moon.

'Cynefin!'

'Apnodens!' he said, hurrying forward, arms raised in greeting. 'Is it you?' He looked past his pupil to the weary train of students behind. 'What's happened? What is it? Why have you come?'

'I need your help, master.' Apnodens said. 'You've heard about the Romans?'

'Of course. One hears of nothing else.'

'They are going to Calleva, but one of the legions will be heading west.'

'That I did not know. Who told you?'

Apnodens drew me forward and introduced me. Cynefin looked as if he were being introduced to an infectious disease. 'You've brought him here, this Atrebatic Romey, to my sanctuary?'

'We can trust him, I promise you. Let us rest and talk at leisure.'

Cynefin acquiesced and led us up the highest of the three knolls, on the top of which was a clearing encircled by ash trees. The grove of the goddess Sulis enclosed a circular temple. It had been built in the form of an ancient Greek tholos but, rather than being made of stone, it had tree trunks for columns, twenty on the outside and ten on the inside encircling the sanctum. Any lingering resemblance to a Greek temple was dispelled in the ambulatory where every niche held a crude wooden figure, not worthy of the name statue, alarming to an eye that expects gods to look human and be beautiful. These spatula-headed figures with unlevel eyes and holes for a nose, upright logs in various stages of decay, some covered in lichen, others sprouting moss, jolt you out of the human world into that of the tree spirits and other divine presences, presences that demand our awe, not our sentimental devotion, presences all around us and never more than at a site as sacred as this.

A meal was prepared while we washed our feet in hot mineral water and changed from our travelling clothes into temple robes. As we ate, Apnodens explained that he had called to the archdruid for advice but had received no reply. 'So far as I know.'

Cynefin nodded. 'The air is ravaged by alarms but a rider came from Vernemeton on the Albios Way this morning. Regalis is advising all druids to go into hiding until we know better what the intentions of the Romans are. I was about to send to you. How much do you trust this man?' he asked, indicating me.

'With my life, I believe.'

'How so? Is he not a spy for Rome?'

'He may be the son of Verica but he is also the son of Innogen.'

'Ah...!'

'He is half-Romey, half-druid, but in truth he is neither. He is his own man, a philosopher who tries always to make the right action. He is also an initiate of Eleusis and part of that ancient tradition we share.'

Cynefin was swayed by this, enough to allow us to talk freely. After the meal, he had the whole college as well as my companions bed down in the temple 'for healing dreams' while he spoke to Apnodens and me alone, late into the night. He told us that, the day before, a party of armed riders had come from Calleva seeking King Esius. 'Sent by Caratacos,' he said.

'Where is Esius?' Apnodens asked. 'We have Branwen with us.'

'Yes, I noticed her. Esius is here.'

By 'here' he meant at the capital of the Dobunni a few miles south, the closest settlement to the temple. Once the Dobunni territory had been split between warring brothers, but Esius had reunited it, giving himself two capitals, north and south. He preferred the northern one, Kyronion, but toured his territory frequently.

'What does Caratacos want of him?' Apnodens asked.

'What do you think? Fighting men. As a vassal of Caratacos and tribute-payer, he is bound to supply a levy on demand but when he was here last he said he could not afford to lose so many men.'

'It is my hope,' I said, 'to persuade him to submit to the Romans.'

Cynefin looked as if he didn't know whether to laugh or bark. 'Submit?' He turned to Apnodens. '*Submit?*'

'Hear him out,' Apnodens said.

I told Cynefin of the plans of the Second Legion to establish the frontier on the Albios Way and of what we thought might happen to any druids standing in their path. 'It will be a stark choice: give up your druidry or migrate.'

'If that is the case,' said Cynefin, 'I must fall in with Caratacos. An honourable death is to be preferred to a life lived under the rule of foreign invaders.'

'That depends,' I said carefully. 'If you only had yourselves to consider, yes, of course, that would be the better course. But you are responsible to your students, the people in your care, not to mention the spirits of the place and the gods of sanctuary. What happens to them when you throw yourselves on Roman swords?'

Cynefin was taken aback. 'The gods are immortal,' he said.

'Are they?' I asked. 'What happened to those ancient gods of the Greeks usurped by the Olympians? What happened to Cronos and the rest when Zeus ousted them? What happened to the ancient Roman gods when the Olympians took over there, too, changing nothing but their names? Everywhere tribal gods were usurped by the powerful senate in the sky which now has its eye on Britain. What will become of our gods, the gods we serve and make sacrifice to? What becomes of them if the druids disappear? The Romans will fill our temples with statues of divine emperors. The trees, the streams, the rocks — who will worship them when you are gone?' I waved my arms. 'Do you want to see these trees slaughtered? Do you want to see that stream polluted and all its sacred fish floating dead? Do you want to see the stones shattered and carted off for building materials?'

The expression on Apnodens's face reflected my own astonishment. Whose argument was this I was rehearsing? But now I was seeing the land as he saw it, and I understood that spirits have no shape or form other than what they inhabit, that the gods of place are the place, are what makes it shimmer with beauty. They are the liquidity of water, the heat of the fire, the sap of the tree, the scent of the earth. Had I seen gods? I had travelled with them all the way from the Sanctuary of the Wheel, but I did not know them as I knew them now, as a ripping of the heart by the vision of beauty that is Britain. And did I want 'my' Romans tramping over this, desecrating it all? I did not.

When I had finished, we sat in stunned silence amongst the dripping sounds of a light rain falling off eaves. Eventually Cynefin spoke. 'I was going to suggest we consult Sulis but there is no need. She has just spoken. And through a Romey!'

'Romey no longer, it seems,' said Apnodens.

'I never was a Romey except in other men's perceptions. I am my own man and I believe there is a way forward that involves neither resistance nor submission; I also believe we can find it, but it will require some sacrifices.'

Cynefin looked offended. He was of the stream of druidry that had long since abandoned the taking of life to appease the gods.

'Sacrifice of our own desires,' I said, to make it clear. 'We will not come out of this feeling satisfied. We shall have surrendered a lot, not least rulership. But — life with honour. That is our aim. And perhaps something new...'

'What is your meaning? Life with honour?'

'I mean learning to live under Roman rule in such a way that we teach our rulers how to govern. Teach them to live in true accord with the land and its spirits.'

The birds were singing by the time we'd agreed on a plan. All the druids, both ours and Cynefin's colleges, would hide in the surrounding hills where there were many caves, while

Apnodens and I went north to Vernemeton to consult with Regalis. I asked Cynefin if he could help the injured men in my party. In the morning, he examined Katuaros's shoulder and said it would be easily fixed, but mostly by rest. As for Mandred...

'Who is this man?' Cynefin asked.

'My slave,' I said.

'Mandred, son of Bethryn of Mai Dun,' Mandred mumbled.

'I remember you. Botched the sacrifice of a man. You cannot enter the sanctum. You will defile the place.'

I glared at Mandred. A man? Not a pig? He had not told me half of it. Mandred trembled with shame.

'Must a punishment last forever?' Apnodens asked. 'He has suffered greatly, been enslaved, all but lost the use of his legs.'

'He should be handed over to the Durotriges and you know it. According to the law, he who fails to perform sacrifice becomes the sacrifice.'

'It is a harsh law. Have we no power to forgive?'

'We have. But the Durotriges?'

'Had he become the sacrifice, they would have taken off his legs. He ran so that they couldn't, but the gods exacted the price. He can barely walk. And the gods, being merciful, put him into the possession of a man of virtue who has cared for him and treated him well. In return, he has proved himself a loyal servant. May we not consult Sulis about his fate, his legs, and the lump on his neck that no one has been able to cure?'

Cynefin agreed reluctantly and ushered us to the inner sanctum where steam rose in coils from a channel in the floor to wreathe about several altars to various gods. 'Sulis!' he said, 'If you reject this man, show your displeasure!' Nothing happened and Cynefin became reassured. At the altar of Sulis we drank ceremoniously of the spring water; the taste was not unpleasant but, then again, not pleasant. Cynefin bade Mandred kneel at the altar, watching with concern as my slave lurched forwards. 'The cyst on your neck we can cure with water treatment, but for your legs, we need the aid of Sulis herself.' He took from a box of votive images a pair of silver legs the length of a finger and, with a prayer, stooped to make the offering to Sulis, laying the image in the steaming channel carrying the spring water.

'Five days,' said Cynefin. 'He must remain alone in the temple five days.'

I bowed my head to the will of the goddess, praying that this treatment might work where everything else had failed and turned to leave Mandred to his five-day incarceration on a diet of powdered soporifics and tangy mineral water.

'Is this Greek healing?' I asked Apnodens as we left. 'It seems Asclepian to me.'

He winced. 'Why must you always look for roots in the mortal world? If a thing is true, its roots are in Annwn, and its shoots everywhere.' He told me that Mandred would be sent to sleep with music on a bed of dried herbs and grasses. 'In his dreams, the demons will come, and Cynefin, purifying the air with smoke, will drive them out. Then the goddess will reveal the cause of his illness and its cure.'

Katuaros, Draumur and I found a cave in the hills to share — not only with each other but also a colony of bats — and secured the entrance with piles of rubble and brash. Up there we could hear the distant wails of the carnyxes calling all fighting men to war and, while Katuaros grumbled about hiding like girls, yet he laid on his back on the ground to rest his sword arm. The pain had stopped but stiffness and bruising remained. Over the following days Cynefin did what he could to mend his shoulder, applying poultices of various self-heals and bone-knitters from his collection of herbs, but nothing would work as well, he said, as rest.

I was sitting at the mouth of the cave at dusk when Branwen approached to lay some food down before me. I was pleased to see her. 'Sit with me,' I said, and she did as she was told, letting her bat flit up to the ceiling of the cave where hung hundreds of what I took to be his fellows.

'Aren't you worried he will choose to join the bat folk who live here?' I asked.

She looked at me scathingly. 'Different kind of bat.'

'Oh, I didn't know,' I said, feeling foolish.

She got up and brushed the dust off her.

'Leaving so soon?'

'You talk to me as if I were a child,' she said, 'and a stupid one at that.' She held out her hands below where her bat was hanging and softly whistled. He released his grip and dropped into her cupped palms with the barest of flutters; she left my cave clasping to her that scrap of leathery ugliness, whose company she obviously preferred to mine.

Unable to sleep on a bed of bat droppings, with our flitting companions squeaking through all the hours of darkness, I took to spending nights in the ambulatory between the inner and outer colonnade of the temple. Sleeping there I hoped to have some healing dreams myself. I might not be physically hurt but I felt orphaned, alone and isolated. In my Asclepian dreams, I met dead parents and argued with them. I dreamt that Claudius pushed me out of Rome into a terrible trap, of Brit-Ana as a great mouth, ready to receive me only to devour me. None of this healed, only strengthened my anxieties. When I woke each morning, whoever came within my gaze appeared disturbingly transient, with one strange exception: Branwen. I could not explain the feeling and did not particularly want to. She was just a sulky, offhand child who blamed me for everything. But she was also my Little Sister and, for some reason, I was desperate for her approval.

35

DIVINE MARRIAGE

One clear night I found Apnodens sitting on one of the smaller knolls gazing at the sky. The waning moon made the stars more visible now and he was able to point out Bran's Raven, the Virgin Maid and the Hunting Dogs. I envied his ability to name the constellations but he was self-effacing and said he knew little, that he would learn more if he could but that would require special training on the sacred isle of Mona. Sitting with him I became infected by his wonder. Stories I'd heard in my boyhood of gods, giants, heroes and beasts moved imperceptibly, silently across the sky.

The priesthood was, it seemed, an order of druidry as subject to division as everything else. Apnodens explained that there were two main streams. One way, the way of rock, adheres to the traditions, specifically the tradition of sacrifice, a most holy devotion to the gods. Any unease we feel, it says, at the death of the victim, is just an indication of our ignorance and delusion, for if, as we believe, we are immortal, why be disturbed?

'It's a reasonable argument,' I said.

'And yet those who hold that idea are often unreasonable, obstinate in their thinking and inflexible. The Durotriges are of that ilk. The other way, the way of water, says that what pleases the gods is devotion to the Mother. If we are to give up anything, it is not life but pride, hubris, our arrogant belief that we can control events. And so the keepers of the river shrines make their offerings by putting what they value into the waters, either treasures or votive images. The gods, they say, are as pleased by a row of stones laid out in a pattern, if done with devotion, as with the blood of an animal. Cynefin is of this persuasion.'

'And you?'

'I am the son of my father and follow the way of water.'

I asked him if he had ever performed blood sacrifice and he said he had. He had killed the bull in the mistletoe ceremony of fertility and had once garrotted a blasphemer in an offering to the gods. He stared up at the stars as if they were his redemption. I told him, then, of my master, Seneca, who I could imagine staying up all night to talk to Apnodens. I explained Stoicism as best I could, and Apnodens hung on all I said. 'I am impressed,' he said at last. 'I presumed Rome to be a fleshpot.'

'As it is. Men of virtue are rare; even rarer now that Seneca has been banished to Corsica.'

Apnodens was shocked at Rome's treatment of the wise.

'Do not concern yourself. Right now he will be sitting out under these same stars, as at peace as we are.'

'Are you at peace?' he asked.

I'd come to Britain with a mission that was clear to me, but the further I went, the more bogged down I became. The fear that the Romans were not behind me, that I was alone in hostile land, had gone, but I had not regained any sense of security. 'Of course I am not at peace, not if I understand what peace is.'

'What do you take it to be?'

'Lack of disturbance, inwardly and outwardly.'

'Surely your Seneca must teach you that our inward state should not depend on outward circumstances?'

'Indeed he does!'

'You should consult Sulis.'

'How?' I asked. 'Do we cast the woods?'

'No,' he said. 'For you...Take a bath. Now. At night under

the stars. Bathe with proper ritual, perhaps for the first time in your life. I think you understand now that water is not just a pleasure for tired bones but is sacred. Consult the sacred waters.'

I entered the spring and washed myself in a rite of purification, my mind given wholly to Sulis. Afterwards I laid back amidst the steam to stare up at the waning moon high above. The moon. The goddess of constant change. Sulis, I whispered, Sulis... What did I expect? A numinous water nymph? Someone to talk to not of this world? There was nothing but the flitting of bats, the call of owls, the cry of small mammals, the wind in the rushes and the hissing spring. Nothing...

I raised my head at the sound of singing and saw two parties coming, one male, the other female. Was I awake or dreaming? I brought my arm down hard on sharp rock, felt the pain and saw the blood. Awake, then. They wore wreaths of flowers on their heads: there was to be a wedding. The man to be married sat enthroned on a stone seat by a plashing waterfall. I knew him by his trident as Neptune but his face lacked the mask-like imperviousness of any statue I have ever seen of him. This Neptune had a sad look, as if he'd done his best but it was not enough. It was the look of my father, Verica. Indeed, it was the face of Verica as a younger man. The water dripped from hair, from beard, from limb, for he was god of all water, not just the seas, god of the springs, the streams, the brooks, the rivers.

Cymbals and reed pipes announced the arrival of the bride. I looked round expecting a sweet maid in flowing chiton, her hair braided with daisies, but was surprised by the vision of a warrior-woman in cuirass and visored helmet, her sword drawn and held upright before her.

Minerva. Minerva? Marrying Neptune? No poet I know has ever mentioned such a heavenly union, and yet it was so. I was watching it with my own eyes. Neptune and Minerva, or, in

Greek, Poseidon and Pallas Athene: the two gods who had contended over Athens, a contest Pallas Athene had won. Here amongst the hot springs of Britain, there was union. The two presiding gods of this place, the god of waters and the goddess of wisdom. When Minerva raised the visor, however, I saw the face of Innogen.

The slap of understanding brought me back to this world. Or did it? In truth, there was no sense of transition. I was still looking at the throne of rock but now no one was seated on it. I could feel the pain of a bruise on my arm. I climbed out of the pool, dressed and returned to the temple to ask Cynefin for an interpretation.

Although it was the middle of the night he was still awake. 'We have watched you since your arrival on these shores,' he said, 'not knowing your real purpose here, whether it is, as you claim, to bring peace or, more likely, to make the way easier for the Romans.' He raised a hand to interrupt my protest at this. 'The dream tells me that your purpose is perhaps beyond even your ken, that you do not know whose servant you are. Apnodens told me that you received a prophecy at Delphi, a riddle from Pythia, saying you must return here to marry your father to your mother. Sulis confirms it.'

'But I don't understand when both are dead!'

'To understand a dream is to kill a butterfly to see how it flies. Do not try to understand. Your way is guided, and not by us, nor by the Romans.'

'I seem to have been misguided from the moment I left Noviomagos.'

'You have not put a foot wrong. Delfos, you are the son of gods, that's all I can say. It's up to you to find out what they want of you.'

330

In the middle of the fourth night there came a terrible yelling from the inner sanctum: Mandred in some extreme of torment, whether physical or mental I could not tell. I hurried to the door where I found Apnodens keeping guard.

'What are they doing to him?' I demanded.

'It's hard to get the truth out of some people.'

'*What are they doing?*' I stormed, but Apnodens laughed. 'He's on his own, Delfos. On his own in the dark. Did you not go through something like this at Eleusis?'

Know Thyself...

Cynefin entered the temple and went into the sanctum to take confession. When he came out he naturally said nothing of what had transpired, only that Mandred was walking freely again.

'What was wrong with his legs?'

'Self-disgust,' Cynefin exchanged a gentle smile with Apnodens.

'Our goddess,' Apnodens explained, 'heals through revelation. And what she revealed to your slave may be revealed to you when he leaves the sanctum.'

The following morning, Esius, King of the Dobunni, arrived at the head of a small force of riders. He was a tall man of about fifty years, wearing a heavy torc around his neck and the bristly hide of a wild boar over his shoulders. On his head, a close-fitting helmet with ribs made of boar ivory; threaded through his long hair and flowing moustaches strings of boars' teeth. Since all these attributes were intended to fill him with the spirit of Moccus, the boar god, it was surprising to see him go down on one knee before Cynefin, saying, 'I need your advice, my master.'

'Caratacos's men found you?'

He nodded. 'I can prevaricate no longer. I am commanded to send a levy at once to Calleva, without any confidence in the survival of my men. Indeed I am told to expect their slaughter. "Better dead than a slave," Caratcos says, but with my farmers dead, my people, my livestock, my whole land will die.' Cynefin held his hands out over the bowed head of the king and called upon the help of Sulis.

When Esius stood, he noticed me and, despite my temple garb, he recognized a Romey and blinked.

'Togidubnos ap Verica,' said Cynefin.

'Son of Innogen? Young Delfos? How long have you been back? And who do you represent? Not your father. That old dotard is reduced to ash.'

'You've heard?'

'I have your fianna wenching and drinking my mead at Kyronion, waiting for you and your foster brother.' He nodded curtly to Katuaros. 'Of course I've heard, but they didn't mention you. So, who do you represent? It's Rome, isn't it?' he said when I did not reply.

'You'd think so,' said Cynefin. 'He thought so himself, but we are beginning to suspect he speaks for the gods.'

'I was sent by Claudius to recommend the kings to submit,' I said flatly. 'It sounded reasonable in Rome.'

'And here?' Esius asked, 'How could I possibly submit to Rome when Caratacos stands in the way? It would be certain death, for me and all of mine.'

We were interrupted by the approach of Apnodens with Branwen. She stood shyly before her father with her head down.

'Branwen?' Esius was taken aback and demanded to know what Apnodens was doing at the Hot Springs.

'By the authority of the archdruid,' Cynefin said on his pupil's behalf, 'all druids are to go into hiding, at least for a while. The bardic college has come here to hide in the caves.'

'No daughter of a Dobunni king hides in caves, not while her father lives. I'll take her back to Kyronion,' said Esius. He picked the bat out of her hair as if it were a louse, twisted its neck and threw it away.

If you have ever seen, ever heard, a catapult breaking when pulled too hard, then you have heard the yowling of the girl bard that morning. Fresh wood pulled apart. She clung screaming to Apnodens.

'Although Kyronion is far from safe, you will return with me, Branwen,' Esius shouted, annoyed by his daughter's obvious preference for her foster father. 'Look at you! When did you last comb your hair? I sent you to the college to make a learned woman of you, not a shrub.'

'And you,' he said to me, in a voice to make my knees knock, 'call yourself a king? You're not even wearing the torc. Come with me...' I followed him nervously into the deep-thatch reserved for his use, for the Hot Springs lay within his territory. Once inside he took off his padded clothes and helmet and, with them, his aspect of terror. 'This peace you advocate,' he said, now just a man weathered by concern, 'what is the benefit? If I were to submit to the Romans, as you suggest, apart from having to live with such dishonour, I would be in constant fear of reprisals from Caratacos. I have to send that levy... even though I may never see my men and my chariots again...'

'There is another way.'

'Speak it out.'

'Send your levy but instruct them to change sides once they reach Calleva.'

He looked horrified. 'Such dishonour! I wouldn't wait for anyone else to kill me — I'd do it myself!'

I felt ashamed even to have had the thought, yet I stood by it. 'What choice do you have? Change sides at the gates of Calleva.'

'Oh, this is the grandson of Kommios talking!'

'Perhaps it is. If you lend your forces to Aulus Plautius, Caratacos will lose the battle. What threat would he be then? Even if he were to survive, he would be in flight and have neither the will nor the opportunity to seek revenge on you.

You would be free of him and his extortionate tributes, and you would have won the gratitude of Rome.'

The king paced about growling. 'Fetch Branwen,' he said to one of his men. When the girl came, she flew at him all claws. *'Why did you kill my bat?'*

'Your bat?' When he understood what he had done, Esius squashed her protests, saying, 'There's no such thing as a pet.'

36

ESIUS THE KING

As dawn bled into the eastern sky, Mandred came out of the temple. It was the first time I had seen him since we'd arrived at the Hot Springs of Sulis and I barely recognized him. The hunched, shambling, sorry excuse for a man had become whole. He was tall, good-looking in his way with small features and pointed nose, and free. As soon as he passed beyond the outer colonnade, he jumped high in the air, kicked out like a horse let loose in a meadow and ran three times round the temple. Finally fetching up in front of Cynefin, who was laughing, Mandred clasped him in gratitude, once, twice, thrice. 'Go and speak to your master,' Cynefin said.

I took him aside and asked him what he had experienced in the temple.

'Ah,' he said, tapping his nose, 'you know how important it is to keep silent about the Mysteries.'

I was not in the mood. 'Tell me then — I insist on it — the truth of what happened to you at Mai Dun.'

'You would not speak to me afterwards.'

'Try me.'

He sat down by one of the bubbling springs and stared into it as silent as a heron; only when I sat beside him did he begin to speak. He told me that an evil man had been brought before the court at Mai Dun, the high place of the Durotriges surrounded by a labyrinth of deep ditches. He had been accused of sadistic cruelty to women and beasts, was found guilty and condemned to the Ordeal of the Ditch.

'The usual sentence was stoning, but this man's crimes had been terrible. We would cut off his feet and throw him in the deepest ditch, where he would die trying to crawl out of the labyrinth. My sister had been one of his victims and so, as a part of my training and test of my mettle, it was given to me to do the amputation. We strapped him down to the altar and I took up the sacrificial axe. With a prayer to Rosmerta who cares for women, I swung it down as if on a log and, to my satisfaction, heard it go cleanly through the bone. The man screamed terribly. Before taking off the other foot I stared him in the eye to prolong his agony with the anticipation of more pain. My sister, after all, had died screaming. His mad, blood-shot eyes caught mine. I lost myself in his gaze and seemed to tip into the Otherworld, the world of all knowledge, all wisdom, all understanding. I returned in the same instant, but I came changed, for I understood now as if in a blaze of light. *Know Thyself* — ha! Believe me, you do not want to. I saw suddenly that I was as bloodthirsty as the victim. I was *enjoying* his agony — couldn't get enough of it. So what was the difference between us? Understanding this, I threw down the axe and walked away.' Mandred had to stop speaking to swallow bile. 'That flash of insight was the god, holding up the mirror to show that I was no better than the condemned man. That is when I dropped the axe, when I saw that he and I were the same, that I was amputating myself.' He gave a juddering sigh. 'The punishment for failing to perform a sacrifice properly is to undergo it yourself. I compounded loss of honour with cowardice, broke into a run, stole a chariot and escaped.' He had lived an outlaw in the forest by the coast for a year before he was captured by the Yew River Tribe and sold into slavery.

I could not speak.

'I have the forgiveness of Sulis,' he said. 'I hope yours follows in time.'

'Forgiveness for what?'

'My lies.'

I breathed in sharply, threw my arm round his shoulders and sorrowed for the man who had sacrificed his freedom and his reputation in obedience to the god, who would rather be an outcast and a slave than a druid of the way of rock. A slave, but for how much longer? Perhaps I should have granted him manumission there and then, but as always, whenever I had that generous thought, it was disabled by fear. I couldn't face the risk of losing him. I could of course have retained him, have paid him for the work he did, but I would not know his choice until I freed him, and he could easily choose to walk his own path. I remembered Branwen's confidence in her bat, that it preferred her company to that of other bats, but I dared not take the risk with my slave.

We rose to our feet when Cynefin joined us. 'He has told you everything? It is good that the truth is known. He may heal fully now, body and soul.'

'But presumably he is still an outlaw and cannot enter the lands of the Durotriges?'

'I sent a rider two days ago to Mai Dun.'

Mandred trembled suddenly and violently. 'You've told them where I am?'

'Have no fear. I have told their chief druid that your self-inflicted punishment has atoned for the deed. We have no reason to dread his reply.'

'What I fear even more than the law,' Mandred said, 'is the restless spirit of the amputated man which has been crawling the earth ever since, seeking me.'

'I think not,' said Cynefin. 'After the botched amputation, the rapist was brought to a swift end with a silver blade in the heart. His body was cast into a deep shaft, over which was placed a large, flat stone. If his spirit survived the silver knife, then it is in agonising captivity for eternity, and rightly so.'

The sun was at its zenith when we heard the calling: wolf howls coming up from the south, hill to hill in a code that

Cynefin understood. 'You are free,' he said to Mandred, and blessed him by making the sign of Sulis on his brow with water.

Having arranged that the bardic college remain hidden in the hills around the Hot Springs in the care of Cynefin, Apnodens, Katuaros and I left as a party travelling with King Esius.

'Innogen's son,' said the king reflectively as we rode together in his chariot along the sacred Albios Way towards Kyronion. 'Your mother was a great priestess who lived in both worlds. She had a magical mirror, a polished bronze disc on a handle, that she would turn this way and that, saying, "This world, other world, this world, other world".'

'I have that mirror. Verica gave it to me.'

'No. That would be an ordinary mirror for seeing yourself in. We buried her with the magical mirror. When she left your father, Innogen came to live under my protection.' He spat into the wayside. 'How I failed her!'

'How did she die?'

'A scratch. A mere scratch from a thorn while she was picking herbs. She didn't notice it at first, not until it grew infected. A mere scratch: she was dead within two days.'

'How could you protect her from an infection?' I asked.

'It was her fate.'

He grunted. 'Perhaps so. We took her body by boat up the river to its source at the Seven Springs. Where the Churn is shallow, we walked knee-deep. Twelve of us, all kin, walking slow through water, carrying the bier-boat on our shoulders. In other deeper, weedier stretches, men on each bank pulled the boat along with ropes. It was most solemn, moving against the current towards the source. Midsummer, and the banks lined with yellow flags and willow herb, elder trees between flower and fruit, willows trailing their branches in the quick-flowing water. She lay in the boat, waxen, covered in flowers. My beautiful cousin, Innogen.'

'You did not have a pyre?'

'By her own request, we interred her whole in the place of the ancestors, dressed in her finery with her most precious objects, and commanded a barrow to be made.' Eisus told me of the rites they performed, the grave goods, her burial place high on the escarpment overlooking the great circular vale they call the Cauldron. 'She was buried with her sacred bronze mirror under her hands crossed on her breast, at her pale lips a bronze bowl holding the elixir of life, around her neck her amber and shale beads, on her shoulder a silver brooch. She was clothed in the finest of plaids and linens and her hair braided.'

As Esius spoke, I could see my mother, her ready smile and wise eyes, her strong flaxen hair; I could smell the scent of herbs in her clothes and the fragrance of her skin. In that moment I was a child again, sitting at her knee, listening to tales of Peredur son of Efrawg, Gereint son of Erbin, stories of Lludd and Lugh. In that moment I was in the forest of her tales, chasing dragons, fighting evil giants, rescuing maidens. My eyes smarted with tears that my mother had died, aged thirty-five, while I was far, far away, living amongst those who considered my people to be barbarians.

'Elixir of life?' I asked. 'Of what use is that to the dead?'

'Have you forgotten so much? Did she not teach you that the soul which drinks the elixir of life is immortal?'

'I remember only snatches of her wisdom, but that, about immortality — it is a lore with which I am familiar.'

'Innogen was familiar with no lore,' the king said, slashing off a branch hanging over the way with his sharp sword. 'She knew the wisdom of our ancestors in the depth of her being. You are a dabbler, O son of Verica. What could your father ever understand of Innogen? He wanted her beauty, he sired a son by her, he gave her a loom to keep her quiet and did not know that her soul was becoming as chaff. The Atrebates with their wealthy ports and fine wines: they were incapable of understanding one such as Innogen. She came home to the Dobunni and when she died we buried her on the lip of Cuda's escarpment, looking out over the Cauldron, the Cauldron in which she was born, out of which she came.'

As we went deeper into Dobunni territory, the land grew ever lusher with brooks flowing fast through fields, paddocks all green with new growth. Lambs played, cows gave of their rich, creamy milk, all living things finally unfurling from the long winter and the clench of spring famine. Esius was impervious to the voluptuous season, grumbling about a flood that caused us to go half a day out of our way to the next ford.

The Cauldron was in the northern territory but, under Esius, the northern and southern tribes had been unified and it was safe to ride anywhere under his protection. 'You should visit the Cauldron, make a pilgrimage to your mother's tomb.'

I told him that I hadn't the time, that I must press on for Venonis.

Coming to the ford, we jumped down from the chariot to wait while the scouts crossed, checking the depth. Apnodens, who was sharing my own chariot with Branwen and teaching her a new hymn, drew up alongside. We all watched the scouts in silence. Deeper and deeper they went, until the water came up to the breast of the smallest horses, causing them to swim. Eventually they all emerged on the far side.

'Sire!' called the lead scout. 'The crossing is easy.'

'And the horses?'

'All well. None stumbled.'

Esius was solicitous of each member of his extensive herd. Every horse had a name, and he knew the mounts of his party as well as he knew their riders. 'Dix did not shy at the current?'

'Steady as her old mother,' the scout called back.

'No such thing as pets,' Branwen muttered balefully, even though she knew her father would put down any animal past its working life.

Esius stood pulling on his beard, looking over the water as the chariots were taken across by able men guiding the horses

340

at the bridle. 'I lost one of my best mares here last year,' he said, turning to me. 'The same year that I had to kneel in surrender before Caratacos, the worst moment of my life. And now you want me to do it again, only this time to a foreign invader.' His mounted one of his horses and led the way into the river. Concentration on the patient wading calmed him and by the time we reached the far side of the ford, he had regained both his posture and his dignity. 'All safe,' he said, stroking the neck of his horse. 'All safe.'

The ancient track ran straight, up hill and down dale, across pastures of grazing cattle and fields burgeoning with wheat, barley and oats. On two evenings we made camp and gathered in a large circle round a leaping fire where wild pigs were roasted. Later we lay down under a velvet sky, lit by stars and the first sliver of the new moon. On neither night did Esius sleep but kept watch with his guards against wolves and Catuvellauni.

I risked the king's displeasure by gently pressing my argument on the benefits of Roman rule. 'One governor, for the whole country.'

'All of it?'

'Not to begin with but eventually, yes.'

'He will have authority over kings?'

'Not personally. He himself is under the authority of the emperor. Let us say that Rome will have authority over kings.'

'How can you offer that and consider yourself a Briton? You are a dog fox!'

'What is a king? A man in constant fear of his life, always watching his neighbours, his brothers, his sons, for the one who will be the next king.'

'The death of kings is part of life.'

'Everyone lives in fear, your family, your people, never knowing what the morrow will bring, which tribe will appear on the horizon to kill your children, violate your women, take all you have. You lead a primitive life, the life of animals, the life of eating, mating, dying. In the south, in Greece and Rome, man has grown into himself, discovered his true stature and purpose. Under good government, people flourish, invent ways to lessen toil, begin to experience leisure. In Italy,' I said, 'and now also in Gaul, rivers have bridges, roads are straight, woods cleared. Verica and I crossed Gaul at an easy pace in six weeks. If we were making this journey in Italy, we'd have reached Kyronion the same day we left Sulis.'

Esius gasped as if winded. He hated travelling, not so much the riding as the overnight camps. Unwittingly, I had just offered him his heart's desire. He did not admit to it. All he said was, 'I can see the benefits. Your argument is gaining weight with me.'

'Public works,' I said.

'Eh?'

'It doesn't sound much, does it? Roads, bridges, aqueducts, systems of drainage.'

'Eh?'

I smiled. 'My friend, the legate of the Second Legion, Vespasian — he has a wonderful way of extolling the virtues of mundane things. I hope you can meet him. In peaceful circumstances.'

To my surprise, Esius the King began to hum an old song under his breath, as if for once enjoying the prospect of the future.

37

KYRONION

Kyronion, a flat-topped hill rising above Churn river, sits where the Albios Way crosses the road to Siluria. At least, it used to. From the fortified dun, Kyronion was now sliding down the hill like snow off a roof to resettle itself in rows of deep-thatches in the river valley; we had passed in through the gates long before we began ascending the hill. The fianna was waiting for us in the new oppidum, as they had been for the past two weeks. They jumped up like hounds when they saw Katuaros and all but barked in their joy. Having entered Kyronion, Esius acknowledging the people coming out to greet him, we began climbing the steep, winding track up to the gate in the original ramparts. While Esius understood the practicalities of the new settlement, he was a traditional man faithful to the ancestors, and kept his house on the plateau where the ground was remarkably flinty and hard underfoot. Nothing much remained here other than the grain pits and forges of the metalworkers, and anything else of value that might need the extra protection of the dykes and palisades in times of trouble; otherwise, since the union of north and south kingdoms, when Kyronion had become the main capital of the Dobunni, everything other than the hall of the king had been removed to the new oppidum below.

The king's house paid due respect to the ancestors. Two rough-hewn poles carved with strange faces flanked the door-way, over which was the tusked skull of a boar. Hanging under the eaves around the outside were human heads with skin of dried leather, enemies of yesteryear immortalised to the glory of the Dobunni, although one of them was Bodvocos, the king's brother, and once the ruler of the northern part of the territory. Succession the British way was a merciless business: rule by the last brother standing.

I complimented Esius on his house but he just grunted. 'This is just a reception house. My preferred abode is deeper in the woods, isolated, on the edge of the plateau.' A procession of elders and chief warriors arrived and, after a meal of roasted meats and barley bread, the king had me address them on the virtue of non-resistance. 'But,' the eldest of the uncles protested, 'we are bonded to Caratacos. The terms of our treaty demand that we send a levy of all our fighting men, every one of them, at his call. And he has called.'

'If we send them, we lose them to death,' said Esius.

'But what will happen if we don't send them? We'll have broken the treaty, laid ourselves open...'

Esius, after deliberating over the past few days, seemed to have decided to take my advice. He set it out before the council. 'We shall send the men but, at the gates to Calleva, they will submit without a fight to the general of the Romans, Aulus Plautius. Togidubnos assures me they will be treated well and taken neither as slave nor hostage, but as fighters on the side of the Romans.'

There was complaint and disgruntlement, especially from the warriors, but Esius was persuasive and told them that, since becoming part of the Empire, life in Gaul had changed for the better, 'according to Togidubnos'. The druids of Kyronion stood apart and silent; Apnodens led them away to speak to them alone. Around the fire the volatile discussion lasted into the night, a night of bickering, arguing, contending and convincing. Nothing was settled until Apnodens returned with the druids, whom he had persuaded to submit to Rome. At least on this occasion. The levy would be sent out the following day and, on reaching Calleva, would present itself to Plautius.

Branwen and two aunts entered to serve mead into the circle of proffered drinking horns. The king asked Branwen to sing for us; she took up her harp, ran her hands over the strings and began a *vocos* to the ancestors. As she sang, she became radiant. Sulkiness was just the shadow of that light.

There are two kinds of bard (naturally). One trains in the schools and becomes a master of technique; the other sings as moved by the gods, is a servant of the gods and often has no technique at all. Because Branwen was the daughter of a king, they had thought it appropriate that she train, but her talent was as natural as a running stream. We listened to the *vocos* and none of us knew whence it came or where it was going, other than into the deep well of loss and sadness. Her pure voice curled in the air.

She remained polite and solemn with me, the Romey; with Katuaros she was more relaxed and natural, as she was with Draumur, whom she regarded as a fellow bard despite his having had no training at all. Since Mandred had come out of the healing temple, Branwen had been teaching him to dance and on this night he found an opportunity to show off. While the uncles sat with dignity at the fire, warriors began to move in a large circle, pounding with their feet, hollering, waving staffs, wands, rattles or knobsticks, their masked faces coming into the light of the fire and passing into darkness again; among them a Durotrigan slave who could jump higher than the rest and holler louder than most. I sat like an old man with the uncles, congratulating myself on a diplomatic victory, while all the time feeling unaccountably vexed. I watched Branwen outlined by the women's fire dancing the fawn dance. 'That was beautiful,' I said in a lame attempt to make conversation when, later, she escorted us to the deep-thatch reserved for guests. Above all things, I wanted her to treat me as she treated the others, as her brother, perhaps even her favourite brother, but she walked along looking out for bats.

'Branwen, what is happening, your imminent separation from Apnodens, do you blame me?'

'Yes,' she said simply. 'Of course. Who else? I will go mad cooped up here with my aunts, weaving at the loom, back and forth, back and forth, the same conversation every day. Every day the same! Oh, my back. Oh, my hips. Oh, my eyes. Oh, this cough. Haugh! Haugh! Oh, my husband and his filthy habits. Oh, my children, running amok.'

I realised suddenly that, as I had been raised as a Roman, she had been raised as a boy, keeping only boys and men company for years, and that she, like me, was uncomfortable to be home.

'Never wear one of our Dobunni mantles, never,' she warned me. 'They have misery in every thread.'

I ran my hand over the soft wrap I'd been given as a gift, dyed pink with dandelion and purple with blackberry. I couldn't feel any misery...

'Believe me,' she said, 'it's there.' She smiled suddenly and, for a moment, I was one of her adopted brothers. 'Take me away from here,' she said earnestly. 'Please. I will die here. My spirit will die. I want to stay with you.'

'You mean you want to stay with Apnodens.'

She blushed and looked away.

'It's too dangerous, Little Sister. Here you will be under the protection of your father.'

'He cannot prevent the death of my spirit. If I can't sing, I shall perish.'

'Of course he will want you to sing! He just has!'

'Performing at the fire — that's not real singing. Real singing is hearing the song from the land and giving it voice. If I can't do that, because people — aunts — keep babbling at me about their aches and pains, what to have for supper and who I should marry, there will be no point in living... Please! Take me with you!'

I remained firm: it was too dangerous. Then her liveliness vanished and sullenness returned to swathe her like a miserable mantle.

'You are your father's only child, Branwen. You must prepare to become queen.'

'I don't want to be queen!' She flounced around like a spoilt child. I laughed suddenly.

'What amuses you?' she demanded.

'I don't want to be king!' I said, and flounced about myself, pulling faces and grumbling.

'Then let us run away together and be what we want to be!'

'And what is that?'

'I'll sing to the deer in the woods and you can sit on your fine horse looking superior. No, no! You can sit in a bare hut like a recluse. You and Apnodens together, staring at the stars. You will sleep all day and stare at the sky all night. Yes, we three will run away together and find a cave somewhere and only come out at night.'

'Sometimes, Branwen,' I said, 'we have to follow duty rather than desire.'

Blowing through tight lips she made a noise like a farting sheep.

At first light the levy mustered, a body of five hundred warriors and twice as many farmers. Esius instructed their captains how to change sides when they reached Calleva. The muttering protests of the men when they learned what they were to do affected the chariot horses, making them twitchy in the traces; mounted men had to turn and turn again to keep their horses steady. Amongst the infantry farmers, no one seemed to care whether they fought with the Britons or with the Romans: they were annoyed that it was now, when the weeds were at their most rampant, when lambing had not yet finished, when there were cheeses to make.

The chief druid of Kyronion conducted a short rite dedicated to Taranis, god of thunder, and with a blaring of the carnyxes, they were off. Off, not like Romans in ordered columns. Off in a trundling of wheels and a cacophony of war trumpets, wrapped in their pink and purple colours under the standards of the boar. From a guard tower on the upper ramparts, Esius watched them go. 'I hope you are right,' he said, and there was threat in his voice. But his mood could change like the weather and moments later he was taking me through the woods to a secluded grove on the northern scarp. It was a perfect circle made generations before by planting a ring of twelve elms. Now the spaces between were filled with blackthorn, hawthorn, silver birch and rowan — trees in fruit for much of the year — while the stately elms soared up to the sky. The sward was kept short by tethered sheep and flowers of the meadow sparkled in the grass.

Inside the grove but not in the centre was a smaller circle, this one a magnificent house newly re-thatched, all wheaten and golden. On the lime-washed walls of wattle and daub were patterns that were familiar to me, because they were my own tattoos. On either side of the doorway, eight-petalled flowers. At first it seemed a house in contrast to its owner but Esius changed in its presence, turning from the crude, greasy hog-king to druid. The only people allowed here were priests, bards and uncles, who sang the ancient stories and performed the sacred rites. Outside the grove, the view was extensive, south to the wavy blue line of the downs; north to the start of Cuda's hills and in between the folds, wolds and combes of rich farm-land. 'This is a very sacred place,' said Esius, 'and no one is allowed here except by invitation.'

'For some reason, standing here,' I said, 'I am reminded of the Sanctuary of the Wheel, as if I hear its echo.'

'It is due east from here. It is in our song of origins that this is a place of eight ways. They are all over the country. Britain is a map of wheels, or stars some say, laid down long ago. We only get glimpses. I've never found eight ways, only four: we stand at the crossing of the Albios Way and the Silurian Way.' He ushered me inside the house where, once my eyes had got used to the gloom, I could see the fine work of its struts and purlins. The beams and poles were so smooth I presumed the use of planes, as in Rome, but Esius said it was done with axes. 'Planes are for those who use axes as choppers,' he said dismissively. He said that most of the wood had come from one tree, an ancient and mighty oak uprooted by the Shee last year during a wild night. 'I put my best carpenters to work on it. Planes! Don't let them hear you say that.' The wood had been oiled and was warm to the touch, as if the tree were still alive.

'Now tell me how much better Roman houses are.'

'I'd rather have this than the imperial palace!'

'It has no bath house.'

But I could build one, I thought. I could see myself living here so strongly. It might not offer the comforts I'd grown accustomed to, but it appealed to my soul. It was gloomy within, like all British houses, but a place of beauty, a house that connected you to the past. I glanced at Esius, appreciating now that the identification with the boar spirit was just a brutish hide covering a man of resonance and deep perception.

'I am concerned about what is ahead for us,' he said. 'Whether it is British or Roman, both options frighten me.'

'You don't strike me as one easily frightened.'

'I am a father. I am frightened for my only child. I am a king. I am frightened for my herds and my people. Since the unification of Dobunnic territories, we have given up war. We never make raids. It is not our way. Instead I send my only daughter to bardic school in the hope that she may intercede with the gods and the ancestors on our behalf. Among my neighbours are the Belgae. Biccos was a friend of mine, and I hope to find another in his son, Katuaros.' He paused. 'It would be good, I think, whatever the future has in store for us, if we were to unite our tribes through marriage.'

Some small thing twanged inside me. Was it jealousy? Of Katuaros? 'She's just a child!' I protested.

'A betrothal of five years. Not uncommon.'

I couldn't imagine Katuaros waiting five years and worried for our Little Sister. So many child brides die in the first pregnancy.

'So,' he said. 'You agree?' He was peering at me strangely. 'Were you even listening?'

'To what?'

'My proposal.'

'To make an alliance with the Belgae.'

'No. With the Atrebates. With you.'

I gazed at him with a frown of incomprehension.

He sighed loudly down his nose. 'You are rejecting my proposal. Refusing my daughter...' His temper was rising.

'I accept,' I said quickly. 'I accept your proposal.' It was, after all, the highest of the seven forms of marriage, the divine form based on an arrangement between father and husband for the good of the people. It would surely appease the gods for my father's marriage, which had been the lowest form, that of snatching a woman through desire.

'Of course I will take Branwen as wife,' I said, trying not to think of her sullenness. 'But she must consent. What makes you think she will accept me?'

Esius laughed. 'Why wouldn't she?'

'There is a cold draught from her every time I pass by.'

'You're too young yourself, if you don't yet know how women hide their feelings. You think she favours your foster brother? Or that wisp-haired harpist, Draumur? No, she just feels at ease with them. As for Apnodens, he's her foster father and she'd much rather be with him than with me. Yes, she made that clear.'

'That was because you murdered her bat.'

'I didn't know it was hers! It was just a bat in my daughter's hair!'

I looked out to the broad skies beyond the circle of trees. The acceptance of the betrothal put a burden on me. I had assented readily enough, because an alliance of the tribes was so attractive, but a child, a morose slip of a girl who needed looking after... Could I do it? Did I even want to? 'She will stay with you for the five years?' I asked Esius.

'Of course. Though, with our future so uncertain... Perhaps she should stay with Apnodens.'

'That would be best, I believe,' I said, 'for Branwen's sake. When we return from Venonis he could take her with him to Sulis.'

On the way back to the dun Esius led me on a detour into a beech wood where, in a secluded paddock in a glade, he kept his mares with the new foals. I realised at once the trust he was placing in me to reveal this hidden herd. He had done well, breeding a fine line of riding horses from a son of Tiberius that Verica had given him.

'Choose a mare,' he said. 'There, that one. Rosmertina. Put Scipio with her next season and you will have the start of the best herd in Britain. You can take her foal, too. He's a good one, strong in the leg.'

I smiled grimly. 'I live nowhere. How can I start a herd?'

'All in good time. She will be yours when you are ready. My wedding gift to you.'

That plunged me into thought, as to what I could give Branwen. Land, livestock, slaves were not in my possession to give. My mother's mirror, yes, she would like that, and a ring of course... Esius broke into my thoughts. 'In time, it will all be yours. You will take all my possessions and my people when the time comes.'

'May that not be for many years.'

When we arrived back at the king's reception house, Esius summoned Branwen for a private conversation. A short while later she burst out of the house sobbing and ran off to a place where no one could find her. 'She'll be in one of her dens,' Esius said, unconcerned when she did not come back even at night-fall. 'Always goes to cover like a wounded deer.'

'What upset her?' I asked. 'Was it the betrothal?'

351

'What betrothal?' Katuaros asked. I told him in an off-hand fashion what Esius and I had arranged.

'You are to marry Little Sister?' He somehow restrained his laughter and just looked at me with merry eyes.

'She ran off when I told her,' Esius said.

'I'm not surprised,' said Katuaros. 'She's probably half way to Caledonia.'

Immediately after the departure of the levy, Esius had ordered the strengthening of the defences, and not against the Romans. He was worried about reprisals from Caratacos. I lent him the manpower of the fianna who, between them, could dig a dyke in a day. Around the base of the hill and at several places on its slope, all available men were out ditching and laying traps while down in the woods timber was being felled to repair the old palisades with sharpened stakes. I tried to reassure the king that Caratacos would not escape the Romans, but he was not going to take any chances. We had arranged that Esius would travel with us to the midsummer gathering at Venonis but he was having second thoughts. He wanted to wait at least until we had news from Calleva. It did not seem right to be on the move while the destiny of our land and peoples was being decided between the Thames and the Kennet. Besides, there was a betrothal to arrange, once we had found the one to be betrothed. Esius and I had decided there could be no formal handfasting, announcement or exchange of gifts. A solemn pledge was all there would be time for: an intention to marry in the future.

We spent most of the following day talking horses and in the evening we watched Draumur groom Scipio until he shone in the dying light. 'Such good hooves,' Esius observed enviously while having his own hair groomed and plaited by a slave.

'He's a marsh horse from the Maremma,' I explained. 'Broad in the hoof and long in the stride.' The bats were coming out, darting and diving. 'Still no sign of Branwen?' I asked. Draumur said he'd seen her earlier and she had been frequently sighted by those felling trees in the woods. Apnodens thought she was making the most of her last days as a child. It may only have been a betrothal, a promise for the future, but it marked a change in her life, a change which her aunts warned her would show on her body. Did she think womanhood would rob her of her powers? Did she spend those two days alone in a form of mourning?

Having evaded all search parties, Branwen wandered back of her own volition in the morning, laden with armfuls of flowers. She was in good humour, clearly resigned to her destiny, and arrived while I was sitting alone on the ramparts, staring out at eye level with a windhover. She lit up when she saw me, like the Silver Maiden and the Golden God.

'There you are!' I said. 'I missed you.'

'Do you really want me as wife?'

'That depends. Are you going to grow up to be an unusual and talented woman?'

'If I can.'

'Then, yes, I do.'

'Can I keep bats?'

'If you want. But not in the house. I don't want bat droppings everywhere.'

She was laughing; we were playing again; playing the future. 'Can Apnodens live with us?'

'If he chooses.'

'What shape is our house?'

'Square.'

'No! It must be round, as round as the moon and the sun. It must be! I can't marry anyone who lives in a house with corners!'

I lunged at her and she ran squealing away.

And so, as the Roman army marched on Calleva, I played with my wife-to-be.

38

BATAVIANS

I walked with Esius in procession along the path, a path Branwen had walked alone earlier to strew with stems of blue-bells and cow-parsley, to meet my bride-to-be in the elm grove. In the absence of knowledge of what was happening at Calleva, our celebrations were muted. We made a sacrifice of flowers to Rosmerta and took seven strides around the altar to say, 'By these seven steps you have become my dearest friend.' Dearest friend. Branwen? The thought of what I was doing made my head swim but I had precious little time to worry about it. We were just arriving back at the reception house on the plateau when, through the still evening air of early summer came shouts, bellowing like bulls from hill to hill, and the light of fire beacons leaping up.

'Calleva?' Esius asked Apnodens, who was pricked like a hare listening to the messages.

'Fallen to the Romans.'

'And Caratacos?'

The messages were contradictory. Some said he had been killed, some that he had been captured, some that he had escaped. The succession of Dobunni messengers that began to arrive were equally confused and it was not until the middle of the following day that we could be certain of events. Those of Caratacos's army who survived the Roman attack on Calleva had escaped east towards Wey river. And Caratacos? He was alive. As was his brother, Togodumnos.

Even though the war had moved east, Esius did not relax.

There might be revenge bands about. He called on his people to come up from the valley to find safety within the ramparts. There was no question now of his accompanying us to Venonis, not while Caratacos lived. He must stay. And he implied I should stay, too, to lend the support of my men to his defences. Apnodens counselled me to be strong of purpose and to continue my journey, and Katuaros lent all his weight to that. I agreed to leave in the morning.

That night, the night of no moon, wild horses galloped across open land as if being chased. We could hear the thunder of their hooves. Our horses at the lines and in the paddocks, Scipio in his stable, were agitated, pulling on securing ropes, kicking at doors and fences. Esius went out with some men bearing torches to the mares' paddock, convinced there were wolves about. Apnodens, however, went up on the ramparts to listen to the distances. When he came down he said he had heard horses neighing and whinnying, crying out to each other the way dogs do. Agitated himself, he paced up and down muttering, urging on the dawn. At first light Branwen burst out of the women's house in tears from a nightmare she'd been having. She ran towards us blindly. I assumed she was heading for Apnodens but it was me she came to, putting her arms out to be held. I squeezed her tight for comfort while she wept into my chest.

The rising sun sent out apricot streamers of alarm from behind a smothering of woad-coloured cloud, turning the land into a betwixt and between place, neither light nor dark. From where we stood, I could see the dust of a rider approaching us on the road from Calleva. He must have ridden through the moonless night — no mean feat on our tracks. The watch at the gate challenged the lone rider, then gave him entry. I had the king called from his bed. When the sweating messenger arrived at the reception house, he faced an Esius who was still half asleep. He spoke of the fall of Calleva, how at first the arrival of the Dobunnic forces had given new hope to the besieged who were hiding behind ramparts being battered by Roman engines and catapults; how despair had followed when the Dobunni changed sides.

'We have already heard all this,' said the king gruffly, interrupting him. 'The Catuvellauni are on the run eastwards?'

The messenger nodded curtly. What he had come to tell us about, what we could not know about because nothing had been called, was the horses. Branwen sat down heavily.

On horseback and in chariot, the Britons fleeing Calleva had gone across country to where the Wey joins the Thames. Both rivers are shallow there and so divided into streams and tributaries that the ground is marsh for a mile or more. The Britons knew ways across and rode sure-footed native horses. They picked their way over sucking bog and slippery grass, leaving the Romans to flounder behind them and, with luck, drown. Achieving the north bank of the Thames, the Britons relaxed, set up camp and picked off any bold legionary who hazarded the crossing.

Auxiliary troops, drawn from all corners of the Empire, bring to the Roman army their own special talents. What the Batavians of the Rhine can do that no one else can is swim across rivers in full armour. Vespasian led the unit upstream to where the water was deep and sent them over. Full armour, they say, the Batavians swim in full armour. Well, that's nonsense of course. I have seen them perform this feat as an entertainment on the Tiber. For a start they don't wear plate metal like legionaries, but tunics of boiled leather, although they do retain their helmets which makes them look like they are swimming in armour. Heavy equipment such as weapons they float across using their shields as rafts while they, themselves, clasp inflated wineskins or pig bladders and paddle like dogs. That's how they do it. That's how they crossed the Thames to outflank the Britons. They came ashore in silence on the night of no moon, but the horses sensed them and snickered in the dark. The dripping Batavians cut the throats of the guards, then started on the horses. They went from beast to beast, cutting hamstrings.

Why didn't they kill them? It would have been more honourable. It would have been quieter. As it was, the Britons woke up to the screaming of their horses, the knowledge that a unit of the Romans had crossed, and the realisation that the enemy was more barbaric than they were. Without horses, without chariots, they were helpless. And not a single Briton was able to send out a call for we have no words for such an act. What is the verb for having to kill what you love because someone else has disabled it? The horses had to do the calling themselves.

While the charioteers rushed to save what animals they could, and put down those they couldn't, the Romans on the other bank rained arrows on the men left in camp and, amidst the disarray, began to build causeways across the marshes. Vespasian's legion arrived first on the far bank. He expected the Britons to flee, but they stood their ground and fought ferociously to drive the Romans back into the river. Caratacos, they said, was roaring to avenge the horses. The Britons might have succeeded except that the legion under Sabinus also crossed and scythed into them. At that point, the Britons fled.

Branwen was haemorrhaging tears. As for Esius, as he listened to this account, his face went grey then darker grey in a huffing, puffing rage. 'The horses?' he said, over and over again. 'The horses?' For him, the Romans might have been attacking the British gods. Having spent his life breeding horses, he knew the effort involved in generations of refining the stock. His own horses, being now on the side of the Romans, were safe, but that did not stop him feeling for his fellow chieftains, who'd had to put their screaming horses down in the water meadows of the Thames. Indeed, I felt the same: horror at the Roman action.

'They had a horse pyre,' the messenger told the king. 'Even though they were engaged in battle, they still sent the horses to the Summerlands on a great pyre.'

'And my horses?'

'Safe, given that your levy had deserted. But the Britons are finished.' The messenger was trying to be impartial in his reports and true to his training, but he blinked rapidly as he said this.

'And Caratacos? Alive or dead?'

'Alive, but Togodumnos was slain at Calleva. Caratacos now is chief of the Catuvellauni.'

Esius jumped to his feet, roaring. 'I should never have agreed to it! I've put my men in the service of monsters! I am on the wrong side!'

'How can you say so?' I protested.

He rounded on me. 'You!' he thundered, stabbing at me with one of his large, blunt fingers. 'You come here with your oily words, making me change sides. Then you persuade me to give you my daughter!'

Branwen jumped between us. 'It's not his fault!'

Esius pushed her out of his way. 'Of course it's his fault.' His small eyes had become bloodshot and his hand moved to the hilt of his sword. Unusually for him, Apnodens stood frozen, his jaw slack, not knowing what to do or say.

'And you!' Esius shouted at him. 'You limp-wristed apology for a druid! I shouldn't have listened to you. Peace, indeed! Long live the druid kings!' As he pushed past Apnodens to reach me, Katuaros shoved me out of the way. He and the fianna kept the old king at bay with their spears while the rest of us ran for the horse lines and the chariot. We set off with Mandred driving. I looked back to see Katuaros and his men leap on to their horses to follow us. My last view of Branwen was her twisting in her father's grip, screaming at him to let her go.

39

THE RIM OF THE CAULDRON

When we came to the Albios Way, we hesitated. Stopping by a shrine to the Mother, we became shrouded in a sudden mist, outwardly and inwardly, for with the mist came profound doubt. It seemed perilous to go on a public track to Venonis. Was it time to admit I'd failed in my mission? Should I ride east to join the Romans? It would certainly be ill-advised to travel in Dobunni lands while the fury of Esius was raging.

'Cobwebs!' said Mandred, brushing wildly at his face.

'Just mist,' I said, but as I did so, it took form before my eyes and separated into three hooded figures, beckoning me towards a more obscure path. Apnodens saw the spirits, too, and bowed to their authority.

'We are being invited,' he said, 'to make a pilgrimage to your mother's barrow.' As diversions go, it was not a great one, just a few miles on a high road across the hills that Esius himself had pointed out to me from the elm grove, the route they had carried her bier.

Katuaros protested, 'Why? Let us not deviate!' The fianna, who were already some way further along the Albios Way, shouted out for us but I called to them: 'We're going west. Further west!'

West to the tomb of Innogen. 'The gods will it,' I explained when they rode back to join us.

The track went over wooded hills until it came out high on a ridge, tipping us, it seemed, into the vast and circular vale below called 'the Cauldron'. Far below, the Severn river, glinting in the light, ran out of the vale like a line of molten metal. From the lofty viewpoint of the escarpment, 'the Rim', we could see forest beyond the great river and, beyond that, the distant hills of Siluria. In the vale, smoke coiled from clusters of steads and, to the north, from the oppidum of Clevo. We did not travel down, however, but kept to the Rim: the Path of the Dead Ones, lined by barrows and shrines.

The tomb-keepers live in their own steads on the escarpment and we were directed to the couple who had been responsible for the interment of Innogen. The old man took my gifts of food and sat to tell us, to intone for us, how the great lady of the Dobunni had died in the prime of her beauty, her spirit gone like tree blossom in the wind, her body beautiful even when spiritless ('tall she was as an alder and like an ash tree neither male nor female but both'); how she had been buried adorned with her treasures, her comb, her weaving bobbins, her mirror, the mirror by which she scryed the Otherworld, in which she could now be seen by seers. The mirror my father had claimed to possess; the mirror amongst my possessions in my saddlebag. So were they lying or did I have another? For all mirrors, whether for women's vanity or their witchery, look alike.

Even this old couple had one, hanging on the wall of their rude hut, fine-wrought in bronze, etched with circle patterns on one side, polished on the other. The old man took it down reverentially, held it aloft with both hands and, slowly turning it, began to intone spells while his wife put herbs on the fire. The air grew sweet and heady. 'I see her now, I see her now,' sang the old man, swaying where he sat, 'the great Innogen, glowing like fire embers.'

'You can see her?'

'She wants to speak to you.'

'What does she want to say?'

'To you, to speak to you. You must drink of the dreaming cup.'

I shook my head. The Dobunni are famed for their spirit-walking. It is said they spend more time in the Otherworld than in this one, and some of them go there never to come back.

'Innogen calls you, I can hear her myself,' said the old man's wife. 'She has a message.' I was about to sneer at the fortune-teller's craft when the old man said, in a woman's voice, 'Delfos.'

Apnodens handed me the dreaming cup. 'All will be well,' he promised. I held out my hand for the shallow bowl and drank its liquor, which had a taste neither pleasant nor unpleasant, a taste of the past, a taste I already knew of the earth and the forest floor. It was but a heartbeat later that the edges of the world began to dissolve, the faces of my companions to grow huge, their voices to drawl. I looked desperately at Mandred, who reached out and took my hand, but I felt nothing, for my world, this world, had become the dream and there was nothing in it that was real. The old woman now held the bronze mirror by the handle, first showing me the back with its beautiful lobes, crescents and off-centre circles, patterns that I could now see about me everywhere as if in the air, and then turning it so that the polished face reflected on the wall like an image of the full moon. Suddenly I was staring into the face of my mother.

I tried to speak but the words came out slurred as if I had tree gum in my mouth sticking my tongue to my palate. 'No need for speech – I know everything in your heart. You still do not understand the Oracle yet its meaning is so simple — why does it elude you? You persist in wondering which side you are on. Rise above the conflict of opposites. The marriage has to take place within you. Only know thyself and it will come clear: you are to marry your Britishness to your Romanity, your heart to your head, nature to empire. That is what it means. Out of this union will come a sacred child.' Then clouds billowed over me like a mighty yet silent tempest.

I woke up, or seemed to, sitting amidst windswept silver birches on the escarpment, my back against the breast of the Mother. The larks were up, trilling, and white clouds went past the sun as slow as elephants. Far, far in the distance, beyond the river and the forest, the grey-blue hills that marked the boundary of the Silurian territory, full of wild people if the stories mothers tell children are to be believed. Small, dark and squat, the Silures snatch any child senseless enough to wander in the mountains alone, roast him on a spit and have him for dinner. But I was feeling so ill-at-ease with all that was behind me, the Britons, even the Romans, that Siluria no longer held any fear. A world of its own. Beyond battle.

There was an ache inside of me, a void, a deep sadness. My soul felt like a dry well. A word drifted up, an invocation. *Mother*... And, immediately, a response.

—Where is my mirror?

—In your tomb, laid upon your breast.

—It is not. Your father sent a thief and stole it. Verica tried to see me in it.

—The tomb keepers...

—They are lying. Too ashamed to tell the truth.

—Then I have it. It is with me.

—Unlike your betrothed.

—I left her with her father. She blames me for the perfidy of the Romans. Her father seems to think that I, myself, maimed the horses.

—Is that really what he thinks?

—Perhaps not. Perhaps for a moment I had persuaded him that Rome is a force for good, and for a moment he believed me. Then we both woke up.

—That is the truth. But why abandon your betrothed?

—I have not!

—And yet you left her behind, and now she is taken by another.

—*Who*? I must go back!

—It's too late. Go forward, not back. Learn to listen to yourself, your truest guide. Always torn between two ways. Learn to drive the chariot of your soul. Steer a new course for this troubled land.'

When I returned from the Dream, I asked Mandred to fetch the mirror from my saddlebag. 'Recognize this?' I asked the tomb keepers, and regretted my tone when both of them began to weep in a mixture of regret and relief.

I went to the tomb with them, not that it was much of a tomb, not the splendid barrow I'd anticipated, just a stone-lined burial chamber sunk into the ground. It took several of the fianna to remove the cap stone and I trembled violently, scared to see my mother in decay, but there was none. Her face was hidden by a fine bronze bowl so all I could see were her hands crossed on her breast and holding a necklace of amber beads. I unwrapped the mirror and placed it face down under her brittle hands. There was a sound like autumn leaves being stirred by a gentle wind, as if a sigh were escaping from the tomb. I looked up and saw two silver birches close-by, their leaves rustling in the wind. The breeze kissed my cheek.

'She is at rest now,' said the old man. 'As are we.'

'When will her barrow be built?' I asked.

'It is no longer our custom.'

I was not happy with the new custom of neglect, the product of a people growing indolent. In the old days, the whole community would have come out to shovel earth for Innogen. I walked around the area where there were a lot of loose stones and gathered what I could to pile on the capstone as the beginnings of a cairn. Indolent they may be, but no one can resist adding to a pile of stones.

We stayed overnight in the tomb-keepers stead and early the following morning set off across country for the Albios Way, to pick it up further north. I was upset and restless. Despite the advice of my mother's spirit, I wanted to rush back and rescue

Branwen but both Apnodens and Katuaros were insistent that I did not. It would be madness. It would be certain death. All major tracks were now busy, mostly with Catuvellauni on the run and going west. We stopped one group of weary, wounded men to ask news of Caratacos and were told he was making his way to Siluria.

'On this track?' Apnodens demanded.

Our informants did not know. One thought this very track, another thought that he'd gone to Kyronion. I looked at Apnodens in desperation.

'We do not go back there,' he said emphatically. 'What would you do if you met Caratacos? I fear it is too late,' he looked haunted by the thought. 'We should not have left her behind.' He groaned with his face in his hands. 'I don't know what to do!'

'It was not lawful to take her,' I reminded him.

We continued on the high track leading to the Albios Way. A few miles on, Apnodens paused at a cairn by the wayside. 'Seven Springs!' he said. 'The sacred source of the Churn. We can rest here and consult the Seven Spirits.' Steps hidden by brambles and hazels led down into a rocky hollow. Apnodens used his staff to push back the brambles, inviting us to go down. He said we all needed to drink of its healing waters. Katuaros went to the first step, peered down into the hollow and declared it too dangerous. These stone steps, slippery with wet leaf litter, were the only way down and up. Anyone could come along and trap us there: he would stay on the path as a protection.

The rest of us exchanged a knowing grin.

'What is it?' he demanded.

'This place is an abode of many spirits, among them the Shee,' Apnodens said. 'So, anyone else want to stay behind?'

Katuaros was about to defend his pride and dignity when he suddenly gave up and smiled wryly himself. 'Even so, my plan is a wise one,' he said, sitting down on the back of the chariot.

Whether through loyalty or fear, the rest of his men stayed with him.

Apnodens advised him to hide the chariot and horses.

'We can protect them,' said Katuaros, bristling.

'It will save you the bother if you hide them.'

'Hide them,' I commanded him, worried about Scipio. 'And hide yourselves. No point in inviting trouble. If anyone threatens us, you can ambush them.'

Leaving the fianna to disappear into the woods, the rest of us went down the steps. Apnodens led the way, wet brown leaves oozing through his bare toes. We could not see the bottom for the gloom cast by the overhanging trees. Only when our eyes grew accustomed could we see the water seeping out from seven mouths along the base of the rock to gather in a gravelly, shallow pool. Apnodens said that the stream that formed here was the source not only of the Churn but also the Thames. 'Such is the sweet, silent beginning of our mightiest river.'

It was a ferny, mossy place and, yes, the Shee were there. I could hear their soft whisperings and Apnodens, having made an offering to the waters and put his question as to whether we should go back to Kyronion or press on to Venonis, had his ear against the rock. Mandred and Draumur had taken their boots off and were paddling like children. Apnodens however had his head cocked like a bird, listening. I saw a frown form on his face and even as it was forming there were sudden shouts from above, a furious clashing of swords, and the body of Katuaros crashing through the hazels to drop into the basin where the springs collected.

Draumur, drawing his sword as he ran, went up the steps two at a time in bare feet.

40

AT SEVEN SPRINGS

'Delfos?' I knew that voice as I knew no other. 'Won't you come up to meet me?' The taunts of Caratacos boomed in the hollow of Seven Springs. All at the same time: I was baffled by Katuaros, whose head seemed to be off the ground, as if lying on a pillow; I was trying to think of a way out avoiding Caratacos; I was wondering what the order of our departure up the steps should be. Who would follow Draumur? It could only be me...

'Delfos? I have someone here to see you. Two, in fact.'

Mandred protested as I went towards the steps. Apnodens was distracted, kneeling in the water beside Katuaros and speaking to him as if to a living though unconscious man.

I have never seen anything so beautiful as the bright little ferns that poked out of crevices of the mossy stone steps. Life in impossible circumstances. If this was to be my last view of anything, it was a good one. The light increased the higher I got and, just as I'd been blinded by darkness a while before, now I was blinded by light and emerged through the hazel bushes wincing. It must have been the same for Draumur, meeting his death in a blaze of light. His body lay there, a spear through his unprotected heart. Of the rest of our fianna there was no sign.

There stood Caratacos, leaning on his sword, holding a bag which seemed to contain a large ball. His men, who had stood back during his one-to-one with Katuaros, remained sitting on fallen trees of the woods to enjoy the spectacle of their leader picking off his enemies as we emerged like moles.

'How is he?' Caratacos asked of Katuaros.

'Alive.'

'I drew no blood. Not my intention of course. I wanted to slice off that horned serpent and leave him with a stump, but he lost his footing and fell. A long and rocky drop. Alive you say?'

'He fell into the lap of the Shee.'

Caratacos laughed hard. 'Here,' he said, flinging the bag at me. I knew what it was as I caught it, the feel of it through the linen, its weight, the brittleness of the fabric where blood had dried.

'Open it,' he said.

Inwardly I called on all the Seven Spirits of the Seven Springs to give me strength to open the draw-string bag; I reached in, felt the coarse hair of a dead man and pulled out the head of Esius. I turned away in grief, guilt and disgust. As I did, I noticed Firebreath in the long grass, where she had fallen from the hand of Katuaros.

'What have you done?' I hissed.

'Taken Kyronion. I had no intention of leaving it in the care of a double-dealer like him. He lost us the battle. I kept him alive while I took his daughter— '

'What do you mean, "took"?' I shouted.

'I mean chained her up. I'm not stupid. Virgins are ten times the worth of any woman.'

I could feel his words in my gut, churning me up, making me ready...

'I kept him alive while we fired his house, killed the children, "took" the women in the usual sense, gathered up a pen full of slaves. Where are the horses?'

'What horses?'

'I got the herd but no foals. Where are the mares kept?'

'Have you not got enough with Verica's herd?'

'A man can never have enough horses.' He came close, was breathing in my face. 'Especially after losing so many. Every mounted warrior who fought with me, every chariot driver, each one of them, needs a new horse or pair.'

He'd clearly been wounded in the battle with the Romans, had healed but was now grey with tiredness. He stood back. 'And so I took off the old boar's head.'

'What do you intend to do with it?'

'Haven't decided. Stopped here, in fact, for some guidance. Either I wash it in the sacred waters and hang it from my bridle as a prize, or I dedicate it to the spirits of Churn river and let it float back home. Thing is, my bridle is already heavy with trophies.'

I glanced around quickly, wondering where the fianna were and at what point they might deign to come and join me. 'By our druid laws it should be embalmed,' I said. 'The head of a king. Your disrespect will have consequences.' So saying, I threw it at him. This caught him off guard, long enough for me to snatch up Firebreath and brace myself in a fighting stance.

Caratacos was so surprised he laughed. 'You?' he said. 'Fight? Fight me?' Deciding I was serious, he lunged. I felt the cut but not the pain. As I had no shield Caratacos threw his aside so as not to have an unfair advantage. Had it not been for this and his weariness, I'd not have lasted the moment. But, though with each thunderous descent of his blade I was beginning to fall backwards, I fought on, not knowing where this strength was coming from. I wanted him dead. I fought because I hated him... because I feared him... because I admired him... because I envied him. Envied? Yes. Envy. I envied his unmuddled view of himself and his purpose in life. He never tripped himself up with self-examination, was never tortured by thoughts of his weaknesses, nor by any conscience. What did *Know Thyself* mean to him? It meant one word: Caratacos.

I wanted him dead. Not to make it easy for the Romans — though if I could kill him now it would all be over — no. I wanted him dead for taking Branwen and selling her into slavery. Where was that wretched fianna? As my power began to ebb, a bramble shoot sprung up and snagged his breeches, ripped into the flesh of his bare calves. I raised Firebreath high to bring her down where his neck met his shoulder. This was it. The Deep Strike my father had named me for. Then Apnodens crashed out of the hazel bushes, his arms raised in the Druid Peace, and we both stopped mid-strike. I'd always thought the Druid Peace, when a priest goes out between opposing armies, was a signal, a sign to desist under the law. But it is more than that. We could not have struck each other even had we wanted to, and for sure we wanted to.

Caratacos was snarling like a cornered polecat, heaving for breath. Blood flowed from the bramble cuts as he leaned forwards, bracing his arms against his knees.

'Where are you bound?' Apnodens asked him, taking his sword.

Caratacos glared at him. 'You! You two-faced traitor to your own kind! If my brother were alive and were here, he'd have you skinned and pegged out for the ants.'

'That's a druid king for you,' said Apnodens calmly.

'But he's dead,' Caratacos pointed his sword at me, 'thanks to you. You had us going in the wrong direction until we were exhausted. The Romans are on their way! They're landing in the east! They're not coming! They're here! By the time Togodumnos engaged in battle, he was already half dead.'

There was no point in protesting that I, too, had been on as much of a run-around, and as much in the dark. Besides, if I were about to die, I might as well have some glory.

'The Dobunni came just when we needed them but, from the walls of Calleva, I watched them submit to Aulus Plautius on his fine white horse. Betrayed! Betrayed!' Caratacos thundered. 'All is lost because of you!'

'You think you are a freedom-fighter,' I said. 'You think you are High King and saviour of Britain. You think you are a new incarnation of Vercingetorix the Gaul.'

'As well I might be.'

'I'll tell you what you are, you are the *cause* of all this, the very *cause* of it. The Romans are here because of you. Your own brother Adminios went to them for help against you. My father did the same. It is because of you, a land-grabbing horse thief, that they are here.'

The colour ebbed from his face then rushed back in. 'Adminios? I would have had no power against him if he hadn't been weak. A bandy-legged lamb weaned too early. Sometimes the first-born is more the runt than the last born. I gathered the strength the others left behind in the womb. Adminios was using the lands of the Cantii as a bridge to Gaul and Rome, ships coming in and out, in and out of his harbours and ports. Through that foot of Britain, the infection got in. There and all along the south coast, the rot, the rot of an easy life, the rot of greed, of luxuries, of trade. Once kings were kings by the strength of their arm and the mettle of their sturdy hearts. Once kings were warriors, were heroes. Once we ate the fruit of the forest and the harvest of the fields, food we had hunted, foraged and farmed ourselves; we were fed by the Mother. Now we import it, some of it, the wine, the olives, the dried figs — that is the food of kings now, and they trade in it. They sell human lives for jars of oil or glossy pottery. That is why I fight, and will continue to fight, even to death. Adminios and Verica had become weakened by trade. If you want to strengthen the tree, you prune it. Land-grabbing horse thief? I, alone, have been cutting out the rot to make Britain strong again. And what do you do? You bring the rot back in.'

One of his fianna, who had been down to the springs to fetch water, now appeared and began to bathe his chief's leg, which calmed Caratacos down.

'How is Katuaros?' he asked him, his voice level again.

'All broken but alive.'

'How many are down there with him?'

'Just one.'

'Where's your fianna?' Caratacos asked me, but at that moment Apnodens noticed the head of Esius staring out of a clump of ferns.

'By Taranis!' he cried, 'What have you done?'

Caratacos shrugged. 'What was due to be done the moment he betrayed me.'

'And his daughter?'

'Shackled and put with an agent. Prime booty, that one. A virgin, a girl bard, daughter of a king. I'm expecting a bag of gold when she's sold at some Roman port.'

Apnodens seemed to double in height as if about to break his discipline and strike him, but then he bent over and howled, a primeval sound, as of a woman giving birth, the eternal cry of unendurable pain. It was picked up by hounds belonging to Caratacos's war band, and by distant wolves. The birds of the woods thrashed amongst the branches and cawed as if joining the lament. That sound vibrating in my innards... it took all I had to check the tears for Branwen and for Draumur both.

Impervious to grief, Caratacos got up and picked up the head by the long grey hair, the boars' teeth clicking. 'So, what shall I do with it? Bridle or river? Or nail it up as first fruits dedicated to these springs?'

Apnodens held out his hands and Caratacos gave him the head of Esius. 'Take it. My bridle is heavy enough with trophies, although a king... always good to have the power of a king.'

'Where are you bound?' Apnodens asked him again, although his bottom lip was quivering.

'Clevo-in-the-Cauldron and then over Severn river to Siluria. The Britons are not finished yet. No. We shall regroup. We shall retreat to the mountains and, when we are strong again, we shall return. Not in any useless attempt to do battle the Roman way. No. You can tell your Roman friends, son of Kommios,' he said to me, 'that they must never relax their guard for a moment. That shadow that falls across their tents at night could be us. That hooting of an owl, that creaking of a branch, could be us. Behind any rock, we could be waiting. We shall maim them, Delfos, cut their ham strings and leave them to die. It's the least we can do. The Romans can stay as long as they like, but they'll have to get used to not sleeping. The spirits are with us, in the sucking bogs, the boiling rivers, the sudden downpours of freezing rain. The nymphs of the misty waters are with us; the dryads of the grove. I would not like to be a Roman in Britain. The way we fight, there is no safety in numbers.'

He turned to his men, calling them to mount up. It was only as they disappeared round a bend in the track that our fianna came out of hiding, Mouse Ears insisting they had been about to burst out and save me when they were checked by Apnodens's spell. Not trusting myself to reply, I went with Apnodens back down the slippery path to where Katuaros lay, conscious now. Apnodens placed the head of Esius reverentially in the basin of the largest spring to be cleaned by the living water. 'How are you?' he asked, turning to Katuaros.

'Very well,' he said, lying like a felled tree. 'What's that? Esius? No!'

'Can you sit up?'

It was a struggle, but he succeeded.

'Hmmm, all seems well. Thanks to the spirits...' Apnodens examined him but found nothing that matched the description of 'broken'. He rose and walked away, then suddenly turned and threw his staff to Katuaros, saying, lightly, 'Catch...'

Katuaros reached out and yowled. His shoulder, which had taken the brunt of the fall but had settled while he rested, jumped out of joint and once again stood at right angles to his back. Apnodens went to him and wrenched it back into place with a snap. Katuaros's cries ricocheted off the rock walls of the basin before he fainted.

'He'll not be fighting again,' said Apnodens, straightening up. 'Nor is he fit enough to continue with us.' It was agreed that we would send him back to Sulis with the fianna. 'We'll not be needing that useless bunch. If Caratacos and his scattered armies are moving into the west, we'll be safe from here to Venonis.'

While Mandred was binding my arm tight to stop the bleeding from the cut, Apnodens picked up the head of Esius, cleaned it with some loose, straggly moss and put it reverentially back in the bag I'd kept. 'Cynefin will embalm him and set him up somewhere honourable in the temple. A brave man, and the father of the girl destined to become your wife.'

I fell on my knees before the druid and begged forgiveness for causing the death of Esius. Had I not persuaded him to change sides... Greeted by silence, I looked up and saw Apnodens staring down at me, tight-lipped. No light words of atonement came from him, just a nod. He inhaled deeply. 'These lands need a king. I shall recommend your election at Venonis.'

'I want to go back to Kyronion, to see what may be rescued or saved.'

'And what of your mission? We have two weeks before midsummer, two weeks in the bright half of the month.'

'My mission? The Romans are here, Caratacos is in flight and my only attempt to win a king over has ended in his death. If my mission ever had any value, it has none now. I will go to Venonis for midsummer, but first I must go back to Kyronion.'

'There is no point. Just because the road is straight does not mean the going is easy. Come north with me now. If we arrive in good time, we'll be able to see my father in private at Vernemeton.'

His plan appealed to reason, but reason at that moment was not strong in me, not half as strong as the pain from the cut, my anger with Caratacos and the grief of loss. I desperately wanted to find Branwen. Suddenly a very long distance separated me from Seneca, a long way indeed from Britain to Corsica. His teaching was beginning to evaporate. Sometimes a cultivated plant reverts to its origins and a rose that has been bred to be crimson sends out pink flowers. My graft was weakening; with my desire to smash out the brains of Caratacos, I was going back to my British rootstock.

Katuaros, who had woken up, lay listening to us, looking from face to face with concern. I told him how Esius had been killed and Branwen taken into slavery. 'Our faithful Draumur, too, is dead.'

Mandred yelped. Katuaros groaned. Apnodens stooped down to make sure his shoulder was still in place and tell him he was to go back to Sulis for healing. Katuaros turned ashen, not with the pain but with the shock of retirement. He knew without being told that his fighting days were over. When I said that I intended to return to Kyronion, he insisted I should not, that I should go as planned to Venonis.

'As soon as I am mended,' he said, 'I will seek Branwen. Delfos, you must go on to Venonis, consult the archdruid, the druid elders, the kings and chieftains. Our future wellbeing depends on you. You alone can stop any slaughter. I will search for Little Sister, and I will find her.'

He was brave as we lifted him out of the hollow by means of a litter hastily constructed from hazel poles by Cow Crippler and Ten Horns. They yoked the litter to a spare horse and set off on the track to Sulis. Katuaros was facing us as they dragged the litter off.

'I'll find her, I promise! We'll find our Little Sister,' he called.

We took the body of Draumur into the woods above the Seven Springs and in a clearing built a pyre on which we placed the body, fully decorated with his beads, feathers and bones. The knot of hair he had taken to wearing tied to his belt we placed back on his head. On his breast, with his hands arranged on its strings, we put his harp. Mandred, who was cast lower than I'd ever seen him, insisted on taking charge of the rite and sang prayers to rise up to the gods with the smoke. Before the flames caught, however, he reached out and plucked from the body the knot of hair which he had decided to keep.

Together we stood back from the heat as our friend melted into tallow and bone. The colours of the flames were more iridescent than a dragonfly: reds and greens and blues shot through with fizzing streaks of orange. But the sights and smells were as nothing compared to the sound of harp strings popping, each on a different note. Mandred sang to the Seven Spirits of the Seven Springs with the seven notes of a burning harp, offering Draumur to Annwn. Later we put the ash into Churn river at its source.

41

VERNEMETON

We spent a day on the Albios Way without meeting any obstacle. It was the most straightforward day's journeying I'd had since returning to Britain. But then, as we led the horses out of a forest on the lip of a hill in the northern part of Dobunni country, we looked down into a vale to see a Roman cohort scouring the farms for hidden fighters. We all fell flat instinctively. Apnodens turned a wry smile on me. 'Who are you hiding from?'

Who indeed? The unit was from the Second Legion of Vespasian. I should have been riding down the hill hollering a greeting, shouldn't I? Imperceptibly the Mother had reclaimed her son. I felt hairy and woolly and unwashed. I felt part of the earth. I laid my brow down amongst the buttercups and sighed. The druid patted me on the back. Mandred found us a detour to avoid Romans.

One night on a beacon hill in Corieltauvi country, Apnodens drew breath and sent a call south asking for news of Branwen. There was none. We learnt, however, that Katuaros had reached Sulis safely. I listened to these ululations and whistles across the wolds, trying to understand them, to recognize patterns and find out how long messages were conveyed in a song as short as a willow warbler's.

The Albios Way, which men in their ignorance think of as the Salt Way, or poetically as 'From Lindinis to Lindum', is one side of the triangle that has the south coast as its base. On it lie Sulis, Kyronion, Venonis and the grove of groves, Vernemeton.

This is the track so ancient that no one knows its origins, the line the Romans are now establishing as the new frontier of the Empire. As we rode — he in the chariot being driven by Mandred, I riding on Scipio — Apnodens discoursed on the movements of the sun and the moon, the annual cycle and the monthly cycle, and how they repeat their pattern every nineteen years. As he taught us, he interspersed his lessons with tales of battling lions, charioteers and winged horses. I felt as if I were lifting off the ground and was halfway to the celestial vault. I realised we were receiving the teaching that our peoples travelled from Gaul and Iberia to learn from the great druid colleges of Britain.

'Understand the Wheel as a diagram of the cosmos on the ground,' he said, 'and you know everything you need to know about time, space and the creation.' Calls coming up from the south interrupted our philosophising. 'Romans. Retreating,' Apnodens said simply.

'*What?* That can't be right,' I said.

'Are they regrouping for a new attack?' Apnodens wondered. 'But why south of the Thames? It was hard enough for them to cross. Why cross back?'

Then I remembered the plan I'd heard discussed in Rome. Once any resistance had been put down, Plautius was to send to Rome for Claudius. That's what Plautius was doing. He was waiting for Claudius.

'And then?' Apnodens asked.

'Conquest will be completed.'

'Where?'

'Camulodunon.'

I sat in silence on Scipio, looking out over the rolling plains of the Lands of Llyr. I did not know what to do about my mission, whether to abandon it or intensify it. 'When you don't know what to do next,' Apnodens said, 'do the next thing.'

I smiled despite my mood. 'Explain your riddle.'

'What is your next thing?'

'Arriving at Venonis.'

'Then that is what we must do.' He nodded to Mandred to start the chariot, ran after it a little to exercise his legs, then jumped on the back.

We arrived at Venonis at sunset of the second day, half a moon before the midpoint of the year. The hill of Venonis is a great swelling in the land without jagged rocks of any kind. Carved with serpentine ditches, it is capped by tall palisades. The lower slopes were densely populated with shrines, set up by the various tribes in honour of their local gods. There were a few people there, erecting market stalls, but otherwise it was quiet. From the main viewing point on the ramparts we watched beacon fires running in lines, lines which I now began to understand, fires on the summits of hills in the eight directions, all leading the way to this assembly place at the apex of the triangle. Glow worms in the dark lighting the way to follow. With at least a week before the kings gathered here, we went on to Vernemeton, a few miles further along the Albios Way, the great grove where the chief druids would be gathering before formally processing to Venonis.

Going beyond Venonis was, to my southern mind, going beyond the known world and my skin prickled as we rode deep into the lands of the Corieltauvi that stretched right up to Brigantia. Those tribesmen we saw about their daily work looked no different from any other Briton and I was beginning to smile at the fears inspired by my grandmother's stories when, in the place where large rocky hills begin to swell out of the land, I saw shadows flitting among the trees above us. 'Crow People,' said Apnodens and my sweat turned cold as I remembered the stories of the black-and-white men with feathers for hair, who can run the rocks like goats, and who, if they catch you, will boil you alive in their giant cauldron. Apnodens smiled. 'They are hunters living amongst the pines and high oaks and are more frightened of us than we are of them.'

And so I went north, accompanied by the two good companions fate had bestowed on me, but inwardly lonely and aching for what was lost. For those who were lost. For she who was lost. The lushness of the wayside, the abundance of the oh-so-late-in-coming hawthorn blossom, the rich texture of birds and their song, all were vinegar in the wounds of loss. I worried for Katuaros. I writhed with guilt at any thought of Esius. I felt sick with apprehension at the fate of Branwen. Where was she now? A child slave penned up with a thousand others awaiting transportation? Little Sister hoping for rescue by any one of her brothers? Such were the thoughts biting at my conscience like horse flies.

The closer we got to Vernemeton, the quieter and more morose Apnodens became. I asked what troubled him.

'If my father and his council decide that I have been disobedient, that in accompanying you here I have broken my vows, I lose everything. Nineteen years of study cut short. I lose the college. I lose any chance of future office.'

'You received the blessing of Cynefin.'

'I did, but what if my father disagrees? Perhaps he will be harsh with me, his son, so that no one can accuse him of favouritism.'

'Why have you risked so much?'

'We watched you from the moment you landed, assuming you to be an agent of Rome, but I soon realised that that is not the case, that you are an agent of the gods. What I see when I look at you is a man of peace. Blundering idiot most of the time, but at heart, a man of peace. I serve the archdruid, but I put the gods first.'

'Then trust them.'

He nodded.

'What will you do if you are sent down?'

He was quiet for a while then, slowly, a smile suffused his face. 'Why, I shall spend my time studying the stars!'

You would not see the Great Grove if you did not know it was there. Following Apnodens's directions, Mandred steered the chariot confidently through expansive woods for a mile or more before we came out into open pasture where a stream ran through an extensive stead. Looking round, it was some time before I realised we were in the centre of the grove. The deep-thatches were laid out in the cosmic plan, the stead a mirror of the heavens centred on the shadow pole. Archdruid Regalis came out of his house to welcome us. He was tall with long grey hair showing black in streaks, same with his beard. Under still-black eyebrows his eyes were steely, stern but not unloving. A just man.

He gazed on his son. As Apnodens had feared, his father was angry. 'I told all druids to go into hiding. In coming here, you have disobeyed me. You've broken your bond to study for nineteen years,' he said. 'Broken at seventeen years two moons!'

'Did you not know it would happen, when you set me to watching Togidubnos?'

'You were told to watch him, not join him. You were supposed to have remained at Sulis.'

'I could not see him getting here without me.'

'Such hubris! Now you can never be archdruid in my place. Was it worth such a sacrifice?'

'It has always been my hope to retire to Mona and study the stars.'

Regalis sighed down his nose. 'The druid kings will take over.'

'Togodumnos is dead.'

'Caratacos is not. It will be a different order, one of violent resistance. He will bring blood and fire raining down on us. It's all I can do to keep everything contained as it is. Perhaps you are right. Perhaps we should all retreat to Mona.'

While they talked, messages arrived at the grove, either called or coming by way of gallopers. Secluded it might be, but Vernemeton was as noisy as a briar bush full of starlings. As the sun began to set, Regalis led us to the open fire to join the elders and tell of what we knew of events in the south. He introduced me as Togidubnos ap Verica, to which there was quite a lot of spitting into the fire.

'I beg your counsel,' I said, which pacified them somewhat.

'Togidubnos,' said Regalis, 'Your father died four moons ago and you did not call it.'

'It seemed unwise at the time. We did not wish to draw attention to my presence in the country.'

'A selfish act. A wise man entrusts his fate to the gods and doesn't interfere with customs just to protect himself.'

'I believe,' said Apnodens, 'that, on the contrary, the fate of my friend is determined by the will of the gods. They say that the gods use us for their own ends. If that is true, then in Togidubnos they are trying to bring about peace.'

'What do you understand peace to be?' Regalis asked me.

'To create harmony from conflict.' I said. 'To resolve two you make three.'

'What is your meaning?'

I hardly knew myself what my meaning was, but it came from my soul as a strong thread is drawn from a distaff. 'The Romans. The Britons. Both sides believe they have to vanquish the other, that unity is the rule of many by one. That is the law of nature. Wolf eats lamb. But the law of the cosmos is different. Two opposites find something in common, and a third is born. Son of the marriage. Son of the King and Queen. Son of the Black and the White. It is entirely possible that there is a future which is neither British nor Roman but a product of both. Something is working here that is not mortal. Is it the Shee? Is it the gods of the place? Or is there something new?'

'I don't know why or how,' Apnodens said, 'but our future depends on this man. And I don't think he knows why or how, either.'

Regalis, moved by what I had said, nodded. 'There have been many signs over the years,' he said, 'but about ten years ago they began to increase. Reports come hither from all the tribes of our people, spread as we are across the world. Reports of strange events in the cosmos, strange weather, strange behaviour amongst the animals. Some great sacrifice has been made, of a man. That is all I know. But do not expect too much from the old gods. Their day is over.'

This was the last thing Apnodens expected to hear from his father and he stood there with his mouth open and breath snatched away. I would have been equally shocked had the words of Regalis not found their echo within me. The grove of great ash trees, festooned with creepers and ivies and peopled by figures carved out of peeled, dead wood, seemed alive with spirits. But veils were parting to reveal another Spirit that, like no other god before it, had love as its substance. That's the only way I can describe it: a new way into a new life. A new life that did not have fear as its basis.

'At this moment,' Regalis said. 'I am being directed to accept you, Togidubnos. And to make you king.'

But he was also directed to strip Apnodens of his college and any future office. I sensed my friend's relief. He would miss teaching, but he would not miss the burden of responsibility. I think Regalis knew this; I think he knew his son well and was not punishing him so much as setting him free.

'As the gods will it,' Apnodens said simply, his head bowed.

I envied him. With the role of king now put upon me, my soul was weighed down as if by lead.

42

MIDSUMMER

Regalis needed to consult the spirits. The dreaming cup was prepared and passed around but I refused it; while he, his council and his son, sipped from the cup and passed into Annwn, I went for a walk. There was a stream running by the grove and there I found a man watching for trout. He had no rod or spear: all he wanted was to catch sight of one. Kingfishers darted past, but he was not interested in iridescent birds.

'What do you look for?' I asked.

'The unseeable,' he said in Greek. He was black of hair and dark of face, from Cyprus perhaps, or the Levant. 'The unknowable: the still trout in the shadows, who is watching me.' I joined him and as I looked for trout I entered a very deep sense of peace. He said his name was Aristobulos.

'What brings you here, so far north?' I asked.

'I was sent.'

'By whom?'

'Look, there! Did you see it?'

I'd seen nothing, but Aristobulos said his trout had just moved from one shadow to the next.

'For what purpose did you come?'

'Is it true,' he asked, 'that the druids have a rite of rebirth, when a young man is taken by the feet and immersed upside down in a grain pit filled with water?'

'Yes, or a cauldron, or just a stream, but I think it has passed out of use. I've never heard of it being done. You should ask Archdruid Regalis.' I decided not to mention the rite of immersion in a cauldron of boar's blood.

'What does it signify?'

'It is symbolic of the birth from the womb but represents the birth of a soul. A newly-awakened soul.'

'Ah. Awakened to what?'

I did not know. Aristobulos took hold of my left hand and laid it on my breast. 'This is who you need to listen to and consult. No one else. You can trust neither Roman nor druid, friend nor foe. No one. Trust no one. Only yourself.' He tapped me on the chest. 'Do you want it? The soul's awakening? Come. I'll perform the rite for you. What do you say?'

This from the man who had just told me to trust no one.

He tapped me on the chest again. 'Listen! What do you say?'

I said nothing but, as in a dream, followed him as he waded into the middle of the stream where the water came up to his waist and the linen of his robe floated about him like a cloud.

'What do you say?' Aristobulos repeated, drawing me into the stream.

'I say yes.'

He placed his hands on my shoulders and pushed me under the water. 'You have made many offerings to water,' he said. 'Now become the offering.' I'd been here before. Nearly drowning for love of a girl budding into womanhood; nearly drowning because of her, by her hands. Now I had no fear but under the water let everything go, everything I loved, everything I held to be true, every precious thing. It all washed away in the current of the trout stream.

He pulled me up by the hair, slapped me to make me breathe, and I wailed. I opened my eyes not to a new world, but the old one, seen as if for the first time in all its stupendous beauty.

'You have a role to play, Togidubnos. Accept it. Son of a king, be a king. Son of a druid, be a druid, son of the master, know thyself.'

384

It was as if all across the ages to time immemorial, the highest thoughts of men, the most skilled arts, all spoke of one truth, across all time, all lands. As if so many ancestors, the builders of stone circles, of pyramids, of temples now lost in sands, the knowers of stars and readers of auguries, the oracles, were all party to the same truth that I had just been born into, the one spirit which Seneca called 'the Logos'.

'The gods are dying,' Aristobulos said. 'And the new is being born. Plough the ground for the new seed.'

Someone touched me on the shoulder. I opened my eyes to find I was sitting alone, cross-legged on the bank. It was almost evening and my clothes were dry. Had they ever been wet?

'Are you alright?' Apnodens asked.

'Shee,' I said. 'Who needs the dreaming cup?'

Back at the fire, music had begun that would last until the dawn of the summer solstice. Regalis looked at me and patted the place beside him. I sat down.

'Tomorrow,' he said, 'we shall be electing kings. The seats of the Atrebates, Dobunni and, perhaps, Catuvellauni, are empty and must be filled. There will be a long debate among the elders, different candidates offered and voted upon. I have a mind to nominate you as heir to Verica, and perhaps to Esius as well.'

I remembered my immersion into the stream and the words of Aristobulos, 'be a king'. 'I accept,' I said.

'I thought you would put up more of a struggle,' said Regalis.

'Stoic philosophers recommend public life as a duty to be borne. Can I be a king without the trappings?'

'A royal hermit? No. But you can have a hideaway — somewhere to go when the business of the day wears you out.'

I knew immediately where that place was, in the elm grove beyond Kyronion. But how could I live there alone, without Branwen?

'What can I do about my betrothed? I need to find her.'

'You are about to be betrothed to your people, your land. They must be your first consideration. If she is due to be returned to you, the god will do the work.'

Many druids had gathered at Vernemeton, coming from all four quarters, some crossing from Ireland and Gaul, for the great assembly in this year of trial, and the procession to Venonis was long and slow. The archdruids wore mural crowns like small walled cities on their heads, the rest, according to rank, horned helmets, bronze circlets, very tall conical hats, silver diadems. The leading priests had their heads shaved in tonsures running from ear to ear over the pate. Their ceremonial dress was woven in colours I'd never seen before, secrets of the dyer's art. Jangles hung from sceptres and crowns and standards. The procession going south along the Albios Way was a bright serpent of men and women that clinked and clattered with every step. They sang as they went, the universal hymn known to all nations. Not one of them carried any weapon, although some priests bore sacrificial knives.

Coming to Venonis, ascending the hill to the assembly within the palisades, the druids arranged themselves in four quarters: the quarter of the Judges, the quarter of the Time Keepers, the quarter of the Marriage Brokers and the quarter of the Healers. When everyone was gathered, assistants helped Archdruid Regalis put on the soft green robe and Crown of Assembly, a headdress of two lobes like giant leaves of mistletoe that made a white berry of his face. In attendance were the chief priests of the Four Quarters: from the north, the Bear priest, from the west, the Crow, from the east the Bull and from the south the antlered Stag. Together they addressed the Four Quarters, turning to each, bowing repeatedly and invoking the gods of the four winds.

The people gathered on the lower slopes were few and mostly the very old and the very young. Those of fighting age who were present, in the service of their pro-Roman chieftains, were subdued, perhaps ashamed not to have fought with Caratacos. Some nations, such as the Catuvellauni, were missing entirely, too engaged in self-defence to attend the midsummer meet. Others made partial representation. Our own Atrebatic camp on the south flank of the hill was particularly desultory with our great family of tribes represented only by some lesser clans. When I walked amongst them, they did not know what to make of me. They wanted a Verica, or a Biccos or, at the very least, a Katuaros.

The Durotriges, a nation of disparate peoples who had only their pride and their pottery in common, were on the south-west flank, next to the Belgae. They were grim, those Durotriges — they looked like Mandred with a hangover. Growling and surly, they bruised anyone in their way as they shouldered through crowds. It was odd that they all spoke the same dialect but couldn't form a lasting federation. When a man thinks he is right, then everyone else is wrong, no matter that every other man thinks he is right, too. And so they argued, shouting across their communal fires, sending their neighbours curses like poisoned spears and calling each other the greatest of all fools. But this year they, too, were thin on the ground and not partaking in the traditional fire-jumping contests or wild horse riding. Whether by instinct or intelligence, they knew their territory was a target for the Romans, including as it does the southern-most stretch of the Albios Way. And I knew it for a fact.

Sending Mandred off to watch chariot racing, I went into the Durotrigan enclave. It was a law of assembly that everyone walked and talked freely without fear. Nevertheless, I had Apnodens with me to lend me courage as I gave my name at the entrance. I was taken to Martoc, chief of the people of Mai Dun, the largest fort in the Durotrigan territory. Impregnable they said, with its labyrinthine ditches; never once overwhelmed by any enemy. For that reason the chief of Mai Dun was chief of the Durotrigan federation.

Martoc had lost an eye in a spear thrust that would have killed a lesser man and the good eye seemed never to blink. 'You have a nerve,' he said when I approached. 'I hope you're not going to waste your breath on words of peace. Ever since your return, you've left a trail of defeat and destruction. Togodumnos dead, Caratacos on the run, Esius dead. So much for non-resistance.'

'It wasn't me who killed them,' I said simply.

'Nevertheless, you travel in the dark times and bring bad luck. I would thank you to leave us. Where's that slave of yours? Mandred does he call himself? Malvynn mab Hedred he is to us, coward and outlaw.'

I tried not to blink at this knowledge, tried to retain an expression of equanimity as if the true name of my slave were no surprise to me. 'Your druids told Cynefin of Sulis that he has atoned for his misdeeds through his sufferings.'

Martoc harrumphed and stared at me with his one unblinking eye. 'He can go free so long as he never tries to return to his own people.'

I thought there was small chance that he would want to.

'So,' he said, brushing the subject aside, 'what are you going to try and persuade me to do?'

'I haven't come to persuade you to anything,' I said, 'but to advise.'

'And are you going to advise me to submit to the Romans?' Martoc laughed, and his warrior companions laughed with him. Clearly wasting my time, I rose to leave. As I did so, I noticed a familiar face in the Durotrigan council: Brocce of Peddre Dun. The tribes of Gifl river, which borders Belgae country, had made treaties with Verica in the past. Brocce in particular had proved himself a reliable friend and shared Verica's belief in an economy based on trading rather than raiding. As I left, I noticed him rise to follow me. Outside the enclave, I went with Apnodens to the nearest shrine where Brocce caught up with us. He greeted me cautiously, glancing around to see we were not being watched, and offered his commiserations on the death of my father. 'A difficult old bugger but a good man.'

Brocce, tall and stick thin, was sprightly for his advanced years. His thin hair he'd cut short, not so much in the Roman style as in the style of balding men. Britons with thin locks are as impressive as dogs with mange. With his hair cropped to his scalp, Brocce made it look like it was his decision to be bald, unlike those who, in a similar plight, wore wiry top-knots held in place by pins and always horribly subject to the wind.

'What is the advice Martoc wouldn't hear?' Brocce asked.

'You should not tarry here but hurry home. The Second Legion is heading south-west to subjugate Durotrigan territory. If you wish it, I can send a message to its legate to inform him that the Gifl people will not be offering any resistance. But you should get home as soon as you can.'

Brocce nodded but said, 'Martoc is right. The example of Esius makes us all think twice about what you say.'

'It was Caratacos who killed Esius, not the Romans.'

'The Romans did not protect him.'

'But what is your choice?'

Brocce shook his head sadly. 'I have no choice. I have listened to what you have said and will leave as soon as I can. To be honest, the Romans do not frighten me half as much as Martoc and the other warlords. Mai Dun, Hod and Spettis — the three fiercest tribes in the territory — they are on no one's side, neither that of Caratacos nor the Romans. All they want is authority over the entire region, and they'll use any trick to get it, threat, intimidation... Just to see them approaching your gates is to lose control of your bowels.' He told of them taking captives from his own people, suspending them by the hair from trees and giving them to boys on the threshold of manhood to practise slashing with their sharp, steel blades. 'Only the heads remained when they were done and were left to festoon the branches in honour of Camulos.'

I assured Brocce that if he submitted to the Romans they would clean up the territory for him. 'You'd live in peace under Roman rule.'

He nodded. 'I can only hope that proves true, for it runs against everything I was raised to believe about loyalty to one's own tribe, but things have gone badly wrong since the days of Caesar. Our trading has collapsed, and we live in fear and poverty.'

It was now clear to me why the Durotriges kept their duns fortified and were not abandoning the hills for the plains like everybody else. They were caught in the past like flies in honeydew and distracted by internecine battles. I encouraged Brocce to side with the Romans when the time came. 'I promise you, I'll get a message to Vespasian, but to be doubly sure, send a delegate yourself and mention my name. Don't worry about Mai Dun. I'll advise the generals that your tribe is friendly: all you'll have to do is to surrender at their approach.' I winced inwardly as I said this, remembering the fate of Esius.

'And what if the resistance wins and the Romans don't come?'

I laughed. 'Martoc will chop you up and feed you to the dogs,' I said, then put my hand on his shoulder and assured him that there was no chance of that happening. 'By the very laws of nature, it cannot happen that the Britons will win.'

'Mai Dun has never been taken.'

'Mai Dun has never been attacked by Roman engines of war.' I described for him the actions of crossbows and catapults and how British defences must crumble under such assault. Brocce nodded morosely. 'Submission does seem the wisest course. Will they enslave us?'

'They only enslave the vanquished. Those who willingly submit are adopted as friends of Rome. That is my promise to you.' And to prove it, I used the power vested in me by Claudius to make and sign a treaty between Peddre Dun and Rome.

'Have this read to the other tribes of Gifl river and invite them to add their signs. For my part, I shall make sure that the Romans are aware of their friends among the Durotriges.' I had forebodings, of course, after everything that had happened thus far, but I was more convinced than ever that they had no choice. If they stayed faithful to Mai Dun, they would be slaughtered.

All around the hill the camps were placed according to the position of their territories. Almost the whole of the north side was 'Brigantia' and Mandred had been there for a day of chariot racing, and not just spectating. He looked filthy, sweaty and somewhat deflated for leaving lively Brigantia behind. I crept up behind him while he was having a wash-down in a horse trough. 'Malvynn mab Hedred!'

He spun round, terrified. To maintain my anger I had to stifle a laugh at his expression. I told him sternly that I had learned his true name from Martoc of Mai Dun and that he was banished from Durotrigan lands for life.

He shrugged. 'What is it to me?'

I turned to Apnodens. 'What happens if I should ever go there? Would I have to leave him at the border?'

'As your slave, he may go wherever you go. The rule of banishment applies to freemen, not slaves.'

'Freemen, not slaves,' I repeated, poking Mandred hard in the upper arm. 'You will never be banished, not while you are my slave.'

He growled and rubbed his arm.

'What else have you withheld from me, Malvynn?'

'Nothing! Very well, I changed my name, but not only to disguise who I was. I changed my name because the day they put the manacles on, Malvynn mab Hedred died.'

'And you knew?' I asked Apnodens. 'You and Cynefin both knew?'

'There is the law of confidentiality.'

'A law of deceit,' I said bitterly. 'So,' I asked Mandred, 'what have you been doing in your day of leisure? Watching men drive round and round in chariots?'

'Only when I wasn't driving one myself,' he snapped. As a spectator, he had been so critical of the other drivers that the Brigantes put him in a race to see if he could do any better.

'And did you?'

'I won,' he said, with the wistfulness of a slave who, in the duration of a race, had tasted freedom. I shouldn't have teased him: I did intend to give him his freedom once everything had settled, but he deserved to suffer at least a little for not telling me his true name. So I let him think his servitude would be forever.

'Cartimandua was watching,' he said. 'She saw me win and wanted to know who I was.'

'And who is that?' I asked cruelly.

'The slave of Togidubnos, who else? She wants you to visit her,' he said. 'Tonight.'

I glanced over at Apnodens. 'Not tonight,' he said, wagging his finger.

'I do need to speak to her, to make sure of her allegiance. The Romans are certain of her, but I'm not. That husband of hers, Venutius… no lover of Rome. I need to speak to them both.'

'You do, but not at night. You know what she wants.'

I shuddered — I seemed to have lost my taste for powerful women — and agreed it would be better to go in the morning to 'Brigantia'. 'After the elections,' I said. 'I'll go then.'

The Meeting of Tribes began officially with the sacrifice of a white bull and feasting lasted until the waning moon was at its zenith. There were so many oblations of wine that even the gods were drunk by the morning, when the clear-headed druid

High Council met to decide various issues, one of which was the filling of three empty kingships.

Following the death of Togodumnos, his brothers Caratacos, Adminios and Arvirargos were considered for election as king of the Catuvellauni, and the council declared for Caratacos. Some proposed he be made High King; others said he'd be lucky to live long enough to be any kind of king at all. When it came to the election of a successor to Verica, my name was the only one put forward, although I did hear some whispering about Katuaros being a 'more obvious choice'. Everything within me longed to step back from this onerous office and be free of the shackles of responsibility, but I stood firm against my own desires.

'And then,' said Regalis, 'there is the kingship of the Dobunni. Esius left no heir apart from his daughter, who would now be queen of the tribe had she not been taken into slavery. Before he died, however, Esius had arranged her betrothal to Togidubnos of the Atrebates and I propose that the two tribes become one, under the kingship of this man here.'

Many of the Dobunni protested at this, and the old north-south divide of the territory that Esius had healed threatened to open up again. Following the murder of Esius and the abduction of his daughter, any promises that had been made, they said, were null and void.

'In the Dreaming two days ago,' said Regalis, 'I met and talked with two spirits. One was a new god...'

A great muttering went around the assembly. A new god?

'... The other was the spirit of a just king. He stands before us now, half Roman, half British, half king, half druid, half single, half married, a man who can heal our land by healing himself. A new order is upon us. We must let go of the old to be born anew.'

'What does that mean?' the Archdruid of the North snapped at him.

'It means we shall behave like Romans and think like Britons. Our administration will be Roman, our dreams and our knowings British. Our governors will be Roman, our free spirit British. But I speak of the southerners. I am advised that the frontier of the Empire will find its furthest reach here, at Venonis. What is north of here and west of the Albios Way will not be affected, not for now. It is my advice for anyone who feels it would be impossible to live under the Romans that you move west or north. I have spoken to the Caledonians, the Ordovices, the Brigantes and the Silures. They will welcome you and give you land to settle in, although it will be poor land, of course, much poorer than what you are used to. Druids yet to fulfil their courses of study are advised to go to the sacred isle of Mona, where new colleges will be established. But for those not directly affected by Roman occupation, I advise you to stay. King Togidubnos is charged with the task of making your lives at least tolerable, we hope much more than that. He is the bridge between Rome and Britain and will carry to the new governor our requests, our complaints, our grievances. It is very likely that, day to day, we shall experience nothing different except this: our laws. We shall be living under Roman law. That has as many benefits as drawbacks. It is for us to carve a new nation according to our needs and wants. May we live in peace with each other; for the health of all, may we live in peace. For this, my friends, is the last assembly. We shall never meet again here for a gathering of the tribes.'

A storm rose, that Venonis would be within the Empire, that there would be no more gatherings, that we would live under foreign rule and law. Then came a blast on several carnyxes and a piercing cry: *Cut down the mistletoe!* And up jumped a priest of the Parisi who took Regalis from behind and drew the sacrificial knife fast and sharp across his throat. 'We shall die free men!' hollered the priest, holding up his dripping knife. 'And not live as slaves! Next year at Venonis!'

'Next year at Venonis!' came a roar of approval from the crowd. I had not realised until that sickening moment how detested the Romans were, and anyone seen to support them. Peaceful submission? It was not to be borne. In that moment, in that election, everyone voted for the druid kings.

Once again I was on the run before I could think what to do, urged on from within, like a deer that runs hither and thither at the scent of the hunter. Following Mandred, I fled for the horse-lines and the chariot. Apnodens, who had been frozen by the murder of his father, had to race to catch us up. Mandred waited until he saw Apnodens coming before starting the chariot off. Everyone was too concerned about what had happened at the shadow pole at the centre of the nations to worry about a few ants running from a disturbed nest. Nevertheless, we sped off. Only when we were out of sight of the Hill of Assembly did we dare to slow. By the time night fell, we were at the place called Three Bridges in the happy lands of King Llyr. We dismounted to massage our aching limbs and took shelter in a wayside refuge.

'Where are we running to?' Apnodens asked when we stopped to draw breath.

'Kyronion,' I replied.

With the blood-lust aroused in the Britons, and the druid kings fully in power now that liberal Regalis was dead, it was too dangerous to travel the populous roads. 'We go directly south,' I said.

'Into the Badlands?'

'At least no one will follow us.'

'Except bad luck,' muttered Apnodens. We left the road and took a path into the broken hills where only goats make tracks. Two days we rode, two nights we slept under a waning crescent moon. As crows fly, the distance was short but on the ground it was long and arduous. Throughout our journey across that rough terrain, we had no news from any direction, did not know the whereabouts of friends or enemies, or of any events taking place. Few lived among these infertile bogs and barren hills and even fewer travelled here. The only human activity we encountered, apart from some desultory shepherding, was iron smelting in the hills and charcoal burning in the woods. Then, on the eve of new moon, we came to the equinox route running from Verlamio to Kyronion, and we came to it just north of the Sanctuary of the Wheel, and the first we saw of it, as we came over the last of the hills, was the long, gilded files, the glowing standards and glinting Eagle of the Second Legion.

V

AND THE LAND
FELL QUIET

43

VESPASIAN

Two cavalrymen were sent out to meet us and make sure we were not armed.

'Druids!' they called back to the legate, who had stopped the march just as our creaking chariot hove into view over the bumpy hills. 'Harmless druids!' They escorted us down to where Vespasian sat in his saddle, hands resting on his reins. He stared at what he took to be three bedraggled strangers until, suddenly, a light came into his creased-up eyes.

'Delfos from Delphi?' he asked. A smile played across his rubbery face, as if life could never surprise him. 'Delphidius! Here I am, stuck in the middle of a barbaric land, not knowing which way to go, and Delphidius turns up in a wicker basket on wheels looking like a druid. Who is this man with you?'

I introduced Apnodens as head of a bardic college and son of Archdruid Regalis, recently murdered.

'Murdered? The archdruid?'

'At the midsummer gathering Regalis was advocating peace with the Romans, but he had opponents who prefer war.'

'How many opponents?'

'Just a few,' I said hurriedly, not wishing to give him the impression that almost all druids were his enemy.

The Second Legion was headed west towards the Albios Way when the track suddenly swung north, in the way of British tracks, and Vespasian had halted the march and sent out scouts to check the trail.

Mandred sought permission to speak.

'Who is this?' Vespasian asked me.

'My slave, Mandred. You know him well enough.'

'I know him only as a limping, cretinous wretch.'

'Do you want to know about the direction or not?' asked Mandred who, since the loss of Draumur, had become angrily indifferent to his own welfare. The legate of the Second Legion nodded. 'Tell me,' he said.

'The track keeps to high ground to avoid wetlands, hence the sudden turn. Long and circuitous but it will get you there.'

'What happens if we go that way?' Vespasian asked, pointing in the direction of the Sanctuary of the Wheel. 'Wouldn't that be a shorter route west?'

'As the raven flies,' I said, 'but we have been that way before and it is treacherous. Thames river runs through, meeting Charwelle river in a tangled skein of streams and rivulets. Go that way and you will be up to your knees in mud for a week.'

'Even at this season?'

'Even now.'

'What is there?'

'Nothing but an ancient temple of standing stones, long since fallen, water-meadows and wild horses.'

'And geese,' said Mandred.

'No one goes that way,' said Apnodens. 'It's a no-man's-land between tribes and best left to wild nature.'

'Is that why the scouts I sent this morning haven't returned?'

Mandred and I glanced at each other, both imagining two Shee-distracted legionaries who would be lucky to see Rome again. 'Give them time,' I said. 'It's difficult to get anywhere in these parts.'

'But this track will eventually lead us to Kyronion?' Vespasian asked Mandred.

Mandred glanced at me; I nodded; he told Vespasian it would.

'Why there?' I asked, trying to keep my voice level.

'It's lost its king and has become a nest of resistance. I need to smoke the rebels out.' Rather than start the march again, Vespasian gave orders to set up an overnight camp and the engineers began measuring and marking out ground. Apnodens and I dined with him in his tent where he told us about the battles along the Thames between Verlamio and Calleva, how he had killed Togodumnos himself but narrowly missed Caratacos, who had escaped and fled.

In turn I told him of my meetings with Caratacos, how he was easy, affable and lethal. 'One moment he is speaking to you as a friend, the next he is taking off the head of your kinsman.' I told him about Esius, about how I had just been betrothed to his daughter when news had come of the horse massacre, which had caused the Dobunni king to regret any alliance with me. 'Why did you do it?' I asked Vespasian, not able to meet his eyes in case I betrayed my emotions.

'Expediency,' he replied. 'A necessity in conquest.'

'You said you'd never crucify a dog, but you're happy to hamstring a horse?'

'We asked you to convince the Britons of the wisdom of submission. If you failed, don't blame me.'

'So the fate of the horses was my fault?' I felt the blood surging up to my brain. My stoical part was breathing deeply. 'Esius certainly thought so,' Apnodens muttered.

'I'm sorry about your betrothed,' Vespasian said, reaching out to put his hand on my shoulder. Vespasian the lover, the married man who adored his wife and his mistress in equal measure, understood my loss. 'Where is she? Do you know where she has been taken?' he asked.

I shrugged. 'My foster brother, Katuaros, who is healing at Sulis, has undertaken to find her, but I think it is impossible. I've seen great herds of slaves being whipped south.'

'Herds indeed,' said Vespasian. 'Their value is plummeting. But a princess…'

'A ten-year-old druid bard and a virgin.'

'The best pupil I ever had,' said Apnodens.

'She has value,' Vespasian nodded vigorously. 'Wherever she is, she'll be treated well. We'll find her. I'll mention her in my dispatches.'

'Kyronion, the lawless place you're going to,' I said, 'is mine by contract. At the midsummer gathering I was elected king of the Dobunni and am on my way there to claim it.'

Vespasian laughed. 'You? Delphidius the king, with a druid and a slave as your Praetorian guard?' In his eyes it was a plan of ultimate stupidity. 'We must thank the gods for our having met, I who need your way-finder and you who need my army.'

Apnodens was not like me, was not vain enough to blame himself for all that had happened; yet he believed that his sin against authority was the cause of the evil repercussions that had led to his father's murder. He seemed to think that we were equally instrumental in the fate of Regalis, as if my sin, of aiding the Romans, was as bad as his in breaking his discipline. He had begun to speak darkly about 'the death of fathers' as if we two were patricides. Was that all we had in common? No, I could not believe that. He was my brother and my friend, my teacher and guide. We were so close, indeed, that I knew his intentions.

'Apnodens...' I whispered as he rose during the night, wrapping himself in his robes. 'Please...' But he went out of the tent without replying. I followed. 'At least,' I said, 'take the chariot and pair.' He nodded, touched my arm in silent gratitude and went to the horse lines, immobilising any guard he met with a click of his tongue.

When Vespasian asked of his whereabouts in the morning, I said that my druid friend preferred to walk alone, not with four thousand others all marching in time.

'Walk alone in a chariot?' Vespasian asked. Then, reflectively, not expecting an answer: 'How come the night watch did not see him go?'

The first centuries formed up; Vespasian nodded to the prefect; the trumpets sounded to resume the march. The legion left camp like a snail extending from its shell. Such was the length of the column that, twelve miles on, the next overnight camp was under construction before the end of the legion had left the last one. A snail or a caterpillar. Moving, bunching, stopping, moving. But inexorable in its intent. More like lava.

The track led over hills and dales, past farms where deep-thatches steamed in their wattle enclosures, where women hid and children ran out to stare at the clanking foreigners. Some of the bolder ones, warriors in the making, taunted the soldiers, but Romans, who can march through clouds of mosquitoes without so much as a twitch, took no notice of them.

'Did you ever solve the Oracle?' Vespasian asked as we rode.

'The Oracle is not a riddle to be unpicked. The words of the god dissolve slowly in the soul to be understood in a moment of insight.'

Vespasian nodded thoughtfully. 'So you haven't understood it?'

'I'm in the process,' I said, guardedly. This was not a topic for saddle-talk. What I had understood at Vernemeton was between me and the Otherworld.

'And you?' I asked. 'Any closer to ruling the world?'

He smiled. 'As you say, understanding dawns slowly. I still long to go home. I seem to be fated always to be apart from my beloved Caenis. Not to mention my wife and son. But ruling the world? I know this much: there is the desire to rule the world that is sheer vainglory; then there is the overpowering desire not to be ruled by others, especially when they are... ' He let the sentence trail off. 'Tell me about Kyronion,' he said to change the subject.

'The original settlement or dun was on a flinty plateau, good ground for training in weapons and chariot-riding. Now a new settlement is being established in the valley at the side of Churn river, which saves the people from hauling water uphill all the time.' I refrained from telling him about the king's house in the elm grove. 'And that's the story behind most of the abandoned duns. Not that the times have grown more peaceful, just that the people have grown more idle.'

'It's the way of things: decline. First we had heroes, then kings, then senators, now emperors. Everything falls into decay.' Vespasian laughed at his own joke and had no care for who might be listening, surrounded as he was by men who, both by training and natural affection, would be loyal to their commander in all circumstances.

'You say Kyronion is yours? I thought you spurned kingship,' he said.

'If I could ask Seneca about it, I'm sure he would say that humility is a good, but should not stand in the way of doing your duty. So I bend my head to what I've been elected to do, which is be king of the Atrebates and Dobunni.'

'Excellent!' said Vespasian. 'That makes my work so much easier.'

After a three-day march, we arrived at Kyronion at nightfall. Caratacos had left behind a force of Catuvellauni to occupy the oppidum and they had retreated up to the defended plateau, seeking the protection of the palisades in apparent ignorance of Rome's mechanical catapults. As soon as the assault began at dawn, the occupiers were trapped within the ramparts. With a masterful display of tactics, Vespasian had them running out like rats from a burning barn by midday. He left it to the auxiliaries to give chase and pick them off or capture them, he did not much care which.

At dusk I entered the upper enclosure with him. What the rebels had not destroyed, the Romans had. There was very little left standing. Looking about I felt a stab I was not expecting;

404

the kind of stab any Stoic would welcome as a test of his powers of self-control. A knife in the heart. Kyronion of the dawn chorus. Kyronion of the lost Branwen. I wheeled my horse away sharply, towards the woods. Good Stoics do not weep. At least, not in view of the Roman army. I dismounted and walked on through the woods to the secret grove of twelve elms. It was untouched. No one knew it was here. The deep-thatch stood as if peacefully slumbering on this summer afternoon amongst a buzz of insects, while the land below the escarpment simmered in a haze of heat. On my way back to the oppidum, I made the detour into the beech wood and found the mares' paddock equally unharmed and in the care of trusty grooms. I assured them that I only intended the best for them but that they should stay hidden until things were more settled.

Back at the oppidum, the people of Kyronion had formed into lines to give their names to the officer of the census, names, land-holdings, taxable value.

'You could at least give them time to recover,' I complained to Vespasian, taking a leather bottle of spring water Mandred had fetched for me.

'And time to work out how to deceive us? For they will deceive us, thinking we are the enemy. But look, what do you see over there?' Vespasian pointed his riding crop at a field kitchen that had been set up to feed everyone. 'Food, that's what it is. Thanks to your rebels, these people are starving, so we are feeding them.' He struck me lightly on the head with the crop. 'That's the difference,' he said, 'between civilization and barbarism.'

'Of course,' said Mandred, walking away with me to get some of that food, 'under a truly just system of government, the people are able to feed themselves.'

'Hush now,' I said. And, forgetting I was king of the place, I sat down to eat a bowl of barley pottage with men of the Second, thinking of ways to keep the mares protected — a legion was a lot to feed and whether it was horse or beef did not matter so long as the meat was fresh. Later I surreptitiously deputed two other trustworthy local horsemen to help look after the mares and begin the work of raising a new herd. I expected that, in time, I could take full possession here and run the place as I wanted, but during this period of Roman occupation it was best to be cautious. When Vespasian told me, however, that he planned to build a fort here, where the Albios Way crossed Churn river, I had no choice but to confide in him about the mares. He assured me he would keep the animals safe from the camp cooks. 'I have a debt to pay Epona,' he said, shouldering the blame for the mutilation of the horses at the Thames.

44

PEDDRE DUN

Having established the siting of the fort, which was the first to be built on the new frontier of the Empire, Vespasian left a unit behind to construct it while the rest of the legion continued south-west. The Albios Way, the path of spirits, the route of pilgrims, the track laid down by the ancestors of the ancestors, had its ruts filled in by a vanguard of engineers, its edges cambered, its kinks straightened out and — in due course — a drainage ditch dug the full length of it, a ditch that has given it its new name of 'Fosse'. That is the name of the frontier: 'the Ditch'. But I get ahead of myself. These were the first days, the exploratory fingering by the Empire of its new boundary. The last free Britons to use the Albios way were the Durotriges and Dobunni returning from the assembly. After that, it was a walkway for military patrols.

Frontiers are for soldiers, not fairies. We were — I was — watched by every tree we passed, as a traitor is watched in silence by the betrayed people. There had been no Shee in my perception since I had joined the legion. This was a different world now, of a different order, and what was going to do more damage to Britain than Roman swords were Roman felling axes, billhooks and slashers. I sat uncomfortably in my saddle, brushing away clouds of persistent flies.

As we approached the Hot Springs of Sulis, scouts were sent ahead. While we waited for their return, Vespasian had me tell him about the place. I kept it brief, said it was treacherous underfoot and had bad air. 'Thermae,' he said. 'Always the same.

The least propitious places are best for your health. Minerals in the water — that's what makes it taste so foul. It will be good to have a healing place on the frontier, but we'll need to smarten it up, build a bath house fit for officers...'

The returning scouts reported that the springs had been abandoned. They told Vespasian of a circular wooden temple and its hideous carvings, shrines to local gods, empty dwelling huts. 'Whoever was here has gone.'

'Do you know who they were and where they might go?' Vespasian asked me.

I shrugged. 'It was a druid medicine college. There was talk of them going west, beyond the new frontier.'

'You think this track is a magic line I can't step over? How far west?'

'Probably over the river and into Siluria.'

'Ah, well...' Vespasian said, dismissing the college from his thoughts. I glanced up surreptitiously at the surrounding hills. All the cave entrances had been covered by brash and you'd not know they were there, but that was surely where my friends were hiding. I imagined Apnodens arriving the day after he'd left the Roman camp, hurtling along the Albios Way without a pause, to warn Cynefin of what was approaching and help him get everyone to safety. All my protestations that the Romans intended the druids no harm had carried no weight with him.

Was Katuaros still here, too? Perhaps looking down on me from some rocky ledge? It had been a moon since we had parted — we were now in the month of Equos — was he still recovering or was he now fulfilling his promise to search for Branwen?

At the rear of the march was an ever-increasing number of slaves, their clothes reduced to filthy rags, their bowed heads roughly shaved, shuffling forwards under the lashes of the gang masters. I regularly rode beside this miserable crowd and had established several times over that Branwen wasn't among them, but it gave me something to do. And in searching for Branwen I met the newly captured — fighting men, women, children — and discovered that boys on the threshold of manhood were castrated; girls taken to serve the soldiers at night.

Vespasian had orders to survey the mines at Vebriacum in the Mendip hills and considered it something worth stepping over the line for. My father had mentioned them in one of the planning meetings, saying they were a good source of silver but hard to access while the Durotriges held the land. He had been looking, of course, to encourage the Romans to wipe his enemies out. Vespasian wanted to explore the territory, especially where the Severn opened into the sea, but he would have to subdue the Durotriges first and they promised to be formidable opponents. He contented himself with sending a well-protected team of surveyors to Vebriacum to assess the viability of the mines. Would it be enough to justify a war on the south-west?

I was used to seeing the eyes of men gleam at the mere thought of gold or silver, but what excited Vespasian was lead. Dull, grey, supple lead. It is the most malleable of metals, too malleable for making torcs or coins but perfect for cistern linings and miles of water pipes. Vespasian's time as magistrate in charge of street-cleaning had made an impression on his soul; I admired him as something of a stoic hero, that where other men dreamed of treasure, he had visions of systems of drainage. It was men like Vespasian who had made the city of Rome inhabitable, but historians find their heroes in others.

While the surveyors made their expedition, Vespasian moved the legion down to the edge of the Summerlands, where the view south becomes all water calibrated by reeds and rushes. Here the Second set up camp and waited for the surveyors who, a few days later, returned in an ebullient mood: they had been able to tell, just from lumps of ore lying about on the surface, that mining at Vebriacum was more than viable. Indeed, they had noted the presence of silver within the lead. Even practical Vespasian could see the economic benefit of the production of silver ingots. Had they met any opposition? No, none. It seemed the place was largely uninhabited apart from the ubiquitous farmsteads.

Vespasian sat in his tent making plans with his officers. He wanted to be free of those dragging slaves at the rear. They were of little value and would be best employed at the mines. So they were sent with a cohort to Vebriacum to establish a settlement for a population of close to two thousand. While they were building the settlement, the lives of the wretched slaves would be almost tolerable, but once the mines were opened, then they would be condemned to live out their days in narrow, foetid tunnels deep underground. Most would never see the sun again but would come out at night like moles only to return to the shafts and tunnels, the hammers and wedges, before the next dawn.

During the time spent arranging this, Vespasian had sent advance scouts south to check the terrain. When they came back it was with grim reports of endless water, bog, marsh, a few islands, sunken trackways, lake houses on stilts and, always looming in the distance, some fortified dun bristling with pointed stakes. 'Only a local will know the way across this land,' they said.

'This is home territory for my slave,' I said, and Mandred was brought into Vespasian's tent. He said that the Albios Way skirted the waters but it was still subject to flooding and was often little more than a single-file track. And after Lindinis? What then? He said there was a road south to the coast over chalk hills but that the best port was Bol harbour, further to the east. Vespasian sent a message to Plautius to arrange for the fleet to come and collect the legion at full moon. I was in awe of his certainty. He had appraised this great stretch of mere with its fortified lumps and bumps, determined his route, anticipated a series of victorious assaults, and asked to be collected in two weeks.

His confidence was shaken when, as the legion formed up, a small British horse arrived with a Roman soldier slumped over its back. It ambled up to the column as if it knew where it was going, or who it was looking for. A silvery horse that could look pink in some lights, blue in others. Amabel... I dismounted, reached out, stroked her between the ears as the wounded man was taken down. She was flesh; she was breathing; she was caked in the soldier's blood. I kissed her blaze and tapped her gently on the rump, sending her back whence she had come.

Once we had given water to the barely-conscious man, he told us that he was the only survivor. The rest of the cohort sent to build a mining township were all slain. 'Caradoc,' he whispered, 'Caradoc.'

'What does that mean?' Vespasian demanded.

'In the dialect of these parts,' I said, 'it is the name of Caratacos.'

The engineers and surveyors who had initially gone to Vebriacum had met no one. The Britons hiding in the hills had not wanted to draw attention to themselves by attacking small fry. They had waited for the cohort and that which, according to their spies, they knew would be coming with it: the slaves. My first thought was that they had captured them as booty but no... After a fierce and bloody battle fought the British way, without the Romans having either time or opportunity to form up, they killed the entire cohort bar this standard bearer, who they had left sufficiently alive to tell us that the slaves had been liberated.

'Liberated?' Vespasian looked baffled. 'Do you mean set free?'

'They took them across Severn river into Siluria.'

Vespasian struggled to contain his temper, but he was not the kind of commander who, in wrath, kills the messenger.

He had a wagon brought up the line for the wounded soldier, but the man did not survive the day. As for the horse...

'What happened to it?' Vespasian wondered.

'It was a wild horse,' I said, 'and wandered off back to its herd.'

'Even your horses are weird,' Vespasian grumbled. 'What kind of colour was that? Sometimes I wonder if those rumours at Gesoriacum, about Britain being a land of mists haunted by spirits, weren't true.'

I got back on Scipio, saying nothing.

Vespasian set aside his ambition to supply Rome with British lead. It could wait for the crucifixion of Caradoc. Meanwhile, the men of the Second Legion prepared to wade. Although it was summer and the land was comparatively dry, as the scouts had reported, there were long stretches where the Albios Way was but a causeway of pegs and planks, enough to carry locals, even a drove of cattle, but not over three thousand men each carrying a heavy weight of kit. We did not have the time to have road builders go in advance. We had to get our feet wet.

The first man to feel the long fish slithering between his legs screamed out, 'Snakes! Water snakes!'

'Eels,' I said.

'Supper!' said Mandred, smacking his lips.

Vespasian put my slave at the front of the column with the scouts for he alone could read the pegs in the water, as to whether they showed the routes of causeways or warned of rivers, and could lead us to the east of the Summerlands to find ground high enough to carry us to Lindinis and Brocce's home, Peddre Dun, which stood at the beginning of the Albios Way.

'Brocce is friendly to Rome,' I told Vespasian. 'As are other tribes around Gifl river. I've spoken to him and he's agreed to submit on your arrival.'

'And the rest?' Vespasian asked, scanning the defended hills that, from a distance, were pimples on the chin of the horizon.

'Presume them to be hostile,' I said. 'The Durotriges are not fond of Rome; nor are they over-fond of Britain; they don't even like each other. Indeed, that will be your main advantage, that they do not fight as one, even though they are all federated to Mai Dun, the greatest hill of them all. There will be no massed ranks to face, but a series of battles fought from individual, well-defended duns.'

Vespasian nodded with what appeared to be satisfaction. Although he saw the wisdom of a bloodless conquest, at the same time he wanted revenge for his losses at Vebriacum, and the soldier in him could not see the point in going to war if he was not to return home with some trophies. He had a mistress and a wife to impress, and even more a four-year-old son...

We waded for a day, past islands where people who lived in houses built on stilts travelled from place to place in coracles made of woven rushes, dredging the shallow waters with nets. The Summerlands are where this world and the Otherworld meet. To die in the Summerlands is propitious and kings have been known to come here in their last days, drawn like dying deer to a special place, to have their bodies cremated in burning boats. To see the sun set over the Summerlands, its redness spilling over the waters like radiant blood, is to know wonder. But the red we saw on the southern horizon was the molten crown of a dun ablaze.

'What is it?' Vespasian shielded his eyes against the sun high in the sky. 'Beacons?'

'It's a dun itself,' I said. I asked Mandred which one it was.

'Brocce's,' he said. 'Peddre Dun.'

Vespasian doubled the marching pace and soon we were approaching the hill. Finding the best vantage point on the slope, Vespasian ordered the scorpions and ballistas to be set up. With increasing desperation I tried to persuade him that Brocce and his people were friendly but his instincts were stronger than my pleas.

Mandred was staring up at the hill. 'I see no one on the palisades,' he said. 'Lift your nose. Do you not smell burned thatch and, worse, roasted meat?'

I sniffed but could smell nothing more than old fires.

'Open your ears,' said Mandred.

Suddenly I could hear a distant thrumming, a low moan, a groaning, a lifeless lamentation.

'What is it?' Vespasian asked, concern adding extra creases to his face.

Mandred said, 'It's the sound men make when they are too exhausted to scream. There's no need to set up your artillery.'

'Send scouts,' I told Vespasian, but he was in no mood to risk losing any more men.

'Then I'll go on my own,' I said. 'I owe it to Brocce.' Especially, I thought, if he had suffered from his allegiance to me and to Rome. Mandred, to whom the word 'alone' meant both of us, stepped forward with me.

'Are you serious?' Vespasian demanded. 'I could subdue this place by sunset, yet you would risk your life to save theirs?'

'It looks subdued already to me, and I owe it to Brocce.' And every other person I had failed since I'd arrived back in Britain.

Mandred and I moved forward up the hill. What seemed to be a lot of scree underfoot was sling-shot: the occupants had put up a good fight on their assailants. Mandred halted suddenly and pointed into the woods, where we saw the first of the heads hanging by the hair from the gnarled branches of old oaks. Martoc! At our approach, wild pigs, dogs, carrion crows, stopped their feasting and carried away what they could, leaving the ground littered with gnawed bones.

It was a long climb up the gradual ascent in the heat of the harvest sun. The wheat in the terraced fields was dry and rattled in the breeze. Cows needing to be milked lowed pitifully. Dogs running loose, caught between the feast and the approach of new masters, loped along with their heads down, as if we might not notice them. I was retching now at the smell from within the palisades and the black clouds of flies. The song of larks in the sky seemed obscene, a song of pure indifference. By the time we reached the yawning, broken gate, I was trembling in waves of fear. At the gate, impaled on a spike, was the cropped head of Brocce. His baleful stare bored into me and almost brought me to my knees, but I staggered on through the gate to be met by a tall wall made of the golden stone quarried from the hill; we could not see ahead but must go left or right, the classic defence against a frontal assault, only it clearly had not worked. We went to the left, stepped beyond the wall, saw together what we had to see.

I cannot speak of what we found within the torn and yawning gates, the smells of butchery and roasting meat. Brocce's people had been, were still being, hacked up or clubbed by men dressed in bearskins. By men who, under the influence of powerful spells, thought they were bears. In a blood frenzy. We turned and fled back to the ordered lines of the army on the slopes below, skidding over the scree of slingshot.

'Kill them!' I shouted to Vespasian as I skittered towards him. 'Kill everything that lives!' For amongst the victims there was no one there who could survive their mutilations.

Vespasian immediately gave the order and the Second Legion went into formation to march up the hill, shields up and swords drawn. The men in bearskins and their victims were too far gone in trance and death to defend themselves. The legion did their work of dispatch coldly and piled up the dead for quick burial.

I had just enough strength to return inside the dun with Vespasian. A few steps in, and coming to the first reeking pile of flesh, the seasoned legate threw up. Some of his men cried out like little boys; some busied themselves propitiating gods; most did their duty and began digging burial pits. The spade that each man carried to dig dykes or roads was put to use to create mass graves. This was not right, to bury them all together, killers and killed, in the jumbled heaps of body parts in which we found them, but I did not know how to say so.

'Who was it?' Vespasian asked me. 'Who did this?'

'Martoc of Mai Dun.'

'Briton on Briton? Why?'

'Durotriges on Durotriges. Martoc wanted the Gifl people to know what happens to those who collaborate with the enemy.'

'And we are the enemy?' His puzzlement was so genuine I almost laughed. 'What kind of country is this?' he asked. 'We've come here to save you from yourselves, it seems.'

Mandred suggested something to me that I passed on to Vespasian who immediately translated it into an order. Beacons were lit to call the Gifl tribes to come and help bury the dead with due dignity. An uncle arrived from Lindinis and sought permission to sing a curse into the land, asking the Mother to stop nurturing those responsible for the massacre and eradicate them with disease and famine.

'There is no need for that,' Vespasian said. 'The legion will do the work. We are on our way to take out Mai Dun.'

Nevertheless, the elder sang his curse and the Gifl people joined together to perform the due rites and ceremonies for the people of Brocce. As to the slaughtered assailants, their bodies went into the mass graves dug by the Romans. I myself looked after cremation of Brocce's head and the release of his spirit to the Land of the Ever Young. Verica, Esius, Brocce — was I the cause of the death of kings? It seemed I only had to touch them with my words of peace for them to fall like rotten fruit.

As we moved on south over the chalk hills, rumours began to circulate through the legion that the killing had been a mass sacrifice made by druids. Some things are too credible to weak minds and nothing I said made any difference. Nor could I stop the blasphemous, ignorant mumblings of those — mostly auxiliaries — who thought the gods were to blame. Two days later we were setting up the war machines again, this time on the flanks of the overpowering and apparently impregnable Mai

Dun. It rose out of a flat landscape, the long, green hill with shallow domed top, its slopes a labyrinth of ditches, death traps to any invading enemy. Although laced together by who knows what inner strength, every now and again Mandred whimpered as his memories reared up before him, of the terrible sacrifice, the hideous victim, the realisation of his own impurity. He rode behind me, using me to block out the view of what was before us.

It took longer than half a day, the destruction of Mai Dun, but we fought without engagement from a place beyond reach of their weapons. While the onager, a catapult made not of twigs, like ours, but oak beams, was set up, sling stones from the Britons whistled through the air to fall well short of us, I stood and wondered at my people, that we had never adopted the bow and arrow. I suppose, before the coming of the Romans, we had never needed them. Slinging was something we were raised to, something boys did for fun and sport before wielding stones as weapons. Slings, swords, knives, spears — who needed arrows? I imagined the young warriors of Mai Dun turning and turning the slings through the air, once, twice, thrice, before releasing, but the impotent pebbles fell on the hillside and harmlessly rolled to a halt at our feet. They must have known, then, the taste of defeat.

After the onager was set up, two men turned a windlass to create torques of rope, twisting and twisting beyond what you'd think a rope or a man's biceps could stand. Once the beast was quivering with tension, Vespasian invited Mandred to load its cup with a heavy stone. The boy in him longed to do it, to release the lever and hurl destruction at the wooden palisades above. The man in him declined, saying, 'I'd enjoy it too much.' He turned to me with a wry grin.

'The last time you shirked a task on moral grounds,' I reminded him, 'you ended up a crippled slave.'

'Whatever the past, whatever they have done, they are my own people,' he protested. I stared at him, wondering what

I would do in his place. Before I had come to a decision, however, he had turned, loaded the stone, pulled the lever and barked as the machine jumped. In silence we watched the rock climb on a high arc for half a mile into the sky before crashing into Mai Dun. A thunderous great strike from Taranis that stopped the pattering of pebbles. The soldiers standing round cheered and congratulated Mandred. In that moment, I plunged into a well of doubt. These people of Mai Dun had destroyed the people of Peddre Dun. They had no virtue. But I was sickened by the inequality of the Roman response. It had no honour. I walked away and Mandred, his vengeance satiated with one shot, followed. We spent the rest of the afternoon watching the fall of Mai Dun from a distance, the palisades destroyed by flying rocks, bolts and fireballs. The place was ablaze by sunset and the people running out were caught and taken to the slave pens. When Vespasian entered Mai Dun, he found that Martoc, the chief, and several others had killed themselves rather than be taken.

After that, the Second Legion scythed through the Durotrigan territory, taking out one dun after another. Twenty, some reckoned, in fourteen days. To be honest, the further we proceeded, the more the duns capitulated at our approach, for we sent ahead word that we would spare any who submitted without a fight. Only Spettis and Hod required serious assault. By the time of the full moon, the land of the Durotriges was under Roman rule, their warriors were being sent to the mines and their farmers put to building a large oppidum on flat ground next to the river.

I hated the Durotriges. I had grown up hating them. They were the bogeymen of grandmother's tales. I'd even had trouble being civil to Mandred in our first days together, such was my prejudice. So why, as Mai Dun was emptied, its ditches filled in, and all the duns of the territory pulled like teeth, did I feel a plunging sense of loss?

We met the fleet at Bol harbour and from there Vespasian

418

and his legion made the short journey across the Solent to the Isle of Vectis to drain it of any Durotrigan remnants. Once Atrebatic, Vectis had been Durotrigan throughout my lifetime. I should have been at least relieved. Instead I felt empty. A small boat carried me along the coast to the creeks of Noviomagos, attended by squawking seagulls.

It was nearly five moons since my return from Rome. I felt I had aged ten years. I looked about to see if what I had promised my people had been true, that they would be better off if they surrendered. Men were out at the farms, cutting the first corn. Women were winnowing the grain. Children helped their parents and played at the same time, running about trying to catch squealing piglets or riding on the backs of horned sheep. Young girls sat by flocks of geese, dreaming the hours away. The oppidum looked cleaner, tidier, the two main streets cleared of mud and chickens. I walked the ceremonial route to the south-west quarter, puzzled by the bemused looks of 'my' people, only to discover at the end of my walk that the oppidum was under the control of a new king who was not me.

45

LUGHNASA

There are two gods of the harvest, the Dark One, a god of the underworld who nurtures the seeds, makes them germinate and thrust upwards, and the Light One, god of the upper world who ripens the corn turning green into yellow. The day I arrived back at Noviomagos, it was the festival of Lughnasa. All the children were up in the hills gathering whortleberries for the god of light, the god of prosperity, the god of overflowing grain pits and barns. Everyone prefers Lugh to Crum Dov, forgetting you need both to get a good crop. Crum Dov and Lugh: Proserpina and Demeter in another land and another story. Whoever the god responsible, the harvest seemed to have been a good one despite all the difficulties of the year.

I walked into the oppidum, just a man and his slave, unchallenged and unrecognized. My hair had grown and, having only stayed here a fortnight when I'd arrived home in the spring, I was not that familiar to the locals; besides, they were not looking out for a king; they already had a king, the man who had protected them during Verica's absence. A natural king who had grown from the soil like the corn.

I went to the king's house, newly-built and twice the size of the previous one, to present myself to him. The interior was honeyed by the light spilling in through the open door. The withered head of Kommios in its niche, the king's regalia glinting on its post, the swirling decorations of the limed walls, the sacred symbols, triskeles, cusps, eight-spoked wheels... Katuaros on the king's chair.

I was angry. He had usurped me. He had not fulfilled his promise to search for Branwen. Yet I longed for him to look up and see me in the queue of clients and petitioners, his eyes to widen, the generous smile... His hair had been shorn to the scalp revealing something of the turtle in the length of his neck, but his eyes, when he did look up: all hound, all horse.

'Delfos?' he yelped, coming from the royal chair, pushing those waiting out of the way and flattering me, as ever, with his one-pointed attention. The bear-hug, I noted, was weaker now and no longer posed a threat of suffocation.

'I thought you were dead! At Venonis!' He was, of course, excusing himself.

'Well, I'm alive.' I tried to remain impervious to his charm but he dipped his head into mine, touching my brow with his, and my anger was doused, as always.

He had come to us at Calleva when we were five, brought by Biccos and formally presented to Verica as his foster son. How my father's eyes had glowed at the sight of him, as if here was the son he had always longed for. Verica lost no opportunity in making loud comparisons between us, and by rights I should have hated Katuaros, even tried to kill him, but there was this slender lad with eyes as bright as stars, saying goodbye to his own father and his life without a blink of regret, a lad who was brave to the core. A lad who could get his way with anyone, especially me. The first thing he had said to me? 'I wish I were clever like you.' Second thing? 'Let's go hunting.'

My own brothers, older by ten and twelve years, used to kick me out of the way as if I were an annoying dog. I wanted to be with them, to walk with their strides, reek with that same ballsy smell, have muscles as hard as rocks, but they just said, 'Leave us alone, you buzz fly.' And then came Katuaros, the brother I'd always wanted, who drew me out of the women's house into the life of men, who stood by me, who protected me. Like a cob swan, he pecked, pulled and beat me until I dared to fly.

'Where are my boots?' I demanded.

Telling everyone waiting to see him to come back later, Katuaros had my boots brought from a cupboard where they had been put amongst the family relics. He knelt as if to put them on my feet himself.

'I don't want this,' I said. 'You have the chair.'

Katuaros declined and said it would be best if neither of us sat in it until there had been a formal election. 'That would not be wise,' I said, omitting to mention that an election had already taken place at Venonis. 'The Romans will just take over if they meet indecision on our part.'

'They'll do that anyway, surely?'

'They will build on old foundations if they are good ones.'

His shoulder had been set by Cynefin at Sulis, who had diagnosed a fractured collarbone, but it was still in the process of healing.

'I'm not supposed to do much,' he said, downcast. 'One good reason for being king...'

'So you've made no attempt to find Branwen.' It wasn't a question.

'But I have! I've made countless enquiries which revealed nothing. I could say that you are not to worry, we shall find her, but the spirit of the summer harvest prompts me to be truthful. It is hopeless, Delfos. She's gone. We have slaves being driven through here like cattle at Beltane. It's the same at all ports. I've asked every trader I've met about her but it's like looking for a leaf on a river and you don't even know which river. She's gone.' He stopped short of saying there were other fish in the sea; which is just as well, for I would not have been proud of myself for punching a man whose fighting days were over. But I could glower.

'What is it?' he asked, alarmed by my expression.

'I don't like your hair cut.'

He snorted with laughter. 'You think I've turned Roman? Cynefin made me do it as a sacrifice. He said my vanity is the cause of all I suffer. I had to do it myself with a pair of shears then burn my hair on an altar to Sulis.' His face fell at the memory of such profound loss but then he grinned suddenly. 'It will grow back, of course.'

'And be even more luxuriant than before, I expect,' I said.

Distracted by the need to hide his students in the caves and close up the sanctuary, Cynefin had only been able to give Katuaros half of his attention and less of his time. Katuaros had been left wincing at any effort that required him to lift his right arm.

'Come,' he said, 'let's go hunting.'

I raised an eyebrow.

'For whortleberries.'

He took me up Lughnasa hill to show me the places where the sprawling bushes were most abundant. We picked and ate the fat, juicy berries as we went along, the memory of being sick as boys restraining our greed. Higher up a man dressed as crooked Crum Dov, who had blackened his face with berry juice, stalked along the sheep trails calling for little ones by name. They squealed in terror and ran in and out of the gorse bushes trying to hide. We heard them whispering and giggling as we passed. Turning the brow of the hill, we met Crum Dov stomping over the heath towards us and there it was, the fluttering in the stomach even while my head told me it was just an uncle dressed up. You could believe two things at once, your head saying there was nothing to fear, it was only a game, while every muscle in your body tensed for flight. Suddenly a small boy burst cover, ran to me and clung to my legs. It was the little mussel hunter.

'What do you want, Crum Dov?' I asked the approaching god on his behalf.

'His whortleberries.'

'He picked them for Lugh.'

'I want them, or I shall eat him.'

The juddering child began to sob. I reached down and took

his basket of berries and emptied some of them into the pannier on the crooked back. 'Half,' I said to Crum Dov. 'We give you back half.'

The god of the underworld took his share and went off in search of more.

Half to the ground. That is what we do with seed. Give half to the ground and eat the rest. I stood on the hill looking out over the land, determined that, somehow, we retain our festivals. I would speak to Plautius about it. As governor for five years he would set the foundation for all that was to follow. I would convince him that the people would be more compliant if they didn't have their traditions ripped from them. As Crum Dov began to pick his way back to Noviomagos, the children came out from their hiding places and ran after him to mob him like crows, pulling off his rags and disguises until the familiar iron-forger was revealed. They jeered at him, they jeered at themselves and, as the sun began to set, they took their berry harvest home, most of them as black around the mouth as Crum Dov himself.

I remembered the fear, and I remembered not being scared anymore, not after my foster brother arrived. Together we had never been caught by Crum Dov. We had run the hills, possessing them, dreaming of growing up to be warriors single-handedly protecting our tribe, driving away the Durotriges from the west, the Catuvellauni from over the Thames. Romans never came into it.

Katuraros suddenly peered at me. 'Are those tears on your face?'

'Wind in my eyes,' I said.

From the hill we could look down on the oppidum all the way to the creeks and the Solent beyond. We could even see the Isle of Vectis where Vespasian and the Second Legion were 'mopping up' the Durotriges. By the will of Katuaros, Novio-magos was being restored to its circular shape crossed by two roads meeting in the centre at right angles. 'Its ancient shape,' he said, 'but lost to mud and land grabbing over the years. The four quarters are back in place, although our tribune friend at the harbour calls them "quadrants". I'd have done more but I've been concentrating on securing the road to Calleva. I'm trying to encourage the refugees to return there.'

'You and the Roman army.'

'Me and a small unit.'

'I have no doubt but that you should be king here.'

'Do you think I haven't heard about the election at Venonis? I am simply holding your place until you are ready to take up your rightful position.'

The harbour was in charge of a military tribune who was organising the building of more granaries and, with surveyors, marking out the road that would carry the Second Legion to Lugh's Dun on Thames river, a small cluster of fishing steads at the furthest tidal reach where the Fourteenth Gemina were building a bridge. The road that began at my coast would cross the Thames at Lugh's Dun and run to Camulodunon, the intended capital of Britain.

I was as disappointed as Katuaros that Noviomagos had not been selected as capital. He had been surveying the mustering ground with a view to laying the foundations of the governor's palace. I had never been to Camulodunon but imagined that the old Trinovantian capital looked much like Noviomagos and was about to be transformed as so many places in Gaul had been transformed: a palace for the governor, paved streets, regimented lines of houses, temples. I found I was relieved. 'Well,' I said, 'it may hurt our pride to be considered the doorstep and not the heart of Britain, but it will mean a quieter life.'

On the mustering ground, I scratched a map in the dust. 'Where are my boundaries now? The Romans will return to me what was originally Atrebatic land and keep the Catuvellauni lands within their original bounds, allowing the Trinovantes to get their lands back. So, we shall have the territory from the coast to the Thames.'

'When you say "we" you mean the Atrebates?' Katuaros asked. 'If everything is being put back as it should be, can I make a claim for the Belgae? Think of us as a buffer between you and the Durotriges.'

'No longer a requirement. The Durotriges are finished. I'll keep the Regni lands,' I said, extending my area across the south to meet the border of the Cantii. 'And of course, I have the Dobunni lands.'

Katuaros stared crossly at my map. 'So, aside from the Cantii in the east, and the Dumnonii in the far west, you have it all apart from my little enclave.'

'I think it would be best if I had all of it,' I said.

'Who do you think you are?' he spluttered. 'Caratacos?'

'It is a very large area,' I agreed, bending to write with a stick TOG.REX in the middle of my dust map. I could hear him breathing rapidly. Before he exploded, I wrote CAT.REX below.

'What's your meaning?' he demanded.

'That we share the kingdom.'

'Share? Two kings?'

'One who stays and one who moves.'

46

CALLEVA ATREBATUM

The road from Noviomagos to Calleva had been, as Katuaros claimed, made safe. Engineers were out, marking a straighter line between the two capitals of the Atrebates and building bridges where once there had been fords. One could sense the future and its busy prosperity like the smell of a storm in the air. I had suggested we take a chariot but Katuaros chose to go on horseback to regain his riding strength. As for the fianna, we disbanded it, giving the men the choice of a farm or joining the Second Legion when it passed through. They all opted for a farm.

Whatever qualms I had about the Romans taking over, it felt good to approach my native oppidum in the woods by a safe road, but we found the settlement largely abandoned. The Catuvellauni, who had enslaved most of the original inhabitants, had now been enslaved themselves and sent off either to the ports or the mines. Refugees were beginning to return from Noviomagos to claim their houses and pockets of land but thus far not many. The shops along the main streets were open, however, to serve their new customers, the legionaries. Calleva seemed to be a site of military occupation but I was assured by the tribune in charge that they were merely rebuilding the defences and putting the streets straight again for me. This, I was told, was Calleva Atrebatum, the *civitas* of my tribe and potentially an administrative hub for southern Britain.

'Do I not get a say in these arrangements?' I demanded.

Plans were hurriedly produced and there was nothing that I could object to: a defensive wall made of stone rather than earth, a forum in the centre, several temples, public baths. I looked at this last with deep satisfaction: my own oppidum with public baths. A sigh escaped me.

'We're following the original plan for the streets,' the tribune said.

'Yes, my father laid it out.' I remembered Verica pacing about muttering, 'North, south, east, west, how the Romans like it best.' There was nothing to object to. The long timber hall of the king remained and was being used as temporary accommodation for visiting officials such as ourselves. Close by was the women's house. Katuaros lifted the door hangings to look in and jumped as rats scuttered past him.

'This is where I first met you,' he said, 'do you remember? Sitting with your mother at her weaving loom, helping her untangle the warps. You looked up at me with eyes full of hope and expectation.'

'I did? Hope of what?'

'Escape. I could see it at once. You longed to escape your mother and the women's house.'

'That's ridiculous...'

'Longed to become a man. That was my task. That was why Verica adopted me, to give you a brother your own age. To make you ready for what was to come.'

'I was perfectly able to become a man without your help.'

'Perhaps, but not without my protection.'

It had been the best four years; four years of running the hills and swimming the lakes with the best of companions; four years of pitting my strength against his, always losing ever improving; of running races I could never win but which made my legs strong. Years of tattoos and drinking the hot blood of a boar I had slaughtered myself. I took hold of his arm, ran my hand up the ram-horned serpent over its puckered scar, up to the shoulder that did not sit so well. 'I am so sorry,' I said, mourning his loss of youth and vigour.

'Don't be. The king that moves and the king that stays still.

You were always the one who moved. When they took you away, when Verica handed you over to the Roman soldiers who had come to collect you, I came into this hut, laid my head in Innogen's lap and sobbed like a baby.'

'Why didn't you return to Ford of the Alders?'

'What, to keep company with my sisters? Those skinny witches? Return to the house of Biccos? I couldn't bear my father; he was always having to get the better of me. Preferred yours. Verica. Yes, here I was part of the Atrebates, and who wouldn't prefer that to being Belgae, whose glory is all in the past? And here at Calleva, just over there by the well in fact, I fought the mighty Caratacos. When Biccos was killed I shed no tears. It was the death of a stranger. I was angry, of course, but only because of honour affronted et cetera. It was Verica I loved.'

'As he loved you, the kind of son he had wanted me to be.'

I remembered the moment I was lifted up to share the horse of a man with bare brown legs and speech I did not understand; of straining to look back and not seeing either my mother or my foster brother, only my father standing broad and proud, swathed in his finest plaids, torc gleaming, the king who had surrendered his youngest son to Rome as a token of his loyalty.

At a tavern Katuaros bought a flagon of mead which we drank cold and, after the fourth cup, I broached the subject of marriage. Not mine, his. 'Have you chosen anyone? Who of all the women you have known would you wish to take as consort?'

Apparently these could be numbered in their hundreds, if you would believe him, but there was one who stood out, one who could headlock a warrior to snap his bones back into place and not quail when he screamed. Debonia of Cuma. 'But she is not of royal blood,' he said.

Given our future as vassal kings, I thought that was of no consequence.

'Yes,' he nodded over his mead, 'she I would choose to be the mother of my children. And you? Who will you marry?'

'The one who was given to me, Branwen.'

'She's lost, I tell you! Wake up. Be practical. Go choose another mare to raise your herd. That singing wisp of strangeness — she will never become a child-bearer.'

'And when you have your children, your sons, will you send them away to be guests of Rome, or to be fostered?'

'It's what happens. You have to drive off the children.'

'We're not swans or owls. We do not have to drive off the children. This is something we could do, you and I, an improvement we could make: in this great wave of change that's coming over us, we could drop at least one odious tradition. If anyone noticed we could blame the Romans. You hated your father because he gave you to Verica. I hated mine because he sent me to Rome. Mandred hated his because he gave him to the priests. Our fathers were only doing what they had to do, according to custom. Who's to say they did not grieve?'

'Verica certainly did.'

'And I would think Biccos did, too. Don't forget he risked his life to save yours at the Battle of Calleva.'

A little mead makes you jolly; too much makes you morose. Katuaros sat with his head in his hands, groaning in misery.

'Just don't do it to your own sons,' I said.

'I won't,' he said, muffled.

'There'll be no need, not with Rome in charge. And no need for brothers to kill each other in the British way of succession. It's all going to be so much better.'

'So much better...'

On the way back from the tavern to the royal hall we passed old Gofannon's forge and, to my astonishment, when I went in I found him there, old now, old beyond days, but still making artefacts in bronze. For some reason the other two did not follow me but stayed outside.

'Old man,' I said, 'how do you work here, unmolested?'

'Unmolested?' Gofannon asked, not looking up from the mould he was making with clay.

'Unmolested by Catuvellauni, by time, by the Romans. Apart from the military and the shopkeepers, the only ones left in Calleva are the beggars, the infirm, the human detritus no one can be bothered with. And you.'

'Delfos?'

When he looked up, I saw the cataracts in his eyes and knew him to be blind. He was doing his work by touch alone. But how was that possible with molten bronze at the casting stage? He must surely have an assistant.

'I am so changed,' I said. 'You can't possibly recognize me, not by voice.'

'Delfos?'

'Yes.'

'King Togidubnos?'

'Yes.'

He creaked down on his knees and began feeling around in a box. 'Here...' he said, holding out a bronze horse, the same as the one I had last seen sinking into water weeds in southern Gaul. 'I made you one when you were a boy. You helped me. Remember? I heard you'd lost it, so I made you another.'

'You weren't angry?' I asked, kneeling beside him.

'Why should I be angry? You think boys never lose things? They lose them all the time. Bronze trinkets, friends, kingdoms, loved ones. Some even leave their boots behind on chairs.' He took me by the face with his gnarled old hands, scarred and burned after a lifetime of metalworking. 'Find her, Delfos. She is with the commander of the Roman army. In his slave pens. You must hurry. Don't go across land. Go by river. Quicker and safer.'

'I will come back,' I said. 'Calleva is to be my capital.'

'I won't be here,' he said with a sigh. 'They only kept me alive for this.'

'Who?'

Did he whisper then, or was it a sigh, just an outward breath? But what I heard was *sheeee*.

I came out of the forge, blinking in the light of day, to rejoin Katuaros and Mandred. 'She's with Plautius!' I cried.

'Branwen?' Katuaros asked. 'How do you know?'

'Gofannon told me. He's still alive! Must be eighty-five years old.'

Mandred blinked. 'Delfos, the place is empty. Just a cold ruin.'

I spun round and found it was so. But I also found I was holding a bronze horse, warm in my hand.

'A Shee dream,' said Mandred, rolling his eyes. I expected Katuaros to flinch at the name but he did not.

'The Shee...' he said appreciatively, taking the bronze horse and turning it over in wonder.

'You are reconciled to them?'

'When I fell at Seven Springs, who was it who saved me? Who caught my head, put a pillow of air and moss between me and the hard rock, if not the Shee? I understand now that the ones who trip us up are also the ones who save us, and we need to thank them for both.' He grinned suddenly. 'And perhaps I have begun to understand that something Verica once told me was nonsense.'

There had been an occasion which I no longer remembered, probably a game of Black Raven, where I had stormed out of the house in a tantrum while Katuaros remained behind. Verica had told him a wild story, claiming that Katuaros was his true son, snatched at birth by the Shee who, in his place, had left me, a changeling child. It was only when Biccos had brought Katuaros to him as his foster son that Verica had become certain of what he had always suspected. 'I recognized you at once.'

Katuaros, still being a child when he was told this story, didn't think to ask how he came to grow up in the house of Biccos. He was too delighted with the discovery that, as he thought, he was not the son of his father.

Over the years he forgot the story and his fear of the Shee until that moment when he was about to jump off the boat at the Sanctuary. 'Then the memory came back in such a rush I lost my footing. My footing, my sword arm, my reason for living...'

We rode together to Kennet river, he to cross and make his way overland to Cuma's Hill to claim his bride, me to go downstream to meet the Thames and from there to go by boat to the camp of Plautius at Lugh's Dun, to find the girl to whom I was betrothed.

47

PLAUTIUS

The Catuvellauni territory that Thames river passes through was all but deserted. Some of the fields had been burned to stubble while others were being belatedly harvested by those labourers who remained. For people always remain, the true natives, born of and yoked to the soil. Their leaders change, their taxes get redirected, but still the land must be sown, tended, harvested, ploughed. Despite the chill spring, the harvest everywhere was a great one, the wheat and barley yellow and abundant. The grain would be scythed, threshed, winnowed and surrendered to the Roman army. The land of the Catuvellauni was under new rule.

As Mandred and I approached the jetties and wharves of Lugh's Dun, we saw soldiers of the Ninth constructing the bridge at the place where the sea tide reaches, while engineers were surveying the extent of the site, its rolling hills and many streams, to determine the place for a new oppidum. As we were being escorted to the main tent in the centre of the Roman barracks, I noticed, on a small hill close to the river, children wearing wild clothes and blackened faces being whipped down to the camp. The leather walls of the commander's tent were rolled up to allow air through and I found the adjutant at his desk sitting in a simple tunic, his armour hanging up on a tent pole. I asked to see Plautius and, with an air of weariness, the adjutant said I would have to wait four days. 'Name?' he asked, stylus poised over his tablet.

'Togidubnos, King of the Atrebates and Dobunni.'

434

'Purpose?' he asked, unimpressed.

What was my purpose? I had none other than to find Branwen. 'Have you had any slaves through here?' I asked lightly.

'Thousands. Hundreds of thousands. We have more slaves than a wood has ants. Is that your business? Slaving? How many do you have?'

'I have a few thousand Catuvellauni penned at Calleva I'd like to sell.'

'I warn you the price has plummeted.'

'I also have information about Caratacos.'

The adjutant twitched and decided my request for an appointment was more urgent than those of the usual petitioners, moaning and carping about their rights. 'I'll fit you in as soon as he's free,' he said, and offered me a seat.

'Where do you keep the slaves?' I asked, as if to pass the time.

'We auction them straight away to the traders, who ship them to Gaul. Some go overland to Rome, some take another ship at Massalia. The more valuable ones go that way. You're a trading man...'

'Usually more of a buyer than a seller.'

'But you understand about supply and demand. I sometimes wonder what our muscle-headed commanders understand. They just keep shipping. Soon you'll be able to buy a slave in Rome for a denarius. Might as well send them all down the mines. That's where the money is, in tin and lead, silver and gold. After all, with this glut of workers, we don't have to worry about looking after them. There will always be more.' He looked at me man to man, as if I would find this information to my advantage. Don't waste your money on slaves, he was telling me: invest in minerals.

His second-in-command disagreed. 'I've heard that more than half of them commit suicide on the way to Rome. Their value is holding up.'

I glanced around the slaves who were in attendance. Long serving, they spoke Roman well enough and yet there was not the flicker of an expression on their impassive faces. 'There's one particular—' I began.

'As for those plaids, those famous woollen mantles,' said the adjutant, 'I'm sending bales of them to Rome, bales and bales. A month ago one of those woolly blankets alone would have cost more than I earn in a year. Next week they'll be cheaper than slaves, if you don't mind bloodstains and holes, that is.'

'I'm looking for a woman—'

'Huh. Go on, surprise me. There's a tent in the north-east quadrant. Help yourself. Have fun.'

'— who is my betrothed.'

'Amongst the slaves? Oh. Well. These things happen. Mistakes are made. And now you want me to identify her I suppose?'

'Her name is Branwen, daughter of King Esius of the Dobunni.'

'We don't take names. Haven't got the time. So many of them plodding through the slave paddocks on their way to auction. They all look the same after a while. You're free to go and look if you like. The pens are in the south-west quadrant, or you could ask at the docks. Any distinguishing features?'

She climbs trees, talks to bats, has wrists I can circle with my thumb and forefinger. 'She sings,' I said.

He laughed. 'Not here she doesn't.'

'She's a female bard,' I persisted.

He looked blank.

'Is she a child?' asked the second-in-command. 'Yes. She was amongst the slaves we took at Verlamio. Sang in lamentation. Don't you remember?'

'Just one big hub-bub to me,' said the adjutant. 'All that miserable moaning, groaning, begging and pleading.'

'She made seasoned soldiers cry,' said the other. 'Plain girl but a voice like a robin in winter. A bard, they told me. British

436

princess and druidic bard. Imagine that on the titulus board round her neck in the slave market.'

'Yes, I remember now,' said the adjutant. 'The commander took her in, said she wasn't for sale.'

'So she's here?' I said, my heart pounding in my ears.

Neither knew. I must wait to ask Plautius myself.

There was shouting outside coming closer, scuffling, some children cursing bitterly in the Catuvellauni dialect. A representative example of them was pushed into the tent where they stood in their Lughnasa costumes, knees knocking but hearts defiant.

'What's going on?' Plautius asked, coming out from his partitioned section at the back of the administration tent.

'Found these vermin gathered on a hill; they were burying an effigy of you made of corn. Rebels! Sons of rebels!'

The eldest could only have been ten at most and leader of a gang of homeless, displaced orphans who were finding what order they could in their lives by keeping the calendar.

'Crucifixion?' the captain asked.

'Stop this!' I said before Plautius could reply. 'It's Lughnasa, the festival of the first corn, and it is very special to this place which is Lugh's own. Two gods contend over the harvest. Crum Dov, who has grown the corn, and Lugh, who wants it for the benefit of everyone. Crum Dov it is they were burying.'

'Why do they have sooty faces?'

'Whortleberries. Show us your mouths,' I said to the children in their dialect. We were treated to a display of blackened tongues and lips. 'They eat whortleberries and smear themselves with them and then they re-enact the battle of the corn gods.'

'Set them free,' said Plautius who, having looked at the list of appointments, beckoned me into his sanctum. 'King of the Atrebates and Dobunni, eh?' he asked with a wry smile. 'Are you well, Delphidius?' He ushered me to a seat. 'Who gave you these titles?'

'I was elected by the druid council at the midsummer assembly.'

Plautius looked tired and his eyes were bloodshot. He was as neat as ever but looked as if he did not sleep too well. The job of conquest all but done, he was not only consular legate but governor now. A governor, a provincial governor — I a king and he a provincial governor, so why did I feel so small, so insignificant, barbaric? Everything about him, even the greyness and smarting eyes, demanded fear and respect. After all, he had the power to crucify children... Not that he would. I'm not sure when it was, whether in Rome or only now, that I knew him to be a practising Stoic, perhaps even a fellow student of Lucius Seneca. Certainly by the end of that interview I had understood — mostly by his interest in the corn gods — that he was an initiate of the Mysteries of Eleusis.

Clearly my titles were only as durable as he chose them to be but for the moment he respected them and we discussed the government of my tribes, the level of taxation, what roads would pass through our territories and where. The Albios Way, now called the Fosse and frontier of the Roman Empire, was also my western boundary, at least from Sulis up to Kyronion. I told him I had been with Vespasian as he subdued the Durotriges. 'Perhaps he mentioned me in his dispatches?'

'Perhaps. I don't read them myself but leave it to the adjutant to tell me what is important. I certainly heard a lot about the defeat of barbarians.'

If Vespasian had, as I had asked, mentioned Branwen, it seemed not to have got to Plautius.

'Governor,' I said to him. 'One other thing. I heard that Branwen, daughter of Esius of the Dobunni, who was abducted by Caratacos, was taken in by you.'

He looked up under his brow. 'Yes,' he said, simply.

'Is she here?'

'What's it to you?'

438

'She's my betrothed. It is by that arrangement I am now king of the Dobunni, since her father was killed.'

'The Dobunnic levies who submitted to me at Calleva — that was your work?' Plautius asked.

'In negotiation with Esius, but he was murdered for it by Caratacos.'

'Ah...' he said. 'Well, she's not here any more. One of the more valuable ones. I had her sent as a gift direct to the imperial palace. The lady Messalina will enjoy entertaining her dinner guests with a British slave who can sing like a dying swan.'

Having Messalina and Branwen share the same sentence caused something to jar in my brain. If Messalina were to discover who Branwen was linked to, her interest in the girl would soon stray into cruelty.

'Got shipped off a few days ago. Yes. Go and ask the recording officer at the dock. He'll know.'

He peered at me, his unmoving face watching my trembling one. 'Delphidius,' he said, 'you are a student of the Stoics, yes? Well, this is an indifferent.' Something I should not let bother me. 'Only virtue matters.'

I wanted to howl. Somehow I contained it. 'Lucius Seneca,' I said as I rose to leave, affecting composure. 'Any news of him?'

'Still in exile last I heard, and shouting to come home. Apparently he's writing self-abasing letters fawning for favours. No one's perfect, eh?'

I'm not sure I'd consider it an imperfection if a man of fine intellect were to conclude that the simple life is unendurably boring.

Before I departed, I explained the arrangement for dual kingship I had made with Katuaros. Plautius was surprised and said it was not a decision for us to make: it had to be put before Claudius himself, who was at Gesoriacum and getting ready to sail to Britain across the strait.

I found the recording officer by the main jetty, surrounded by busy scribes making tallies of goods in and out, interviewing sea merchants, checking seals. He consulted his papyrus rolls from the week before, the time when I had been travelling slowly down the river from Calleva, and told me she had been loaded on to the slave ship Salacia bound for Ostia.

When we were alone, Mandred tried to calm me down, saying nothing would happen to her, she was too precious. No one was going to reduce her value by molesting her.

'But on arrival?' I asked. 'After the sale?' I felt as if the bowels had been taken out of me and, beyond pain, was uncaring of anything that might happen now, but not in a stoical way. It took elephants to rouse me from the stupor of hopelessness.

48

CLAUDIUS ARRIVES

The Ninth Hispana under Plautius had camped on the south side of the Thames while they cleared the Catuvellauni territory on the north. That had all been done now, a bridge built, a new camp started on the north bank, but symbolically this drama was to be played out with the great river as the divide between civilization and barbarism. While we waited for the Princeps to arrive — he had landed at the coast of the Cantii and was riding at the head of Twentieth Valeria — I had crossed over to see how, from a cluster of huts and boat-sheds, an oppidum was being built. Who would live here, given the clear-out of the Catuvellauni? It would be a Roman camp served by the native stock, presumably, those people who had been overcome by mine just a few generations ago, as the Romans were now overcoming us.

I often reflect on the differences between Romans and Gauls. In fact, there is much that is the same, but the difference centres on the question of individuality, or the lack of it. What the Gauls captured became the possession of various tribes; what the Romans captured became the possession of the Empire. These legionaries didn't impress themselves by heroic deeds but by threat, fear and overwhelming numbers. When an empire rules, individuals cannot bring it down, even by killing the emperor. The only thing that will destroy an empire is another empire; or plague, famine, earthquake, time and decay. It is never threatened by a squabble of resistance fighters. The Romans were here, the Romans would stay: we had to find a way of living under their rule; we had to find our freedom within.

Waiting for the Princeps were elephants that had been sent in advance. They are by nature placid creatures. You can imagine unleashing panthers on an enemy, but not elephants.

'You could say the same about horses,' Mandred said, stroking a grey trunk and giggling when the trunk stroked him back. They seemed to tower over us but were only a couple of feet higher than me at the shoulder; it was their strangeness that turned them into giants in our perception.

'They have a dramatic effect on the bowels of the enemy,' said their keeper. 'Have one of these charging towards you, especially if you've never seen one before, and you can't keep anything down or in.'

'How do you make them charge.'

'Goads, of course.'

It was all theatre. Claudius needed to be seen conquering barbarians in order to be awarded a triumph by the Senate; he wanted to do it in style — and comparative safety. Had elephants helped Hannibal in his war against Rome? Little if at all, but they made the exploit of the Carthaginians crossing the Alps legendary.

At Venonis, Fourteenth Gemina was holding the area with a line of forts and starting a road that would lead to Camulo-dunon. For now, to greet the emperor they had sent their legate and a cohort to Lugh's Dun. Similarly with the Second: Vespasian arrived having left most of his legion behind in the west, deployed in vexillation forts along the Fosse to secure and maintain the Empire's new frontier and extending it south to Isca. His reputation was wreathed in glory after the subjugation of the Durotriges. I met him among dignitaries milling in the vestibule of the imperial tent awaiting the arrival of Claudius. 'You can add the Isle of Vectis to your territories,' he said, 'O King of the Atrebates and Dobunni. I'll have a word with Plautius to see that it comes under your jurisdiction.'

The bridge across Thames river was completed in time for the arrival of the Princeps with his voluminous entourage consisting of most of the Senate, whom Claudius had not dared risk leaving at home to conspire against him in his absence. Having rested, he met and conferred with Plautius and the other legates in the camp on the south bank and, a day later, with a blare of war trumpets two full legions with the Princeps at their head crossed the bridge to wipe out barbarism.

The choice to use elephants was only partly theatrical. With his infirmities, Claudius found sitting on one as comfortable as sitting on a chair, once you'd got on to it. Elephants could walk through marshes without getting the Princeps muddy, and keep him high above the swords of the enemy, but their main virtue was instilling terror.

Two legions plus auxiliaries plus two cohorts — seventeen thousand men in all — marched into the eastern lands to meet no organised resistance. People fled from their settlements to hide in woods and forest. They were not Catuvellauni, who had either been destroyed in battle or had fled; they were Trinovantes, the people the Catuvellauni had dispossessed when they took Camulodunon as capital for Cymbelinus. In my opinion we should have been restoring the lands to them, not finishing off what the Catuvellauni had begun.

As soon as any group was large enough, they roared out of the trees to take on the Romans, making as pitiful a stand as I hope ever to see. I saw their faces, red and distorted with frustrated rage, as they hewed left and right before they and their chariots were crushed by solid ranks of soldiery. I saw children killed by their fathers rather than be yielded up as slaves. I saw women killing themselves. The Romans beat the woods as if to flush out game and Claudius made his way to Camulodunon in a blood lust of one minor battle after another.

Riding with the cavalry I did not engage in any fighting. I just watched and became increasingly distressed by what I was seeing. I realised this is how it could have been in the land of the Atrebates had Katuaros and I not steered our people on the course of least harm. The rage and the massacres were all in the east and the west. That southern Britain was in more or less peaceful transition was down to us. As if in response to this vanity, there was a flash of light, sun off a helmet perhaps, which jarred my brain, took me elsewhere. For one incandescent moment, I was back in Greece, in the Temple of Apollo at Delphi, gazing up at the Greek letters carved into marble: GNOTHI SEATON. Simultaneously, Fate hurled a British spear through the air to smash into my chest and send me flying backwards off my horse. I crashed to the ground and lay winded, thanking Apollo-Belenos for Roman armour. Mandred bent over me with concern.

'Just as I was just beginning to understand,' I said, struggling up on to my elbows. 'Where's my horse?'

'Not far. Gone off to crop grass with mine.' The skirmish had moved on and things were quiet around us. I tried sitting up and found everything to be well apart from the pain of bruising. Mandred helped me get the armour off. The spear had not punctured anything and there was no blood but I'd effectively been smacked in the chest by a high velocity metal punch. My cuirass was dented where it should bulge.

'What did you understand?' Mandred asked, picking up the offending spear.

'Know thyself. I have spent all this time wondering if I were British or Roman; passionate or rational; barbarian or civilized. I realise I am neither.' I felt curiously limp without the support of the armour.

Mandred stared at me. 'What do you mean?'

'In the *Phaedrus*, Plato speaks of a chariot drawn by two horses, one self-disciplined, the other governed only by its appetites. I am always wondering which horse I am, but now I see I am neither. That's the point of the allegory. I am the driver. We all have both horses to contend with; we are all drivers. Like the writhing dragons at the Sanctuary of the

Wheel, like Pythia and Apollo at Delphi, there is no good or bad, just contending dualities that are brought under control by a third. That is who I am. That is who you are. Druid or charioteer? Neither. Both. And Claudius — learned scholar or drunken gambler? Neither. Both.' I struggled to my feet, wincing with the effort.

'Do you want to keep this?' Mandred asked, wielding the spear.

'Why should I?'

'Draumur would have done, would have made an ornament of it.'

'Fetch the horses. Let's get on.' Mounting Scipio was a nightmare of pain and I could only go at a walk, catching up with the legion at the overnight camp they were building at a river ford. On the way we passed shrine after shrine being abused, wooden figures of spirits burning in scrub fires, soldiers pissing in sacred wells. At the camp, however, all was orderly.

Claudius invited me to join him for supper along with several other guests. Vespasian impressed the company with a record of his conquest of the south-west and of the Isle of Vectis, somewhat embellished (the falsification of history begins with those who were there). He said, in his opinion, Vectis should be given to the Atrebates. Plautius agreed, saying it made sense if the south was held by a British chieftain. I frowned. Since when had I become demoted to chieftain? Was every local man of any consequence to be reduced to a state prefect? I imagined that many royal hides would bristle at this.

'I hear you had varied success in your mission,' said Claudius to me. 'How do you feel about your native land, now that you've been reintroduced to it?'

'It needs bath houses,' I said, unable to think of anything more intelligent while I was distracted by the pain of lying on my side on a supper couch. Claudius looked at me askance and asked what difficulties I'd encountered; he was particularly interested in the druids, but, suspicious now of his interest,

I said as little as possible, only relating those things he would already have known. The supper lasted twice as long as I considered endurable. When eventually I was allowed to stagger to my bed, Mandred helped me undress and whistled appreciatively at the bruising: great spreading circles of saffron yellow and woad blue flecked with amethyst and orange. 'Now that's what I call a painted barbarian,' he said, and sent for the camp doctor, saying that the King of the Atrebates needed help. A man with bad acne arrived who, having established that no bones were broken, decided I was using my privilege to waste his time. 'I have twenty men waiting for me, one of them with half his face cut off,' he said, dismissing himself. I saw his point and let him go.

Unable to ride because of the pain in back and buttocks from the long fall from Scipio, I travelled in a wagon at the rear of the march, understanding now Katuaros's distress at his loss of vigour. I was feeling it myself and trying not to spit at Mandred when he said I wasn't being very stoical. Many of the wagons around us were heaped with spoils. After each minor skirmish I saw more beautifully wrought swords collected as treasure, more mighty shields of chased bronze piled into the wagons.

There are no straight lines in nature. Everything flows like rivers, clouds, waves on the sea, billowing in serpentine lines. Amongst the wagons were those carrying the machinery of war, catapults and ballistae made of beams of wood squarely jointed. Straight lines were making war on curves and winning.

Covering a vast stretch of open land on a plank track, fields and pasture to the left, wetland marsh to the right, we passed great pyres being built of chariots. Splintered wooden shields provided the kindling for chariot poles reaching up like the outstretched necks of swans, yokes of ash rising like wings, spoked-wheels turning on their axles in the heat, every surface of wood, leather or metal lovingly and masterfully carved in the circles and spirals, three-quarter moons and partial eclipses, which is how my people understand the cosmos, how they invoke the gods, inviting them to cross from their world to ours, how we make our world inhabitable by the divine. All those cusps and curls carved in an act of worship being devoured by Roman flame.

On the fourth day of the march we came within sight of the dun of Camulos —such as it is, more a wen on the face of the land, being a promontory that divides the estuary of Colne river. Within view of the earthworks and palisades of Camulo-dunon the Romans set up camp on dry land. I was summoned to Claudius 'immediately' thus, to cover the distance between the back of the line and the front quickly, I had to go by horse. Scipio was too tall, his saddle too hard. Amongst the camp baggage and the spoils was a small herd of British horses, a walking larder of fresh meat. I chose a small, gentle mare, put a double blanket on her back and, with the help of Mandred and a mounting block, got on. After the initial shock of pain, we got into our stride and her running gait carried me smoothly to the Princeps. If I was wearing no armour it was because of the sores that had formed where buckles had broken my flesh in the fall, so I arrived looking like… a Briton.

'Have you gone feral, boy?' Claudius asked.

'Just a hybrid.'

'What, like a mule?' Claudius laughed at his own joke and his attendant senators laughed with him. 'You're certainly riding one. Where's that beautiful stallion I gave you?'

'At the rear. Keeping safe.'

'See that?' he pointed to a grove of ash trees. 'It's in the way. We need to put the cavalry there. But when our men went to fell the trees, druids rushed out like hornets and drove them off.'

'How? With what weapons?'

'No weapons, just curses. Plautius can't get anyone to go near. They don't seem to speak the dialect of our local guides. Go and see if you can speak to them. Tell them that, if they don't leave of their own accord, we will set fire to their cover from a distance.'

I rode to the grove and called out a greeting in the Trinovantian dialect. The response came in my own, Atrebatic one. The master came forward to speak to me and I learned that this college, dedicated to healing, was part of the diaspora caused by Verica's banishment of the druids. I gave him the message from the Romans and received a haughty response, but even while he was spitting his curses, stiff with pride, clearly aware whose son I was, he was a doctor looking on a sick man.

'Save this grove,' he said, 'and I will save your life.'

'It's only bruising!'

'But it is deep — right to your soul.'

I returned to Claudius. 'Caesar, it's a healing college. Please spare their grove.'

'They are conniving conspirators dedicated to keeping Rome out of Britain. All groves are to be destroyed by my order.'

'Caesar, druids are famous for their rare gift in healing. People come from all over the world to study with them here in Britain. I haven't been able to get to the bottom of it, but either the first druids were disciples of the god Asclepius or, as some claim, the god Asclepius studied here.' I saw his eyes twinkle with interest: here we were again, in speculative discourse based on my research and study. 'Who does not need a doctor?' I went on and was about to point out how many he had consulted himself in his lifetime when I thought better of it. 'Every man yearns for good health. Let them live, Caesar.'

'They may certainly live, but in the capital of Britain we intend to build here, not skulking in the woods. Their trees will not be spared.'

'Caesar. That grove is not only the home of druids. The god Camulos himself resides there, I am certain of it. He threatens certain death for anyone who harms his trees.'

Claudius looked at me through narrowed eyes. 'Oh, really?'

'Try it,' I said. 'Send a fiery bolt in.'

Plautius ordered a scorpion to be set up and, once it was done, sent in one flaming bolt after another. Then came an unearthly screeching that had every Roman in the vicinity on the run. No flame took hold. Once the Romans had decided to let the grove be and set up the cavalry camp elsewhere, I slipped away, back to the druids. Their master, who had trained with Apnodens, looked pleased with himself. Flames had been put out with water; Romans sent fleeing with a *vocos* I hoped never to hear again. His name was Dravidos and, going down to my knees before him, the proper supplication of the wounded to the healer, I gave myself over to his care.

I was there five days, lying on a bed of hides and moss staring up at the canopy of eight ash trees. The doctor and his students made up poultices for bruises and sores while I wondered drowsily why trees do not touch each other. The canopy had rivulets of space between one tree's crown and the next through which the light shone. It was airy, it was watery, it was leafy; I was in and out of sleep. In the waking times, Dravidos came and said prayers over me to Belenos, calling on the god for help to remove the painful shadows from my soul.

'Son of Verica,' he said to me. 'I hear you have done what you can to atone for your father's crimes, that you performed a funerary rite so profound that the Others came to help. There is no need to carry your father any longer: set him down now.'

Was I still carrying Verica? If not, what then was the source of my oppression? Tears began to well out of the sides of my eyes.

'What is your pain?' Dravidos asked.

'I fear my actions, done for the good of my people, have brought about their destruction.'

The druid sat back on his heels and laughed. 'You? The cause of our destruction? What vanity is this? Does Fate know you are usurping her powers? Fear not, Togidubnos, you are as much a beneficiary of Fate's caprices as the rest of us. Just another mouse to her cat. You are not the cause; nor do you have the power to prevent.'

'But I can help?'

'In what way?'

As we talked, in the not-too-far distance was the roar of battle, the cries of men trying to defend what was theirs; the bellowings of those trying to take it. 'When this is over,' I said, 'take your college and slip away. Return to my territories where the druids will be safe, at least as long as I have any power at all. Mandred will tell you the best route. Where is he? Is he here?'

Dravidos nodded to where my slave was sitting, his back against a tree, trying to hammer the dents out of my cuirass. Scipio was standing in a small stream, looking pensive in the way of horses who have nothing to do, with him the little mare, whom I'd bought off the camp quartermaster to save from the butcher's knife. My slave and my horses were my only remaining possessions, yet I felt I had no right to possess any of them. Better to be bonded by friendship... I stared up at the trees, enjoying their dappled shade, listening to their whispers, and out of the smoke of memory came a couple of lines from Plato's *Timaeus*: 'In its centre he set a soul... and he set it to turn in a circle, a single solitary heaven... whose knowledge of and friendship with itself is enough.' The leaves trembled in the light. Friendship with yourself is enough...

War trumpets sounded the defeat of the enemy. Camulodunon was won, the last battle in the conquest of Britain. I closed my eyes and went to sleep.

49

THE DUN OF CAMULOS

In the centre of the oppidum was a temple dedicated to the ram-horned god, Camulos, and the shadow pole was engraved with his image. All deities speak to something within, are a colour on the palette that is the soul of Man, and for Camulos that colour is red. He is the rage of a warrior in battle, the crest on a centurion's helmet, the tunic of a Roman general, the blood of a dying boar. He is the stiff back of resistance, the fearlessness of a man, the sword arm, the sword. 'The invincible sword' is one of his names. Conferring at the temple we agreed this was the one the Romans call Mars. I glanced at Mandred, who raised his eyebrow as if to say, 'Believe that if you will.'

Claudius did not sleep well in the royal deep-thatch with its disturbingly barbarian house shrine and said the place was flea-ridden. He retreated to his tent which, from the inside, looked like a palace. I wandered the capital of the Catuvellauni, the place that had seemed the source of all evil, now just the defeated oppidum of proud Cymbelinus, father of Caratacos. His capital was being reduced to mud by Roman feet pacing the ground, hastily laying out a camp fit for an emperor. I was surprised by the riches in the houses. I had, of course, expected piles of spoils the Catuvellauni had taken from their conquered enemies, such as my own people, but these riches were the spoils of trade. They had pottery of many colours that I had never seen before, not even in Rome, and brightly-coloured beads and amber glassware from Italy. Their women had used the sacred mirrors for applying cosmetics and perfumes. And the men had been literate. No matter that the druids forbade reading and writing as being detrimental to the powers of memory, these people kept records as extensive as those of any civilized harbour master. Cymbelinus had been raising up a new breed of men, until his own sons rebelled. Rebelled and regressed.

There was a forlornness to the place that ran deep. The feel of the sea close by, that low, low horizon, the cry of curlews: it struck the gut with an insatiable hunger for something out of reach. It was a place of lost dreams and broken promises. I could not imagine being happy here, but for the strategically-minded Romans, who thought of us as an island beyond Ocean, it was perfect, and they began building at once what was intended to become the capital of the province of Britain. In two days the army built a house for the Princeps, a platform, a gilded throne, and had begun on the barracks, all centred on the temple of Camulos, now called Mars.

Messages had gone out to all the kings of Britain to submit formally to Rome at Camulodunon at the new moon. By the fourth night, the barracks had been constructed and the kings had begun to arrive. The first was bandy-legged Adminios, the brother of Caratacos who had inspired Caligula to mount his futile expedition. He was keen to regain the lands of the Cantii his brothers had taken. Cartimandua of the Brigantes followed, along with her husband Venutius of the Carvetii tribe. While Cartimandua went amongst the senators greeting many as old friends, Venutius kept apart with his fianna, drinking and boasting, and making it clear that in his opinion the Romans were dung beetles. Invited by the Princeps to dine with him and the British kings, Cartimandua caused an uproar when she arrived in the imperial tent wearing a toga. 'The proper costume of kings,' she said, brushing off all suggestions that she might change into something more becoming of a queen.

When Claudius had been softened by wine, Cartimandua asked him why, being a woman, she could be a queen but was not eligible for the Senate? While Claudius struggled to find an answer, one of the senators said loudly that the Senate 'will never be defiled by the presence of a woman.' Cartimandua turned her noble head to face him, to stare at him until his arrogance wilted, and then, in public, invited him to defile her bed with his presence that very night. 'For you need to know that power is not the prerogative of elderly men sitting in semi-circles,' she said.

The king of the Iceni, Antedios, bellowed with laughter and advised the senator to accept the offer and discover the truth of what she said. Claudius, however, suggested they might like to meet the following night since it was his right to be the first to be converted by Cartimandua to a British way of thinking. With Antedios was his son Prasutagos and daughter-in-law Boudicca, who was staring at Cartimandua with feline intensity. I heard later that, while Cartimandua was changing the minds of Roman autocrats, Boudicca was in the bed of Venutius. These things may seem strange now, but I remember it from my childhood, the openness of a British marriage, with both my father and mother readily sleeping with anyone except each other. It was the Romans who were shocked. Naturally they referred to it as 'a barbarian practice', omitting to say how much they enjoyed those hot nights while Claudius was in Britain.

In council with my fellow kings I forged an alliance with Cartimandua who expected me to seal the pact in her chosen way. I modestly declined. Someone advised her in a low voice that, as a Stoic, I was very well practiced in self-denial. She then gazed on me as if on a challenge. 'We'll enjoy putting that to the test,' she said. However, I found self-denial peculiarly easy when faced with a woman in a toga with hips like those of a heavily laden pack donkey. Of all my alliances, that with Cartimandua seemed the shakiest. I advised myself never to rely on it.

Apart from the Brigantes, these gathered kings represented only that portion of the British Isles the Romans now possessed, the fertile triangle we had drawn on the sand bed in Claudius's chambers, its western frontier the Fosse, its apex Venonis. Naturally the Durotriges and Dumnonii were not present, nor any tribes west of the Fosse, no one from Ewyas, Siluria, or Ordovicia; none from north of Brigantia, the Caledonians or Picts. 'Britain' was, for the Romans, that lush triangle. As for Brigantia — those wild mountains, moorlands and bear-infested forests —Cartimandua renewed their alliance with Rome but they remained beyond the frontier of the Empire.

Katuaros arrived, fresh from his marriage at Cuma, his wife by his side and a small entourage of Cuma warriors. Suddenly the intimidating midwife was my sister and I tried to embrace Debonia fondly but, although interested in all the pomp and ceremony surrounding the Princeps, she did not yield her position as being the intimidating one. A critical glance from Debonia had even Cartimandua blinking. 'That woman needs to lose weight,' Debonia said to her husband of the queen of the Brigantes. Katuaros grinned and said he'd be sure to tell her. He glanced at me with his bright eyes as if to say, 'See how well I've chosen!'

I formally requested of the Princeps that, for his services to the Empire in the pacification of the tribes, my foster brother be made a Roman citizen. At the same time I broached the idea that we share the kingdom of the Atrebates between us.

'And you think that would work?' Claudius asked.

'We are like true brothers.'

'It seems to me that in Britain "brother" is a euphemism for "deadly enemy", especially where land is concerned.'

I had to agree that this was so.

'And even if you do break that tradition with the strength of your kinship,' Claudius continued, 'could the people be happy under two kings? Would they not be forever playing one off against the other, or stating a preference that would antagonise you?'

That, too, was true, and made me wonder if my noble wishes were, in fact, hopeless idealism. Claudius leant forwards. Appreciating my desires, he wished to offer a third way. 'Divide the tribes,' he suggested, tapping the back of my hand.

Thus I was confirmed king of the Atrebates and Dobunni by the Romans, and Katuaros king of the Regni of southern Britain, a territory which also includes Ford of the Alders, the lands of the Belgae and the Isle of Vectis. Katuaros has his parcel and is content. As I write, he is busy with his house near the coast which has a foundation nearly twice the size of the Temple of Apollo at Delphi and is more like the imperial palace than a domestic villa. I could not tolerate living in such an extravagant house, where you would either have to shout if you needed to be heard across the courtyard or send a runner. I have chosen to live in the grove of twelve elms beyond Kyronion where I know everyone employed here by name.

When he gave Tiberius Claudius Catuarus his citizenship, the Princeps also gave him a gold signet ring like mine. I expected Katuaros to have it engraved, as mine is, with a sacred symbol. Instead he engraved it himself with his own name in his own letters. 'Magic!' he said, pressing it into warm wax for the first time. I almost envied him his open-hearted, open-faced delight at these things. There is nothing hidden or twisted in Katuaros. I allowed him to strut about in a toga for two days, referring to himself as Tiberius Claudius Catuarus, or Catuarus Rex, and designing coins with his image on one side, the triple-tailed horse on the other, before I sternly recommended the virtue of humility.

At Camulodunum — the spelling of its name already changed from the British version — there was a service of manumission for those slaves able to buy their freedom. I presented Mandred to the magistrates and stated that, though he could not afford his freedom, I would give it to him in gratitude for his loyalty. While I held Mandred by the shoulders, the lictor laid a rod on his head and made a few formal declarations. Then I turned Mandred round by the shoulders to face the world, saying, 'By my will, this man is free', and let him go.

Mandred stood still facing the world with the wonderment of a wild animal when the cage door is lifted. I nudged him. Without looking back, he walked off into the crowd, not even interested in collecting the few paltry possessions he had, or the little mare I had given him. I watched his disappearing back, not quite able to believe what I was seeing. Had he wanted his freedom so much all this time? Had his loyalty been a pretence? I looked about me, at those faces amongst the Romans that were familiar to me, but there was no one I could count on here as friend. Only Katuaros. He stood staring at me as if he, too, could not believe the manner of Mandred's departure.

'Well,' he said, 'perhaps we should go to the slave pens and find you somebody else.'

'Perhaps I, too, also want to be free,' I said, not without bitterness. 'Slaves can tie you down.'

After several days of state business, Claudius invited me to dine with him alone, to relax as we had been wont to do in the old days, discussing things of mutual interest, seeing how reality accorded with the written accounts we had studied together. But it was not like the old days. I remembered once when I'd caught him watching me with a look on his face of a vengeful demon: half-shut eyes, cruel line at his mouth, as if planning some act of retribution. He had us all fooled, limping about with his head hung low like a whipped dog but in that moment, I saw that other Claudius, the one who had spent his life biding his time. Now his time had come. Now the half-shut eyes and cruel mouth were official. He might want to relax with me, but I was on my guard.

'Is Britain what you expected?' I asked.

'I had no idea until I met your kings how diverse a people the Britons are. Like your gods you are only understood in your own localities. Gauls, Germans, Belgae — are there any indigenous people here?'

'Only the peasants. None among the warrior class. Even west of the frontier, where they claim to be an ancient people, their songs of origin speak of Iberia.'

'And they are...'

'Silurians, Ordovicans and Decangli, all of them proud, resourceful and ready to fight to the death. Leave them be. And leave the northerners, too.'

'The Brigantes?' A look came over his face at the memory of his night with Cartimandua. Had he been a cat, he would have purred and cleaned his whiskers.

'No, further, beyond the Brigantes.'

'What is there?'

'Wild belligerent people, the Caledonians and Picts. Like the Silurians and Ordovicans, best left alone.' I unrolled his largest map showing the triangle of conquest. 'Forget Brigantia. She will always be your ally but it would be a waste of time and r esources to possess her. Here is Roman Britain. Fertile, hilly but not mountainous, fed by many streams and rivers. Here, salt. Here, silver. Be content.' And leave my people, I thought, somewhere to escape to.

He asked me about the druids.

'Their power is broken and they are melting away beyond the frontier. There is nothing for you to worry about from the druids.'

For a moment Claudius stopped being the princeps. His face softened into its old self. 'I've missed you, Delfos, missed our discussions. Are you fully transplanted back into your home soil? No tempting you back to Rome?' Ever gullible when it came to Claudius, for a moment I thought he meant it.

'I would go tomorrow, Caesar, if I thought I could find my betrothed.' I told him about Branwen and how Plautius had sent her as a gift to Messalina.

Claudius listened, nodding and was thoughtful. 'Your place is here,' he announced at last. 'We need you here to keep the centre steady. Hold the centre —that's your job and only you can do it. I'll write to my wife and have the girl returned to you.'

I sat back with a sigh of relief. 'You are right. My duty lies here.'

'Spoken like a good Stoic.'

'Speaking of which...'

'Be politic, my friend, and do not ask.'

I asked, 'Is he still in exile?'

'He was never in exile. Do you really believe that story? *Ah, poor me, cast out to some barren island, just like Ovid.* He was relegated, and to Corsica. Corsica. Where half of Rome goes in the summer for a holiday.'

'Even so,' I said. 'He'll still be missing the Senate and the Forum.'

'Of course he will. He writes to me at least once a week begging forgiveness.'

'I don't know why he should do that. He was not guilty, and you know it. Seneca? Adultery?'

'You don't know him very well, do you?'

'Come on,' I said, rising anger making me forget myself. 'That charge was a joke.'

'My wife made it. Would you call her a liar?'

'Of course not, but she was affronted by some remark made by Julia about her hair.'

Claudius laughed without taking his eyes off me. 'Really? I never heard that version, but it could be why she picked on Julia. But it was Seneca she was after. He'd had the temerity to write her a letter on adultery. Adultery! My lovely, loyal Messalina! I can't imagine who she would find in preference to me. Can you, Delfos?'

I said I could not. It was impossible to imagine... And yet I now knew beyond doubt that Claudius was aware of my

458

infidelity. It was in his eyes, in the tone of his voice. 'You know Seneca,' I said. 'He's always writing on subjects that interest him as moral questions. I'm sure he didn't mean to imply anything by it. He's an innocent man,' I said, 'and doesn't deserve exile.'

'Relegation,' Claudius corrected me. 'Hypocrisy deserves no less. And so dear boy,' he said, reaching forward and pinching my cheek, 'on those grounds I'm relegating you to Britain. Indefinitely. To this wet and windy isle of painted head-hunters.'

50

THE CRYING LAND

I tossed and turned sleeplessly: should I stick to principle and shrink from office, or should I take part in public life for the greater good? I had taken on the kingship, and a much-debased kingship at that, when all I wanted to do was to walk barefoot among the trees with Apnodens. Deep in the night I went to the temple of Camulos for advice. God of war he might be, but what was this if not war with myself?

As my eyes adjusted to the dark, illuminated by a few small lamps on the altar, I was startled by the presence of a naked woman, naked but for her long and luxuriant hair which covered her like a cape. She had under one arm a large swan, its hissing head held down out of harm's way. The wife of Prasutagos, Boudicca, was performing a rite to the god of war. She had been ignoring my presence until, as she drew the knife, I snorted in disgust.

'Does it not trouble you,' she asked, letting the blood drain from the neck into a silver bowl lit by the flickering lamps, 'how everyone is kneeling before that jug-eared abomination who somehow survived a miscarriage? How has it come to this, that we, the proud Britons, are governed by an ill-formed monster?' She laid the swan down and, entering the trance, turned her questioning on the god. 'O Camulos, god of the warriors, answer me! If we were destined to fall like the Trojans, then why not to a mighty warrior such as Achilles? Not a gibbering, twitching buffoon on an elephant…'

She held a pair of shallow bronze spoons, one in each hand.

One with a hole in it she dipped into the bowl and scooped up some blood. She held it over the other spoon that was quartered by an engraved line. With her eyes closed she blew softly on the blood and then opened her eyes to see where it had fallen on the lower spoon. Most was in the south-east quarter.

'Sometimes things work backwards in this world,' she said, showing me the spoon, 'and we have the conquest before the battle.'

A little of the blood had spattered in the west.

'Caratacos...' she sighed, as if invoking him, and licked up the blood.

Suddenly she stared at me through her green, cat-like eyes. 'Collaborator!' She spat the blood straight into my face, the most powerful of curses. 'You have abandoned the daughter of Esius, you the indifferent man and she the Silver Maiden!' She fell deeply into trance, collapsing on the dirt floor and leaving me alone with the body of the swan drooping over the altar, its soft white feathers reddened with its blood. I left, my prayers unsaid.

The next morning Claudius called me to him again and, as if he had been eavesdropping on my own troubled heart and wished to burden me further, offered me Verlamio. 'Plautius will have charge of Camulodunum and Lugh's Dun but I thought, for old time's sake, not to mention revenge, you might like to hold the ancient capital of the Catuvellauni? Add it to your kingdoms? It's the least I can do for relegating you here. Vespasian tells me that the horse herd of Caratacus is there, largely the herd of your father I believe. A good place, then, to start a line of your own.'

'I have no wish to take on even more responsibility.'

'Well, your wishes don't come in to it, but would it help if I changed the relegation from "indefinite" to "five years"?'

Given that would allow me to return to Rome, I agreed.

Verlamio... It seems that every time I am tempted to renounce my possessions, they increase. Thus he who would

461

hold no office is now King of the Atrebates, Dobunni and what's left of the Catuvellauni.

I never saw Mandred about. He seemed to have dissolved into the oppidum that was being churned into mire by thousands of soldiers coming and going. There was no bath house as yet and I was directed to the local springs at the foot of a low hill. I was advised that I would need a slave to guard my clothes, but at the slave market I stared at the lines of helpless wretches and found I was unable to choose. Some stood with bowed heads, others stood proud with insolence in their eyes. Who would I rescue next like an abandoned dog? Who would I bring back to life through care and just dealing? All of them, or none? Unable to bring myself to purchase a replacement, I wandered the oppidum looking for a man to hire, though I doubted I could I trust anyone picked at random.

Katuaros found me grooming Scipio and, to lift my spirits, took me out for an afternoon of chariot racing. There was a large stretch of ground that had been levelled and covered with sand, and laid out with a rudimentary circus marked by staves from a broken palisade. Several races had already been run between Roman teams. In Rome chariots are raced by slaves or gladiators: strong men with broken noses and cabbage ears, expendable men who rarely saw the age of thirty. Here at Camulodunon the drivers were mostly drawn from the auxiliaries. By the time we arrived there had been two deaths, four horses put down and three chariots wrecked beyond repair. The race Katuaros was keen to see was Romans versus Britons. Four-horse teams versus 'two foals and a basket' as Vespasian described our native vehicle. A rowdy group had gathered in the British camp around a young man trying to get himself elected as a driver. 'Isn't that Mandred?' Katuaros asked. They were testing him by getting him to run the pole on a chariot being driven at full pelt but each time he tried, he had to jump off half way along. He had still not regained full trust in his legs.

All the seats on the wooden stands had been taken but a box

above that of the Princeps had been reserved for British kings. We sat between Cartimandua and Prasutagos. Once the track had been cleared of wreckage from the last race, the next was heralded with a blare of trumpets and began in a burst of astounding violence: wheels coming off, appalling injuries, the crowd cheering, gasping, making that sound that is half repugnance, half satiation. I wanted to be anywhere but here. Katuaros and Cartimandua were shouting support for her muscular slave who was vying for the lead against a gladiator.

Once the great stampede of grinding metal and wood had diminished to two chariots, it was one Roman with a team of four against one Briton with a pair, and that Briton was Iceni. Below us, Claudius was failing to sit still with imperial dignity but was shouting and beating the air with his fist. Round and round the track they went, the Roman trying to ram the Briton, but the Iceni pair were nimble and took the bends easily. The Roman, all leathery skin and grey stubble, snarled into the wind and bellowed at his horses, whipping them ferociously. The Iceni raced in silence, but on the final turn the Roman stopped battering against his opponent's wheels and took the lead. When the Briton lost, we cheered him — Romans and Britons alike — as if he had won, such had been his display of courage and skill.

And then, as the Roman chariot made its way out of the arena, and people were standing to leave, the Iceni chariot rode a lap of honour, this time driven by the Iceni queen. The British horses, shaggy and long-maned, were urged into their running trot by a shaggy driver whose hair flared out behind her like a red banner. We were all caught like wasps in honey by the sight of her. Boudicca rode the chariot well, flexing her legs, taking the turns with grace, showing how Britons and chariots are welded together like centaurs. Then, once the horses were at their highest speed, and keeping hold of the reins, she stepped forward on to the pole. Now everyone fell quiet, the Princeps, the legates, the tribunes, the centurions, the thousands of legionaries, but only for a moment. When Boudicca hitched up her woollen skirts and ran the length of the pole, right up to the yoke, a cheer went up, and carried on going up until it was more like screaming, because no one had ever seen anything quite like this. Boudicca showed the Romans just what it was they had 'conquered' so easily.

Mandred was watching the race on the far side of the circuit, looking resentful that a woman could do what he could not. Later I saw him at the practice ground, running a chariot pole that had been set up across two fixed mounts. He was fine, but then most men are when the pole isn't moving. Even I can do that…

Ten days after the submission of the kings, Claudius set off to return to Rome, a return that would be celebrated by a triumph for his addition of Britain to the Empire. I had not been able to speak alone with him again. I made a formal request for an audience but was turned down. 'Ask Caesar,' I told the secretary, 'to remember his promise to return Branwen of the Dobunni to Togidubnos of the Atrebates.'

As I packed to leave I came across Mandred's meagre possessions — a comb, spare tunic and boots, a red scarf, Draumur's knot of hair and a hooded cape. These I did up in a bundle tied to the ash spear that had felled me; he'd kept it, he said, to remind himself of my immortality. I'd found out that he was staying in an old deep-thatch being shared by several of the dispossessed and went there to find him but without success. I left his bundle and the little mare, trusting his lodging mates to do the honourable thing and give them to him.

In a sour mood I left Camulodunon with Katuaros and Debonia, knowing I could not trust Claudius to return Branwen. 'I'll write to him,' I said, 'and to every man of influence I know.'

'Let her go, Delfos,' said Katuaros. 'You have the dowry — you don't need the bride. Find someone else.'

'I am responsible for her and the plight she is in. I brought about the downfall of her father. It's my duty to do what I can.'

'A nation needs a mother,' Debonia said. 'And the sooner the better for this one.'

'The Dobunni will want and deserve their own queen,' I said.

'We can surely find him someone?' Katuaros asked his wife, ignoring me.

I stopped listening as they began to make a list of eligible women who, for one reason or another, I rejected.

'Of course,' said Katuaros. 'He's not being honest, making us think that love and duty are the same thing. Trouble is, the lady who has his heart is unobtainable, even more unobtainable than Branwen.'

My heart began to thud at that, and a boyish blush started up under my neckerchief.

'Is she married already?' Debonia asked her husband.

'No.'

'A priestess, then?'

'Theana the witch!'

'No!'

And as those two brainless gossips had fun at my expense, I became too choked with embarrassment to deny it.

'She had him in a pond,' Katuaros told his wife. 'Took his virginity down amongst the fishes.'

'Is that possible?' Debonia began to stare at me with professional interest. As midwife she was expert in the science of birth, but she wanted to extend her expertise to include the study of conception. Unlawful couplings, in her opinion, produced monsters like Claudius. 'I'd like to know who his mother slept with,' she'd said of the Princeps one evening in Camulodunon.

'His father of course!' I'd said.

'Of course. But a different man, presumably, to the one who sired his brother who, as I've heard it, was as handsome as Claudius is not.'

Debonia's theory wasn't ridiculous. I thought back to Claudius's mother, Antonia, and her hatred of her son. Was it because he was ill-formed? Or because she'd hated his father, whoever that had been? I told Debonia to keep such theories wrapped in silence. 'People have died for less.'

Now, while she and Katuaros laughed at my discomfiture, I rode on in gruff silence, trying to summon up an image of Branwen to douse that of Theana, which was having an effect on my body.

'Imagine,' Debonia was saying. 'The sister of Caratacos!'

'And she's sweet on him, too.'

'No!'

'It wasn't me that freed him from Caratacos at Beltane.'

'No!'

'Yes, Theana came in the night ...' and Katuaros wittered on while I looked for an excuse to ride alone. Then the chance for revenge got the better of me.

'Did you sleep with her as you claimed?' I demanded of him.

'Ah, now he's getting tetchy,' said Katuaros. 'We've rattled him!'

'Did you?' Debonia asked her husband. 'Did you sleep with Theana?'

'What, and have my pride and joy shrivel? Of course not. He assumed it: I didn't put him right.'

'You two have only been married less than a moon,' I said, 'and already you are keen for your friends to make the same mistake.'

'Oh, oh, oh!' Katuaros crowed. 'We *have* rattled him. Doesn't take much to unseat a Stoic.'

We had intended to ride together to Noviomagos but, after a decent interval of time, I announced a change of plan. I thought I should visit Verlamio to acquaint myself with the place and the administrators in charge. At a parting of the way, I left Katuaros and Debonia to cross Thames river and go south while I continued westward. As they rode off with their entourage,

I was left alone. No friends, no fianna, no wife. No Mandred.

The bright-eared wheat and barley in the fields, sown with such effort in the spring, had been fired by retreating warrior bands so that the Romans could not have the crops. The horizon was grey with rising smoke. Neglected sheep roamed free, goats bleated to be milked, cattle, whose ribs stood out like the branches of winter trees, staggered in search of water. All this devastation was blamed on the Romans, and anyone I passed kept his head down as if I, in my Roman tunic on my Roman horse, were a reviled foreigner. An ache in the heart of me worsened with every step.

I was not in the position, let alone the mood, to go into Verlamio and claim it as my new capital; instead I followed a track running westwards through extensive beech woods, heading for Kyronion as a wounded hound limps home. There was nothing on the forest floor but brown leaf litter, fallen trees covered in moss and the first fungi of the season. Bird song and the skitter of squirrels were the only sounds until I came out into the open, high up in the hills with an oceanic view over the vale of Tamessa, its green fields and silver river. There were columns of smoke in several distant places: woods were being cleared of rebels, groves were being fired.

What harm had those trees done anyone? On the march, scouts often returned from reconnaissance with lurid stories of groves dripping with human gore; I'd never seen anything except circles of yew, ash or oak, their branches entwined, tree elders embracing those that loved them. Ancient, venerable trees that stood for Truth. For that is what druid means in my language: *dru-vid*. Truth or Tree Knower. Can be either; can be both.

The escarpment below me was zig-zagged by sheep paths and the setting sun was throwing long shadows. A shimmering carpet of blue butterflies rising and falling over the juniper scrub caught the last light of the day. Above me kites wheeled, filling the air with their plaintive calls. And then it rose up in me, like a serpent, like a dragon, this force so strong that we spend our lives burying it. I did not so much dismount as fall from Scipio, sliding down his warm flesh to the hard ground where I lay on my face, arms splayed, crying into the soil an oblation of unstoppable tears. Tears that welled like blood from a wound, or a spring from a hillside, a pulsing wetness as if my heart were dissolving. I cried the tears that the ten-year-old could not cry when he was sent from home, from his dark, mysterious, beautiful home of the moon to the land of the sun. The tears of fright, the tears of grief.

It was a warm evening promising a warm night and I didn't bother to make camp but lay there until exhaustion took me into sleep. When I awoke just before dawn, I heard a subtle sound as if from the hills and vales, the *vocos* of Nature herself lamenting. A deep, deep and ancient sorrow. The cry of a woman raped. How long will it be before her beauty is destroyed by utility, her sacred tracks become military roads, her trees felled for building forts, her rivers dredged of fish, her duns abandoned for a soft life in valleys, the old stone temples and the tombs of the ancient ones ploughed up? The cry, the lament, was of Brit-Ana herself.

High on the escarpment I threw back my head and cried out my own *vocos* to reach the end of Britain, not a sweet call as Branwen used to make but something more like the howls of a lone wolf. Nature cried and I yowled with her. At once there came an answering call from below, at the foot of the escarpment. Was it an echo? I waited a little and then once again I let the sound out. And there came its echo…

In a light rain I made my way down the sheep trails, in and out of thinning woods, and saw no one until I came to a place where two tracks met on the plain. There I found my echo sitting on his small mare, wearing a hooded cape.

'I thought I'd got rid of you,' I said.

'You gave me my freedom,' said Mandred, 'and presumably the choice to spend it how I wish? Sounds to me like you could do with some company.'

I reached out and touched him. His arm was warm, human. 'What is it?' he asked.

'Just checking,' I said, heeling Scipio and setting off west.

Four years have lurched past in this land where the wheel of time has been broken. No longer do our months fall according to the phases of the moon or have names such as 'Sowing Time' or 'Windy Month'. Now they are irregular in length and are called after gods, emperors or numbers. Our rulers insist that the year begins in January and we, knowing better, mutter in our beards and carry on as we have always carried on, ploughing, sowing, hoeing, reaping, according to the laws of the moon and stars. This year, the first day of January saw a total eclipse of the moon in Rome.

The druids have gone two ways, either deep into the woods or beyond the frontiers. Even the ones I welcomed back into my territories have since vanished. Gatherings are no longer held in the ancient sanctuaries but on the sacred isle of Mona beyond the frontier. Apnodens, however, remains with me, sharing this secluded grove of twelve elms beyond Kyronion. He lives in the royal deep-thatch, while I have built for myself a small rectangular house with a tiled roof (corrupted by Rome I find I cannot live without windows).

No one knows about this place apart from my trusted friends and retainers. Any dispatches for me get left at the oppidum of Kyronion, now a Roman town in the valley of the Churn. Those in charge respect my privacy and don't come looking for me. I tell them I am busy breeding a new herd of horses, which I am: Scipio is happy at stud in the mares' paddock.

This life is tolerable. I spend the summer touring my lands, holding court at Calleva or Verlamio, giving judgements in disputes, dealing with all matters administrative as the local representative of the governor. Plautius and I have worked together to keep central southern Britain at peace but he has reached the end of his tenure and will leave for Rome at the end of this month. And then what? Or, rather, who? The fate of my people depends on the nature of the man in charge but no one has known his name, until today. On a visit to the oppidum I found a message from Vespasian awaiting me. He said nothing critical, nothing that might incriminate him, but the name was enough: *Ostorius Scapula*.

The very sound of it is cold water on my spine. I've never met the man but his reputation runs before him. He's the ambitious kind who will tread on the faces of friends to get to the top. Ostorius Scapula. A name to shoulder you out of the way. Outside my territories, Britain is a simmering cauldron. It won't take much heat to bring it to the boil. I must write to Claudius. He has betrayed me, yes, and did not keep his promise to return Branwen, yet I will plead with him not to persecute the Britons with Scapula. Everything depends on the governor, his nature, his virtue. I must write to Claudius and beg him to reconsider this appointment. My land needs to be wedded to the Empire, and the way to do it is not by rape. My mother country and my father country need to be married lawfully if I am to fulfil the Oracle and preside over the birth of something new.

Back at the grove and standing looking out over the Fosse, I wonder if it as permanent a frontier as I'd supposed. Apnodens joins me. I tell him about the new governor and my fear that, for reasons of personal glory, Scapula will want to extend the Empire west.

'It is time,' he says, 'for the king who moves to come out of hiding.'

HISTORICAL NOTE

A major difficulty in writing this book has been the imbalance of the historical record. While we know so much about ancient Rome, we know almost nothing about ancient Britain. For many centuries all we had of Togidubnus was a brief mention in Tacitus's *Agricola,* where he tells us that the king lived a long life and was loyal 'down to our own times,' i.e. AD 70s. Then in the eighteenth century an inscribed stone was found at Chichester which records the foundation of a temple to Neptune and Minerva by the guild of smiths under the authority of 'Togidubnus, Great King of the Britons'.

Apart from that, we can only speculate. He was probably, although not certainly, an heir of Verica, and ruled at least the areas that are now Sussex, Hampshire and Berkshire. That the history of central southern Britain, in the first three centuries of the Christian era, is one of relative peace and prosperity, I have taken to be the legacy of this forgotten king.

As to the druids, the little we know has been enhanced by the scholarship of Miranda Aldhouse Green and Anne Ross. There are veins of gold in the essentially medieval texts of the *Mabinogi* and the *Tain bo Cuailnge* — to be mined with caution. It is generally agreed that the more lurid tales of druidic rites are Roman propaganda, but unfortunately modern archaeology has a tendency to dig up weird and inexplicable things such as skeletons of humans without feet or heads, or animals with the body parts of different species mixed up like a chimera. And then there are the bog bodies, the victims it seems of ritual killings. I give a passing nod to this material but feared that to concentrate on it would distort a novel — at least, *this* novel.

We know nothing of the daily life of druids. *Dru-vid* is Sanskrit for tree- or truth-knower and it is possible that this priestly caste share a steppe origin with those who moved eastwards into India. Given that India has maintained its traditions over thousands of years, still worshipping the same gods, in the same language, it seemed to me that I could do worse than look to ancient Vedic texts for inspiration for the daily life of druids. The levels of marriage, for instance, I found in the Laws of Manu. Apnodens's extraordinary powers derive from a contemporary account of Himalyan holy men (Swami Rama, *Living with the Himalyan Masters*) but once again I had to tone down the material to make it fit for a novel! Irish literature has preserved details of life in druid colleges and Caitlin Matthew's *Celtic Visions* was invaluable for these, particularly the arduous exercises in memorisation (if anyone doubts my connection of the druids with Brahmins, the Mahabharata, the longest epic in the world, has come down to us as the fruit of such exercises).

The idea of druid kings was based on many historical and contemporary cases of religious militancy. In Chapter 7 of the Laws of Manu it states that a Brahmin may engage in the occupation of a warrior in times of adversity. I imagine that the druids were bitterly divided between those who wished to maintain peace and those who wished to resist the Romans.

The word 'Celt' is a hand-grenade with the pin pulled out. One needs to handle it with great delicacy. The exhibition on the Celts held at the British Museum in 2016 created an authentic flavour for this culture while, in the final room, giving space to the story of the 'Celtic Dawn' of the 19th century. To avoid pitfalls or offence, I've called my Celts 'Gauls' – an etymologically related word and more descriptive of where the Britons came from. Studies in DNA are challenging many sacred cows and with every passing day more is being

472

discovered but it is already clear that ideas pumped into children of all four nations of the United Kingdom require examination, leading perhaps to a greater sense of kinship and unity. There is no black and white, no good-guys-bad-guys, nothing simplistic about our history. It is probably best to view it as a muddled story of successive changes of ruling elites: the Gauls, the Romans, the Anglo-Saxons, the Vikings and the Normans. Apparently no invasion has significantly affected our ancestry since that of the Beaker People, 4,500 years ago, which, as has only recently been discovered, accounts for 90% of our DNA. For the man in the British field, it is likely that the only difference in his daily life after any change in the ruling elite was the language spoken by the tax collector. Some incomers mingled with the natives and created new populations, some kept apart in their castles. The Gauls were probably as foreign to these shores as the Romans, but they were closer in culture to the Britons.

When you stand back from it all, it is clear that there is a northern European culture that is different from the southern one. The Gauls, the Belgae, the Germans, the Vikings, the Anglo-Saxons — all would have found their languages, their religion and their art to have a lot in common, akin perhaps to the 'English-speaking world' of today, with the distinct possibility of a steppe origin. From the amazing lunar geometry of the Celtic era through to the carpet pages of the Lindisfarne Gospels is but the tracery of a family tree: knots, animals, intricate patterns — this is the cultural heritage of the north, and unfortunately it is one that Britain more or less surrendered, not so much in the time of the Roman Empire as in the time of the Roman Church (although we still see its echo in the Romanesque carvings of Norman cathedrals and churches, but then the Normans were North men). We took on the Mediterranean ways, their gods, their calendar, their laws and philosophies and, ultimately, their new religion. Our indigenous customs were not snatched from us; we traded them in.

Tacitus puts it baldly in *Agricola*: 'And so the population was gradually led into the demoralizing temptation of arcades, baths and sumptuous banquets. The unsuspecting Britons spoke of such novelties as "civilization", when in fact they were only a feature of their enslavement.' (The same is surely true today when we cheerfully exchange our privacy — and our freedom — for the wonderful convenience of smart technology.)

NAMES

Some original place names are still known to us. Cirencester, for instance, was known to the Romans as Corinium but behind this is Kyronion (now the site of Bagendon). They are not always easy to discover and sometimes I've made them up. It is the names of rivers that are best preserved but perversely I've stuck with the ones we know. I found that if all names of places, landmarks and rivers, were changed then it created a marsh of the unknown that was difficult for any reader to navigate, but if I left the names of rivers as we know them, it gave at least a framework of familiarity.

The names of historical characters are spelt the Latin way, at least while the story is in Rome, but as it moves across Gaul to Britain, the spellings become more Gaulish to reflect the rehabilitation of Togidubnos. I have spelt Katuaros and Kommios with a 'K' for a prosaic reason: there are too many names beginning with 'C'.

With words that have survived in Irish or Welsh, to avoid difficulty in pronunciation for English readers I've transliterated them to a close approximation, thus *sidhe* become Shee and *Crom Dubh* becomes Crom Dov.

Whether our narrator is Togidubnus or, according to the old school, Cogidubnus, is not so much a matter of conjecture in the academic world these days as choice. I chose Togidubnus on the ground that the 't' keeps the 'g' hard whereas the 'c' could make it soft. I think it is a national shame that we have forgotten one of our great kings and find his name strange and unpronounceable. Without doubt we gained much from Romanization but we lost just as much, not least our calendar, our ancestral gods and spirits of place, and our stories.

SOURCES

The major historical characters of Rome each has his or her own biography, easily come by. The following provided more by way of inspiration.

The Origins of the British by the geneticist, Stephen Oppenheimer, gives the new picture of our history emerging from studies in DNA (but, published in 2006, it is being superseded by later studies in this burgeoning field of discovery).

The Ancient Paths by Graham Robb makes a study of the 'lost map' of the Celtic civilization.

The discovery of a henge in Oxford was published in *Oxoniensia* no. LXXVIII (2013), George Lambrick, *Prehistoric Oxford*.

ACKNOWLEDGEMENTS

Throughout the six years of writing this book, I have had enduring support from many friends who I came to think of as 'Team Chariot'. They kept me going both with practical help and with their encouragement.

I first met Togidubnus in Martin Henig's *Heirs of King Verica* (2002, 2012). Professor Henig has provided help and guidance throughout the writing of this novel but I haven't *always* stuck to what he advised, for which I hope he forgives me. Memories of his contribution are of urgent whispers in the Sackler Classics Library, Oxford, followed by coffee and cake in the bar of the Oxford Playhouse.

My beloved husband David listened to every draft read out loud and raised very useful queries. He was also my companion in visits to many of the sites and never complained when I suddenly needed to go back to Cirencester from Seven Springs, or find out how to get to Birdlip from Bagendon (so long as each trip included a picnic).

Geoffrey Parkes, geographer and explorer, with special interest in Mongolia and Somerset, has helped me imagine terrains long gone. To locate what is now called 'Ditches' (Elm Grove in the novel) required his expertise and an OS map, followed by fish and chips at the Bathurst Arms by the Churn. I have to thank Geoffrey, also, for the cover image, delivered at a fine dining pub near Uffington, so fine we were reduced to tapas portions.

Joanna, Lady White (nee Migdal), my sundial-making friend, suffered being quizzed about shadow-poles, solstices and moon phases several times over. During one memorable night of such conversations at the Chelsea Arts Club, she introduced me to gin and tonic done the modern way and put me on the road to ruin.

The Harrison family offered unstinting help over the years, especially in the practicalities of life for legionaries, drawing on Graham's knowledge as a heritage consultant and experimental archaeologist. Towse and Graham both read a draft of the MSS and gave me much to chew on, not least some excellent home-made falafels. Frequent meetings with Towse and Bron at the Plough, Wolvercote, kept up my confidence and calorific intake.

With the first sketching of the story I had the help of 'beta readers' — a group who will give you feedback not of the grammatical kind so much as, 'this works' or 'I'm lost'. It seems inconceivable now that Seneca got only a passing mention in the first draft. Someone's annotation, 'Hope we hear more of him', was the root of what turned out to be a major character. So my thanks to the reading group of Wessex, led by Jane Quick. Thanks also to the Scotts for putting me up when I was looking into Noviomagos (Chichester) and taking in Fish-bourne Palace and the Butser Iron Age Farm at the same time.

Hugh and Dorothy Venables, who live in the shadow of Ham Hill (Peddre Dun), invited us to stay and participated in my hunt for local archaeological detail. Hugh taught me how to cook 'parcels' and, with Dorothy, helped with the task of proof-reading, for which I am very grateful.

Sally Dunn showed infinite patience waiting for us — with cake, and tea in bone china — while David and I got lost trying to find the Ancient Technology Centre (it's 'up behind the school' in Cranbourne, should anyone want to go looking for it). The ATC is a fantastic resource for ancient buildings, and through their own experience and experiments, confirmed what I already had 'seen' in my imagination, that some round houses would have had an upper gallery. It was also at ATC that I saw a small Roman house from London on which I have based Togidubnus's house in his grove retreat.

Martin Lubikowski of ml designs managed to make enough sense of the glossary to produce a fine map. Jean Maughan set the type and, as ever, provided serenity at the trickiest stage. She also, in the course of research, gave us a fabulous tour of the Mendips, taking in Charterhouse, the site of the ancient mines, and treated us to a first rate pub lunch.

Lastly my thanks to all my writing buddies who suffered having their brains addled by draft after draft, not least Judy and George Thomson of Chicago, particularly for George's wonderfully gentle-but-firm editing. Not to mention his cooking...